Margaret Mayhew w~~as~~ ~~her~~ earliest childhood me~~mories are of~~ ~~th~~e London Blitz. She began writing in her mid-thirties and had her first novel published in 1976. She is married to American aviation author Philip Kaplan, and lives in Gloucestershire. Her previous novels, *Bluebirds*, *The Crew*, *The Little Ship* and *Our Yanks*, are also published by Corgi.

Also by Margaret Mayhew

BLUEBIRDS
THE CREW
THE LITTLE SHIP
OUR YANKS

and published by Corgi Books

THE PATHFINDER

Margaret Mayhew

CORGI BOOKS

THE PATHFINDER
A CORGI BOOK: 0 552 14823 7

First publication in Great Britain

PRINTING HISTORY
Corgi edition published 2002

3 5 7 9 10 8 6 4 2

Set in Sabon by
Phoenix Typesetting, Ilkley, West Yorkshire

Corgi Books are published by Transworld Publishers,
61–63 Uxbridge Road, London W5 5SA,
a division of The Random House Group Ltd,
in Australia by Random House Australia (Pty) Ltd,
20 Alfred Street, Milsons Point, Sydney, NSW 2061, Australia,
in New Zealand by Random House New Zealand Ltd,
18 Poland Road, Glenfield, Auckland 10, New Zealand
and in South Africa by Random House (Pty) Ltd,
Endulini, 5a Jubilee Road, Parktown 2193, South Africa.

Printed and bound in Germany by
GGP Media GmbH, Pößneck

For Moira and Colin

Acknowledgements

I should especially like to thank Sir John Curtiss, who flew in the Berlin Airlift, for suggesting it as a subject for a novel and for his kind help. I am also grateful to Geoff Smith, Alan Melvin and Phyllis Parsons who all served at RAF Gatow during the Airlift, to Dr Helmut Trotnow and his staff of the Alliierten Museum in Berlin, and to Han Geurts and Hans-Gerd Troue for their translations. Ann and John Tusa's superb book *The Berlin Airlift* has been my bible. My thanks, as always, to Diane Pearson, my editor, and to my husband, Philip Kaplan.

Foreword

At the end of the Second World War, the victorious
Allies – America, Russia, Great Britain and France
– divided up the defeated Germany between them
into four separate zones, each occupied by one of
the Allies. Berlin, the capital city, which lay a
hundred miles inside the Russian zone, was similarly
carved into four sectors. The subsequent disagree-
ments between the western Allies and the Russians
over the control and administration of the new,
post-war Germany threatened a Soviet blockade of
all land and waterway access to Berlin, leaving only
three narrow air corridors for the western Allies to
supply their sectors of the city.

The seeds of the Cold War had already been
sown.

Prologue

1943

The target was Berlin. The Big City. Headquarters of the Third Reich. Hitler's lair. The black heart of the enemy. If it hadn't been such a bastard of an op, it would have been a positive pleasure. So far they'd clobbered Essen, Düsseldorf, Bremen, Mannheim, Frankfurt, Hamburg, Cologne, Bochum, Hanover, Kiel and done a couple of fairly boring trips to Italy. They were all the same to him. You flew there, you dropped your bombs, you got the hell out as fast as you could and flew back again. But Berlin had a particularly nasty reputation. First, it was a bloody long way away and, second, it was much better defended than most. New radar devices, decoy targets, fighter flares and a whole lot more flak guns. The chop rate was pretty high. As Harrison and his crew rode out in the truck he knew they were all jumpy, though naturally they didn't show it. Nobody ever showed fear. Not done. Personally, he'd stopped worrying about dying round about their fifth op. Given the known odds, it seemed more or less inevitable that he'd buy it, sooner or later.

They clambered up into the bomber and he settled himself in the pilot's seat, went through some checks and started up the four engines, one after the other. The Lancaster rolled out onto the perimeter track and joined the queue of other bombers heading for the marshalling point. Waiting to turn onto the runway, he went through a whole lot more checks before it was their turn to take off. In the beginning this had been the moment when he'd always wondered whether they'd make it back to earth alive; now he didn't give it a thought. All that was in his mind was the job in hand. The laden bomber started down the runway and he increased power until she lifted from the ground and rose majestically into the night.

They crossed the enemy coast north of Bremerhaven and then turned east over the Elbe, droning on across a blacked-out Germany towards Berlin. As they approached the target, searchlight beams groped for them and flak exploded round them, tossing the aircraft violently like a ship on a stormy sea. He held her as steady as he could for his bomb aimer until their load of high explosives tumbled out and fell towards the target. As he turned the Lancaster away hard to port he glanced down for a second at the city below: at a great mass of leaping flames that lit up the buildings and the streets and the river; at a raging inferno. Serve the bastards right, he thought. They asked for it and, by God, they've got it. They sowed the wind and now they're reaping the whirlwind.

*　　*　　*

She crouched in a corner of the cellar with her hands pressed over her ears. In the opposite corner, her mother was clasping her small brother close against her, shielding him with her body, and, near them, her grandmother and grandfather were clutched tightly in each other's arms. Her other brother was standing defiantly upright shaking his fist at the ceiling and shouting. She couldn't hear what he was saying but she knew he was cursing the British Royal Air Force, using up all the bad words he knew. She cursed them, too, for the hideous suffering they were inflicting night after night, and for the merciless destruction of the city; for the deaths of thousands of defenceless old people, women and children, and for the hundreds more who would be dead by dawn. On and on it went. The whistling shriek of bombs raining down, the ear-splitting explosions, the seismic shaking of the ground beneath her. The paraffin lamp on its hook was swinging violently to and fro. Another terrific explosion close by brought down a cloud of debris and dust and at another, closer still, the lamp went out, leaving them in total darkness. She began to pray, babbling the words to herself, *Oh God, in Thy infinite mercy, spare us. Mary, Mother of God save us . . .*

The next explosion was so great that, at first, she thought a bomb had come right through into the cellar. She lay stunned, the breath knocked from her body, unable to move. She could hear her grandmother screaming hysterically and her mother's voice trying to calm her. Then she could hear the roar and crackle of flames overhead and feel heat fierce as from a blast furnace penetrating into the cellar, sucking at her lungs, choking her. Her mother was shouting now, telling them to get out. *Hurry, hurry, hurry.* She struggled to her feet. Her little brother was thrust into her arms. *Take Rudi, Lili. Look after him, whatever happens.* She stumbled up the cellar steps after her other brother and into the courtyard. The apartment building was a mass of flames and they ran out into the Albrecht Strasse, into a tunnel of fire. The flames were leaping across the street from one building to another and a great wind was blowing a blizzard of charred paper. She saw a woman framed inside a window on an upper floor, her hair and clothes alight; saw her jump and crash onto the pavement and burn. People were running down the street with bundles of belongings, fleeing from hell. She ran, too, with her brothers. Ran and ran down to the banks of the Spree.

One

1948

The convoy of British army lorries left Hanover shortly after first light on a morning in early April. Harrison travelled in the leading vehicle, up in the cabin, and the driver, a tough-looking corporal, was somewhat surprised to find himself sitting beside an RAF squadron leader. 'Thought you'd've gone in by air, the comfy way, sir.'

He would have thought so, too, but he had no intention of discussing it with the corporal or of satisfying his curiosity. Instead he lit a cigarette and smoked in silence, staring out of the window. He was glad to have left the city behind. Seeing the massive destruction in central Hanover, close up and at ground level, had been a more sobering experience than he had expected. By the end of his second wartime tour with the squadron he had notched up a good number of ops there and revisited it later as a Pathfinder, marking the targets for the bombers coming after. He'd come to know Germany rather well by night from the air and had flown over it low in broad daylight in the first months after the war was over, taking ground crews on a kind of Thomas Cook's sightseeing tour. The army corporal was, apparently, reading his thoughts.

'First time you've 'ad a close-up at what the RAF did to the Jerries, I expect, sir? Clobbered them good and proper, didn't you? You and the Yanks. With Bomber Command yourself, were you, sir?'

'Yes.'

A quick sideways glance at his wings. 'What did you fly, sir?'

'Lancasters mainly.'

The corporal nodded. 'One of the best, sir, an' no mistake about it. You can keep your 'alifaxes and your 'udsons an' all the rest of 'em, an' those Yankee Flying Fortresses an' Liberators. The Lanc 'ad 'em all beat – that's the way I see it.'

He was inclined to agree. He'd loved flying the Mosquito for its sheer daredevil speed but the Lanc would always have a special place in his heart. Strong, sturdy, reliable. Mile after mile, hour after hour, op after op, ploughing steadily through night skies, through swarms of fighters and barrages of flak and coming back home battered but unbowed. With his crew, at least. Their luck had held out.

'I was in the Desert myself, sir. With Monty,' the corporal went on. 'We 'ad respect for Rommel and 'is lot. They fought decent. Don't know as I feel the same about any of the rest of the Jerries – not after 'earin' an' seein' what they done in them camps, an' all that. The SS an' them Gestapo blokes. Wicked, I call it. A crime against 'umanity. I reckon they deserved everythin' they got from us, an' more.'

Again, he agreed but he didn't say so. The man wanted to talk and, if given any encouragement, would probably chatter all the way to Berlin.

'First visit to Berlin, sir? On the ground, that is.'

'Yes, as a matter of fact.'

'Wait till you see it, sir. Blimey, they really copped it. Bad enough what we an' the Yanks done, but the Ruskies went an' finished off the job somethin' shockin'. You wouldn't 'ave wanted to be a Berliner when they came marchin' in, specially not a fräulein. Not from what I've been told. Never ever felt sorry for a Jerry till I saw Berlin. Stayin' there long, are you sir?'

'No idea.' They hadn't told him because they'd had no idea themselves. He'd been summoned by the CO and told that he was being posted forthwith to RAF Gatow in the British sector of Berlin as an operations officer, responsible to the wing commander in charge of flying. Apparently the Russians were making life increasingly difficult. Their Yak fighters were buzzing RAF aircraft, doing aerobatics in British air space and generally playing silly buggers and, on the ground, garrison supplies passing through Russian hands were being deliberately held up with some flimsy excuse. Nothing particularly new about that so far as he could see; the Russians were a tricky bunch and had been all along. The Red Army had stolen a march on the western Allies and been the ones to take Berlin, and they'd acted like a dog with a juicy bone ever since. He distrusted them as much as he distrusted the Germans and that was saying something.

He watched several miles of uninteresting countryside go by. Flat fields with some kind of root crop growing, pine woods, the odd, dilapidated farm here and there. A depressing scene under dull, grey skies. An old woman and an old man, dressed in shapeless black peasant garments, were toiling away in a mucky yard. The man wore a beret, the woman a headscarf knotted under her chin and both turned to watch the convoy pass. He half expected them to scowl and shake a fist but their faces were blank – wiped of all emotion.

The corporal had noticed the old couple too. 'Still in shock, some of 'em. Can't believe they didn't win the war, like 'itler promised them they would. It's given them somethin' to think about all right.'

The pre-war autobahn stretched ahead, pitted with bomb craters; the convoy snaked its way slowly past them. Three years since the war had ended, he thought, and the country was still on its knees; still in ruins. He felt no sympathy whatever for her people but the stark fact was that if Germany wasn't helped back on her feet she would be easy prey for the Russians, and Communism would spread even further west across Europe.

'How far to Helmstedt, Corporal?'

'Another forty miles, I reckon, sir. There'll be a nice little Ruskie reception committee waitin' for us. Last trip I did they went through everythin' with a toothcomb an' kept us 'anging about for hours. They've been givin' us the real runaround lately.'

'So I've heard.'

His CO in England had been quite specific. 'The

Russians want us out, Michael. That's it in a nutshell. They'd like the Allies to pack up and get out of Berlin so they could take over the whole damn city, as well as their part of it. And they're up to all kinds of games to try and squeeze us out. We only have one road, one railway and the canals to get supplies across their zone of Germany to our sectors in the city, so they're having a lot of fun slowing up our freight consignments, impounding barges, stopping trains, turning back our vehicles at the border with any old trumped-up pretext . . . And we *have* to cross their zone. Berlin's slap bang in the middle of it. There's no other way.'

'Surely there was a signed pact with them about access at the end of the war?'

'Believe it or not, there wasn't – not for overland. Apparently we trusted them. A gentlemen's agreement. Staggering, isn't it? There was some kind of cobbled-together arrangement about the waterways – not that the Russians are taking much notice of it. The only firm guarantee was for three air corridors twenty miles wide and they're not safe either. That Russian Yak that collided with our Viking coming into Gatow had been buzzing it, though the Russians flatly denied it, of course. Even tried to make out it was our fault.'

They had both stared at the map of Europe on the wall of the CO's office. The four zones carved out of a defeated Germany by the victorious Allies at the end of the war had been dotted in heavily with black ink: the British zone in the north, the French in the south-west, the American to the south and the

Soviet to the east. The capital city of Berlin – itself divided into four Allied sectors – lay one hundred and ten miles inside the Russian zone, a tiny island in a large Red sea.

'They'll only let seventeen trains through each day and the railway's jammed up with stuff, so we'll be taking this lot of RAF chaps in by road, together with garrison supplies. Boat from Harwich to The Hook, train to Hanover then a convoy along the autobahn from Hanover to Berlin.' The CO had tapped a forefinger on the map. 'This is where there's likely to be trouble: Helmstedt. That's where the road crosses over into the Soviet zone. They'll try anything: papers not in order, road blocked, some daft new permit needed. We're sending in some pretty useful bods on this trip – controllers, radar operators, electricians, mechanics. That's why I'm asking you to go along with them, Michael, and to take charge. Make sure there's no monkey business along the way. Don't put up with any nonsense from the Russians. Get our people and the supplies there asap.'

The Russians at the border would be armed – to the teeth, he'd been warned. He carried his old service revolver and the last man at the back of each lorry had been given a rifle to brandish with menace, if necessary. Only one Russian officer and one soldier were supposed to go on board to inspect papers. Any more and they were to be thrown off, but no shots were to be fired.

'So, you're expecting trouble, Corporal?'

'Yes, sir. I've been doin' this trip backwards and

forwards for months and every time they've got somethin' up their sleeve. Crafty lot, they are. They make out the autobahn's bein' mended, or it's got blocked, or somebody's papers aren't in order or we haven't got some stupid licence . . . You wait an' see. Still, there's a NAAFI on our side so we could stop an' get a cup of tea first, sir, if you like. Cheer us up a bit.'

'No, we'll press on straight through.'

'Like I said, sir, I don't think we'll be doin' that exactly.'

He could tell that the corporal was grinning to himself.

At Helmstedt the convoy left the British zone and crossed the few hundred yards to join a long queue of other vehicles – Allied and German – waiting at the barriers at Marienborn which marked the start of the Soviet zone. The Russian foot guards had closed faces and sub-machine guns slung across their chests. The corporal whistled through his teeth. 'Not what you might call charmers, are they, sir? Never a smile, let alone a joke.'

It was nearly an hour before they reached the front of the queue and a Russian officer came round to the corporal's window: a stocky, flint-eyed man with hair cropped short as stubble.

'Identity papers.'

The corporal handed over his paybook and pass and went on whistling while the officer examined them slowly, like a child with a difficult reader. Harrison said sharply, 'Stop making that noise, Corporal.'

21

'Sorry, sir.'

The papers were handed back; the officer jerked his head at him. 'Yours.'

He took them out of his tunic pocket and offered them; they were snatched rudely from his hand. 'You are Squadron Leader Michael Harrison?' His name, easy enough to pronounce, was mangled. 'Yes.'

'Why you are here?'

None of your damn business, he wanted to say. 'I'm in charge of this convoy. We're travelling to RAF Gatow in the British sector of Berlin.'

'What people you have in lorries?'

'RAF servicemen. And supplies for the British garrison.'

'You have a list?'

'I have a list of the men on this convoy.'

'And of supplies?'

'There is a list, yes.'

'I see this list, please. We must know all items.'

'I'm afraid not. You have no authority over consignments to the British sector in Berlin. None whatever.' He stared at the Russian, who glared back.

'We inspect. Each vehicle. Each man. Come.'

He climbed down and followed the officer. It took another hour for the Russians to work their way slowly through the convoy. He waited beside the lorries while they pored over IDs and military passes and prodded at crates and boxes. The officer came up to him waving an RAF paybook.

'Is not in order.'

'What do you mean, not in order?'

'Name is not good. We cannot see. You look.'

He took it. 'The ink's smudged, that's all. It says Sergeant Simmons.'

'We cannot read this. We cannot let convoy pass. Regulations are not complied with.'

'That's nonsense. The paybook is perfectly correct.'

'Is not. You must go back. All vehicles. Come again when papers are put in order.'

Harrison strode over to the back of the lorry. 'Sergeant Simmons?'

'Sir?'

'Get down here, please.'

The sergeant scrambled down and saluted. 'Sir?'

'This is your paybook?'

'Yes, sir.'

'Did you realize that the ink's badly smudged where your name's written?'

'No, sir. It wasn't before, sir. Definitely not. Must've just happened.'

'Do you have your Movement Order?'

'Yes, sir. I've already shown it.'

'Give it to me, please.' He turned back to the Russian officer. 'This man is Sergeant W.S. Simmons, radar operator with RAF Transport Command. This is his paybook with his photograph, stamped by the Royal Air Force authorities. And this is his Movement Order, in both English and Russian.'

'I have seen this.'

'Then you will have seen that his name is clearly typed and that all the details are correct.'

'How we know this is same person?'

'The identity numbers on both the paybook and the Military Order tally.'

'Is not enough. Photograph in book is not good. Is not like this man.'

The chap was playing silly buggers all right. 'Hand me your dog tags, Sergeant.' The sergeant pulled out the two ID tags hanging round his neck under his uniform. 'As you see, these are also in the name of Sergeant W.S. Simmons.'

'Is still not proof. Photograph is looking different.'

'I vouch for this man. You have my word that this is Sergeant Simmons.'

'Not proof.'

He said coldly, 'Is it your custom to doubt the word of another officer? I thought the Soviet Army understood the meaning of honour. Perhaps I was mistaken. I should point out that this Movement Order has been issued by order of the Commander-in-Chief, British Military Administration of Occupied Germany and signed on his behalf. It certifies that the holder of this order belongs to an agency of the British Occupation Forces. It says so very clearly in your language as well as in English. Are you also doubting the word of our Commander-in-Chief?'

The Russian hesitated and then turned away. 'You all wait. Perhaps you can go. Perhaps not.' It was another twenty minutes before he returned. 'OK, you can go. But next time if all things are not in good order you do not pass.'

The corporal grinned as Harrison climbed back into the lorry. 'Couldn't think of nothin' else, could he, sir? Lucky you was there.'

From Marienborn the autobahn continued dead straight for more than a hundred miles across the Russian zone of Germany to Berlin. A deep ditch ran along each side and the surface had been badly damaged by bombs and artillery fire. The convoy passed through wooded hills and then across a long stretch of more flat land. There were occasional clumps of birch trees but few settlements and few signs of life except for sporadic straggling groups of weary-looking German civilians on foot, laden down with bundles and bags and suitcases and walking the opposite way, westwards.

'Gettin' out,' the corporal remarked. 'They'll sneak through into the British zone. Don't blame 'em, do you, sir?' Towards Magdeburg they passed mile upon mile of cabbage fields. 'For the sauerkraut, see, sir. Live on it, they do. Cabbage an' potatoes an' pigs' feet. 'Orrible.'

They crossed the Elbe at Magdeburg, grinding slowly over the one-track bridge still not properly restored since the war's end. It had started to rain, heavy drops blurring the windscreen. The corporal switched on the wipers which hummed slowly to and fro. Sixty miles or so further on the land became a swampy network of lakes and inland waterways and so they came, at last, into the ruined city of Berlin.

Two

Lili Leicht finished work in the early evening. She had spent the past eight hours with a gang of other women clearing rubble from Litten Strasse in the Soviet sector, shovelling it into wheelbarrows, carting it to the trolleys that ran on rails along the streets and loading it up onto them to be taken away to dumps. Undamaged bricks had to be extracted by hand, scraped clean with trowels and stacked into orderly piles. For her toil she was paid some near-worthless Reichsmarks and given a ladle of soup and a hunk of black bread to eat on the spot, but at least it was employment where there was almost none. And from those piles of bricks it was hoped that a new Berlin would eventually be built. One fine day.

She walked the two kilometres back through the ruins to her home, crossing the River Spree at the bridge by the Friedrich Strasse Bahnhof and passing under the railway arch. As she turned into Albrecht Strasse a soldier was approaching from the far end of the deserted street, heavy boots ringing against the cobblestones. She drew back into the shadow of a wall, trying to conceal herself, her heart pounding in fear. *Frau komm!* Woman come! It was still known to happen, even now, three years after the Russians had taken the city and, with it, their revenge. But when the soldier drew nearer she saw that he was not Russian, after all. He was British. A young man in khaki uniform and a forage cap, strayed out of his sector and whistling a little to himself as though he were equally nervous. She walked on, averting her eyes and stepping into the gutter as they passed each other. He said something to her in English but she didn't look at him or answer. No fraternization: those were Allied military orders to their troops. No handshakes or acknowledgements. No speaking to German civilians who must make way respectfully to the victors. But there was no order compelling the vanquished to reply. She walked on fast down the street, past the blackened shells and the heaps of rubble, until she reached a doorway set in a surviving fragment of wall and opening onto an inner courtyard. Once upon a time a fine old nineteenth-century brick apartment house, five storeys high with ironwork balconies and stone-embrasured windows, had stood round three sides of the courtyard but now only a small corner section of it remained; the rest was burned out, roofless and floorless. A double door, panelled and with a snarling wolf's head of carved wood decorating each side, led to the only habitable part of the building: three rooms on the ground floor.

Grandfather was asleep in the armchair, head

sunk on his chest, and Rudi was lying on the couch, reading a book. He was always reading – any book he could lay his hands on, whether he could understand it or not. He had gone through all the ones that had survived the bombing raids and the Russian soldiers – novels, essays, poetry, plays, Father's heavy philosophy tomes, travel books, the English novels of Charles Dickens that Father had so admired, dictionaries, even Mother's fashion magazines. It had helped to make up for all the schooling that he had missed. Today, it was an old atlas. He looked up.

'Sumatra and Java have an annual rainfall of three thousand millimetres, did you know that, Lili?'

'No. I'd no idea.'

'So does Borneo. It's because of the monsoon, you see.'

She took off her jacket and untied the cotton scarf from around her head. Her back and arms were aching, her hands bleeding, her fingernails broken and filthy. It seemed a very long time since she had sat in a classroom and learned about such things. 'Yes, I suppose it would be. What else have you found out?'

He turned some pages. 'This is interesting too. Siberia has lots of forests with all kinds of trees. Fir trees, spruce, larch, oak, elm, maple, walnut, wild apple, stone pines, pitch pines, Manchu pines . . . I never knew that, did you?'

'If I did, I've forgotten.' She went over to the couch. It was a huge old thing with plush upholstery and scrolled mahogany ends that had once stood in her mother's shop and had somehow survived with only a few bayonet swipes and slashes. She looked down at her brother. 'Are you feeling better?'

'Yes, much.'

He didn't look it. He was still very pale with dark rings under his eyes. They were all thin, but Rudi's arms and legs were like sticks. She felt his forehead, which was quite cool.

'See, Lili? I'm fine now. I'll go to school tomorrow.'

'Perhaps.' She drew the blanket up to cover his bare legs. 'You must keep warm.'

'I *am* warm. It's not winter. It's April.'

'The air is still cold. Has Grandfather been asleep for long?'

'All the afternoon, I think.'

'I'll wake him soon, when I've started the supper.'

'What is there?'

'We have some potatoes and carrots and a little sausage. We'll have soup and bread. You must eat all you can.'

The room had once been the formal *salon*, now it was simply the room where they lived. One part was the kitchen, another the part where they ate and sat; the couch in the corner where Rudi was lying was also her bed at night, with a tattered screen dragged round it. Her grandfather and brothers all slept in the second room; the third was a bathroom. For a long time after the bombing there had been no running water, but now there was cold water at least. And electricity where there had been only candles, if they could find them.

She tied an apron round her waist and began peeling and dicing the potatoes and carrots. When they were cooking in the saucepan on the stove, she went over to her grandfather and shook his shoulder gently. He stirred and looked up at her in his confused way. 'Irma?'

'It's Lili, Grandfather. Time for you to wake up. Supper will be ready soon.'

His eyes were sad. 'I thought you were your mother – just for a moment.' He had grown more and more muddled in his mind over the past year – sleeping long hours and retreating into a world of his own. At other times, though, he was still clear-headed and like his old self. 'What time is it, Lili?'

'Past seven o'clock.'

'In the evening?'

'Yes.'

He began to struggle up from the armchair. 'We must listen to the wireless . . . the news . . .'

The black and red *volksempfanger* – one of Goebbels's thousands of people's receivers manufactured to spread the Nazi propaganda into every home – stood on a high shelf. He reached up to switch it on and fumbled clumsily with the tuning wheel. After a moment, when it had warmed up, a blast of American swing music filled the room, then loud squawks and more crackles, and then a flood of Russian from Radio Berlin. 'But where is the BBC? We must know what is really happening. Find it for me, Lili. It is very important.'

She leaned across and switched off the set. 'The war is over, Grandfather, don't you remember?

Three years ago. That's only the Russians talking their stupid nonsense. Come and sit down at the table.'

He looked bewildered and then nodded. 'Ah yes, of course. It's all over. Finished. I forget these things when I have been sleeping. So many dreams, you see, so many . . . and so real.'

She led him to the table and he sat down, staring vacantly into space, still wrapped up in his dreams. She served the soup and the bread, urging both him and Rudi to eat. The vegetables had been old and had a musty taste and the bread was stale but they were well used to that, and the sausage helped. Dirk's share of the soup had been left in the pan and they had almost finished theirs when he came in. By the look on her brother's face, she could tell at once he had been up to no good.

'Where have you been, Dirk?'

As usual, he was airily evasive. 'Here and there.'

'Doing what?'

'This and that.'

'I thought you were going to try and get some work.'

He shrugged. 'There is only labouring. They pay nothing, you know that. Look at the pittance you get. I can do better. Make much more money other ways.'

'You mean on the black market? You know how dangerous it is. If the Russians catch you, you could be put in prison.'

'They won't catch me. I'm very careful. Look what I've got for you.' From the deep pockets of his old raincoat he produced items like a magician and laid them all triumphantly on the table, one after the other. 'Tinned beans, Spam, cigarettes, chocolate, and something specially to please you, Lili – soap. American soap. There!'

She stared at the haul. 'Where did you get all this?'

'Some American soldiers over by the Gate. I traded a couple of my watches – not the very best ones, but they liked them. Just smell the soap.' He picked it up and thrust it under her nose. 'Feel it.' It was very smooth with a silky sheen, not dull and gritty like German soap, and it smelled of spring flowers. 'Here Rudi, have some chocolate.' He unwrapped the bar and broke off a big piece for his brother, who crammed it into his mouth eagerly. 'You too, Grandfather. And you, Lili.'

She shook her head. 'No, Dirk. I don't want it. I want you to stop doing this. It's not worth the risk.'

'It's no risk, I told you. I take care.' He met her eyes. 'Besides, it's a lot better than some other sorts of trading, isn't it? And we need these things. The rations are a joke and there is nothing in the shops to buy anyway.'

'But we survive.'

'That's all we do. Survive. We don't *live*. And we don't enjoy anything. Come on, Lili. Everybody's doing the black market.'

'In the western sectors, maybe, but not over here with the Russians. I told you, it's much too dangerous to bring stuff back. You know what they are like.'

'Of course I know. We all do.' He looked away

from her. 'You, of all people, know it. They're peasants. The scum of the earth. Animals. We have seen that.' He opened the pack of American Camels, tapped one out and stuck it at a jaunty angle in his mouth, feeling in his pocket for his prized American Zippo lighter – the one thing she knew he would never trade for anything. It had a dent in one side that someone had told him had been made by a bullet, which, unlike many black market fairy tales, was probably quite true. He held out the pack. 'Try one. They're good. Let's enjoy them. Enjoy something, for once. *Please*.'

He was seventeen years old and at fourteen he had been manning a machine gun at the end of their street when the Russians had entered Berlin. He was right about surviving, not living. She could remember something of the good days of peace, but, like Rudi, Dirk had known little else but war and deprivation. She took the cigarette and bent her head towards the Zippo flame.

Three

RAF Gatow lay in the British sector, fifteen miles from the centre of Berlin on the south-westerly edge of the city. The Havel See, a large inland lake that connected to the River Spree and the Berlin canals, was close by and the border with the Russian zone only half a mile away. Harrison, who had pictured a collection of war-battered tin huts in mud, was pleasantly surprised to see an impressive arched entrance to solid pre-war buildings with rendered walls, shuttered windows and tiled roofs, all laid out in a way very similar to peacetime RAF stations in England. There were paved roads, lawns, trees, shrubs, tennis courts, an indoor swimming pool, badminton court, gymnasium, cinema . . . no expense had been spared. He discovered that it had been the Luftwaffe equivalent to the RAF College, Cranwell. Goering had boasted of it and, apparently, the Führer himself had opened it in 1934. The station operational headquarters was sited at a considerable distance from the living and messing area, near a group of hangars, crewrooms, storerooms and workshops. The ops room was on the first floor, a huge map of northern Europe occupying one wall. The control room was one floor higher. Above that, a flat roof gave a panoramic view of the whole airfield.

Wing Commander Flying put him in the picture. 'The situation's gradually getting worse, I'm sorry to say. We've got Dakotas flying in three times a day from Bückeburg up in our zone carrying food and mail, but that's not going to be near enough if the Russians step up their antics and there's no sign of them backing off at the moment.' He jabbed his pipe at the big windows looking out to the runway. 'There's a Soviet army camp just outside our perimeter, beyond those trees over there where their zone begins, and they're making a thorough nuisance of themselves.'

'In what way, exactly, sir?'

'Anything they can think up. One of their latest wheezes is to lob dud shells over here. Then they send a party round to apologize, pretending it was all a big mistake, and have a good snoop to see what we're up to. A couple of weeks ago some of their soldiers set up a roadblock at a crossroads in our sector, if you please. Started stopping our vehicles and holding our drivers. We sent one of our chaps round to sort it out. He closed three of the roads so the only way they could go was back home. And we get their air force fighters buzzing around like bloody wasps.'

'I gather they want us out of Berlin.'

The wing commander said drily, 'So it would seem. And I think they'll get up to every devilment they can think of to achieve it. The worry of it is we're depending more and more on our supplies coming in by air and if the situation gets any worse we're in real trouble. They can make it impossible for us to stay, if they want, simply by blocking our overland supply lines. That way they'd starve us out. We're at their mercy. Nearly all the food has to be brought in and we have to feed ourselves, not to mention the German civilians in our sector. At the moment there are stocks of food for only forty-five days.'

'Doesn't the Russian zone provide something? I saw crops growing as we came through.'

'They've flatly refused to supply any food to the western sectors right from the very start. Made all kinds of excuses about the land being devastated by the fighting and being short themselves. They barely keep the civilians in their own sector alive: just subsistence rations. And it's not only food they won't help with. They won't let us have any of their coal so we have to bring all ours in from the Ruhr. Overland, of course. Rail or barge right across their zone.'

'If we had to increase our air traffic considerably, could the system cope?'

'Not a hope at the moment. Our new runway's making progress, as you can see, but it's a long way from being finished. Gatow was just a grass airfield when the Luftwaffe was here. We put down pierced steel planking on top but, of course, that won't take much weight or wear. The only plus is our radar and radio set-up. We've got the best there is and some first-class men and women to work it.' The wing co paused to relight his pipe and smiled at him. 'Now, thank God, we've got some more.'

Harrison settled into the station routine quickly, familiarizing himself with the layout, the personnel, the names. There were over two thousand men serving at Gatow, occupying former Luftwaffe quarters which were luxurious compared with many he had endured in wartime England. There were also fifty WAAFs serving as radar operators, telephonists, clerks, nursing orderlies and cooks, as well as two flight WAAF mechanics – something he had never come across before. The Waafery had the ill luck to be sited not far from the Russian army camp and there were constant complaints that the Russian soldiers kept them awake with drunken singing at night. Apart from the British, a number of German civilians worked on the station, both men and women. The women were employed in the kitchens and as waitresses in the messes, and as cleaners; the men on the airfield worked as labourers. Quite a number of them, he noticed, were obviously well educated and must once have been accustomed to a very different kind of employment. All of them worked extremely hard, as though their lives depended on it. Which, he thought grimly, they pretty much did.

In the Officers' Mess bar he came across a squadron leader whom he'd known from his wartime service in England. Tubby Hill was an older man and had flown a desk in admin throughout the war. In the four years since Harrison had last seen him he had grown greyer and a little tubbier, but was otherwise unchanged. Tubby gave him a beaming smile.

'Well, well, Michael, what a small world the RAF is. What brings you here?'

'Orders.'

'Nobody in their right mind would come of their own volition. The food's terrible and the whisky's getting scarcer all the time. Next thing we know they'll be rationing it.'

'Will you have one, if there is such a thing?'

'I don't mind if I do.'

The German waitress was a stolid girl with hair coiled in thick flaxen ropes round her head – just the sort of Gretchen he'd seen in Nazi photographs gazing adoringly at her Führer. She brought the whisky for Tubby and a German beer for himself and he thanked her politely. She neither looked at him nor smiled.

'They resent us,' Tubby observed placidly, accepting a Player's. 'When we arrived here they were very upset at being treated as the enemy and horrified at being regarded as Nazis. Our energetic de-Nazification programme has ruffled a lot of feathers.'

Harrison lit their cigarettes. 'What else are they?'

'Berliners tend to think of themselves as staunch opponents of Hitler.'

'Christ, they voted him into power didn't they, like the rest of the country?'

'They'll tell you that plenty of them didn't. That they tried hard to get rid of him and suffered for it.

Apparently, Hitler hated Berlin and never trusted the Berliners. Had them all labelled as either Jews or Commies. Lots of them refused to do heil Hitlers and wouldn't turn out to cheer Nazi troops. Hitler was furious. Another line is that they weren't fighting the British, only the Russians.'

'Come on, Tubby. We've all seen the newsreels. The cheering crowds in Berlin . . . all those hands reaching out to the beloved Führer driving in state through the Brandenburg Gate. They were all for him and I can't feel very sorry for any of them, I'm afraid.'

'No, I can see you can't. Nor do I particularly, all things considered – and there's a lot to consider – but the civilians here have had a pretty rough time of it, especially the women. When I came here in late '45, Berlin was like a city of the dead. The people were living in the cellars like rats, scratching around for a few potatoes and some sticks to light a fire. The Russians took everything they could carry off and smashed almost everything else. It's a bit better now. The women have cleared mountains of rubble and there's electricity and water and gas back on in most places, and the food situation's improved somewhat. There's a thriving black market, of course. They'll trade what few possessions they have left for food, and cigarettes will get you anything. Twenty Player's is the going rate for a fräulein, I'm told, but that's only hearsay. I'm too old now to find out for myself.'

Harrison's first sight of Berlin had shocked him. The widespread destruction had looked bad enough from the air, but as the convoy had wound its way through the devastated city, he had seen that it was actually far, far worse than anything he had imagined. But while he had stared, appalled, he had reminded himself again of the unspeakable misery that the Germans had inflicted upon millions.

'They asked for it, Tubby.'

'Of course they did, dear boy. And the Russians would be the very first to agree with you. *They* gave them no mercy at all. Vengeance was theirs. The Red Army had a field day when their tanks rolled in to settle the score. It's a wonder they'd left a brick standing or anyone alive by the time we and the Americans finally arrived. Actually, there's a bit of a flap on with the Ruskies, as you must have gathered.'

'That's why I'm here.'

'Well, it's brewing up into something jolly unpleasant. There's been talk of getting the service dependants out – all the wives and kids – but they're afraid of sending the wrong message to the Berliners: that we're going to abandon them. That would be playing straight into the Russians' hands, you see. Likewise, they don't want the Ruskies to think we're going to cave in. First-rate fighters those chaps, of course – I very much doubt if we'd ever have won the war without the glorious Red Army – but they've been giving us a lot of gyp.'

'They've got one hell of a cheek, Tubby. We've got a perfect right to be here.'

'Most certainly we have. We're all agreed on that – the Yanks and us – and the French, for what *they're* worth in the equation, which isn't much; too many home-grown Commies of their own to cope with.' Tubby flourished a hand. 'We stand firm together. Only we stand in a tricky spot, slap in the middle of the Russian zone with our supply lines being slowly strangled at their pleasure.'

'There are still the air corridors.'

Tubby chortled. 'A handful of Dakotas trundling around and an American Skymaster or two. I can't quite see them keeping us in the necessities of life for long – let alone our Germans as well – can you?'

'I imagine we could bring in a lot more by air, if necessary.'

'A drop in the ocean, Michael. A mere drop. Apart from the Allied garrisons, there's three and a half million German civilians in western Berlin. That's a lot of mouths to feed.' Tubby drained his glass and signalled to the waitress. 'My round. You see, the fundamental difference between us and the Russians is that *they* don't want Germany to get up off her knees – they want her to stay there, ground down under their Communist boot. The French rather agree with them, reasonably enough. They'd like Germany to be reduced to a collection of agricultural states with not an industry in sight, so there's absolutely no chance of her invading them yet again and France can make a grand recovery. Whereas we and the Yanks are trying to haul her up – give her a chance to live, as our own dear Foreign Secretary so touchingly put it. Recreate her democratically. And get her industry going again. Two drastically opposing attitudes. That's really why we're in this appalling mess.'

'And isn't it a fact that we need Germany to act as a buffer against Communism?'

'Oh, absolutely. Our interest is vested, as well as noble. Naturally it is. We're not complete fools, however much we may look it.' The sullen Gretchen brought more drinks and Tubby raised his whisky. 'Enough of that. Your good health, dear boy. Tell me, what have you been doing with yourself since we last met? You were a mere flight lieutenant then. How many missions did you chalk up in the end?'

'Over a hundred.'

'Quite a score.'

'I did a couple of tours and the rest was with No. 8 Group.'

'The Pathfinder chappies. I thought that was their exclusive little badge that you're wearing. No wonder you're covered in glory. DFC and bar, and DSO, I note. Did you come this way often?'

'Twenty times, actually.'

'The dreaded target. I remember the groan that used to go up at briefings when the crews learned it was Berlin. Nine hours' slog and guaranteed a very nasty reception from Jerry. How does it feel to be down at ground level this time?'

'Safer.'

'Interesting to be able to view your handiwork at close quarters, I imagine.'

He shook his head. 'The word is shocking, Tubby. The city looks like a moonscape. It's horrific. Unbelievable. But I still think they asked for it. Modern war is total. The whole bloody German population was fighting us whether they were civilians in munitions factories or troops in the front line.'

'Quite so. And I gather the ones in the factories worked their socks off so they wouldn't be put in uniform and sent to the front. One can't really blame them, especially if the front was Russian. Well, what happened to you after the war, when it was all over?'

'I was transferred to Transport Command. Spent some time ferrying troops home, mostly from the Far East.'

'Bit of a comedown from the old glory days.'

'It was rather a pleasant change, actually. I was slightly surprised to find myself still alive and kicking and likely to remain so for the foreseeable future – that took some getting used to. After the ferrying I did a spot of flying training and was eventually shunted into a staff job.'

'You're going to stay in the jolly old RAF, I take it? Make a career of it?'

Harrison shrugged. 'Possibly. I've nothing else in view. It's a fairly decent life.'

'It certainly has its advantages. A lot of the chaps who went back to Civvy Street are having a tough time of it, from all accounts. Damn hard to settle down tamely to a nine to five office job after what they went through. You'll go far, Michael, I'd lay even money on it. You're just the sort the RAF needs. Not married?'

'No.'

'Thank God for that. I always knew you had sound sense.'

Harrison smiled. 'Well, not yet, anyway. But I've someone in mind.'

Tubby rolled his eyes. 'Don't do it, I beg of you. You'll rue the day.'

He wondered if he would. He was twenty-eight years old and there'd never been a shortage of girls around. He'd progressed from one to the next without feeling the least desire to marry any of them. There'd been some agreeable affairs with WAAFs that had ended equally amicably when he or the girl was posted away. He was not completely sure that he wanted to marry Celia but he certainly liked her a lot and there didn't seem any good reason not to. He'd known her for years; she was practically the girl-next-door, her home close to his parents' house in a village outside Reigate. She'd served in the WRNS in the war and occasionally he'd come across her when he was home on leave. After her demob she'd started working as a secretary in the War Office. He'd taken her out several times when he was in London and enjoyed her company. She was attractive, intelligent, uncomplicated and he'd been on the point of asking her to marry him on his last leave. His mother had made no secret of the fact that she'd love her as a daughter-in-law, nor that she thought it was high time he settled down. Though she had never said so, he guessed that she desperately wanted more grandchildren to help assuage the loss of Harry and Benjy, and that Celia could go a long way towards replacing Elizabeth.

He changed the subject. 'Tell me what *you've* been up to, Tubby.'

'Nothing much, dear boy. Shuffling papers around on a desk, as usual. Actually, if it weren't for the Russians making life so tedious for us, this wouldn't be such a bad place really. Post-war England isn't exactly the lap of luxury, is it?'

'Hardly.'

'It doesn't pay to win a war – you end up picking up the tab. Our poor old country is practically bankrupt but we still have to shell out for everything and we'll have rationing for years to come – long after everybody else. Mark my words.'

'The alternative wouldn't have been much fun either.'

'Losing? Very true. And I rather doubt that the Nazis would have been giving us the same sort of helping hand that we're giving the Germans. Or trying to. Not the easiest task when we don't see eye to eye with the Soviets on how the country should be run.' Tubby wagged a finger. 'We've got to hang on to Berlin. If the Russians turf us out they'll run the show their way. And after Berlin they'll probably try to take over our western zones too. With the whole Eastern bloc already in their pockets, we'd be in a bit of a jam if that happened. The Iron Curtain would have shifted almost up to our doorstep. They know that and we know that, though everybody pretends they don't. It's all a game.'

'A damned dangerous one.'

'Ah, there you have it, dear boy. Damned dangerous. So we've donned our kid gloves. Mustn't provoke Stalin, at all costs. It would never do to start a Third World War.'

*　　*　　*

Over the next days Harrison had several opportunities to see the Russians up to their games. Their Yak fighters appeared without warning in the skies over Gatow, performing aerobatics and buzzing the RAF Dakotas as they came and went. More dud shells were fired from the army camp beyond the perimeter, followed by the arrival of a small Red Army deputation full of apologies and bearing bottles of vodka. Rumours circulated of continuing harassment to British and American transport to and from Berlin. The Russians had issued yet more regulations, insisting that all passengers – civilian or military – travelling across their zone produce additional documentation and that all freight must carry Russian authorized permits. Trains were stopped and shunted into sidings where they were left for hours on end and then sent back, vehicles refused entry at borders because of some arbitrary new ruling. Parcels sent out of the city by post had to be presented to Russian sector post offices for permits and wagonloads of them were confiscated. Flying mail out instead was no solution – neither the British nor the Americans had the aircraft for the job. It was easy for the Soviets to inflict all kinds of petty but effective humiliations. The question was how far would they go? Nobody knew that answer.

It was a while before Harrison found time to make a trip one evening into the city centre. A fleet of black Volkswagen Beetles served as free taxis for all the Occupation Forces and he took one of these from outside the Gatow gates. The driver, an elderly

German, spoke little English and his own German was minimal; the half-hour drive in through the outlying, pine-wooded suburbs passed in silence. That suited him fine. The non-fraternization rule had been relaxed somewhat but he had no desire to converse amicably with any German. He studied the back of the driver's head: the bullet-like Teutonic shape to it, the beefy neck, and the hunched shoulders. *They resent us*, Tubby had said. *They were very upset at being treated as the enemy.* Personally, he didn't give a damn how the Berliners felt or what excuses they made. So far as he was concerned they were all tarred with the Nazi brush. Even so, as they approached the centre, he was shaken again by the total devastation. The city was a corpse: bled of life and colour, rotting and horrible to behold; street upon street of ruins, wooden crosses marking where the dead still lay entombed, empty shells of what must once have been busy and thriving shops and cafés and restaurants. Occasionally, vestiges of the name above had survived: *Bettina Damen Moden, Brunen Parfumerie Kosmetik, Café November, Bar Oskar.* Gangs of women, from old to young, were labouring away like navvies with pickaxes and heavy shovels, clearing and carting rubble.

There was practically no traffic – a dilapidated tram swaying along on its rails, a British army Bedford, an American staff car, an army jeep, a civilian truck or two and a few people on bikes.

He had asked the driver to set him down near the Brandenburg Gate. The Reichstag, he knew, was close by – or what the Russians had left of it – and he was curious to see both. The East-West Axis, a long, wide boulevard, ran through the middle of the Tiergarten towards the Gate. The name conjured up a romantic image of charming and peaceful gardens where Berliners could stroll at leisure. The reality was a ravaged expanse of scrub and mud and tree stumps.

The Brandenburg Gate – backdrop to frenzied Nazi torchlit rallies and Hitler's triumphant parades – was exactly as he had envisaged: massive and forbidding. It stood just inside the Russian sector and he walked past the sign announcing *You are now leaving the British Sector* and crossed the white line painted in the road, marking the boundary. The Russians could play silly buggers with the roads and railways across their zone, if they wanted, but there was nothing much they could do to stop movement about the city. The Red Army might have got there first, but the victory and the defeat of Nazi Germany belonged equally to all the Allies. And so, by international agreement, did Berlin. A Russian soldier standing on the other side gave him a curt salute which he answered equally curtly. He spent some time staring up at the Gate and thinking of the newsreels and the newspaper photographs that he had seen. The great stone columns and capital were badly battle-scarred but still awesome and defiant and Victory still rode her four-horse chariot on the top. The old Reichstag, though, a short distance away, was a sorry sight. Burned out, bombed, and pounded remorselessly by shells in the battle for

Berlin, the old German parliament building had been left a shambles, the ribs of the great dome where Russian soldiers had raised the Red flag high over a devastated city, a tangle of twisted metal. It was a powerful symbol of savage vengeance. But who could blame the Russians for what they had done to Berlin after what the Germans had done to them? He thought, once again, they asked for it, and they got it.

He went on through the Gate's centre archway, where the Führer had passed so triumphantly in his open car, and down the Unter den Linden – another broad boulevard that must have been elegant before it was bombed to bits. There were no longer lime trees to walk beneath and not much left of anything else. The Adlon Hotel, famous for its pre-war sybaritic splendour, had been destroyed.

He was conscious of his RAF uniform, sensing that it was noted instantly by every civilian that he encountered. They avoided his eye, stepping out of his path – whether from hatred or the deference of the defeated, he couldn't say. He felt no guilt and certainly no shame at his uniform, but the woman with the sad and careworn face whom he had just passed, for instance, might have every reason to hate him.

Most of the people looked grey-faced and malnourished and many were dressed virtually in rags. A few of the girls, he noticed, had somehow managed to dress up in hats and spring costumes and high-heeled shoes. One of them smiled at him – a bright-red-lipsticked, inviting smile. Unfairly, he despised her for it. In front of the wreckage of what had been a restaurant, a one-legged man, propped up by a crude wooden crutch, was playing 'Lili Marlene' on a harmonica. Harrison found some Reichsmarks in his pocket and put them into the hat on the pavement. The playing paused, the man bowed to him. He wore the shabby remnants of the Wehrmacht uniform and there was a medal ribbon on his chest. *Danke, mein Herr. Danke.* Harrison strode on grimly. God, it was all pretty depressing.

At random, he turned into a narrow side street where grass and weeds sprouted up from between broken cobblestones. The lower floors of some buildings had survived intact and a shabby-looking café had a mismatched collection of tables and chairs set outside for customers. As he approached, a man reading a newspaper at one of the tables glanced up.

'Good lord! It's Harrison, isn't it? Michael Harrison?'

He paused. The man seemed vaguely familiar but he couldn't place him. 'Yes. I'm sorry, I'm afraid I don't remember . . .'

'We were at school together. Haven't seen each other for years, of course.' The chap had stood up and was holding out his hand.

'Nico Kocharian,' he said, smiling. 'I was a year below you.'

He remembered him then. The Armenian boy in his house. Bit of an oily type, rather podgy, hopeless at sport and not exactly popular. He was considerably podgier now, dressed in a foreign-looking civilian suit, a too-loud tie and a narrow-brimmed brown felt hat pulled low over his forehead – a distinctively German-shaped hat with a green feather stuck in the band. There was a definite whiff of some exotic cologne. The newspaper, he noticed, was in German: *Der Tagesspiegel*. 'Of course, I'm sorry. I remember you well.'

'Once seen, never forgotten, eh? Take a pew and have some coffee. It's ersatz, of course, but actually not too putrid.' The schoolboy slang grated. He spoke colloquial English like an Englishman but could never, ever, be taken for one. Harrison sat down reluctantly. The zinc table top was gouged with what looked like shrapnel hits. A waiter was summoned and addressed in fluent German, a gold cigarette case produced, snapped open and offered. 'They're Turkish. Jolly hard to come by over here.'

'I'll stick to Player's, if you don't mind.' He groped for his own.

'No offence taken. These aren't everyone's cup of tea.' Kocharian fitted one of his own cigarettes into an ebony holder – an affectation that Harrison deplored. A gold lighter appeared, snapped into flame and was held out to him. 'Cigarettes are currency in Berlin, I expect you've discovered that, Mike. You can buy almost anything with cigarettes.'

The 'Mike' grated as well. 'Yes, I've gathered.'

The Armenian leaned back in his chair. 'So . . . squadron leader in the Royal Air Force, if I read the rank correctly from those rings on your sleeve. Are you with the Control Commission?'

'No, I'm out at RAF Gatow.'

'Not a bad place, is it? It was the Luftwaffe version of Cranwell, you know.'

'So I've been told. What brings *you* to Berlin, then?'

A dimpled hand waved – the nails manicured and polished, Harrison noticed with some distaste. An elaborate gold ring shaped like a knuckleduster and set with some kind of red gem glinted on the little finger of Kocharian's left hand. His own signet ring was plain and simple. 'A little venture. I'm starting up a publishing business.'

'Isn't that rather risky? I should have thought the Germans had other things on their minds than buying books, at the moment.'

'Ah, but I intend to specialize in school textbooks, you see. The Nazis wrote their own history books for schools, did you know? You should see them. Swastika and dagger on the cover, Nazi indoctrination throughout. Naturally, the Allies have pulped the lot and new textbooks are much in demand, written from rather a different angle. You follow me? Here's my card.'

He glanced at the small white card printed in German, English and French: *Phönix Verlag, Phoenix Publishers, Édition Phénix*. Somehow the thought of such blatant opportunism rising out of the miserable ashes of post-war Germany offended him even more than the manicured fingers. 'Very astute of you.' He tried to give the card back.

Another wave of the podgy hand. 'No, keep it. I've plenty of them. I have a small office at that address, here in the Russian sector and you can always get in touch with me at that number. I live over the shop, so to speak. Pretty basic, but one's lucky to have a roof over one's head in Berlin, let alone a telephone. And it's jolly convenient.'

Harrison put the card away in his wallet, intending to chuck it out later. 'When you say the Allies, I take it you meant the Americans, British and French. What about the Russians?'

'Not really a market there. They have their own version of events. Oddly enough the French are the ones doing most to help education in their sector. The German kids in their schools have twice as many textbooks as ours. The Americans are bottom of the class in that respect. Quite surprising.'

'Wouldn't you be better off operating in one of the western sectors?'

'Not necessarily. I rather like this part of Berlin. Actually, I prefer it to the west. Not much left of the old buildings, of course, but there's still bags of atmosphere. It was a fascinating place before the war, you know. Chock-full of writers and artists and intellectuals. Opera, theatre, cinema, not to mention restaurants, bars, cabarets . . . all that sort of thing. Paris had cornered the market in straight sex so Berlin felt it had to diversify, to put it politely, to attract visitors. You've read Isherwood, of course, so you can get the picture.'

He was curious. 'You came here before the war?'

'I spent the summer hols here in '38 – learning a spot of German. Of course, the golden years for Berlin were in the Twenties and early Thirties. By the time I knew it the Nazis were throwing their weight around and the writing was on the wall. Some prophetic chap said that Berlin's dancing partner would turn out to be Death itself. He got that right on the nail.'

The waiter arrived with the coffee. It was black as night and bitter but he'd tasted worse. 'A pity the citizens didn't listen to him.'

'By the time they realized the prophecy was coming true, it was probably too late. Once he'd got a toehold Hitler was unstoppable. Brilliantly clever chap, in many respects – the way he manipulated the whole thing . . . suspicion, secrecy, terror, all kinds of rumours flying about and those incredible speeches. Absolutely mesmeric. One has to take one's hat off to him.'

'Does one?'

'I can see you don't agree, Mike.'

'It's rather hard to admire his methods, in any form,' he said coldly. 'Especially the concentration camps.'

'A great many Germans didn't know a thing about those, you know.'

'Frankly, I find that difficult to believe. And even if some didn't, they're all responsible, in my view.'

'Bit of a harsh judgement.'

'I don't think so. They allowed Hitler and his henchmen to come to power and they let them stay there.'

'Berlin was actually pretty anti-Nazi. There's a joke they used to tell: what's the perfect German? Blond as Hitler, slim as Goering, tall as Goebbels. Rather good, don't you think? No?' Nico Kocharian

54

spread his hands deprecatingly. 'Let's change the subject. What did you do in the RAF during the war?'

'I was a bomber pilot.'

'That's a DFC you're sporting, isn't it? And that little silver thing in the middle means you got it twice over. A DSO too. What's the little gilt eagle underneath?'

He said shortly, 'The Pathfinder's badge.'

'*They* were no slouches, by all accounts. Well, I can't say I'm surprised, Mike. You were always brilliant at everything when we were at school. I was a complete duffer, I'm afraid, except for languages.'

He'd annoyed everyone by showing off in French classes, Harrison remembered; rattling away pretty much like a Frog. 'You were rather good at them, I seem to recall.'

'Well, I had a bit of a head start in that department, of course. Armenian father, half-French, half-Russian mother. It helps. I find I can pick them up quite easily.'

'How many do you speak?'

'Armenian, Turkish, Russian, French, German.' The fat fingers ticked them off. 'I've added a couple more recently: Polish and Hungarian.'

'That's quite a lot.'

A shrug. 'It comes naturally to me. Actually, it was quite handy during the war. I did my bit with the Army Intelligence Corps. They seemed to find me useful.'

'Really?' Harrison said politely. 'It must have been interesting. When were you demobbed?'

'Late '45. I stooged around for a bit, doing the odd bit of interpreting and translating, and then came here early last year. Of course, the place was like hell on earth.'

'It still is, isn't it?'

'My dear chap, you should have seen it then. The Berliners were literally starving and utterly demoralized. The Americans, sweet innocents that they are, simply couldn't get it. They've never been bombed to smithereens or starved out of existence. Couldn't understand why they kept finding wretched Germans scrabbling around in the trash cans behind their canteens. The British, at least, do know about being bombed and what it's like to go without, of course. We can empathize, if not exactly sympathize. Berliners are only just beginning to pick themselves up out of the gutter. They've seen a glimmer of hope for the future. What sort of future rather depends, though, in which direction it lies. To the west or to the east. With the western Allies, or with the Soviets. It'll be interesting to see.'

Harrison frowned. 'The city's governed by all four of the Allies equally. It's international.'

'In theory, yes. But the British, American and French Occupation Forces are making rather a hash of it, aren't they? They haven't a clue how to handle the Russians who are running rings round them, and the Berliners are losing faith. They all think the western Allies will eventually give in and quit Berlin.'

Harrison said tersely, '*All* think? That's rather a sweeping statement, surely. There's plenty of evidence that the western Occupation Forces have no intention of leaving. Why should we? We've got every right to be here.'

'Of course. But it may prove to be increasingly difficult to stay. The Russians can pull the plug on access in and out any time they choose, as you must know. The British are always resourceful in a crisis, but there are limits. What could you do if that happens?'

Harrison repressed a retort. He was not going to discuss what the British would or would not do, at any level. Nico Kocharian might have worked for the Intelligence Corps in the war – if he was telling the truth – but he could be up to anything in Berlin. The city was a hotbed of intrigue. He wasn't the sort of chap one could trust. Or like.

The light was fading and he looked at his watch and held it to his ear. The bloody thing had stopped again. 'Do you have the time?'

The Armenian was wearing a flashy-looking watch – gold casing with a heavy gold mesh bracelet. 'It's nearly eight.'

He drained his coffee. 'I ought to get a move on.'

'Having trouble with your watch?'

'It keeps stopping. Damn nuisance. I must get it fixed.'

'Easier said than done in Berlin. The few watch-makers still alive and in business simply don't have the spare parts. I can find you a good replacement, if you like. As a matter of fact, I can find most things in this city – good food, good booze, good women . . . I know my way around pretty well.'

He said coolly, 'I'm sure you do.'

'The kid I got this watch from is a sort of Berlin version of the Artful Dodger and some of his stuff is first class.'

'Black market, you mean?'

'Well, naturally. Don't look so disapproving, Mike. That's the only way to get hold of anything in Berlin. It's not so terrible. Everybody trades in it, one way or another. This isn't Tunbridge Wells.'

'I'm aware of that. Thanks, but no.'

'In fact, Dirk comes from a perfectly respectable family. Professional middle class, we'd call it. They've had to survive somehow. You've no idea what it's been like for them and the rest of the population. You really should meet them and see how these people are living and coping against the odds. I could introduce you to the Leichts. Have you actually met any Berliners? Talked to them?'

'No.'

'Rather a special breed. They are *Berliners* first, Germans second. Fearfully proud of their city – even in its present sorry state. Always cracking jokes. A bit like the cockney Londoners. As I say, you really ought to get to meet some of them. It might help you to understand them better, Mike, old chap.'

He looked round for the waiter to pay his bill. 'I'm afraid I'm not particularly concerned about understanding any Germans. And it's Michael, not Mike. If you don't mind.'

'Sorry. Silly of me. Of course it is. And probably *Sir* Michael one of these fine days when you're an air marshal, or something exalted, which I'm quite sure you will be. Your father was knighted, wasn't he? I remember that happening when we were at school. He's a general.'

'Retired now, actually.'

'And expecting equally illustrious things of you, no doubt. It often runs in families, doesn't it?'

'Not necessarily. And the RAF is rather different from the army.'

'Same fine military tradition, though. Service to the Crown, and all that. King and Country before everything else. All mapped out since birth.' Nico Kocharian smiled at him. 'No, I suppose you wouldn't be at all interested in meeting any wretched Huns.'

It was said without apparent irony, but he knew that he was being mocked for being stuffy and bigoted. 'Frankly, I don't see any point, and fraternization is discouraged.'

'That's rather old hat now.'

He said stiffly, 'Not as far as I'm concerned.'

'A bit of a narrow view, Michael, if you don't mind my saying so.'

He *did* mind. Quite a lot. He'd never thought of himself as narrow-minded. In fact, he rather prided himself on having a pretty fair and open mind on most things; on being somewhat different from his father in that respect. He stubbed out his cigarette. 'Where is this family then?'

'Only a stone's throw from here.'

It proved to be rather more than that – several throws, in fact – and he regretted his capitulation every step of the way. Penetrating deeper into the Russian sector, he saw that it was in even worse shape than the western ones: a squalid wasteland of abandoned ruins and evil-smelling rubble. The cobbled side streets were deserted except for one old woman, bent double, and dragging a home-made cart behind her, full of what looked like filthy rags. He could see no traces of the pre-war vitality that Kocharian had spoken of. The light was going rapidly and the street lamps, few and far between, were still unlit. He wondered uneasily how safe the area was. They crossed a bridge over the River Spree – a narrow stretch of dark and scummy water, choked with rubbish – and as they walked beneath a railway arch one of the city S-Bahn trains thundered overhead. The archway bricks were marked with trails of green slime slithering into pools of water and there was a stink of urine. What a hell of a place to live in, he thought. Mean and drear.

They turned into a narrow, cobbled street where a few buildings were apparently inhabited. Upper storeys were wrecked and open to the weather but he could see lights burning in ground-floor windows and down in the basements. At the far end of the street an old flak tower rose black and menacing into the skies. Odd to think that he must have been on the receiving end of those guns. The Armenian beckoned him through a door in a wall which led into a courtyard flanked on three sides by the burnt-out shell of a red-brick apartment building. Here again, a small part of it, in one corner, appeared habitable. A short flight of steps led to an elaborately panelled double door with a carved wolf's head, lips drawn back in a snarl, in the centre panel of each door. The brownish paint, faded and peeling, was peppered with shrapnel marks. A dark blue and white enamel plaque on the lintel bore the number 8. Nico Kocharian tugged at an iron bell pull.

While they waited, Harrison looked round at the courtyard. It might have been rather a pleasant place once. He could see the remains of stone-embrasured windows with iron balconies and there was a stone fountain and basin in the centre and urns that had probably held flowers. Were there any flowers now in Berlin? None that he could remember seeing. No living colour. Nothing to lift the spirits and cheer the heart. All grey, grey, grey. Devastation and desolation. He thought of the bombs cascading down, of the blazing inferno he'd witnessed from thousands of feet above. *Oft have I struck those that I never saw and struck them dead.* The Shakespeare line learned long ago for a school performance of *Henry VI* seemed apt. One side of the double door had opened and he turned.

The girl standing there was small and slightly built – very different from his mental image of the typical German woman – and her hair was dark, not blond, and held back with combs behind her ears. No Gretchen plaits. Kocharian was addressing her in rapid German. His name and rank were spoken and she glanced at him. He sensed her hostility. Nico Kocharian said to him. 'This is Fräulein Leicht. She speaks very good English.'

She held out her hand, but reluctantly. 'How do you do, Squadron Leader. I am pleased to meet you.'

She clearly wasn't. 'How do you do,' he said. 'I'm sorry we're intruding like this.' Her hand felt unexpectedly rough.

'You don't mind us calling on you, do you Lili?' Kocharian was all smiles. 'Is Dirk at home?'

'No. Did you want to see him?' She seemed wary.

'If possible. Do you think he'll turn up soon?'

'I'm not sure. I never know.'

'May we come in?'

She nodded and stood back to let them in, obviously unwilling. Harrison couldn't blame her. They went from a small, dark hallway into a large room which, like the courtyard, must have seen much better days. Bare electric bulbs gave a dim and grim light, showing strips of lath and plaster dangling like stalactites from a high ceiling. Planks of wood had been nailed across one of the four large windows, a threadbare carpet across another. The furniture consisted of a single armchair, wooden beer crates, upended and containing books, and a large old-fashioned couch with a screen standing beside it. There was also a dining table, one leg broken and supported on bricks, and four odd chairs. In another part of the room, he noticed an enamel-topped work table and, beside that, a pot-bellied stove, much the same as those found in every Nissen hut in wartime England. A hole for the flue pipe had been clumsily punched through the outside wall. There was a smell about the place that repelled him. An odour of decay that he would always associate with Berlin. More than ever, he regretted letting Kocharian drag him there.

He could see the girl better now. She wore a jumper and skirt, both darned in several places with thread that did not match. Her stockings were darned too, and she wore clog-like shoes. 'My grandfather is sleeping,' she said, indicating an old man sunk in the depths of the armchair, chin on chest, dribble sliding from the corner of his mouth. 'I will not disturb him. This is my brother, Rudi.' A skinny, white-faced boy of about eight or nine, sitting at the table, stood up politely. Harrison nodded to him and the boy grinned. 'Royal Air Force. RAF. I am most interested, sir. What aeroplane do you fly?'

'I don't actually fly any at the moment.'

'But you have the wings.' The boy tapped his own chest. His hand was almost skeletal – bone with a transparent covering of skin. 'That means that you are a pilot. In the war, perhaps? You fly Liberators?'

'Liberators are American.'

'*Ach*, I am stupid. Lancasters, I mean.'

Harrison hesitated. He said crisply, 'Yes, as a matter of fact, I flew Lancasters.'

The boy looked delighted. 'I have pictures of these bombers.'

'Really?'

'He's plane mad,' Nico Kocharian said, amused. 'I should have warned you.' The German hat had been removed. Underneath his black hair was glassy with oil.

'*Ya*, I make a collection of pictures. Especially I like the Messerschmitt 109 and the Spitfire. You have flown a Spitfire?'

'No. I'm afraid not.'

'Only the bombers?'

He was spared from answering by the old man, who woke up with a start and struggled to his feet. He tottered across the room and began fiddling with a wireless up on a high shelf, turning the tuning wheel fretfully to and fro and muttering to himself. The set crackled and shrieked and whined and suddenly a stream of Russian blasted their ears. The girl went over and reached up to switch it off. He saw then how workworn her hand was, with broken nails and cuts and bruises. She said something quietly to the old man in German and led him back to his chair.

'My grandfather forgets sometimes that the war is over. Towards the end we listened to the BBC broadcasts. He is trying to find the station.'

The old man nodded eagerly. 'BBC. We hear English news. From London.'

Kocharian said in a low voice, 'They took a hell of a risk. It was a crime to listen to foreign broadcasts. The Gestapo punished anyone they caught at it.'

I'll bet they did, he thought. 'Where was that Russian coming from?'

'Radio Berlin. It's controlled by the Russians. They broadcast from the *Rundfunkhaus* in the British sector.'

'What was it all about?'

Nico smiled. 'They were putting their point of view to the general population.'

'Propaganda, you mean. Against us.'

'Rather amusing considering their location.'

He didn't find it remotely amusing.

The girl said to him, 'I am sorry but we have nothing to offer you to eat or drink.'

He could feel himself flushing. The whole thing was crazy and extremely embarrassing. These people didn't want to meet him any more than he had wanted to meet them – except for the boy, who was gazing at him as though he was some kind of hero. Kocharian was watching him, too – with sly enjoyment, he fancied – and he was suddenly furious at being put in the situation. He turned to the girl.

'We are inconveniencing you, Fräulein Leicht. We should be leaving. I have to be getting back in any case.' He moved firmly towards the door. But as he reached it, it opened and a youth entered the room. He saw at once that it was Kocharian's Artful Dodger.

He was small and slightly built, dressed in a shabby raincoat about two sizes too big for him and he wore it tightly belted with the collar turned up around his ears, like some film gangster. He stopped, his eyes widening. 'The Royal Air Force visits us again.' An exaggerated bow. 'Good evening, sir. Welcome to what you have left of our home.'

Kocharian said, 'This is Dirk – the one I was telling you about.'

'What were you telling, Nico? Everything good, I hope.'

'Squadron Leader Harrison needs a watch, Dirk. His old one has broken. What have you got to offer?'

'Actually, I don't need one at all,' Harrison said curtly. 'And I really must be going.'

The youth blocked his path. 'Please stay for a moment more, sir. I may have just the watch for you. All work very well. I make sure of that.' He smiled disarmingly. 'And, of course, for you to buy is food for us.'

He was trapped. Common decency obliged him to stay and probably pay through the nose for some dubious watch that he didn't want in the least. His service Omega had seen him through the war and he was sentimentally attached to it. He had every intention of getting it mended and keeping it. He waited, fuming inwardly, while the youth left the room. The girl said, 'Please do not feel you must buy anything, Squadron Leader. Please leave, if you wish.'

She seemed sincere, discomfited even, but he did not trust her either. The younger brother started asking him more questions. What plane did he like best? Which was the fastest? How long did it take to learn to fly? What were the medals he was wearing? He answered them all with as good a grace as he could muster. The kid looked more than undernourished: he looked ill, as though there was something chronically wrong with him, and he kept coughing.

After a while, his brother came back with a battered leather case, slightly larger than an attaché case. He put it on the table, snapped open the clasps and lifted the lid with a flourish. Inside, arranged on a piece of worn and rather dirty velvet, lay half a dozen watches – wrist and pocket. 'I deal most in ones for the wrist,' the youth told him. 'The Americans want those. They like best Swiss. The Russians like those too, but most of all they like the American watches with a Mickey Mouse on the face. Such as this.' He picked one out and held it up by the strap. 'See the hands are Mickey Mouse's hands with the big gloves. It's very funny, no?'

Personally, Harrison thought it crude and childish but he said nothing. He didn't care for any of them.

'You do not like these?'

'Not particularly, I'm afraid.'

'Please, I may see your old watch?' Reluctantly, Harrison held out his wrist. 'Ah, Omega . . . one of the best. I am very surprised that it is working badly. All the RAF were given these, it is so?'

'Only pilots and navigators.'

'So, when you came to bomb us you knew the time very well?' The youth laughed as he said it. His sister said sharply, 'You should not joke about such things, Dirk.'

'Oh, I do not joke, Lili. It was most important for the bombers to know the exact time. That is why the RAF gave them all very good watches. Isn't that so, sir?'

'There was no point in issuing dud ones,' he said stiffly.

The boy piped up. 'And before each raid everybody made their watches to the same time. I am right? You start them all together. How do you say this?'

'Synchronized them. I'm sure your Luftwaffe did exactly the same.'

'But not with Omegas, I think.' His brother was delving into a side pocket of the attaché case. He pulled out another watch. 'With German ones like this. This is my best one. A Hanhart *Flieger-chronograph*. Hanhart are an old watchmakers in Schwennigen. For more than seventy years they make them. Very famous in Germany. A very good name.' He laid the watch reverently on the table and beckoned. 'Please come to look, sir. This is not a watch for anybody – just for pilots. Made specially for the Luftwaffe. It is the most precise watch in the world. It gives all the time information you need. See the way the bezel can revolve, with the two buttons so well placed, and the leather strap with the strong rivets. This certainly belonged once to a Luftwaffe pilot. Look, the strap is a little worn from being on his wrist . . .'

He had all the slick salesman patter and, in spite of himself, Harrison was intrigued. He went closer and picked up the Hanhart watch and examined it. Stop/start and reset buttons. Steel casing with a ridged bezel, black face, white numbers and hands, two smaller face dials – one for seconds, the other for minutes, stitched and riveted black leather strap. It looked a superb piece of craftsmanship.

The young German hovered at his elbow. 'You see this red mark on the bezel? You can turn it forward however many minutes you want so that you can easily see when they have passed. And this button here is to press to start the big hand for seconds. Press again and it stops. The bottom button is to reset to zero.'

'Yes, I know how it works.'

'And if you turn it over, sir, you will see that it has the Nazi insignia. Very interesting.' Harrison looked at the back of the watch. Engraved in the steel was the Nazi eagle, wings outstretched, clutching a swastika in its claws. 'You like it, sir?'

He said guardedly, 'It's rather unusual. Where did you get it?'

'Oh, from someone who got it from someone . . . It is the first Hanhart I find. It is most special, I think. You would like to buy it?'

Harrison hesitated. 'Maybe.'

'You would not be sorry.'

'How much is it?'

'Four hundred Player's. The tins of fifty are best.'

He put the watch back on the table. 'I'll think about it.'

'Three hundred and fifty.'

Kocharian said, 'It's a wonderful watch. Must have cost a packet new.'

The Artful Dodger picked it up and displayed it by its strap. 'If you want, I keep it for you while you think. One week.'

They were all waiting; watching him. 'All right.' He looked at his own watch, forgetting that it had stopped. 'Now, I really must be going.'

Kocharian was following him. 'I'll come along with you, old chap. Show you the way. You don't want to get lost in the Russian sector after dark.'

Harrison shook hands politely with the grand-father, who stared up at him with vacant eyes and mumbled something in German. The boy, Rudi, caught him up near the door. He was dressed in shorts and his bare legs looked pathetically wasted. 'I hope very much you will come again, sir. If you have pictures of British aeroplanes, please bring them as well – for my collection.'

He shook hands with the girl. She was as slight as an elf, much shorter than himself, and her rough hand was as small as a child's. He noticed that she had a scar on her forehead above her left eye. 'I'm sorry to have disturbed you, Fräulein Leicht.'

'Goodbye, Squadron Leader.' She didn't invite him to return.

The elder brother had put away the watches and snapped the case shut. He called after him confidently, 'We see you again, sir.'

The old gas lamps were lit but set so far apart that they left long stretches of darkness. Harrison switched on his torch. 'What's the name of this street?'

'Albrecht Strasse. Thinking of coming back for the watch?'

'I doubt it.'

'It was a good deal.'

'I dare say.'

'Interesting that it belonged to some Luftwaffe pilot.'

'If it ever did.'

'Oh, I think so. Dirk can spin some stories but I'm sure that one was perfectly true. Hanhart did make watches for the Luftwaffe. The eagle and swastika on the back was rather a nice touch, I thought. Tell me, what did you think of the family?'

'They seemed pleasant enough. How is it that they speak such good English?'

'School, of course. And the father was a university professor and spent some years at Cambridge. Apparently he used to speak it all the time with them. I never actually met him myself. It's a bit of a sad story. Father, mother and grandmother killed during the war. The grandfather has gone dotty, as you saw. Lili has kept the rest of them together and they've survived somehow. They've had to fend for themselves.'

'In that terrible place?'

'It was their home. They've nowhere else to go. People live like that all over Berlin. I say, old chap, how about a nightcap? There's a club I know just round the corner where you can get almost any booze you want – illegal, of course, but who cares? It's rather like Berlin used to be before the war.'

'No, thanks.'

'Getting to be a bit of a stick-in-the-mud these days, aren't you, Michael? I suppose that's service life in peacetime. You forget what the real outside world's like.'

He said, goaded, 'We deal with the outside world all the time, as a matter of fact.'

'But from a distance now, isn't that so? Like the Americans. You live cocooned in camps and quarters, eat your own kind of food, drink your own kind of drink and play in nice, safe service clubs with your own people. That's no fun.'

'I'm not sure I share your idea of fun.'

'You don't know till you try it, old chap. What's

the saying? When in Rome, do as the Romans do. Well, now you're in Berlin and the club is down these very steps. Goes by the name of *Der Kellar*. You'd never find it if you didn't know it was there – which is the general idea, of course. Take a quick dekko? Just for a moment.'

The Armenian was already halfway down a flight of stone steps and for the second time that evening, Harrison found himself going where he hadn't wanted to go in the very least. The steps led down to the basement level of a building that looked a virtual ruin. His torch showed a door that had been crudely mended with long pieces of wood, nailed criss-cross from top to bottom so that it looked more like a portcullis. In response to a knock, it opened and they went inside.

The club lived up, or down, to its name – a low-ceilinged, brick-walled, stone-floored cellar with supporting archways and lit mainly by candlelight. Tables and chairs had been salvaged from somewhere and a crude stage erected with curtaining strung on wire and drawn across the front. A three-piece band was playing beside the stage: some melancholy German tune. The atmosphere was thick with cigarette smoke, and the place was packed with customers. The unsavoury-looking man who had opened the door showed them to a small table at the very back of the room, against the brick wall. 'He says this is the only one free,' Kocharian said. 'We're lucky to get it.' It was obvious from the way he had been greeted that he was well known there and he kept waving and smiling and calling out in German. 'What'll you have, Michael? Name your poison. They've got pretty well everything.'

It was a real dive, he thought with distaste, looking round. The band was third-rate and he couldn't for the life of him see the attraction of the place. The patrons were all civilians except for a noisy group of American servicemen lolling round one table, clearly the worse for drink. The few women present were dressed like whores. He could see no other British uniform apart from his own. 'I'll have a beer, please.'

'They have jolly good schnapps. Have one as a chaser.'

He suppressed his irritation. 'Just beer, thank you.'

Fingers were snapped at a waiter, the order given in German, Turkish cigarettes offered. 'Sorry, I forgot you prefer your own.' The gold lighter appeared. 'Beautiful girl, Lili, isn't she?'

He lit his own cigarette. 'Yes, she's nice-looking.'

'The Berlin girls have a lot to recommend them, actually, and they've all had a miserable time of it. The Nazis, the round-the-clock Allied bombing, the Red Army and now the Occupying Forces. Growing up and living in these frightful post-war conditions. Half-starved, no pretty clothes, no fun. You can't blame them for exchanging their favours for some extra food and nice things.'

He wondered if Lili Leicht had done just that with Nico Kocharian; the thought was repulsive. 'How did you come across that family?'

'I ran into brother Dirk. He was flogging watches in the Alexander Platz. Quite a character, isn't he? Of course, Lili hates him doing that. She's terrified the Russians will catch him and send him off to some labour camp. More than likely, one of these fine days, I'd say. He sails pretty close to the wind. Anyway, I bought this watch off him – a jolly decent bargain, actually – and we got chatting and he took me back to their apartment. I could see what a tough time they were having. I do what I can to help.'

'What does the girl do?'

'Lili works as a *trummerfrau*, clearing away rubble. You'll have seen the women out on the streets, no doubt. Terrible job, but it's all the work most of them can find and they do get given some food.'

It explained her hands. 'Can't they get men to do it?'

'My dear Michael, there aren't many able-bodied men left in Berlin. They've all been killed or are still POWs or too old and doddery to work, like Grandpa Leicht. Poor Lily should be doing something much better, of course. She's well educated and her English and French are excellent, but there's no chance of it at the moment. No Government, no Civil Service, not much industry or business, hardly any shops, almost nothing.'

'The young boy, Rudi, seems in pretty poor shape.'

'He is. There was a frightful polio epidemic in Berlin last year and he caught it. Hundreds of children died but he was one of the lucky ones to survive. Thanks to Lili. She's a devoted sister and she'd do anything for him. The kids here are *all* undernourished, of course. Rickets and retarded growth and riddled with TB. You're something of a hero to him, being an RAF pilot, did you notice? Rather ironic, isn't it?'

The waiter squeezed his way between tables, tray aloft, and set the drinks down: a beer with a tall head of foam and a glass of schnapps. Nico said, 'I ordered *Bernauer Schwarzbier* for you. It's made on this side of the city. The stuff they brew in west Berlin now is undrinkable.' He raised his glass. 'Cheers!'

The beer was about the best he'd ever tasted, which was some consolation. 'This place seems very popular.'

'They've come to see Helene. It's a very good act. Almost as good as the great Marlene.'

'Dietrich, you mean?'

'Who else? She *is* Berlin. They haven't forgiven her for deserting them, of course, but she still belongs.'

The curtains jerked back on their wire and a glaring white spotlight was switched on to illuminate the stage. A roll of drums announced a juggler dressed and made up like a clown, who proceeded to juggle plates and spoons and knives and forks and balance them on his forehead. Harrison watched, bored. After that some character, even more unsavoury than the one who had let them in, came onto the stage and told what were presumably funny jokes for an interminable length of time. When he finally went off and the laughter and clapping had died down, Harrison finished his beer and stubbed out his cigarette. He stood up.

'If you don't mind, I'll get going now.'

'Hold on a moment, old chap, Helene's about to come on. You mustn't miss her.'

The spotlight, which had been switched off, went on again. There was a murmur of excitement round the cellar and some eager handclaps. After another prolonged roll of drums, a figure emerged from somewhere in the shadows at the back of the stage and stepped forward into the bright light. Long chorus girl's legs in black net stockings, suspenders, high heels, top hat, blond hair, heavy-lidded sultry eyes, plucked eyebrows, scarlet Cupid's bow lips; complete silence fell. Harrison sat down again slowly. The voice, when she started, was a perfect imitation of the real Dietrich – low and husky and not so much singing, as speaking the words.

Ich bin von Kopf bis Fuss auf Liebe eingestellt . . .

He had seen *The Blue Angel* film years ago, before the war, when Dietrich had sung the song in English, 'Falling in Love Again', and this imitator was good enough to give him the same frisson he had felt then, aged about seventeen. It could have been Marlene herself. He listened, captivated. To his ears, German usually sounded harsh and rather ugly, but not when it was delivered like this. As he joined in the thunderous applause at the end, Nico Kocharian leaned towards him. 'I thought you'd enjoy it, Michael, old chap.'

The performer sang several more German songs which were unknown to him and, finally, 'Lili Marlene'. For this she left the stage and moved among the tables. When she reached the group of Americans she paused and switched suddenly to English for their benefit, circling their table slowly.

The Americans were lapping it up, grinning and clapping and the audience were laughing. She's mocking them, Harrison thought, watching her sway from one Yank to the next, picking up their drinks, sipping from each glass, stroking their hair, draping herself across their laps. Playing with them. Showing them up – though they don't realize it. Her route back to the stage took her by Harrison's chair. She spotted his uniform and, again, she stopped and caressed his cheek with her hand; he could feel the sharpness of her long red fingernails. Up close, he saw how heavy her make-up was: the patches of rouge on her cheeks, the lipstick thick and glistening, the false eyelashes jutting like long black spikes. '*Royal Air Force.*' She bent to hiss the words low and her eyes gleamed at him; he read amused malice in their depths.

After another number and two encores she finally left the stage to roars and whistles and the spotlight was switched off again.

'Pretty good, eh, Michael, didn't you think?'

'Yes, she was very clever.'

'You didn't realize?'

'Realize what?'

'Helene is a bloke, old chap. I happen to know him rather well. He's very amusing. Amazing legs, hasn't he? Far better than most women. You're looking quite shocked.'

He was annoyed to find himself reddening. Christ, how could he not have known! 'I'm not in the least shocked.'

'The Germans love all sorts of variations. Helene is very tame stuff. I could take you to some places that would probably make your hair stand on end. Every perversion known to man.'

He got to his feet again. 'I can well believe it. And now, I really must get back.'

'If you insist . . . I'll take you to the Gate. You'll be able to pick up one of your free taxis there.'

For two pins he would have told the chap to shove off – one way and another he'd had more than enough of his company – but he wasn't sure if he'd be able to remember the way back to the British sector and it would certainly be foolish to go wandering about Berlin at night. It started to rain as they walked along dark, deserted streets. Harrison thought he had never been in a more ghastly city. All the evil, all the hatred and terror and cruelty and suffering and misery seemed to lurk in every corner, to cling to every stone and every brick. He wondered if Berlin could ever be cleansed of its hideous past. They turned into the long, wide street that he recognized as the Unter den Linden and to his relief he saw the dark mass of the Brandenburg Gate ahead. Just beyond it lay the British sector.

'We must meet up again, Michael,' Kocharian said.

'I doubt that will be possible. I'm kept pretty busy.'

'Yes, the Soviets will make sure of that. They'll be tying you up in knots if you don't watch out. You have to remember that they didn't go to English public schools and that they think quite differently. I gave you my card, didn't I? Keep it safe, just in case you need anything.'

He didn't answer. He had no intention of doing so, or of ever seeing the chap again if he could help it.

'I owe you a good turn from our schooldays, you see.'

'Really?'

'Don't you remember?'

He shrugged. 'It was a long time ago.'

'You rescued me from Conway and Turner and that lot. They were indulging in their idea of a little amusing sport, sticking my head down the lavatory and pulling the chain . . . You came along and put a stop to it. Sent them all packing. Surely you haven't forgotten?'

'I'm afraid so.' He'd always cracked down hard on any bullying but he couldn't recall that particular episode. Unfortunately, the Armenian had been pretty unpopular.

'Well, it was nothing much to you, I suppose, but it meant a hell of a lot to me and I don't forget things like that. So, if I can ever do anything for you, you have only to ask. By the way, how's that charming elder sister of yours? I remember her coming to Speech Days. All of us chaps fancied her.'

He hated even to speak of it. 'She was killed in the Blitz. With her two sons.'

'I say, old chap, I'm frightfully sorry. How ghastly! Simply tragic. Your parents must have been awfully cut up.'

So was I, he thought. So was I.

He picked up one of the Volkswagon Beetle taxis in the British sector and tried to shrug off his black mood during the ride out to Gatow. The transvestite singer seemed to him to epitomize the cruel vileness of Berlin and he had an unpleasant feeling that all the way along the line, from the seedy café to the Leichts' apartment to *Der Kellar*, he had been made a fool of.

Four

Harrison put his encounter with Nico Kocharian and the Leichts out of his mind. There was plenty to occupy him on the station. The number of Dakotas ferrying in supplies had been increased and so had the ways in which the Russians were making a nuisance of themselves. There were more stoppages on the only railway line into Berlin, with freight wagons being detached because their labels were supposedly incorrect. On the canals, barges loaded with perishable goods were held up for days while their papers were processed at a snail's pace by the Russian authorities.

Meanwhile, Intelligence reports warned of more Soviet troops patrolling the zone frontiers.

In the Officers' Mess, Tubby Hill shook his head gloomily. 'They've got us by the short and curlies, Michael, and they know it. There's not a thing we can do.'

'We can bring in a great deal more stuff by air.'

'So you said before, dear boy, and again, I say, nowhere near enough. The new runway's not even finished yet and we can barely handle the present traffic. And the Yanks are no better off. It's a lost cause.'

'It's not like you to give up without a fight, Tubby. You were all for hanging on like grim death.'

'I'm getting too old for these war games, that's the truth. I'm ready to settle for a quiet life, pottering about the garden, spraying the roses and doing *The Times* crossword.'

'I don't believe it.'

'Wait and see. I'll be first in the queue when they start ferrying us out.'

'You really think we should leave the Berliners to their fate? Let the Russians just walk in and take over?'

'Three years ago you were busy bombing the city out of existence, dear boy, and with gusto. They deserved everything they got – those were your very words, I believe.'

'And I meant them. But this isn't the same situation at all, Tubby. We won the war and with it the right to be here. If we don't stand up to the Russians now, where will it end? They won't just stop at taking Berlin, they'll want the rest of Germany. And then what next? You said so yourself. The Iron Curtain will be on our doorstep. We've *got* to stay.'

'I know, but it's easier said than done. Picture the scene if they choose to blockade us completely. No food, no fuel, no raw materials, no nothing coming into the western sectors. That means nothing for our German civilians either. Less than nothing. No work, no pay, no hope of survival let alone recovery

. . . back to square one. The Berliners are probably going to end up begging us on their bended knees to get the hell out.'

'I think they have more guts than that. Look what they've already survived.'

'First time I've heard you say anything nice about them, Michael.' Tubby sighed deeply. 'Of *course* we have to stay – that's the bore of it. We've got to get the Jerries back on their feet again somehow and make sense out of the whole damned mess.'

Harrison had tried, unsuccessfully, to get his watch mended and found himself thinking again about the Luftwaffe pilot's chronograph. Three hundred and fifty Player's was a reasonable deal and he had actually liked the look of it rather a lot. The Nazi emblem on the back was an added attraction. It amused him – in the same way, he supposed, that a naval friend of his was tickled at possessing a U-boat captain's Zeiss binoculars. A trophy of war. He debated what to do. If he called on the Leichts again he could take the boy something. He'd seemed a decent kid and he must have had a pretty rough time of it. Maybe he should take some chocolate, too. The street had been Albrecht Strasse. There were few signs in Berlin and one ruined street looked much like another, but he could get the taxi driver to find it for him.

Another week passed before he made the trip into the city in the late afternoon. The driver dropped him at the bottom of the cobbled street and he walked down it in the direction of the old flak tower. He could see it clearly now: a massive square block of reinforced concrete, fifty or sixty feet high with a flat roof where the anti-aircraft guns would have been mounted, and rows of slit windows in its walls like some medieval castle. It looked almost unmarked – impervious to the shells and bombs that had destroyed practically everything around it – and would probably be standing there for hundreds of years to come.

He found the door in the wall that led into the courtyard and the double door in the corner with the snarling wolves' heads. It was the boy, Rudi, who answered his tug on the bell pull and his face instantly lit up in a smile.

'I do not think we see you again, sir. Please to come in.' He followed him into the big room. As before, the grandfather was fast asleep in the armchair, chin on his chest. There was a buzzing from a cluster of large flies on one of the window sills. 'Lili is at work, but she comes back very soon. Please to sit.'

He refused the offer of one of the wonky chairs at the table and took out the pictures of various RAF planes that he had cut out of a magazine. They were nothing special but the kid seemed thrilled to bits.

'Thank you very much, sir. Wellington, Halifax, Lysander . . . I have not these. They will be new for my collection.'

He handed over the two bars of Fry's chocolate. 'It's English, I'm afraid. You probably won't find it as good as German or Swiss.'

'I do not know. I cannot remember how that was. But I have tried American once and it was very nice.

Thank you, sir. I give these to my sister. We . . . I forget the word in English. To each take some.'

'Share.'

'*Ya*, share. We all share. Always we share with everything.'

The grandfather stirred and woke up, muttering. The boy showed him the pictures and the chocolate bars, speaking to him excitedly in German. The old man nodded vaguely and glanced in his direction without recognition or interest. Just as well, Harrison thought. He might not share his grandson's misplaced enthusiasm for the RAF. There seemed no point in waiting around and he was about to take his leave when the sister came back. He could tell by her face that she was equally surprised to see him. She, too, was shown the photographs and the chocolate by her brother.

'It is very kind of you, Squadron Leader. Thank you.'

'Not at all.'

'We did not expect to see you ever again. Is it the watch that you have come about?'

He said awkwardly, 'Actually, I did think I might take another look at it – if your brother still has it.'

'I am not sure, but I think so – yes. He was very certain that you would want it in the end. But he is not here and I do not know when he will return. He does not tell me.'

She took off her jacket and the flowered cotton scarf she was wearing, tied up turban-wise round her head in the way that factory girls in England did. He thought how attractive her hairstyle was –

soft and simple and with none of the tortured curling and crimping that usually went on with women. Her skirt and blouse, he noticed, were smeared with dust and dirt; the thought of her having to do such hard manual labour dismayed him.

He said, 'It doesn't matter. It wasn't that important.'

'If he has it, I will ask him to keep it for you, if you wish. You can come back again?'

'Yes, I'll do that. It might not be for a while, though.'

'He will keep it.'

He picked up his cap from the table. 'Well, I'll be getting along, then.'

She accompanied him politely to the outer door. 'Thank you again for the chocolate, Squadron Leader Harrison. And for the pictures for Rudi.'

'I'll bring some more next time.'

'Please do not trouble. There is no need.'

She shut the door quickly and firmly behind him. The boy had been pleased to see him, but the sister had not. Blow the watch, he thought, striding away down the street. I'll find another one.

Dirk did not come home until past midnight. Grandfather and Rudi had gone to bed but Lili stayed up, always unable to sleep until she knew that he was safely back. When, at last, she heard him come in, her growing fear turned instantly to anger.

'Why are you so late? Where have you been? I've been worried sick about you.'

He protested in his maddeningly airy way. 'Don't

make such a silly fuss, Lili. It's not so very late.'

'It's nearly half past twelve. What have you been doing?'

'Meeting somebody. Doing some very good business.' From the inside pocket of his raincoat he drew out a small box and opened it. 'Just look at this.' She stared at the ring embedded in its soft cushion of black velvet. 'It's a ruby, set in pure gold. Isn't it beautiful?'

'It must be worth a fortune.'

He smiled at her. 'No, not a fortune. A hundred American cigarettes and a tin of British dried milk. It once belonged to a Jewess, I was told. I can imagine what happened to her.'

'You're crazy to do this, Dirk. The Russians will catch you in the end. And if they don't someone else will. Don't you ever read the newspapers? Every day people are murdered and robbed in Berlin. Or they just disappear. And what use is a ring? You can't eat it.'

'But one day I can sell it for a nice lot of money. I shall keep it. Hide it in a safe place for a rainy day. Or I may barter it instead since every day is rainy. For some meat, perhaps. It's a long time since we had any meat to eat and it will do Rudi good. So you've no reason to make such a song and dance.' He returned the ring to the box and his eye fell on the half bar of chocolate on the table. 'Hallo, what's this?'

'It's your share.'

He picked it up, reading the wrapper. 'This is English chocolate. Fry's Sandwich. How did you get this?'

'The British squadron leader was here again earlier. He brought two bars of it and some aeroplane pictures for Rudi. He wants to buy the pilot's watch. I told him I wasn't sure you still had it.'

'Yes, I still have it. I always knew he would come back for it.'

'I don't see why. I never thought he would.'

'Two reasons. He liked the watch. And he liked you.'

She said crossly, 'You talk such nonsense, Dirk. He doesn't like anything German. He never wanted to come here in the first place, anyone could see that. It was all Nico's doing. You know how he loves to meddle with people's lives. To manipulate. I think he gets a kick out of it.'

'Well, it was lucky that he meddled with ours. He's a lot of help to us.'

'But I hate to feel beholden to him in any way. I don't like him bringing us things. I don't like him coming here at all.'

'We need him. He's good for business. He knows everyone. Everything that happens in Berlin.'

'Then I wish he would find you some proper work instead of this dangerous game you play.'

'What would I do? Sweated labour for peanuts, like you do? Dig drains? Cart rubbish? Is that what you want for me?'

'You'd get extra rations.'

'I can get extra rations without doing that. Look at all the things I find for us. So long as I can do that, you don't have to sell yourself to any more Americans.' He stared at her thoughtfully. 'I think you should encourage the squadron leader. I told you – he admires you. I saw the way he was noticing you. Very politely, of course, like an English gentleman. Very correct. But he noticed you, just the same. If you play your cards right you could marry him and go and live in England and drink tea all day.'

'Don't say such stupid things. It's not funny.'

'But it's not so stupid. Just be sure not to tell him anything, that's all. A lot of girls in Berlin are getting out that way. Why not you?' He grinned. 'Only you will have to work fast because the British will be leaving soon. The Russians are driving them out like frightened sheep. You could take Rudi with you. I'll look after Grandfather. He's too old and gaga to move.'

She said quietly, 'I don't want to leave, Dirk. This is our home. We are Berliners.'

He nodded. 'So we are. Suits me.' He picked up the half bar of chocolate from the table. 'Is this any good?'

'Yes. It's got a different layer in the middle.'

He bit into the bar, chewed and swallowed. 'Not bad. I never knew the British could make decent chocolate.' He smiled at her. 'Perhaps he'll bring some more when he comes back for the watch.'

It was almost two weeks before the squadron leader returned one evening. Dirk opened the door to him and he came into the room in his smart blue uniform with medal ribbons and badges, holding the Royal Air Force cap in one hand and carrying a large brown paper bag under his other arm. Lili knew from seeing the British Occupation Forces in Berlin that they were by no means all tall and fair-haired, as she had previously imagined, but the squadron leader was both those things, with blue eyes. Even out of uniform, she would have instantly known his nationality. So reserved. So stern-looking. So unemotional. So correct.

Grandfather had not felt well and had gone to bed early but Rudi was up and the squadron leader had, indeed, brought more chocolate. He took it out of the paper bag: not the sandwich kind this time, but a different one in a purple wrapper. He laid it on the table. Cadbury's Whole Nut Milk Chocolate. 'I'm sorry I couldn't find any more pictures,' he told Rudi. 'But I brought this instead.' He handed her brother a metal model of a two-engined aeroplane. 'It's an American DC3. A Dakota, we call it in the RAF.'

Rudi was overwhelmed and, for a moment, speechless. 'It's really for me?'

'Yes, that's right.'

'To keep?'

'Yes, of course. Not very exciting, I'm afraid. It's a transport plane mainly. Bit of a workhorse. But very useful and extremely reliable.'

'Thank you, sir. You are very kind. I like it very much. I think perhaps I have seen this aeroplane in the sky over Berlin.'

'Very probably.'

Dirk had fetched his suitcase and set it on the table. He unsnapped the clasps and took out the

Hanhart *Fliegerchronograph*. 'Here you are, sir. Please try it, if you wish.'

She watched the Royal Air Force pilot unbuckle his own watch, which he put in his pocket, and fasten the Luftwaffe watch round his left wrist. Dirk was watching him too – motionless and intently, like some animal with its prey. 'You like it, sir?'

'Yes, it's fine. Three hundred and fifty Player's, you said?'

'Yes, sir. It is a very good bargain for you.'

The squadron leader handed over the brown paper bag. 'Seven tins of fifty. I think that's how you wanted them.'

Dirk checked quickly – a mere glance inside the bag so as not to offend the squadron leader. 'Thank you, sir. And if you know other people who would like a good watch, I can help them too. It is all extra food for us.'

The squadron leader flushed. He said, 'I understood civilian rations were better here in the Soviet sector than in ours. We have to bring in all our food from miles away. Surely the Russians can feed you much more easily.'

'The Russians do not want us fit and strong, sir. They want us weak and feeble, so they keep us on just enough calories a day to survive.'

'Why not move to a western sector? We try to do rather more than that.'

'There are not many places to live anywhere in Berlin, haven't you noticed, sir? And this is our home – isn't that so, Lili? Home sweet home. It means very much to us. It's all we have. All that reminds us of our mother and father.'

The flush spread further and deepened. 'Yes, of course. I'm awfully sorry.'

Dirk started to take the tins of English cigarettes out of the paper bag and arrange them in his case. 'It's not so bad. We have electricity now and water from the tap. Quite luxurious. Besides, to move to your sector would not help us. We do not believe that you British will stay here for much longer. Or the Americans or the French. The Russians are making it too difficult for you all, so you will give up and go in the end and the whole of Berlin will become Russian. That is what will happen. That is what we believe.'

The squadron leader said stiffly, 'I can assure you that we have no intention of leaving.'

'Intention is one thing to have. But you may be forced to. After all, like us, you must eat. So must the civilians in your sector.' Dirk snapped the suitcase shut and lifted it off the table. 'Excuse me, sir, but I must go out now.' He nodded to Lili and said in German, 'I won't be long.'

She answered, also in German, 'Where are you going? It's getting late.'

'Not far. I'll be back soon.'

He was gone before she could argue, slipping out like quicksilver. The squadron leader moved towards the door as well but Rudi wanted to show him his collection of aeroplane pictures, pasted with flour and water into a home-made scrapbook. The Englishman sat patiently beside him at the table and she noticed that he was able to identify all the planes.

'You must go to bed now, Rudi,' she said in German when he had reached the end of the book.

'Oh, no . . . there are many questions that I must ask.'

'Not now. The squadron leader has to leave. You have kept him long enough. And if you do not rest you will not be well enough to go to school in the morning. Say goodbye and thank you and make sure you don't disturb Grandfather.'

He went off reluctantly, carrying his scrapbook and the prized aeroplane model and his share of the nut chocolate.

She said politely, 'Thank you for bringing the plane. It means a lot to him.'

'Nico Kocharian told me he's not been well.'

'He caught polio last year. There was a big epidemic in Berlin and a lot of children died. It was a miracle that he recovered. His health is still not good, as you can see. He has a cough and there are all sorts of problems . . . It is the same with many other children in Berlin. When they are growing they need good food but this has not always been possible.'

He looked uncomfortable. 'I'm sorry. I hope things will soon improve.'

'It does not seem very likely, does it? If the western Allies leave.'

'Is that what you all *really* believe? That we'll give up Berlin? Throw in the towel?'

'Towel?'

'Sorry. Let the Russians push us out?'

'They surround you. They make a ring round the

city with their tanks and soldiers. Berlin is like an island now and you could be cut off completely.'

'We won't let that happen.'

'How can you be so sure? How could you stop it?'

He said levelly, 'We're not in the habit of letting other countries dictate to us.'

'Yes . . . I know that. You have shown the world so.' She folded her arms across her chest. 'It's not the Berliners you really care about, is it? It's not permitting the Russians to bully you. You do not want that to happen at any cost.'

He frowned. 'The western Allies want peace in Europe, not more war. A democratic peace. For everyone.'

'I do not think you can comprehend how it is in Middle Europe. How it has been for centuries. Always wars. Always frontiers changing. Always revolutions. Always refugees. In England you are on a safe little island of your own. In America they are in another world altogether. There can never be a lasting peace here, you know. However much *you* may want it. Perhaps you waste your time and it is better that you do leave.'

'Surely you don't want the Soviets to take over the whole of Berlin? To be ruled by them – after the way they've treated you?'

She said fiercely, 'The British and the Americans did not treat us so well during the war either. You bombed us by night and by day until thousands and thousands were dead and our city was in ruins.'

'The Nazis had to be beaten.'

'By deliberately killing old men and women and

94

innocent children? The Luftwaffe bombed only military targets.'

'Is that what you believe?'

'It is what we were always told.'

'Then you were told lies. Nazi propaganda. A great many civilians were killed by the Luftwaffe in England – in London and other cities.'

'But your cities were not completely destroyed like ours. We were on our knees, already defeated, but still the bombers came, day after day, night after night, until there was nothing left.'

'Germany refused to surrender.'

'So did England. But we did not bomb you to dust.'

'Only because we stopped you.'

She found she was shaking, either from anger or distress; perhaps both mixed up together. 'You flew in those bombers – the Lancasters. The ones that came at night. I heard you tell Rudi so. You were the pilot. Perhaps you came to Berlin?'

'Yes, as a matter of fact I did.'

'Many times?'

'Yes. Many times.'

It could have been him up there that night. His plane that had dropped the bombs. 'Didn't you feel *any* pity for the people you were killing?'

'I'm afraid not. I imagine your Luftwaffe didn't feel much either when they bombed our women and children. It was war. Total war.'

'So, you pressed a button from high up. You saw nothing of what happened and you felt nothing? How easy for you!'

'*Easy*. You think any of it was *easy*? Do you know how many RAF men died getting rid of your beloved Führer for you? More than fifty-five thousand. And I haven't included the umpteen thousands of Americans who lost their lives having to do the same ghastly job.' He, too, was angry now. Very angry. White-faced with it, not flushed like he had been before.

'He was *not* my beloved Führer. I hated him. So did others.'

'Well, I'm terribly sorry but it wasn't exactly possible to pick out the few who may have been against him and not drop bombs on *them*.' He took a deep breath. 'We don't seem to understand each other very well, Fräulein Leicht. There's absolutely no point in continuing this discussion.' He picked up his cap from the table. 'I ought to go at once.'

'Yes, it would be best.'

She shut the door after him and went to sit in Grandfather's armchair to wait for Dirk to come home safely. She was still shaking. The rest of the English chocolate lay on the table. Rudi and Dirk could have her share. She didn't want any of it. Not a crumb.

Five

May turned to June. The new runway at Gatow was progressing but not expected to be ready until the end of July at the earliest. Meanwhile the Russians stepped up their harassment of all road and rail traffic. The autobahn bridge over the River Elbe into Berlin was closed by them on the pretext of necessary repairs. The only alternative way to cross the river was on an ancient ferry pulled by cable which could hold only two buses or six cars at a time. The situation was becoming critical.

At a dance at the Officers' Mess, Harrison found Tubby Hill slumped morosely in an anteroom armchair, glass in hand. He raised his head. 'Do you feel what I feel, Michael?'

'It depends what that is.'

'That we're fiddling while Rome burns. Heads stuck in the sand.'

'Mixing your metaphors a bit, aren't you, Tubby?'

He nodded towards the dance music. 'There they are all cutting a rug as though we've got nothing whatever to worry about when any day now the

Ruskies are going to pull it from under us.'

'You've got a very short memory. We never let the war stop our station dances, did we? No reason to now.'

Tubby wagged his head slowly from side to side. 'I told you I was getting old. Things bother me now and I don't like being bothered. Have you heard all these rumours about the new western currency we're going to spring on them?'

'Well, the Reichsmark is more or less worthless. We have to do something or the economy will never recover.'

'The Russians are going to be hopping mad about it, mark my words. They'll never accept western currency in their zone. They'll put up the shutters, lock the doors and throw away the keys and that'll be that.'

'It's a risk we have to take. We can't go tiptoeing around doing nothing because we're afraid of what the Russians might think. Of course they'll cause trouble – bound to – we've just got to stand up to them.'

'You make it sound so simple but it isn't, you know. As, no doubt, we shall soon discover. By the way, what is that very fancy watch you're wearing? Not RAF issue, I'll be bound.'

'It's German. My old Omega conked out. A *Fliegerchronograph*.'

'Speak English, dear boy.'

'A pilot's watch. I bought it from some German kid who does a bit of black market trading.'

'Tut, tut. *Et tu*, Michael. I'm surprised at you. I

thought you were above such things. Does it keep good time?'

'So far.'

'You had better luck than me, then. I was flogged a gold Cartier cigarette lighter once in the Potsdamer Platz. Turned out it was neither gold nor Cartier and it didn't even work properly. I chucked the damn thing out in the end.' Tubby waved a hand. 'Go away and leave me to drown my sorrows. Do your duty and dance with some of those charming, hard-working WAAFs and be nice to them – they deserve it.'

He smiled and went and found one of the cipher girls he'd noticed around the station. She was rather pretty and from her ready smile and the alacrity with which she accepted his invitation, he thought she had probably noticed him too. He danced several dances with her and toyed with the idea of asking her out but, in the end, decided against it. After all, he was more or less committed to Celia and it would only complicate matters.

'Good evening, Lili.'

'Dirk isn't here, Nico.'

'Actually, it wasn't Dirk I came to see. It was you.' His German was very fluent, almost unaccented.

'Me? What about?'

'I have brought you a present.'

'I had much rather you hadn't.'

He smiled at her. He had a smile like a toad, she thought; or how one imagined a toad would smile – wide and thin-lipped, the lower lip always moist and smooth and shiny – slightly open, as though his tongue might dart out suddenly to catch some insect. 'My dear Lili, it's my pleasure. A lovely girl like you should have nice things. May I come in?'

He followed her into the big room. Both Grandfather and Rudi had gone to bed which meant that she was alone with him, and Dirk might not be home for hours. He produced the present out of a pocket of his flashy suit. 'From Paris, Lili. The French make the best.'

It was scent. A small bottle of Chanel No 5 contained in an elegant white cardboard box with black lettering. Her mother had worn the same kind. She could go on refusing but he would go on insisting. 'Thank you, Nico. However did you get it?'

'Ways and means. I know how to get almost anything in Berlin.' He often boasted of that and it was probably true. He was that kind of person. He offered a cigarette from his gold case – the Turkish brand that he always smoked.

'No, thank you.' She could, at least, refuse a cigarette; he could hardly insist on her smoking it. She watched him fit the cigarette into his ebony holder and flick the wheel on his gold lighter with his thumb. It was always gold with him. Gold case, gold watch, gold pin to his tie, gold nib to his pen, gold fillings in his teeth, the flashy gold ring on his finger. The very first time that she had met him she had disliked and distrusted him. He was too smooth, too glib, too Mr Know-All. Dirk had brought him home late one evening in the summer of the year after the war had ended. 'This is Herr

Kocharian,' Dirk had said. 'He is British.' She had taken one look at Nico and known that if he was of British nationality then it was only by adoption. If things had been different she would have forbidden Dirk to bring him home again, but at that time they had been desperate for any extra food they could get and Nico had given them things – tins of American Spam and corned beef and powdered milk and eggs. And Dirk had gone from doing a little bartering here and there to becoming a fully fledged black marketeer.

The smoke from the Turkish cigarette was almost nauseating. She sat down by the table, at a distance, and Nico took Grandfather's chair. His dark eyes, black as olives, gave away nothing of his thoughts. 'I also came to warn you, Lili.'

'About what?'

'The Russians are going to blockade the western Allies at any moment. They will close all roads, all canals, every access in and out of Berlin. It will be impossible for the British, Americans or French to bring supplies into their sectors and there will be a big crisis.'

'How do you know this?'

'You don't need to know that – just to know that it will certainly happen. The Russians are very angry about the new western Deutschmark. They want only their own currency to be used for the whole of Berlin but the other Allies will not agree. At all costs, Lili, you must stay here. There will still be food for everyone in the Soviet sector but not in the western sectors.'

'What will happen to those people?'

'If the Allies do not get out the civilians will starve. And they will be starved of raw materials, as well as of food, and what products they can still manage to manufacture for export will be unable to leave the city. Everything will be affected. Everything will collapse. But so long as you stay here in the Russian sector you will survive.'

Survival. *Überleben*. She knew too well exactly what that meant. To survive was to stay alive somehow. Somehow to find enough food and water and warmth to sustain life, to struggle through each day until the next. 'Squadron Leader Harrison says the British will never leave.'

'They may have no choice. You have seen Michael again, then?'

'He came back to buy the Hanhart pilot's watch from Dirk.'

Nico smiled. 'I rather thought that he might. What do you think of him?'

'He's a Royal Air Force bomber pilot. What should I think?'

'You mustn't hold that against him. He's a jolly decent chap.'

'He has killed hundreds of innocent people. Perhaps thousands.'

'Dear Lili, that applies to countless men, on both sides. He was only doing his job. In war, one obeys orders. He was extremely brave, that's how he earned his medals. Haven't you noticed them? The ribbons on his uniform?'

'They don't mean anything to me.'

'He won the DFC twice as well as the DSO. That's quite impressive, I can tell you. And that gilt eagle badge he wears under them is a Pathfinder's badge. That's even more impressive. Amazing bravery and outstanding devotion to duty – I believe that's the description generally used where they're concerned.'

'A Pathfinder? What is that?'

'What it says. Literally. He found a path for the bombers. Went ahead of them and dropped coloured flares on the target to show them precisely where to release their bombs.'

'My God! He did *that*? Made very sure they didn't miss?'

'Well, they were usually trying to hit vital targets – factories, railways, docks.'

'And often they did not care what they hit, so long as they destroyed a city and killed as many Germans as they could. They were barbaric.'

'The Nazis were not exactly civilized.'

'I know that,' she said bitterly. 'You don't have to tell me.'

'Poor Lili.' He spread his hands, the smoke from his cigarette curling up from the ebony holder slotted between his fingers. 'It was a terrible war. Everyone suffered. The Germans, the British, the Americans, the Russians. Everyone.'

Except you, Nico, she thought. Somehow I think you have escaped it all. You have learned how to turn everything to your advantage; how to tiptoe a path through the middle of all the misery. She stood up. 'If you don't mind, I'm rather tired . . .'

He stubbed out his cigarette in the tin lid ashtray and got to his feet. 'Of course, Lili. Of course. But you will remember what I said? Don't leave this sector, whatever you do.'

She went with him to the front door. He stopped there for a moment and she kept her safe distance. She could smell the smell of him – Turkish cigarettes mingled with musky cologne and whatever oil he used on his slick black hair. He had never touched her, or even tried to, but because of the gifts there was always the dread that he might expect – even demand – her to allow it.

'If there is ever anything you need, you have only to ask me.'

She said, 'I wish you would stop Dirk from what he is doing – that's what I ask. It's so dangerous. The Russians arrest black marketeers. They are dragged away and never seen again. I live in fear of this happening to him.'

'It would be very hard to stop him. Dirk will do as he wants, you know that.'

'But you have encouraged him.'

'I have not discouraged him, that's all. This is a cruel city and only those who help themselves will survive. But I will urge him to be more careful, if you like.'

'Please do.'

'If Dirk gets into any trouble, let me know at once.'

She couldn't keep the scorn from her voice. 'What could you do?'

'Something.' He smiled his toad's smile at her.

'I can always do something. Goodnight, Lili.'

She went and sat in Grandfather's chair and closed her eyes, feeling very tired and very afraid. She had no doubt that what Nico had warned was true; he always knew everything that was going on. The Russians would blockade the city and the British, Americans and French would eventually have to leave and when that happened Berlin would be lost. It would be even worse, if possible, than living under the Nazis. The whole city would be put under Communist rule with brutal commissars and a Secret Police force, without freedom or justice or mercy. They would be allowed only the barest necessities for existence and they would live in constant fear. The Russians hated them and had a mountain of scores to settle. She had not forgotten – how could she ever – the terrible days when the Red Army had reached Berlin at the end of the war. She covered her face with her hands at the memory of it.

It had been the day after her sixteenth birthday when their tanks had come rumbling like thunder through the streets. What little there was left of the city had been burned and pillaged. Men had been rounded up and transported to labour camps in the Soviet Union. Women of all ages had been raped and tortured, mutilated with bayonets, savagely murdered. The few treasures remaining to families had been looted by Russian soldiers and what they could not carry away, they had destroyed. She and Grandfather, Dirk and Rudi had hidden deep in a U-Bahn tunnel, living off bread and water for days on end, and when they had finally crept out they had witnessed a scene of hell. People were shambling about dressed in rags, scavenging like dogs for scraps of food in the still-burning ruins and queuing for water with buckets in long lines, numb despair on their faces. The most terrible thing of all had been the stench of the rotting corpses – a stench so sickening it made you retch and retch and retch. They had returned to the apartment in Albrecht Strasse and found it stripped almost bare of anything that had previously survived the bombing. Pictures, silver, ornaments, jewellery, clothes had all gone. The piano had been chopped to pieces, china smashed, books kicked about and hurled out into the courtyard, upholstery slashed and fouled, furniture wrecked beyond repair, even the taps in the kitchen and bathroom had been wrenched off and taken away by Russian peasant soldiers who had believed they would still provide running water. By some strange miracle, Mother's hats, kept in the old trunk in a corner, had not been touched. She had lifted the lid to see them all still there, as beautiful as ever with their rich colours, their swathes of gossamer silk veiling and their glossy feathers. The sight of them had made her break down and weep.

Somehow they had carried on. They had cleaned up the mess and combed the ruins again for pieces of usable furniture and utensils. Clothing and blankets had been very hard to come by and the worst problem had been finding food. There was almost nothing to eat except a meagre ration of potatoes and bread dispensed to long queues by surly Russians. They had gnawed at mouldy carrots and made soups out of weeds and nettles and tree bark. Finding fuel for warmth and cooking was another impossibility. Nearly all the trees in Berlin had been either destroyed in the bombing or chopped down for firewood. Every branch and stick and twig had been gleaned. Dirk had walked miles out into the country with an old wheelbarrow to look for more.

Sometimes he came back with a few potatoes too, or some swedes, and, once, a whole cabbage. One day a loose horse had come clip-clopping down Albrecht Strasse. Before it had reached the end of the street it had been surrounded and caught. A man who had worked in a butcher's shop had cut its throat and skinned it, and the crowd that had quickly gathered from nowhere had fallen onto the carcass with kitchen knives and hacked it into bloody hunks of meat. Within minutes the dead animal had been stripped to bones – nothing left but head, tail and ribcage. She had managed to grab a hunk of the thigh and carried it home in an enamel washbasin, slopping around horribly in a pool of crimson.

But Rudi had grown thinner and frailer and Grandfather had become more and more senile. And the Russians were no less brutal. Whenever she had gone out of the apartment she had made herself look as ugly as possible – rubbed dirt into her face, painted herself with false blemishes and dressed in old women's clothes or worn Dirk's trousers, done anything to escape the notice of the Soviet soldiers. It had worked – until the time when she had been carrying buckets of water back home from the standpipe and a group of them, drunk as lords, had come staggering down the street, seized her and dragged her into the ruins. Hours later, Dirk had found first the upturned, empty buckets and then her, lying where they had left her unconscious. The bruises had faded and the deep cut on her forehead had healed but the nightmare had never gone away and never would.

And then, at the beginning of July, the British and the American troops had arrived in the city. They had brought with them law and order, doctors, medicines, employment, and food. Most important of all, they had brought hope. Hope of a future where there had been almost none.

For a while, life had seemed a little brighter, but Rudi was still no better. Each day he seemed to grow thinner and weaker. There was no fresh milk or eggs or fruit for children and the Russian-run hospital had no vitamins or supplements to spare. *Take Rudi. Look after him, whatever happens*. Her mother's last words to her: a sacred trust.

She was at her wits' end when one day, when she had been working in the ruins, a young American soldier had stopped to photograph her and then started talking. He could get fresh food, he'd told her, smiling a white-toothed, easy-going sort of smile – if she was nice to him. After him, there had been other American soldiers and, when Rudi had been so close to death with polio, an army doctor who had provided medicine and vitamin pills. Always Americans because she'd learned that they had the most food and supplies. The British were too poor, the French too mean. Compared with the Russians, the Americans were decent human beings. It was not *frau komm!* but *hi, fräulein!* She had learned how to be nice to them and she had taught herself to see it as a simple business deal. The daily toil in the ruins, digging and shovelling, carting and scraping, helped her not to think too much about anything else.

Nico had not stubbed out his cigarette properly; she could smell it still smouldering away. She got up and, reluctant to touch with her fingers what had touched his lips, carried the ashtray to the open window and tipped the cigarette end out.

Then Dirk came into the room. By the swagger in his step, she knew he had made some black market deal that had pleased him very much. He was cock-a-hoop, as though he had achieved something wonderful. Once, long ago, there had been talk of him going to university to become a lawyer; of herself studying languages to become a teacher. Such plans. Such dreams. All come to dust. She was glad that her mother could not see what they had both become. 'Nico was here,' she told him. 'He came to warn us that the Russians are going to blockade Berlin.'

'It was bound to happen.'

'The British and Americans will have to leave, he thinks.'

'I told you so.'

'Then we're lost.'

He shrugged. 'We have come through everything this far, Lili. What's the difference?'

Six

From the control tower windows at Gatow, Harrison watched the Dakota descending out of thick cloud. It was the last of the thirteen to fly in that day from RAF Wunstorf in the British zone of northern Germany and, between them, the Daks had brought in about forty tons of food. There had been a mad scramble, both by the British and the Americans, to organize the airlifting of supplies into west Berlin. Nobody was pretending that the civilian rations could be provided by air once the present food stocks in the city were exhausted; the general view was that it need only be a short-term affair – a ten-day operation, at the most, while negotiations took place with the Russians to open up the lifelines again.

Harrison was not so sure. So far as he could see the Russians had shown themselves to be obdurate and they had outmanoeuvred the western Allies at every turn. They held too many aces. Not only was it going to be impossible to feed three and a half million west Berliners by air, but other things, equally vital to the life of the city, would soon run out – coal, petrol, diesel, oil. The city's main power station lay in the Russian sector and its output to the west had been cut off as summarily as the roads and railways and canals. Extra generators were being flown in but eighty per cent of the electricity supply had been lost. The mayor, Ernst Reuter, had made a brave speech to a huge crowd of cheering people in a stadium in the French sector, rallying them to stand up to the Russian bully-boys. He'd called upon the world to help the Berliners in their fight for freedom.

'Well, we're doing all we can,' Tubby had commented drily. 'Jolly ironic, isn't it? Not so long since the RAF were popping over to kill all these people and now we're popping over to help them stay alive. Quite a volte-face. It takes some getting used to, don't you think?'

'It's not just for the Berliners,' he'd said. 'It's for everything we fought for. I'm damned if we'll let the Russians get away with it.' The thought of what the Soviets were doing – the sneaky, outrageous game that they were playing – enraged Harrison. Thousands of good, brave men had died in order to win the war against Hitler and tyranny and now it seemed that it had been in vain. Tyranny was not dead at all. It lived on and flourished in the shape of Stalin and Communism. Liberty was still far beyond the grasp of every man. Realistically, he held out little hope for Berlin; in the end, it would probably disappear into the Soviet zone. Be swallowed up and lost. There was only so much they could fly into the city. What would happen when the stocks of coal, for instance, ran out? No power, no electricity, no gas, no heat. The only sane hope lay in the Russians being willing to negotiate and kindly lift the blockade which he thought was about as likely as pigs flying.

He watched the Dakota touch down in the pouring rain, sending up a long wake of water, more like a boat than an aircraft. The wet weather was an added problem. The new runway was still unfinished and the alternative landing strip was made of pierced steel planking laid over grass which was not designed to withstand heavily loaded aircraft, especially in soggy conditions. The only other western airfield was Tempelhof in the American sector, a pre-war civil airport. A third was being built in the French sector, but how long would that take? A lot longer than it would take for all stocks to be exhausted. The Dakota had reached the end of the runway and turned off towards the unloading hardstands. It was carrying sacks of flour – three tons of the stuff, its maximum-load capacity. A drop in the ocean, as Tubby had so rightly said.

The Russians didn't hold *all* the aces, though. There was no shortage of either British or American pilots with wartime flying experience to call on and the Americans, particularly, had large numbers of transport planes. And one more thing – the trump card in their hand – was their first-class system of radar-controlled talk-down. A controller sitting out in a cabin on Gatow airfield had been able to direct the Dakota through heavy low-based cloud from the Frohnau beacon ten miles out and bring it safely down onto the runway. All thirteen aircraft had been landed that way, and there was no reason why controllers couldn't handle a steady stream of them. They could certainly increase the traffic by a hundred per cent and the long summer hours of daylight would help. Come to that, with radar there was no reason why they couldn't fly at night as well. All night. And all day. The logistics would be a nightmare, but seemingly impossible military rescues had been miraculously achieved before – Dunkirk, for one.

He had been too busy to get into the city since the crisis had begun but he'd heard that things were pretty bad already. There'd been big power cuts, down to only four hours of electricity a day, cuts in the gas supply, cuts in public transport, cuts in food rations, breakdowns in services . . . western Berlin was sliding back into its former miserable, desperate state. Tough luck on the civilians. Bizarrely, there was no restriction on moving about the city. The Russian soldiers, apparently, still goose-stepped several times a day to change their guard at the Soviet war memorial on the western side of the Brandenburg Gate, acting as though nothing had happened, and the Russian-controlled Radio Berlin, also in the British sector, continued to pour out a never-ending stream of Soviet propaganda from the *Rundfunkhaus*.

The Leicht family would be all right in the Soviet zone, of course. There would be electric lighting, the same ration of food as before, everything pretty much as usual. There was enough rubble left to provide Lili Leicht with manual labour for decades to come. And Dirk was a survivor. The Leichts would be all right, he thought dispassionately. They were lucky.

Somehow Dirk had got hold of an old bicycle. He had come back with it from one of his forays into the country and refused to give a proper explanation.

'It was in an outhouse. Rusting away in a corner. I could see this old couple didn't want it any more.'

'You mean you stole it?'

He looked injured. 'It wasn't like that, Lili.'

'Did you ask their permission?'

'I didn't have to. They were past riding it and, anyway, it wasn't fit to ride. The chain was off and the brakes didn't work.'

'Did you give them something for it?'

He shook his head, grinning. 'Actually, they gave *me* something. Beetroots. A whole lot of them. Look.'

He produced the sack from behind his back – at least three kilos' worth. She didn't ask what he had given for them, or if he had given anything at all; he could easily have simply dug them up. But it was hard to find any fault when they needed the food so badly. For all the Russian promises of good rations and the propaganda comparisons to the stark situation in western blockaded Berlin, they had been without any meat or fresh food for nearly two weeks. They'd been living on old potatoes – green ones, sprouting eyes – and stale bread. The beetroots looked firm and must have some goodness in them – vitamins of some kind. Vitamin C, certainly, and perhaps others, too. They would surely help Rudi. She would grate the smaller, better ones and they could eat them raw, the rest she would turn into soup. She showed them to Rudi who was lying listlessly on the couch. He kept on coughing.

'Look what Dirk has found for us.'

He turned his head to look, but without much interest. The plane that the English squadron leader had given him was still clutched in one hand; he had been making small swoops in the air with it earlier – but feeble ones. His pallor was frightening.

'I have forgotten the name of that plane,' she said in an effort to cheer him up. 'What is it?'

'A Dakota. That's what the RAF call it. The Americans call it a DC3. It's funny, they often call the same plane different names.'

'Do they? How strange.'

He lifted the plane up and let it flop down again. 'Do you think the squadron leader will come back here again?'

She thought of their last bitter encounter. 'I very much doubt it.'

'I'd like him to. He was very nice. And he knows all about planes. He might even bring me some more pictures.'

'I'm sure he would. But I don't think he'll have time to come back, Rudi. He must be very busy.'

'Could you ask him?'

She hesitated, not wanting to disappoint him. 'I

really don't think so. In any case, I don't know how to get in touch with him.'

'Nico would. He knows everything. We could ask him.'

She shook her head firmly. 'No, I don't want to do that. It's better not. Look, we're going to have beetroots for supper. You like beetroots, don't you?'

'I can't remember.'

'Well, you must eat as much of them as you can. They'll do you lots of good.'

He turned his head away again and presently closed his eyes. She sat with him for a while until she saw that he had drifted off to sleep. She wondered what on earth to do. It was a risk to take Rudi to the hospital. She did not trust them there. The Russians ran it and they did not care if German civilians lived or died – or so it seemed to her. In fact, they much preferred them dead. She went to find Dirk who was in the hallway, tinkering with the bike. 'I'm going to see that doctor who lives down the street, Dirk. Dr Meier. He might come and look at Rudi.'

'He's a hundred years old and dotty.'

'Even so . . . there's nobody else. Rudi's asleep at the moment, and so's Grandfather. Will you stay here and watch them both?'

'How long will you be? I have to go out.'

'Not long. I'll be back as soon as I can.'

He nodded. 'OK. I'll wait till you get back.'

'Must you go?'

He went on fiddling with the chain. 'It's business.'

'Will you ride out into the country tomorrow and

see if you can find some more fresh vegetables? For Rudi.'

'I'll do my best. It's not easy. The Soviets have stripped everything bare. Nothing's easy since the blockade.'

'Anything, Dirk. *Anything*.'

He looked up, alarmed. 'You don't think Rudi's seriously ill, do you? I mean, worse than he often gets?'

'I don't know. That's why I'm going to see Dr Meier.'

'It won't do any good.'

She went, nonetheless.

The old man lived alone in the cellar of a building at the river end of the street. Before, he had lived in one of the apartments above but a bomb had destroyed them all. He had been dug out of the ruins, the only occupant to have survived.

Occasionally, Lili had seen him out on the street, always wearing a long, old-fashioned overcoat and black beret, whatever the weather, walking slowly and carrying a brown canvas bag for his rations. He was a widower and had been so for years – that was all she knew about him. That, and his name. It was also rumoured that he was a Jew, but she knew that must be false. If he had been Jewish he would not have been overlooked by the Nazis or spared. They had taken away very old people, just as they had taken very young children. Age had made no difference whatever. She remembered the time when the SS had come in the middle of one night to arrest the family who had lived on the floor above. How Frau

Gross had begged and wailed and wept and the two little girls, Elsa and Christel, had screamed with terror. The wails and the screams had sounded all the way down the stairwell and then outside in the courtyard and then in the street when they were being pushed into the back of a lorry like animals going to market. And then still more cries when the lorry had been driven away, growing fainter until, finally, there had been silence.

The entrance to the cellar was down stone steps from the pavement – a dark, dank and dismal well littered with all kinds of rubbish and filth accumulated from the street above. Lili knocked gently on the door and waited for several minutes before knocking again, louder. At last the door was opened and the old man stood there. Without his beret and long coat she scarcely knew him. He looked different: not so doddery. The beret had partly concealed a fine head of silver-white hair and his blue eyes were piercing.

'Excuse me, Herr Doktor. My name is Lili Leicht. I also live in Albrecht Strasse.'

'Yes, I know,' he said. 'I have seen you passing in the street, Fräulein. What can I do for you?' His voice was quite firm, not quavery at all. As she hesitated, he took a pace backwards. 'Would you like to come in?'

She stepped inside. Where they lived was bad enough but this cellar was worse. Like a prison cell. One small, barred window, set high in the wall, let in a little daylight and the few sticks of furniture were even more rickety than their own.

He dragged forward a bentwood chair – the kind that belonged in cheap bars and cafés. 'Please sit down, Fräulein.' He sat on the only other one himself, moving slowly and stiffly. 'How may I help you?'

'It's my brother, Rudi. He is nine years old.'

'I have seen him too. And you have another brother, I think?'

'Dirk.'

'He would be about seventeen, I think. And your grandfather still lives?'

'Yes.'

'But your father was executed in the war. In a Nazi camp. And your mother and grandmother died when your apartment was bombed. Is this all correct?'

'Yes.' How could he know so much about them? They had only nodded to each other, never spoken more than a polite greeting: *Guten Morgen, Guten Tag, Guten Abend.*

'So, now you must be mother and father to all the family. That is a big responsibility. What is it about your Rudi that worries you so much?'

'He's not well. For a long time he has been in poor health. Last year he got polio and nearly died. I'm not sure what is the matter with him now but I am afraid for him.'

'Forgive me, Fräulein, but much as I sympathize with you, I do not know how I can help you.'

'I thought perhaps, Herr Doktor, that you would be kind enough to come and see him.'

'For what purpose?'

'To give an opinion. Of course, you will have been retired for many years, but I am sure that a doctor does not forget everything he has learned.'

He shook his head. 'But you are under a misapprehension, Fräulein. I am not a doctor of medicine. I am a doctor of music.'

She blushed at her stupid mistake. 'I'm sorry. I have disturbed you for nothing.'

'It is *I* who should be sorry that I cannot help you. To be a doctor of medicine would be much more useful, especially since I can no longer play any music.' He held up his mittened hands and she saw that the fingers were bent like claws. 'I suffer badly from rheumatism.'

'How sad for you.'

'It no longer seems important. I am an organist, or was; regrettably there are not many churches left in Berlin. Do you play an instrument, Fräulein?'

'The piano,' she said. 'But the Russians chopped ours to pieces.'

He gestured round the cellar. 'They came here too but there was nothing much for them to destroy. They were quite annoyed.' He smiled at her. Once, long ago, she thought, he must have been very handsome. 'I met your father once or twice – at the university. Our paths did not cross often but I remember him well. He was a most gifted man. Much respected and admired. And most courageous. I deeply regret what happened to him.'

'Thank you.'

'It's a pity that there were not many more like him. If there had been our country's history might have been quite different. As it is, we find ourselves in a pitiable state, do we not, Fräulein? Defeated and disgraced. Unable to hold up our heads because we are all Nazis – that is how our conquerors perceive us.'

'But it's not true.'

'That may be so but I am afraid our former enemies will never believe it. Why should they? They have seen the photographs of the big rallies, the swastika flags flying, thousands of people saluting our Führer; and, most damning of all, they have seen film of the death camps and the great piles of corpses. The camera does not lie.'

She shuddered. 'We knew nothing of that. Nothing.'

'Nevertheless, we are seen to be guilty as a people, Fräulein, if not as individuals. Your father did everything he could against the Nazis and paid for it with his life. You can, at least, remember that with pride.'

'I do,' she said. 'I remember it always.'

'It should give you strength. Courage.'

She said wearily, 'But there is so little to hope for. When the British and Americans arrived, I thought for a while that everything was going to get better, but now they are sure to abandon us because of the blockade and it will be just as terrible as it was before. Worse. We will have to live under the Russians for ever.'

'You are so certain that the western Allies will go?'

'Aren't you?'

'No. Not at all. I think they will stay. The British

and the Americans are not the kind to give up easily. Have you met any of their people here?'

'A Royal Air Force officer – a bomber pilot in the war. He dropped bombs on Berlin and he didn't care a bit about killing civilians and reducing the city to rubble.'

'They saw it as the only way to defeat the Nazis. And who knows, perhaps they were right. In any case, we must look upon them as our allies now – the only hope we have against the Russians. Our fate lies in their hands.' He looked at her thoughtfully. 'The children of Berlin have suffered badly. They have gone without the food they need to grow up straight-limbed and healthy. You are afraid for your young brother. You want, above all, for him to get his health and strength back. You love him dearly and doubtless you would do anything for him. Am I right?'

She nodded.

'If I may suggest it, you should find a friend among the Occupation Forces here in Berlin. I believe the Americans have plenty of supplies and are very generous.' He paused as she was silent. 'You understand me?'

'Yes, perfectly. I already know this. There was no need to tell me.' She stood up. 'I am sorry to have taken your time.'

'I have all the time in the world.' He waited until she had reached the door before speaking again. 'I am afraid that I have offended you, dear Fräulein.'

She shook her head. 'You didn't offend me, Herr Doktor. And it was very good advice.'

Dirk was bent over the bike in the apartment hallway, doing something to one of the pedals. He looked up. 'Well?'

'He's not a doctor of medicine. He's a doctor of music.'

He spun the pedal backwards very fast so that it made a whirring sound. 'I told you it would be a waste of time.'

Tubby, growling away like a bear in his corner chair in the Officers' Mess, was in a belligerent mood. 'That Yank general, Clay, has a point, you know, Michael. Why not use an armed convoy and force a way through on the autobahn? *Make* the buggers give way? I'm on his side. I've decided that all this pussyfooting around, trying not to upset the Ruskies, is a lot of bloody nonsense and I've had enough of it.'

'And risk starting another war?'

'They'd never dare. They'd back down, like all bullies.'

'We can't be sure of that, Tubby. We've only got something like a third of the number of troops in Berlin that the Soviets have and there are thousands more of theirs out in their zone, surrounding the city. We're not equipped to start any kind of a show-down, let alone a full-scale war. Nor are the Americans. And the first thing the Russians would do would be to take Berlin – the very thing we're trying to stop.'

'They may have hordes of troops but most of 'em are badly trained peasants. And they haven't got the technical know-how, have they? No long-range aircraft. Obsolete weapons.' Tubby wagged a finger. 'And *we've* got the atomic bomb. The Yanks haven't sent those B29s over to England for nothing and they made damned sure Stalin knew about it.'

'The bomb's a deterrent, that's all. A bit of sabre-rattling. It would be unthinkable to use it in this situation.'

'Well, *I'm* thinking of it. How much longer is this tomfoolery going to drag on? Damn it, they're rationing the whisky and the food's uneatable. Everything's bloody dried. Dried eggs, dried potato, dried milk, dried meat, dried carrots, dried peas . . .'

'Water's heavy,' Harrison said mildly. 'Dehydrated foods are much lighter to transport and take up less room.'

'I know that, but is it worth all the effort, I ask myself? We can't possibly fly in enough stuff. Only two airfields we can use in Berlin and some chap from out at Wunstorf told me that it's a shambles their end. Flying Control there can't cope with the traffic. Not enough people to run the show, everything keeps breaking down and they're chronically short of spares. Chaos. Pretty chaotic here, too, I'd say.'

'It was at the start but those days are past. We're getting some sort of proper system going and it's beginning to work. And we'll have a third airfield before long when Tegel's finished.'

'Huh! I was over there the other day. Looks like a bomb site. Hundreds of German fraus in frocks hauling tons of rubble about. It'll be next year before anything can be flown in there.'

'I bet you they'll get it done a lot sooner than that. Those women work damn hard.'

'I know they do. I've seen them at it all over the place. But there are limits to their muscle power, especially on their measly rations. Soup and bread, that's all they get given. Not exactly body-building fare. Let's be realistic.'

'I am,' Harrison assured him. 'You're forgetting their will power, Tubby. They know it's their only chance to beat the Russians. So do we, come to that. And now we've got the Yorks and the Hastings as well as the Daks, we're carrying far bigger loads. And the Sunderlands are doing a damn good job coming in on the lake. The Americans have thirty-five C-54s as well as their C-47s. Between us we're bringing in a pretty steady flow.'

'Not enough, dear boy. Nowhere near, is it?'

'Don't be such a Jeremiah. I didn't think it would really be possible at first, either, but now I've a feeling it just might be. It'd help if the bloody weather would improve. Rain, hail, fog. Christ, this is supposed to be midsummer.'

'Wait until it's winter. The winters here can make England seem positively tropical. What happens then? When we've run out of fuel? We can't run the power stations on dried eggs.'

'We've already begun flying in coal.'

'I know, but you can't dehydrate *that*, can you? A ton of coal is a ton of coal. And it'll take a hell of a lot of tons to keep western Berlin going all winter.

I still say we should do what General Clay wants – storm the ramparts.'

He knew that Tubby had a point: the reality was that they were probably fighting a losing battle. The two airfields in western Berlin could barely cope as it was, and if they were to have any serious chance of success the number of aircraft had to be vastly increased. In the early days of the airlift there had been a frantic scramble to recruit more trained men and all stores had been ransacked for radios, spare parts, tools, ropes, steel planking, pots and pans – anything that could conceivably be put to use in any way. They'd rounded up lorries and jeeps and signed on thousands of German men and women as labourers and loaders.

He knew the bald facts and figures. There were forty-three RAF Dakotas available from Transport Command and forty Avro Yorks. The daily RAF target had been increased to eight hundred and forty tons and the Americans were bringing in three thousand more than that with their C-47s and C-54s. This was the minimum considered necessary to support the three and a half million western Berliners and the Allied forces in their sectors. Apart from the basic food consignments, salt – apparently essential for the human body as well as for industry – had to be carried. Thirty-eight tons of it were needed every day. And salt corroded aircraft. Fortunately, the Sunderland flying boats, designed to get round this very snag, had come to the rescue, landing on Lake Havel, close to Gatow.

The problem of carrying coal was an even bigger

headache. First, it was heavy. Second, it took up a great deal of space. Third, it had to be carried in something and there was a serious shortage of sacks. Fourth, and trickiest of all, the black coal dust was not only unpleasant, it was dangerous. It leaked from the sacks and got into every nook and cranny of an aircraft, eroding wiring and jamming controls. Hosing down simply made matters worse, and the only way to keep the menace at bay was for every coal-carrying aircraft to be swept out by hand with brooms and brushes.

But the biggest nightmare of all was controlling the constant stream of air traffic. The three air corridors across the Russian zone into Berlin were only twenty miles wide and the British and American aircraft were of disparate types and capabilities, flying at different speeds and heights. To prevent mid-air collisions they had to be spaced horizontally as well as vertically. There was no chance of flying in dense formations and the only safe and efficient way of bringing them down in a confined runway space was one at a time. In Flying Control they had worked out that theoretically it should be possible to allow an aircraft to land and another to take off every five minutes but in practice it was more like every fifteen minutes. The bad weather had hampered them too much. So had difficulties in loading and emergency repairs and teething problems with ground control. There had already been two RAF crashes involving Yorks, one at Wunstorf and one at Gatow. The Americans had lost three C-54s in one day, landing at Tempelhof in bad weather, and two other Skymasters had crashed on Berlin – one hitting an apartment block, the other landing in a street in the Friednau district. Men had died and would go on dying.

He finished his beer and saw that Tubby's glass was empty.

'Same again?'

'As long as it lasts. Mark my prophetic words, Michael, we'll soon be drinking water.'

Seven

Lili opened the lid of her mother's trunk slowly, half afraid that the hats might somehow have vanished. But they were still there, in all their glory. She lifted one or two out, trying them on in turn. No looking glass had survived in the apartment, but her mother had kept a silver-backed hand mirror in the trunk and she used this now to see her reflection.

Since childhood, as a special treat, she had been allowed to try on the hats – exquisite, extravagant, beguiling concoctions following the Parisian styles and made with the finest materials and the greatest skill. Before the war in the Twenties and early Thirties her mother's little shop in Dessauer Strasse had been patronized by some of the most elegant women in Berlin. When the Nazi Secret State Police had moved into premises just around the corner and begun their reign of terror, the shop had stayed open. It had remained open for the first year of the war, when the victories had come easily and Berlin women had worn the latest fashions from France and draped themselves in Norwegian silver fox furs, and when every streetcar had smelled divinely of French perfume. And then the bad news had started and the bombs had begun to fall and instead of the smell of French perfume there was the stench of corpses. The shop had closed. Nobody was buying such hats any more. It was thought profligate; wasteful; unpatriotic. In her mother's opinion, though, the opposite was true. Beautiful hats on beautiful women would do more for morale, she had declared, than any nonsense that Herr Goebbels could think up. In times of crisis it was the duty of women to look their very best. One had only to follow the example of the French who had never allowed defeat and enemy occupation to lower their sartorial standards. The Nazis, though, had thought otherwise. Clothes had been strictly rationed: lists drawn up for men and women of the number of items permitted to be purchased and the points required for each. Materials were cheap and shoddy, the clothes ill fitting. Only two pairs of shoes were allowed and the Gestapo would visit homes to count them. If they found more the shoes were seized and a fine had to be paid.

Apart from her wooden-soled shoes, Lili possessed only one other pair. They were of soft navy blue leather with high heels and had belonged to her mother and been made before the war. She had one good dress: a dark blue silk with a pattern of small black dots and a heart-shaped neckline. One of the hats in the trunk suited it perfectly: a little black cap of grosgrain, made to perch at the front of the head, with a wisp of black veiling to cover the brow and the eyes.

Rudi had felt too poorly to get up that morning and lay on his truckle bed in the room he shared with Dirk and Grandfather. He had a book beside him but it was shut and he had his eyes closed. She knelt beside the bed.

'I'm going out for a little while but I shan't be long. Will you be all right?'

He nodded. 'I've been listening to see if I could hear the American planes landing at Tempelhof but it's too far from here. I should so much like to go and watch them. And the RAF out at Gatow.'

'When you're better perhaps Dirk will take you on the back of his bike.'

'He says he saw the big flying boats landing on the Harvel See. The British Sunderlands. There was a huge crowd watching on the banks and everybody cheered. They are bringing in salt, you know. The other planes are bringing food and even coal. It must make the Russians very angry, mustn't it?'

'I should think so.'

'They can't stop them flying though, can they?'

'Not very easily. Not unless they shoot them down and I don't think even they dare do that.'

He smiled faintly. 'It's rather funny, isn't it, Lili? They thought they were being so clever shutting the roads and railways but they forgot all about the air.'

'Yes, it doesn't always go their way.'

'Only Dirk says the British and Americans will never be able to fly in enough of everything. Do you think he's right?'

She said slowly, 'I think it will be very difficult to do so for very long.'

'But they might manage it?'

'They might.'

'What if they don't? Dirk says the people who live in their part of the city will starve.'

She ruffled his hair. 'Don't listen to everything that Dirk says. Don't worry, something will be sorted out. Shall I fetch your scrapbook for you to look at?'

'Not now. Is that one of Mother's hats?'

'Yes. I thought I'd wear a special hat today as it's Sunday. Do you like it?'

'It's pretty.'

'Do you remember how she used to make them? The little shop she had?'

'No, not really. I can hardly remember her at all now. What was she like?'

He had asked the question several times before and it was always hard to answer. Only one or two photographs had survived to show him – fuzzy snapshots that couldn't really give him much idea. 'Beautiful to look at and full of life and energy. Always laughing.'

'I think I remember that – her laughing. And Father, what was he like?'

'Much quieter. An intellectual. Rather serious. Very kind and also very brave.'

'Do you think he was afraid – before he died?'

'I think he had a great inner strength which helped him not to be.'

He stared up at the ceiling. 'I've been thinking . . . when the bombs killed Mother and Grandmother it was at night, wasn't it? So it must have been the

Royal Air Force because the Americans only came by day.'

'Yes. It must have been.'

He was silent for a minute. 'I still like the English squadron leader, don't you?'

She said obliquely, 'It was kind of him to bring you the pictures and the model.' She stood up. 'Grandfather is snoring away in his chair. Try to sleep a little, too, if you can. It will do you good.'

She took one more look in the silver hand mirror, tilting the hat further forward and adjusting the veiling over her eyes. It gave her the comforting feeling of being concealed: to be able to see without being wholly seen. As a final touch, she opened the bottle of Chanel No 5 that Nico had given her and dabbed the scent behind her ears and at her throat and wrists. Her mother's hat, her mother's shoes, her mother's favourite scent. So strongly did she feel her presence that she might have been there in the room standing beside her. *Look after Rudi, whatever happens.*

The sun came out as she walked down Albrecht Strasse but a cool wind made her shiver in the silk dress. The See was running fast, swollen from the heavy rain and dotted with all kinds of debris. When the zoo had been bombed and the cages damaged, the crocodiles had tried to escape into the river but had been hauled out and shot. She could remember how sorry she had felt for them: to have been so close to freedom. As she crossed the bridge, she could see some poor dead animal bobbing along half-submerged. It could have been a dog or cat or perhaps a rabbit; it was impossible to tell from the glimpse of sodden fur. Few dogs and cats had survived so it was probably a rabbit. Berlin had once been full of them. They had run wild in the Tiergarten and hopped about courtyards and alley-ways – until, like anything edible, they had become food.

Now, instead of rabbits running everywhere, there were rats: thousands of rats that had fed off the corpses buried in the ruins and grown fat and strong. When she was working in the rubble, turning over stones and great lumps of masonry, they would run out; once one had scampered straight over her foot. Some of them had grown fear-less and would sit at a short distance, grooming themselves and watching with their beady little eyes. Almost worse than the rats were the flies in summer – great shining green flies that nobody had ever seen before. They rolled around in horrible clumps on the pavements and warmed themselves in the sun on the broken glass. In the apartment, she could hear them rustling and humming in crevices and in the roof space overhead and sometimes they gathered on the window sills, fouling everything they touched. The only respite from them came with winter.

She walked down Friedrich Strasse. Once, before the war, the street had been a beautiful place to stroll and window-shop and, if you had the money, to buy, and then to eat in one of the wonderful restaurants. Now it was a ghost street. She turned into the Linden towards the Brandenburg Gate where there were often American soldiers hanging around; it was where she had picked up the army doctor. Foreigners always wanted to see that Gate, to photograph it and be photographed standing in front of it. It fascinated them. Dirk said that some of them were so naive that you could offer to sell them Adolf Hitler's watch and they'd believe you.

She reached the Gate and walked through one of the archways to the open platz beyond and the boundary between the Soviet and British sectors. Before the blockade there had only been a white line painted in the road, now there were coils of barbed wire and a long striped pole. The Russian guard stopped her, demanding her ID papers. She took them out of her handbag and waited impassively while he examined them. Officially, there was no restriction against movement from one sector to another and thousands crossed in each direction daily, but the Russians always made trouble for German civilians if they could find the slightest excuse. And the fear was always there. He handed back her papers, thrusting them at her rudely, and raised the pole.

She walked across the white line into the British sector. There were no American soldiers to be seen, only a handful of German civilians – an old couple walking slowly arm in arm, a mother leading a young child by the hand, some small boys playing with old piping on a piece of wasteland. The wind was worse here, sweeping up the broad expanse of the East-West Axis from the Tiergarten so that she had to hold on to her hat. She stood, pretending to admire the Gate, when in reality she hated the very sight of it.

After a while, one of the black Volkswagen Occupation Forces taxis drew up, and from the corner of her eye she saw that the man who got out of it was wearing an American uniform. She went on staring up at the Gate and he came and stood a few feet away from her, hands in his pockets, chewing gum: a sergeant with a striped chevron on his arm and wearing a forage cap, somewhere in his late twenties. She could tell, out of the corner of her eyes, that he was looking at her as well as at the Gate, and presently she turned her head and smiled at him. He smiled back and walked over. She saw that he carried a camera in his hand. 'Say, Fräulein, you speak English?'

Thank God she did because they never spoke German. 'Yes, I do.'

He nodded at the Gate. 'Maybe you could tell me about this place.'

'The history? It was built in the eighteenth century and is a copy of an ancient triumphal arch in Athens.'

'Gee, that so?'

'There were other gates in Berlin too, but this is now the only one.' She pointed. 'You see the statue of the chariot with four horses on the top, facing the other way, towards the Russian side?'

'Yeah.'

'They are being driven by Victory.'

'Sure seems like they got that wrong.'

She smiled politely at the joke. 'Napoleon thought

so too. When he conquered the city he took the statue home to France with him. It was only returned after his defeat.'

He chewed on the gum, staring upwards. 'Guess I never thought about Napoleon havin' anythin' to do with it . . . just Hitler. This is where he'd hold those big Nazi rallies, that right?'

'Some of them, yes.'

'Spooky . . .'

'What does this word mean – spooky?'

'Give you the shivers . . . you know.'

She knew exactly.

'Tell you the truth, no offence, but the whole damn city does that. It's a helluva spooky place.' He fiddled with the camera. 'Mind takin' a shot of me in front of the Gate? My folks back home would be real interested.'

'Of course.'

He showed her how to operate the camera and when she had taken several pictures of him, posing in front of the Gate, he wanted to take one of her. She could imagine him showing it off to his family in America, pointing out the German fräulein he'd met – unless he was married, of course, in which case it would be shown only to other men with much elbow-digging and mirth. Soon he would want to know her name and, sure enough, it was his next question. 'Cute name,' he said when she had told him. Cute she had learned already from the other Americans. It meant *suss*, more or less. Sweet. He grinned at her, still working away at the gum, jaws chomping steadily like an ox. He was not so bad-looking but somehow he repelled her. 'Mine's Donald but everyone calls me Bud. Say, can we take a walk, or somethin'?'

She steeled herself. 'The Tiergarten is very close, if you like.'

'Suits me.'

Once it had been such a pleasure to walk there; now to do so was only sadness. The lovely trees had been hacked to the ground and all that was left were scrubby bushes and mud and puddles. The famous Goldfish Pond had no fish and the beautiful tree-lined waterways where Berliners had gone boating in summer were bleak and bare.

'This was a hunting place for royal princes before it became a park for the people. It was landscaped in the English style,' she told him.

'You don't say?'

'But I am afraid, of course, that it is not very nice now. All the trees have been cut down, the wood all taken for fuel.'

'Well, I guess you needed it. You get some pretty cold winters here, that right?'

She knew he would not really understand at all how terrible it had been. 'Yes, they can be very bad.'

'Where I come from, in Texas, our winters ain't nothin' to worry about. Summers are real hot, though. We have a big problem stayin' cool.' He looked around apprehensively. 'This place safe?'

Perhaps he suspected that she was luring him into some sort of trap where he would be robbed, even murdered. For all she knew, it was not so safe for an American who would be bound to be carrying cigarettes and dollars. 'We will not go far, if you prefer.'

A cold trickle of water had seeped through a hole in the sole of her left shoe; she prayed it would not get worse. 'You are in the American army, Bud?'

'Sure thing.'

'What is your work?'

'I'm a cook.'

Her heart leaped but she kept her voice casual. 'That's very interesting. Do you like the work?'

'Yeah. Matter of fact, I get a real kick out of it. 'Course lately we've had to tighten our belts since the Soviets stopped our supplies comin' overland, but we're gettin' stuff in by air all the time, so we ain't starvin' yet – no sir.' He glanced at her. 'I guess you folks are findin' the same. Our boys are gettin' the food to you all right. That so?'

'Actually, I live in the Russian sector. We are given Soviet rations.'

'Gee . . . what're they like?'

'Bad. We get only dried or very old things. And my little brother is not at all well.'

'Sure am sorry to hear that.'

'If only he could have some good fresh food I think he would get better.' The break in her voice was genuine; she had no need to pretend. 'But I do not know how this can be found in Berlin.'

He looked at her, longer this time. 'Mebbe I could help some . . .'

'Oh, do you really think you could?'

'Like I said, it ain't so easy now.'

She stopped on the muddy path and gazed up at

him through the hat veil. 'I'd be *so* grateful, Bud.'

He nodded. 'Yeah, I guess you would. Say, this park ain't much of a place. You live near here?'

'Quite near. We could easily walk there.'

'OK by me.'

'It is not much of a place either.'

She took him back to the apartment and saw how it shocked him. He stood staring round the room as though he couldn't believe his eyes.

'Jeez, you folks really have to live like this?'

She unpinned her hat and took it off. 'There are many much worse.'

Grandfather was fast asleep in his chair. 'He will not wake up,' she said. 'Excuse me, I will just see if my little brother is all right.' Rudi was asleep too. She drew the blanket closer round him and shut the bedroom door. When she went back the American was lighting a cigarette. He had taken off his cap and his hair was cut very short, the same length all over like the bristles of a brush. He held out the Camels to her. 'Smoke?'

'Later, perhaps.'

'Here, have the pack.'

They were always very generous. 'Thank you.'

He looked round the room and she knew he had noticed the couch bed in the corner. 'So, who lives here – apart from Grandpa and your kid brother?'

'Just another brother. He is older. He is out at the moment.'

'No Mom and Dad?'

'They are both dead.'

'And no husband?'

141

'No. I am not married.'

'Didn't think so. I guess there ain't too many German guys left around for you fräuleins.' He was looking her over as he spoke. 'You sure are a pretty girl, Lili. Real cute with that hat on and just as pretty without it.'

She managed to smile at him. 'Thank you.'

'You met many Americans?'

'No,' she lied. 'You are the first one.'

'No kiddin'?'

It was rather hard to understand him; his accent was strange. Very nasal. She said, 'We have a little ersatz coffee left – if you would like some.'

'No, thanks. I've tried that stuff. Mebbe I could get you some of the real thing. How about that?'

She shook her head vehemently. 'Not coffee, *no*. That is not necessary. Only food for my brother. That is what we need so much. Food that is good for children to help them grow. I told you. Some meat, if it is at all possible. Fresh eggs and milk . . .' She had gone too far. He was frowning, not so pleased. She said quietly, 'I am sorry. Anything would be wonderful for us. Anything at all. I will be very grateful, you know.'

He came close and stood looking down at her. He was not very tall but built heavily, with power-ful shoulders, and he had large and ugly hands. A shiver of revulsion ran through her but she made herself look up at him – forced herself to smile invitingly. The frown vanished and he smiled too. 'Well, I guess we both know what we're talkin' about. You've got yourself a deal, Lili.' He nodded towards the armchair. 'How about Grandpa?'

'He won't wake up if we are quiet. And there is a screen.'

'OK.'

'Your cigarette . . .'

'Sure.' He ground it out on the floorboards under his shoe.

He was clumsy, seizing hold of her, tugging at her clothes. The big hands were rough and his breath smelled of the Camel cigarette. She shut her eyes and turned her head away, clenching her teeth. With the Russians there had been the terror of mutilation or murder; with the other Americans she had not been afraid, only resigned. This time it was sheer disgust. She braced herself to endure it, willed herself to pretend to enjoy it, prayed it would be over quickly. He was panting like an animal now, thrusting himself against her; he would be inconsiderate, brutal even. Then suddenly there was a lot of shouting: Dirk's voice yelling in German, the American being dragged off her and shouting too, in English, demanding to know what the hell was going on. What the hell sort of a game were they playing? Dirk went on yelling crazily – in English now, fists flailing, and the screen crashed over. The American punched him away and was dragging on his clothes, buttoning his trousers, grabbing his cap, shouting back obscenities as he left. The front door banged.

Grandfather had woken up and was mumbling away in his chair and Rudi had come from his bed and stood anxiously in the doorway. She got up shakily from the couch, straightening the silk dress. 'Go back to bed, Rudi. Everything is all right. *Go on*, please.' She put her arm round Grandfather's shoulders, soothing him. To Dirk, she said, 'It wasn't the American's fault. It was mine. I asked him here. You should not have interfered.'

He stared at her, white-faced, blood trickling from his nose. 'For Christ's sake, Lili, there is no need any more.'

She said wearily, 'He was a cook. He would have been able to get things for Rudi.'

'I can get things.'

'Not fresh eggs and milk. Not fresh fruit and vegetables and meat. How often do you find those?' She righted the screen. 'He would have got them for me. He said he would.'

He wiped the blood away from his nose. 'Listen. I tell you what I will do. I have heard that the Americans are taking on extra German labour at Tempelhof. They need more men to load and unload the aircraft. Shift work and with extra rations. Tomorrow I will go there on the bike and get work. I will bring back the extra rations and whatever else I can find.'

'Steal, you mean?'

'What's the difference? That Yank would have stolen stuff for you. You didn't care about that, did you? Besides, the Americans have never suffered like us. If things get too bad for them, they can always pack up and leave and go back to their land of plenty. To their steaks and their eggs and their fresh milk. They are lucky. Lucky, lucky people. So that's what I'll do – if you swear you won't do this again.'

'Supposing the Russians stop you?'

'How can they stop me? Thousands of Berliners go to work in the western sectors every day. Besides, I'm not exactly going to tell them I'm off to help the Americans with their airlift, am I?' Dirk smeared away another trickle of blood with the back of his hand. 'He tore your dress, the bastard.'

'It doesn't matter. I can mend it.'

'Poor Lily. It was your best dress.'

'He left some cigarettes,' she said. 'Over there on the table.'

'Well, we may as well make use of them. I could do with one.' Dirk went to the table. He turned, grinning now. 'He also left his camera.'

Eight

The two Ground Control Approach cabins at Gatow were parked at the side of the runway. When the weather was bad, GCA took over from the tower controller to talk the pilots down. Harrison went to check on things. The crew of six were squashed together in a tiny space and hunched over four radar screens – two directors, two trackers and a controller in charge. Between them, they could locate an aircraft in the foulest weather, manoeuvre it onto its approach and guide the pilot to land precisely on the runway. Now it had to be done at night as well. There was no sign of the Russians being willing to negotiate a lifting of the blockade, and flying in supplies during daylight hours alone was no longer enough. As Harrison had envisaged, the airlift had become a round-the-clock operation.

The problem of controlling different types of aircraft flying at different speeds had been solved by keeping the types in a pack together – usually in tens. Even so, with other aircraft ahead or astern, above and below, there was no room for anything but meticulous flying. In a twelve-hour working day, pilots were flying as many as three trips. Some were flying a seven-day week on little sleep and poor food gobbled between flights and the strain was beginning to show. The aircraft were landing faster and more bumpily and taxiing was careless. Pilots were fumbling at the controls, forgetting to put down flaps, getting irritable – showing all the signs of exhaustion. There had been accidents and injuries. Harrison had tried to equate it with his own wartime ops experience but there were big differences and one in particular. Nobody – not even the Russians, as yet – was trying to shoot these aircraft down; it was more a question of asking too much of too few, of the need to improve conditions of food and sleep, for realistic rotas to be drawn up and leave given, before the airlift flew itself into the ground.

He left the GCA cabin and walked back to the tower. The Dakotas were coming in from Lübeck with their coal load. They were also carrying newspapers, cigarettes, tinned meat and powdered milk. And sacks of mail from home.

There were two letters for him: one from his mother and one from Celia. His mother's was characteristically chatty and cheerful – just as her letters had been throughout the war. All about the garden and the dogs, the cats and the village happenings. There had been a cricket match and a flower show and the vicar had said special prayers at Matins for the people of Berlin. *Your father didn't approve, I'm afraid. He says his prayers are reserved for all the Allied aircrews risking their necks for them. We're both so thankful that you're not flying this time. At least we don't have to worry about that.*

In many ways, he wished very much that he was. Whenever he saw the crews climbing down out of their planes and walking together across the tarmac to the canteen for their coffee and cigarettes, he felt a sense of loss. That uniquely close comradeship had gone from his life and he knew that nothing could ever replace it or compare with it. *Celia was home last weekend and came to have Sunday lunch with us. She's looking prettier than ever and is delightful company. We're so fond of her.* He smiled. Sledgehammer hints. *We talked about you a lot, of course. When you are next home on leave we must have a special celebration dinner all together.* He read on about the roses and the greenfly and about Muffy, the old labrador, and his visit to the vet, and about Mrs Millis the doctor's wife who had been in hospital with gallstones but was much better now, and about Mrs Lewis, the daily, whose corns were not.

It was worlds apart from the grim struggle that was going on in Berlin. Lili Leicht had called England a safe little island and the inference, as he'd seen it, that it was due to geography still rankled. England was only safe because she had fought long and hard to stay that way, and he'd done his share of the fighting, come to that. He finished the letter and turned to the one that Celia had written. Unlike his mother, she was careful not to assume anything. Its tone was light: she wrote about a new play that had opened in London, about her brother's promotion in the Navy. The Sunday lunch with his parents was mentioned only briefly. He could see her face and hear her voice, as though she were speaking the words to him, but she, too, seemed to belong to another world.

He put both letters away in a drawer until he could find the time and energy to answer them, and lay down on his bed to try and get some sleep. He was tired after being on duty all night but, even so, he lay awake for a while, listening to the sound of the planes landing and taking off in the distance, identifying them by the sounds of their engines. They never disturbed him. Like everybody else on the station, he was well used to it and the past nine years of his life had been lived against a background of aircraft noise. He found himself thinking of Lili Leicht.

He had thought of her quite frequently over the past weeks. She had made him extremely angry with her remarks, but he acknowledged now that they had been talking from two quite different points of view and that she was perfectly entitled to hers. Nico Kocharian had implied that he was narrow-minded and prejudiced, when he'd always considered himself the reverse. It was a grim idea and one that nagged at him. Not that he cared a row of beans for the chap's opinion – he was a fairly odd customer. He wondered just what he was doing skulking about Berlin. The publishing venture could be perfectly genuine, and then again, it could be a cooked-up story. Black-marketeering was more likely, or some kind of skulduggery. He'd said he'd worked for the Army Intelligence Corps during the war. Maybe that was true. Maybe not. He wouldn't trust him at any price.

Nico's business card must still be in his wallet, since he'd forgotten to throw it out. He got up and fished it out. *Phönix Verlag, Phoenix Publishers, Édition Phénix*. He toyed with it for a moment, tapping it against his hand. An address was printed below and a telephone number. It would be rather interesting to see if the place even existed. Tomorrow he had a day off. He'd go into the city and take a look. Kocharian had said it was in the Russian sector so perhaps he'd call on the Leichts afterwards. Take something for the boy, Rudi, to make amends for having lost his temper. And he ought to apologize again properly to the sister.

The Volkswagen taxi driver had difficulty in locating the street; there were few names and fewer numbers. It was a simple matter, though, as it happened, to find number fifteen because it was the only building in the street still more or less standing and apparently occupied. A card, the same as the one he held in his hand, had been tacked up by the door. The bell beside it produced no sound or response and so, after a moment or two, Harrison tried the handle and opened the door. He stepped into a dark hallway with another door, slightly ajar, leading off it. Someone was talking fast in German in the room beyond, and he recognized Nico Kocharian's voice. He waited for a moment until there was silence and pushed the door open further.

The Armenian, seated at a shabby desk, was replacing a telephone receiver on its cradle. He looked up and Harrison caught his startled expression before it was replaced at once by a beaming smile. 'Michael, my dear chap, how nice to see you. I *am* surprised to find you here. Do come and sit down.' He was round the desk, bringing forward a chair and dusting it with his handkerchief. 'Not exactly luxurious premises, I'm afraid, but that's Berlin for you. We all have to make do with what we can get. Coffee? I have some of the real stuff, believe it or not.'

'No, thank you.' He sat down on the dusted chair and looked about him. Apart from the desk there was a table with an ancient typewriter and shelves containing rows of books – school textbooks, so far as he could make out, and all in German.

Kocharian had returned to his chair behind the desk. The gold case of Turkish cigarettes was held out politely and, as before, declined. 'So, Michael, what brings you here?'

He lit one of his Player's. 'Curiosity, you could say.'

'About what, exactly?' A cigarette was fitted into the ebony holder and lit with the gold lighter.

'I wondered how your publishing business was getting along.'

'I'm flattered you should be so interested. Slowly, slowly is the answer. I've collared a rather distinguished university professor who is very busy editing out great chunks of Nazi propaganda from a history textbook. You wouldn't believe the sort of tripe they put in. There was a Nazi department of education, you know, as early as '34. I have a copy of their teachers' manual somewhere.' He reached behind him and pulled out a book from the shelves. 'Here we are. Listen to this. I'll give you a rough translation. *Curricula for children should be planned to make them youthful members of the Nazi community. History, geography and biology offer the best opportunities to mould children in the Nazi pattern . . . the lessons in history must be planned to create a foundation of race consciousness. History must be presented to make German children hate Jews, Catholics, Freemasons, Communism, pacificism and the Versailles Treaty. They must be taught that Nazism corrects all evils,* et cetera, et cetera.' He turned the page. 'Here's a particularly choice passage. *Nazi youth must be told about Jewish usurers. Contrast must be presented between the fate of the German worker under the Jews and that under Nazism . . . German foreign policy from 1890 to 1914 must be taught to disprove the lie that Germany was responsible for the World War . . . German youth must be told that all culture is dependent on race . . . Hitler must be presented as the saviour of Germany.* And so on.'

'It doesn't surprise me,' Harrison said. 'Catch them young, isn't that the usual method of indoctrination?'

'Of course. Tried and true. Whatever else they were, the Nazis weren't fools in that respect.' The Armenian replaced the book and took out another.

'This is their history textbook. Do listen to the preface: *Dear German Youth, your eyes should gleam with pride and your heart should flame with enthusiasm when you read how the paths of history always have led through sacrifice to victory . . . the Fatherland must be able to rely on its sons and daughters.* And here's another interesting bit in the first chapter. *There is only one will, the will of the Führer who led the Germans from dishonour and bondage to honour and freedom.* All that sort of tosh. It ends with *Sieg Heil!* by the way. Hail Victory!'

'I imagine it was all pretty effective.'

'On the mind of a ten-year-old – yes, certainly. The biology textbooks are instructive too. The teachers' manual ordered classes to be planned to aid youth to realize its obligation to keep the inheritance of their fathers pure and to remain true to the eternal laws of blood and race.'

'They didn't miss a trick.'

'Not one. No flies on them at all.'

'Will you be able to find someone to print these new textbooks that you're planning? I thought the Russians had made off with most of the machinery when they arrived here – or smashed it.'

'Luckily, not all of it. As I told you, I can usually find things in Berlin. I've unearthed a small printing firm who are still in business.'

'How about paper? Isn't it in rather short supply at the moment?'

'It's still tricky to find the stuff, of course, but there are always ways and means.'

'Fortunately for you.'

Kocharian smiled. 'Fortunately for me.'

The telephone rang and Harrison waited while Kocharian carried on a conversation, this time in Russian which he also seemed to speak like a native. With German, Harrison might have understood the general gist of the exchange; with Russian he hadn't a clue. When the exchange finally ended he said, 'How on earth did you manage to get a telephone line installed here?'

A wave of the ebony holder. 'I happen to know someone . . .'

If he was prejudiced, Harrison couldn't help himself. The chap was like some greasy trader in an Eastern souk, rubbing his hands and smiling false smiles. 'Lucky again?'

'Not so much luck, perhaps, as knowing the ropes. Berlin is a tricky place if you don't. But then you don't have to worry too much about that, do you? Being with the RAF. Tell me, Michael, how are things going out at Gatow? I gather you've got planes flying in night and day, loaded down with stuff.'

'We're coping.'

'Even coal, so they say. That must present quite a challenge. But without it you may as well give up and go home.'

'We've no intention of giving up.'

'No, of course not. The Dunkirk spirit and all that. Quite ironic that it should be all about saving Germans this time. The Berliners see the joke, too, you know. They're saying it's bound to work. If the

Allies could manage to drop all those bombs on them before, then they should be able to manage to drop enough food. They have quite a good sense of humour, as I think I told you.'

'Actually, it's all about saving liberty.'

'Oh, absolutely, old chap. That's usually what these things are about, when it comes down to it. The Yanks are doing a jolly good job too, by the sound of it.'

'They're certainly pulling their weight.'

'More than their weight, I hear. But then they've got rather more planes and pilots to call on, haven't they? And rather more money. How's the watch going, by the way?'

It was an abrupt change of tack. 'It keeps good time.'

'I thought it might. Have you seen the Leichts lately?'

'No. I've had no reason to.'

'Rudi has been ill again. Worse than usual. Lili has been distraught.'

'I'm sorry to hear that.'

'The kid needs proper treatment and lots of good fresh food – all that sort of thing. Virtually impossible here at the moment.'

'The Soviets are always claiming that they have much better rations for the people in their sector.'

'In fact it's a big problem for the Russians too. Stocks are right down. It's mostly bread and potatoes these days.'

'Ever since the blockade started they've been trying to bribe the civilians in the western sectors to sign on with them for extra rations. Get them onto their side.'

'So I've heard.'

Harrison wondered how Nico managed to look so sleek and well fed on a diet of bread and potatoes. 'Actually, you don't seem to do too badly.'

Another wave of the holder. 'I get by. And I do what I can for the Leichts, of course. As soon as my business gets off the ground properly, I'll be able to offer Lili a job. She'll be a great asset, don't you think?'

He said shortly, 'I imagine so.'

'Dirk has found some work with the Americans at Tempelhof – loading and unloading aircraft. Not quite his style, but the pay and extra rations help and, of course, Dirk being Dirk, he takes whatever opportunities come his way.'

'You mean he pilfers stuff?'

'Oh, pathetic amounts really. A little sugar, some powdered milk, a tin here, a tin there – nothing that would make any difference in the whole scheme but it makes a difference to them. Especially to Rudi.'

'It's still stealing. And those food supplies are intended for civilians in the western sectors.' As he spoke, Harrison realized how pompous he sounded, and he saw, by the faint smile that crossed Nico Kocharian's face, that he thought so too.

'Unfortunately, Michael, most Berliners can no longer afford the luxury of such fine, upstanding feelings.'

'As a matter of fact, we get very little pilfering at Gatow.'

'Perhaps English grub is less appealing.'

He said drily, 'Believe it or not, the Germans like our Pom potato best.'

'Better Pom than Ivankomm – I believe that's what German parents tell their kids in the British sector. The Russians are the big, bad wolves so the children eat up all their dried potatoes.'

'I don't blame them.' He stood up. 'Well, I'm glad things are going well.'

'I wouldn't go as far as to say that, Michael. But it was nice of you to call by. Will you be calling on the Leichts now, by any chance?'

The question sounded casual enough but he suspected that, in some way, it was calculated. 'Why do you ask?'

'Because I have something for Lili. I may not get the chance to deliver it myself for a day or two. Could you take it for me?' He opened a drawer in the desk and took out a small bottle. 'Vitamin C pills.' He shook it, making them rattle. 'For Rudi.'

The carved wolves' heads snarled at him from the Leichts' front door. He wondered if they were a presage of the reception he was going to receive. To his surprise it was the old grandfather who opened the door. He seemed almost normal, smiling and nodding and beckoning him inside. Rudi was lying on the couch in the corner, reading a book, but immediately struggled to his feet, coughing. Harrison was dismayed at how much worse he looked. 'Squadron Leader, sir, I am very pleased indeed to see you.'

He felt guilty at the boy's obviously genuine pleasure. Somehow he'd got lost on the way and wandered fruitlessly around for nearly an hour in the Soviet sector. The people he had stopped to ask for directions had simply shrugged and walked on. Either they couldn't, or wouldn't, help. Maybe it was his uniform, or maybe his bad German. If it hadn't been for the pills, he might easily have given up. The grandfather was asking him something, but his German wasn't up to whatever it was. Rudi translated. 'He wants you to sit down – in his chair. The best chair.'

'*Nein, danke.*' He searched for some appropriate German words and failed. 'Please, tell him to sit down in it. I'm fine standing.'

The boy spoke to his grandfather and the old man sat down reluctantly, still talking.

'He says it's not polite to sit when a guest is standing. Perhaps you could sit in one of these chairs at the table, sir?'

To please the old man he did so, laying his cap on the table. He took the pictures he had cut out from magazines and newspapers from his pocket. He had taken quite a lot of trouble to track them down. 'I thought you might like these, Rudi.'

'Thank you, sir.' The boy looked delighted and came to sit beside him. He went through the pictures, examining them carefully. 'This one I know well, sir. It is a C-54. American Skymaster. And this is a Stirling perhaps?'

'No. It's an Avro York. A transporter. It was actually developed from the Lancaster bomber.'

Rudi studied it carefully and solemnly. 'It is not as nice-looking as the Lancaster, I think.'

'But very useful for transporting supplies. It can carry a hell of a lot. And it's very easy to unload and load because of the high wings and the low cargo doors.'

'This plane is coming to Gatow now?'

'Oh, yes. Rather.'

'I wish I could go to see but it is too far for me to walk. Dirk says he will take me on his bicycle one day. I should like also very much to see the Sunderlands – the flying boats – coming down onto the Havel See. Dirk is working with the American planes at Tempelhof, you know. He is very lucky.'

He wondered if it would somehow be possible to arrange for the boy to get a ride out to Gatow. There was always a crowd of civilians by the perimeter fence, including plenty of children, watching the planes coming and going from the airfield, and also beside the lake where the Sunderlands were a big attraction. It must help to shore up the Berliners' resolve. They could see with their own eyes and hear with their own ears the huge efforts that were being made by the western Allies to help them. The Russians, watching from the other side of the airfield, presumably had thoughts of their own.

'I don't suppose you know what this one is?'

'No, sir.' The boy shook his head regretfully.

'No reason why you should. It's a civilian aircraft – not military. A Handley Page Halton. We have one that flies into Gatow now.'

'I think I like better the military planes.'

'So do I, but we need civilian ones to help us with the airlift too.' They had come to the last of the pictures – one that Harrison had found in a stack of old *Picture Post* magazines in the Officers' Mess. 'Here's one you'll like.'

The boy smiled. 'It is a Spitfire.'

'No, it's not a Spitfire. It's a Hurricane. They are rather alike at first glance but, if you look closely, you'll see there's quite a difference. The cockpit canopy is a different shape – a Spitfire's is like a bubble – and the Hurricane has this humped backbone, see. And, of course, the shape of the wing is completely different. It's not as beautiful as the Spitfire but it's a wonderful fighter.'

'Does it go fast?'

'Not quite as fast as a Spitfire or the Messerschmitt 109, but it's very steady. And the fuselage is fabric so it's easy and quick to mend. It has eight Browning machine guns, just the same as the Spitfire.'

Their heads were bent over the picture and Harrison didn't hear the door open. Then the grandfather started talking again and he looked up to see that the girl, Lili, had come in and was standing there. He got to his feet, very unsure of his welcome. 'I hope you don't mind, Fräulein Leicht. I brought Rudi some more pictures.'

'That's very kind of you.' She took off her scarf. Her voice was cool.

He groped in his pocket. 'Also, Nico Kocharian asked me to give these to you. Vitamin C tablets for Rudi.'

She took the glass bottle. 'Thank you for bringing them. Where did you see him?'

'I called at his office.'

'I have never been there.'

'Well, it's not much to see.'

'I thought perhaps it would be quite smart.'

'Not at all.'

'I suppose that would be difficult in Berlin, even for Nico.' She looked at the label on the bottle. 'These are American. I wonder how he got them.'

'Ways and means. I believe that's how he usually describes it.'

She gave a ghost of a smile. 'Whenever I ask him he says much the same in German. He has ways and means for everything.'

He realized that she didn't like Kocharian either and he was relieved. And glad. He risked a smile. 'Rudi wants to come out to Gatow to watch the planes. I think he'd enjoy it. Do you think he's up to it?'

The boy said eagerly, 'Of course I am. Dirk will take me on the bicycle.'

'It's a pretty long way on a bike,' Harrison said.

'Too far,' Lili agreed. 'Tempelhof is much nearer. Perhaps he will go there one day with Dirk. We'll see.' Her brother protested in German and she answered him soothingly. 'He says he would much sooner see the Royal Air Force planes. And he specially wants to see the flying boats landing on the Havel See. I will try to take him when he is stronger. It should be possible for us to go part of the way by S-Bahn out to Spandau and perhaps the

161

rest by bus – if there are any buses running still in the British sector.'

He'd seen the German labourers trudging out to Gatow on foot. 'Not many, I'm afraid. There's a terrific shortage of petrol, of course. It all has to be flown in, like everything else.'

'It must be very difficult for you to do this. To carry enough supplies by plane for so many people.'

'Yes,' he said. 'It's very difficult. But we're doing our best.'

'Dirk is working at Tempelhof for the Americans now. Loading and unloading their planes.'

'So Nico Kocharian told me.'

'He is given a free hot meal at the airfield. And coffee and doughnuts. He brings the doughnuts back to share.'

She didn't mention the pilfering, he noticed. 'That's good. How are you coping otherwise?'

'The rations were very bad for a while but now they are a little bit better. We manage, don't we Rudi?'

The boy nodded. 'Yes, we manage. We are OK.'

'You all speak jolly good English,' he said heartily. 'It's amazing.'

'Thank you. Our father was at Cambridge University and spoke it almost perfectly. He insisted that we talk often in English. Also, my grandmother was half French and so we learned that too. Grandfather speaks good French, but only a few words of English.'

The grandfather stirred in his chair. 'But I listen always to the BBC. Some I understand.'

'And we have many English books,' Rudi said. 'All of Charles Dickens, Anthony Trollope, H.G. Wells, Aldous Huxley, Thomas Hardy, P.G. Wodehouse, Rudyard Kipling and the plays of William Shakespeare.' He recited the names proudly. 'Some of them are difficult for me to understand, especially Shakespeare. I like P.G. Wodehouse the best.'

Harrison smiled. 'I like his books too. Have you ever been to England?'

'No,' his sister answered. 'None of us. Only our father. Have you been to Germany before? I mean,' she added hurriedly, 'as a tourist.'

He shook his head. 'No. I know France reasonably well. We used to go on family summer holidays there. Before the war.'

'Then you speak French?'

'Not frightfully well, I'm afraid.'

'You manage?'

He smiled ruefully. 'Yes, I manage.'

'But you do not speak any German?'

'Only a few words. I'm pretty hopeless at languages.'

'Perhaps it does not come naturally to the English. Except for some, like Nico.'

'He's not actually English. His father is Armenian.'

'Yes, he told us. And I could see he was not really English, but he was born there, he says. Is that where you first met him?'

'We were at the same school, as a matter of fact. But he's a year younger, so I can't say that I saw a great deal of him. In fact, I scarcely remember him.'

The old man stirred again and muttered.

'He wants to know when supper will be ready,' she said. 'I must start to cook it.'

He picked up his cap from the table. 'I ought to go, in any case.'

'I would invite you to stay,' she said politely. 'But it's only cabbage soup. I think you would hate it.'

'Yes, you would,' Rudi pulled a face. 'I do.'

She saw him to the door. In the hallway he said quietly, 'Nico Kocharian said that Rudi has been a bit under the weather lately.'

'You mean not so well?'

'Sorry, yes, that's what I meant. He looks rather peaky.'

'He has not been good at all but I think he is a little better now. We have been able to get some decent food for him and it helps. And your visit has cheered him up very much, Squadron Leader. He is very pleased with the aeroplane pictures. Thank you for bringing them. And the vitamin C pills.'

He hesitated. 'Actually, I also came here to apologize to you. About our last conversation . . . I'm afraid I lost my temper.'

'So did I. So we are equal.'

'Perhaps we could agree to disagree?'

She nodded. 'That would be fair.'

He looked down at her. She was so small and slight and fragile; it seemed incredible that she had somehow survived. Or that any of them had. He thought again of the great mass of leaping flames that he had looked down on from the Lancaster, of the Russian tanks storming into the city, the barrage of shellfire, the bitter street-to-street, house-to-house struggle, the almost total, savage, ruthless destruction of Berlin. 'Would you mind if I dropped by again? I could bring the odd thing. We can't get much – not like the Americans – but there's usually chocolate and cigarettes. And I could keep a lookout for some more pictures – if that's all right?' He paused. 'I quite understand, if it's not.'

'Yes, of course, if you like. Rudi would be very pleased to see you.'

He cleared his throat. 'And I was wondering . . . the British here are putting on some kind of entertainment. It's supposed to be an Elizabethan Festival.'

'Elizabethan?'

'Sixteenth century. When our Queen Elizabeth was on the throne. Plays and madrigals and concerts, poetry readings, talks . . . all that sort of thing.' He was uncomfortably aware of the ludicrousness of it, but he plunged on. 'The idea is that it will be good for morale. The Americans are getting comedians and film stars over to entertain people, so I suppose our people thought they ought to do something as well. I'm afraid it won't be as exciting as the Americans' show but the thing is, there's going to be a performance of *Measure for Measure* by the Marlowe Society. You know, the Shakespeare play?'

'Yes, I know of this. It is in our father's book, though I have never read it.'

'Well, I was just wondering if you'd like to come to a performance. It's for Berliners, too, you see.'

She looked bewildered. 'In this situation . . . with the blockade and people half starving and the Russians about to enslave the whole city, you are doing old English plays and old English music, and reading poetry, as though nothing bad is happening? A *festival*?'

'It's meant to cheer people up.'

She started to laugh. He'd never seen her laugh before; she had scarcely even smiled. 'But this is so funny.'

He said sheepishly, 'I suppose it is a bit ridiculous.'

She put a hand over her mouth. 'I'm sorry. It's wrong to laugh. Very rude of me. It is a very good idea, of course.'

'Would you like to come? To the Shakespeare play?'

'I'm not sure that I would be able to.'

'The performances are at six in the evening at the Renaissance Theatre, every day next week.'

He saw the indecision in her eyes and was certain she'd refuse, but after a moment she said, 'Yes, I think I could be there. It is a very long time since I went to a play. It would be very nice.'

'I'll meet you at the theatre then, shall I? What evening would suit you?'

'Tuesday would be best, I think. Dirk is on a day shift then and he could be home to look after Grandfather and Rudi, if I ask him.'

'Tuesday it is, then,' he said briskly. 'Jolly good.'

At the Officers' Club he had dried pea soup, reconstituted mashed potatoes, reconstituted meat stew and tinned pears. He thought of the cabbage soup and was rather pleased it was nothing better.

Tubby was no longer quite so tubby. 'Lost half a stone, dear boy. If this blockade goes on much longer I'll fade away.'

'That's old soldiers,' Harrison reminded him. 'Not airmen.'

The sullen waitress in the Mess actually smiled as she brought the beers. 'They've changed their tune,' Tubby said. 'Haven't you noticed? We're the saviours now, not the conquerors. We're on their side. Their protectors. We're jolly good chaps, after all. Have you seen the stuff they keep bringing here? Bunches of flowers, grateful letters, home-made presents – it's all rather touching. I pray to God we don't let them down.'

'We won't.'

'I've never had your blind faith, Michael.'

'It's not blind, Tubby. The airlift's starting to work. We're getting the supplies in. And we'll be doing a lot better, as time goes by.'

'And as time goes by, winter will be upon us. A Berlin winter. That's going to be the rub.'

'We'll have more planes by then.'

'From thin air?'

'No,' Harrison said. 'From the Americans. They've got them. They'll have to send them over.'

'No *have* to about it. The Yanks like to take their time about these things, as we know. I imagine that little demonstration the Berliners gave at the Brandenburg Gate the other day might help to impress them, though. A quarter of a million good citizens gathered together, all those rousing speeches: *Let us fight for Berlin's democratic rights and freedom* . . . *Berlin calls the world* . . . *help Berlin not just with the thunder of aircraft but with lasting common ideals* . . . Then burning the Red Flag as a final grand gesture under a hail of Soviet bullets. All good stuff guaranteed to touch the heart of Uncle Sam, with any luck. They're rather a plucky bunch, our Berlin burghers.'

Nico Kocharian had called them a special breed and likened them to cockney Londoners. Harrison wasn't sure he necessarily agreed, but they certainly had one thing in common – guts.

He was waiting for her when she arrived at the Renaissance Theatre in the British sector. She caught sight of him in the foyer crowd, standing to one side, smoking a cigarette and wearing his stern expression. Lili almost turned and left. Her first instinct had been to refuse the invitation; her second, that the idea of going to see an English play in Berlin was something rather extraordinary to do; her third, that to do so with the squadron leader would be even more extraordinary. He greeted her in his stiff, polite way and she sensed that he was also uneasy. She noticed that the British had invited a great many Berliners as their guests and that the Berliners had made valiant efforts to dress up for the occasion: to put on whatever decent clothes were left to them, to wear whatever jewellery had not been lost or sold, to polish their worn-out shoes and

168

dress their hair. Good for morale, he'd said, and she could see the sense in that. They could all pretend – just for a little while – that there was no blockade, no shortages, no terrifying uncertainty of the future. She wondered if this was how the British had behaved in their own country during the war – as though nothing whatever was wrong. Perhaps it was, in some way, a classic demonstration of the sang-froid, the stiff upper lip for which they were famous.

When they had taken their seats she looked at the programme and saw that the play was being performed by the Cambridge Marlowe Society. Her father might have known of them, perhaps been to see them act in England. Whoever they were, they were obviously not afraid to come to Berlin. She found that rather moving. Most people would want to stay far away.

The play's title was familiar to her from Father's big volume of Shakespeare, but the story was not. When she asked the squadron leader to explain the plot, he looked apologetic: 'To be honest, I can't remember much about it. It's not one of Shakespeare's best-known plays. It takes place in Vienna and somebody's condemned to death. I think there's a duke who keeps disguising himself and some nuns and friars . . . all a bit of a muddle. Rather an odd choice, really, but still.'

'I am afraid that I may not be able to understand it.'

He smiled. 'Don't worry, you won't be the only one.'

She listened very hard to the old-fashioned English, to words she had never heard before but spoken so poetically by actors in such beautiful costumes that whether she understood or not didn't seem to matter much. It was enough to sit and watch and listen to something so far removed from the grim reality of her daily existence and to let herself be enchanted by it.

In the interval wine was served – good German wine that the British had somehow conjured up. She had never drunk wine of any kind before. A portly, older man in Royal Air Force uniform came up to them and was introduced.

'This is Squadron Leader Hill. Also from Gatow.'

He bowed gallantly over her hand. 'Delighted, Fräulein. How are you enjoying the play?'

'Very much – except I don't understand everything.'

'Nor do I, my dear. You, me and half the audience haven't the foggiest what's going on. Luckily, nobody seems to mind.'

Although he was very friendly and genial, she felt that he was studying her closely while they talked. He is suspicious, she thought. Perhaps he can tell what sort of fräulein I really am. Perhaps he has noticed the mended tear in my dress and guessed.

When the play was over the squadron leader insisted on taking her in one of the Occupation Forces taxis back to the apartment. The Russian guard at the sector border tried to make some silly difficulty over her papers but the squadron leader spoke to him sharply and he backed down. He switched on a torch and walked with her through the courtyard as far as the front door. It was a long time since she had felt so safe. She held out her hand to shake his. 'Thank you for the play. I enjoyed it very much.'

'I'm sorry it wasn't something a bit easier.'

'It didn't matter at all. It was a very good idea. Everybody had a wonderful time.' It was perfectly true. The applause at the end had gone on and on as though nobody had wanted the evening to finish. 'Good night, Squadron Leader.'

'My name's Michael,' he said. 'Please call me that.'

'In Germany we are always very formal – until we know somebody better.'

'Yes, of course. I'm sorry.' He let go of her hand. 'Good night Fräulein Leicht.'

Dirk had his suitcase open on the table and looked up as she came into the room. 'So, how was it?'

'The play was very well done. It was a lovely evening. They even had wine to drink.'

'And the squadron leader? How was he?'

'Quite well, I think.'

'I didn't mean his health. How was he with you?'

'Very polite. Very correct.'

'Are you going to see him again?'

'He says he will try to bring more pictures for Rudi.'

'That's just a good excuse for him. I told you, he likes you. But he is an English gentleman, so he will behave very properly. Not like the others. You don't need to worry about that. If you are clever, you will make him like you even more and then you can marry him and escape from Berlin for ever.'

She was angry and upset now; the pleasure of the evening spoilt. 'You said that before, Dirk, and it's so silly.'

'Is it?' He stared at her over the open lid of the case. 'I wasn't joking, Lili. You always say that this is our home, but if you get the chance to leave, why stay here? Berlin is a doomed city. You know that. Whatever happens – whether the Allies go or stay – there will always be trouble. You should go, if you can. Take Rudi. I can look after Grandfather. It's all the same to him where he is.'

She put her hands over her ears. 'Stop it! I won't listen to you any more.'

He shrugged and closed the case lid, snapping the locks shut. 'Well, I'm off.'

'Now? At this time of night?'

'I have some business.'

'I thought you'd stopped all that – now that you have the work with the Americans.'

'It's not enough. And this is very good business.'

'What sort?'

'I can get things here in the Russian sector that they do not have any more at all in the west – not since the blockade started. People will pay big prices.'

'You'll get caught. They are stopping people now. Searching them. There are road blocks. Police everywhere.'

'Stop worrying so much, Lili. I use the back streets

and I'm like a shadow. Nobody notices me.'

It was useless to try and stop him; all she could do was beg him to be careful and pray.

Grandfather and Rudi were both asleep and she undressed and lay down on the old couch in the corner of the living room, the tattered screen pulled around her, the crumbling ceiling above her head. She thought about the squadron leader. She was not sure if he had asked her to go to the play because he was sorry for losing his temper or whether Dirk was right – because he liked her. He had never shown her that he did anything of the sort. He had been very polite to her and very kind to Rudi, but that was all, and if it was hard for her to like him, then it must be equally hard for him to like her. All Germans were seen to be guilty, Dr Meier had said. All guilty of those unspeakable Nazi crimes. And if he knew everything about her – the whole truth – then he would never want to see her again.

To think of going to live in England was absurd. An impossibility. She would like to see it, though, one day. Her father had talked about it a great deal. He had described the greenness of the countryside, the softness of the landscape, the antiquity of the buildings, the gentleness of the people. And he had admired the English way of life very much – liberal thinking, tolerance, politeness and humour. But they were not so gentle. Father had been deceived in that. Very deceived. Look what they had done to Germany. They had been completely ruthless. And the squadron leader, for all his good manners, had shown that underneath he was not gentle at all. She had seen that very clearly when he had spoken about the bombing. Nor had he won his fine medals for being gentle. *It was war. Total war*.

She turned over restlessly. And now Dirk was up to his tricks again. Something else to worry about when it took all her strength and will power to keep going from day to day. She felt swamped by the hopelessness of it all and almost ready to give up. And yet that was another impossibility. She had to keep going. Getting up, going to work, labouring away with an aching back and lacerated hands, coming back, queuing for hour upon hour for a loaf of bread, a few potatoes, a half-rotten cabbage, a tin of this, a small bag of that. Contriving some sort of meal for them to eat, washing their clothes when there was neither soap flakes nor hot water, mending and patching when there was no wool nor thread for darning and nothing to patch with, tending to Grandfather, nursing Rudi, fretting about Dirk . . . the days followed each other in an unending and exhausting struggle.

And there was no escape.

Nine

In early October the Russians cut the electricity supply to Gatow airfield. The supply came from a power station in the Soviet sector and although back-up supply cables had been installed from another source in the British sector, these were not powerful enough to provide more than a weak and intermittent current. In the Operations Room there was much grinding of teeth and despair until somebody pointed out that the Russian airfield at Staaken as well as the Radio Berlin building and its transmitters, spewing out non-stop Soviet propaganda, were supplied by power from the British sector. This was also pointed out, in turn, to the Russians who quickly restored the supply. Everybody at Gatow breathed again.

To Harrison, the episode demonstrated that they were fighting a war of nerves, as much as anything else. Unlike the kind of warfare he had known, this fight wasn't about might or strength; it was about beating the Russians at their own game. A psychological struggle. The Soviet fighters kept up their own particular game of buzzing the British and

American planes flying up and down the air corridors and their air force kept staging mock battles over the city and carrying out target practice in the corridors. There had been anti-aircraft exercises by the Russian army on the airfield perimeter, firing away so heavily that the windows at Gatow rattled in their frames.

More flying accidents had happened. The Americans had lost six more aircraft and a York had crashed on a night take-off from Wunstorf, killing all five of the crew. But it was remarkably few considering the constant stream of aircraft flying backwards and forwards to Berlin – one landing and taking off every three minutes now, twenty-four hours a day. If, for any reason, a pilot couldn't land in his appointed turn the new rule was that he had to go round and fly back to his base with the load still on board. In that way there were no hold-ups and less risk of collision. The procession kept going. Practice was making it, if not perfect, a whole lot better than the shambles there had been at the start of it all.

Even Tubby was cautiously optimistic.

'We might be in with a chance, Michael. Just a slim chance. I'll say no more than that.'

'That's a lot better than none at all.'

'Mind you, there's still the one thing we can't do much about.'

'What's that?'

'The weather. Winter's round the corner. Fog, snow, ice. It goes down to minus twenty and more in these parts, you know. We'll never keep up with the supplies in bad weather conditions. I hear there's a store of food and coal stocks for thirty days. That's running it damn close. How are the Berliners going to survive a bad winter with no heating and nothing to eat? They won't think we're quite so wonderful by next January.'

'Haven't you heard, Tubby? The Americans have promised another sixty-six C-54s. They're due next month, and they can carry nearly ten tons each. That makes a hell of a lot of coal.'

Tubby raised his glass. 'God bless America! Jolly good for them. Without Uncle Sam there wouldn't be a hope. But I still say the weather could defeat the whole thing. And General Winter's always been on the Russians' side – if you'll recall from your history books.'

'We'd better start praying for a mild one, then.'

'Personally, I don't have a lot of faith in prayer, dear boy. We'll just have to hope that Dame Fortune is on *our* side, against the general.'

Harrison had paid several more visits to the apartment in Albrecht Strasse, taking cut-out pictures of planes for Rudi as well as bars of chocolate. He had stopped trying to persuade himself that this was his only reason. He liked the kid and he was sorry for him because he'd had a pretty raw deal in life, but it was Lili he went to see, though he was convinced that she only tolerated him for her brother's sake. He was the enemy: one of those who had bombed her city to dust, killed thousands of her fellow citizens, including some of her family. For his part, though he might regret the killings, he could never regret the role he had played in defeating the Nazis. Or apologize for it. On the contrary, he was proud of it.

He had found another model aircraft – bought from an American pilot who had flown into Gatow with a crate of them to hand out to German children. At the first opportunity, he took it to the Leichts. Lili opened the door to him.

'Good evening, Squadron Leader.'

She gave him a smile but it was still Squadron Leader: never Michael. He removed his cap and followed her through the dark hallway and into the living room where her brother was lying on the couch, reading a book. The grandfather was sitting awake in his armchair, staring vacantly into space, a dribble of saliva at a corner of his mouth.

Rudi sat up at once and got off the couch. As always, he seemed excited to see him but Harrison thought he looked in no better physical shape. He handed over the silver metal plane with its American stars and the boy cradled it carefully in his palms, examining it.

'This is a C-54, sir? I am right? A Skymaster.'

'Yes, absolutely right. Well done.'

'I know this from the photographs you have given me. American, of course. Wright engines?'

He shook his head, smiling. 'Wrong.'

'Ach . . . then I do not know.'

'Pratt and Whitney. How about the makers?'

'Douglas, I think.'

'Yes. What other planes do they make?'

'Ummmm . . .'

'It begins with D.'

'*Dakotas!*'

They had fallen into the habit of playing a sort of aviation quiz on his visits and the boy was learning fast. Harrison went on with it for a while until Rudi seemed to tire and started coughing. His sister made him lie down on the couch again and tucked a blanket over his legs – the sort of threadbare thing that his mother would have consigned to the dog's basket. She bent over her brother for a while, speaking to him quietly in German. Harrison moved away. When she came over, he said, 'Would you like me to go?'

She shook her head. 'No, it's all right. He just needs to rest for a bit. He wants to show you his latest scrapbook later, if you don't mind. He's been working on it very hard.'

'I don't mind a bit.'

'Thank you. This time we have something to offer you, Squadron Leader. Real coffee. Would you like some? Dirk has stolen it from the Americans, I am sorry to say.'

'No, thank you.'

'Because it is stolen?'

'No, because you need it.'

'No, we don't. It is a luxury. We don't need it at all. I will make some.'

He agreed because it bought him time. Time to sit at the table and watch her at the stove in the kitchen corner, boiling the water, fetching cups, making the coffee, bringing it to him. The cups had no saucers and hers had no handle. 'As a guest, you must have the best one,' she said when he tried to change them round. She sat down opposite him. He offered her a Player's and lit it for her, and then his own. The simple, companionable act gave him infinite pleasure. He put away the lighter in his tunic pocket. 'How are things? Are you still managing?'

'Oh, yes.'

She wouldn't tell him if she wasn't, he thought. 'And your work?'

'The same as always.' Her hands, he saw, were in a worse state than ever, the nails broken and split, the skin callused and dotted with small cuts and bruises. Even so, they were beautiful hands with very slender fingers. Hands never made for scraping away at bricks and shovelling rubble.

'I'm sorry that you have to do such a terrible job.'

'It's not so terrible. And it's useful. Berlin will be built again from our bricks.'

He said encouragingly, 'One day, though, when things are better, you will be able to get a different job.'

'One day, perhaps.'

'The economy will recover. Eventually. Some factories in Berlin are still making things, in spite of everything. Telephones, valves, light bulbs . . . As a matter of fact, we're carrying as much of the stuff out for export as we can. As soon as we've unloaded the supply planes we fill them up with goods.'

'I have heard this. It's very generous of the Royal Air Force.'

'Well, we thought there wasn't much point

sending back empty planes. And it helps the outside world to know that Berlin is still alive and kicking.'

'Dirk tells me that at Tempelhof the Americans don't generally do this.'

'They have a different theory. They believe that backloading slows the turnaround time of aircraft. They think the object of the airlift is to bring supplies into Berlin, not waste time taking stuff out. It's a valid point. That's about the only thing we don't agree on, though. They're terrific chaps.'

'And instead they have been dropping chocolate and candy to the children . . . That's very nice. Very kind. Dirk has seen the little parachutes made of handkerchiefs and scarves coming down. Of course, it's wonderful for the children. They have never known anything like it.'

He glanced round at Rudi in the far corner; he was holding the model Skymaster to his chest and seemed to be half asleep. The old man had nodded off. Harrison lowered his voice. 'It isn't only goods we take out, as a matter of fact. We've been carrying people too. We took a lot of civilians out at the start of the blockade – mostly west Germans who'd got trapped in Berlin. Since then we've been taking others – whenever we can – business people and politicians, people who need special medical treatment, all that sort of thing . . . And lately, we've been carrying elderly people and children. The ones who are sick or undernourished.'

'Where do they go?'

'To hospitals, or relatives, or special homes in the British zone. The thing is, it's really easier for us if

those sort of people can be safely out of the way . . .
before the winter comes.'

'Yes, of course. The winter is going to be a big
problem. Last year it was not so bad but the year
before it was so cold that people literally froze to
death.'

'I know. I've heard about it.' He paused. 'And this
one could be the same. It might be a good thing if
Rudi could go – perhaps your grandfather, too. Do
you have any relatives in the British zone?'

She shook her head. 'None. None anywhere that
I know of.'

'No aunts or uncles?'

'My parents had no brothers and sisters.'

He felt desperately sorry for her. To have had
some sort of family could have helped her. 'Well,
something could probably be arranged.'

'But we live in the Russian sector. Surely you
would take out only those from the British side.'

'Even so, it might be possible to manage it . . .
would you like me to find out, at least?' She fingered
the handleless cup and was silent. 'There's no
charge,' he went on. 'It's completely free.'

'It isn't that. Whatever it cost, somehow we
would find it. But I do not know what would be
best. Rudi belongs with us – we are all that he has –
and Grandfather is so confused and gets very sad
sometimes. It might be *worse* for both of them.'

Behind them, on the couch in the corner, Rudi
started coughing. Coughing and coughing.

Harrison said quietly, 'He'd be given treatment.
Proper food. Lots of care. Your grandfather too.'

'They might be unhappy.'

He said bluntly, 'Do you think they'll be able to get through another winter here – if it's a very bad one? I think that's what you should consider.'

'I must talk to Rudi.'

'Do you want me to find out about it, meanwhile?'

'Yes . . . if you would. Thank you.' She still seemed uncertain. 'But why should you bother?'

It's for you, he wanted to tell her. For Rudi, too, and the old man, but mostly for you. I want to do something for you. Instead he said, 'It's no bother. Squadron Leader Hill – that chap you met when we went to the play – is involved in that department, actually. I can ask him. See what he could do. I can't promise anything. It might not be possible at all.'

'Out of the question, I'd say, Michael. We're up to here with applications from our own sector.' Tubby drew an imaginary line under his double chin. 'We can't start spiriting out the Ruskies' lot. Could cause all sorts of ructions. You know what they're like. Any excuse to make a rumpus.'

'It's just one kid of nine and a doddery old man. Both pretty sick. The kid's got all kinds of problems, TB included, I should say. I don't think either of them have a chance of surviving the winter if they stay here. On humanitarian grounds, I think they should be given a chance to live.'

'The Russians are supposed to look after their own civilians – not us.'

'For heaven's sake, Tubby, you know bloody well

that they don't. They don't care if they live or die. And if they die it saves them the trouble of feeding them.'

'Steady on, dear boy. Steady on. Don't lose your rag. Whatever possessed you to get involved with these people in the first place? Are they by any chance connected to that charming young lady you introduced me to at the play?'

'They're her brother and grandfather, as it happens.'

Tubby raised his eyebrows. 'You're sticking your neck out for some little fräulein? You've gone crackers, Michael. You've got your career to think of, remember? Don't make any waves, for God's sake. No blots on the old escutcheon. Everything by the book. Stick to the rules like glue.'

'I'm not aware that there *are* any rules about this.'

'Not precisely. Not in black and white, but obviously we're only shifting our own people out. That goes without saying.'

'All *I'm* saying is see if you can get their names on the list. Only the two of them. Pull a string.'

'It's a very long list.'

'How long?'

'Weeks long. Months maybe.'

'Do your best, will you?'

'I don't promise a thing.'

'Fine. Just try.'

Tubby sighed. He took his fountain pen out of his pocket and unscrewed the cap. 'Give me their names, then.'

*   *   *

'What do you think of the idea, Rudi?'

'I don't know. I'm not sure if I'd want to go away from you and Dirk.'

'It's only an idea and it may not be possible anyway.'

'How long for?'

'Just for the winter months. You would be some-where warmer, with good food and doctors to see that you get well again. That's what the squadron leader says. He thinks it would be much better for you and Grandfather. He said the RAF are taking a lot of children out.'

Rudi brightened. 'In planes? I'd go in a plane?'

'Yes, of course. It's the only way to leave west Berlin.'

'What sort of plane?'

'I've no idea. One of the RAF ones. A Dakota, perhaps.'

'It might be a York.'

'Yes, I suppose it might.'

'But where would I live?'

'I'm not exactly sure. They are taking the children to special homes in the British zone, or to hospitals, if that's necessary. Perhaps you might go to a hospital for a little while and then to a home. The doctors would do what would be best for you.'

He turned one of the American plane's propellers slowly with the tip of his forefinger. 'But I'd come back?'

'Certainly.'

'And the squadron leader thinks I should go?'

'Yes, he does. He's trying to arrange it.'

'Then it must be all right, mustn't it?'

Towards the end of October, Harrison flew to England on leave. The weather in Berlin had already started to deteriorate and before he left there had been several days of thick fog which had caused plenty of headaches in the Ops Room and frustrating delays in the targeted coal deliveries. Ominously, news had come of ice already forming on the Rhine near Wiesbaden. He flew by Dakota to Bückeburg in the British zone and then on to Northolt aerodrome outside London where he took a taxicab to his flat.

The flat was in a Victorian mansion block on the Fulham Road and he had bought it at the end of the war with a legacy from a fond and rich godmother. It was a rather sombre place and somewhat sparsely furnished. His mother had wanted to cheer it up, as she called it, but he had declined the offer firmly. It served as a useful base – somewhere secure to store his clothes and books and records while he was away and to use when he was on leave. There had been minor bomb damage to the building during the war – nothing more serious than cracks in the ceilings and broken windowpanes which had been mended or plastered over. His eyes had grown so accustomed to the devastation of Berlin that London, by contrast, seemed relatively unscathed: a comparison that he would never have made before. There was evidence everywhere of the Luftwaffe's night-time raids – plenty of bomb sites and gaps and rubble-strewn wasteland – but nothing like Berlin.

He let himself into the mansion block and took

the creaking lift up to his flat on the first floor. Here were solid walls and ceilings, radiators, running hot water, tins of food in one kitchen cupboard, a full set of china in another, his clothes in the wardrobe, Irish linen sheets and merino wool blankets on the bed, carpets on the floors, curtains to draw over the windows, a drinks cabinet with, if he remembered correctly, some sherry left in it, and a telephone.

He called his mother. She sounded thrilled to hear his voice.

'Darling, how simply wonderful! Why didn't you tell us you were coming?'

'Sorry, it wasn't certain till almost the last minute.'

'How long?'

'Ten days.'

'You'll come down this weekend, won't you?'

'Yes, of course.'

'We'll have a lovely celebration. I'll get some people in for drinks after church and wheedle something special out of the butcher for Sunday lunch. I've been saving up ration points, hoping you'd get some leave soon.'

'Don't go to any trouble.' It was a waste of breath saying that; he knew she'd go to all kinds of trouble for him. The butcher and the grocer would be charmed into delving under the counter, the greengrocer coaxed for the freshest vegetables, the garden combed for late autumn flowers, Mrs Lewis instructed to give his old room a thorough going-over. And he knew what was coming next.

'Shall I see if Celia will be home as well? We

could ask her over to lunch, if you'd like that.'

'Yes, by all means.'

A little pause. 'Will you be seeing her in London before, do you think?'

'I've only just arrived. I haven't spoken to her yet.'

'Well, when you do, darling, perhaps *you'd* ask her if she'd like to come on Sunday? Tell her we'd love to see her.'

'I'll do that.'

'I'll invite her parents, too. Keep it in the family.'

The conversation turned to other things: his father who had had a letter published in *The Times* about the lasting benefits of military discipline on young men, the new puppy who chewed anything and everything, the old Humber car that kept refusing to start. He listened to his mother chattering on gaily. During the war, when he had been doing a tour of ops, with death constantly at his shoulder, he had found it all a curious comfort. So long as the daily's corns were playing up, the cat had had kittens and frost had got at the camellias, everything was pretty much OK.

When he had said goodbye to her, promising faithfully to be down on Friday evening, he poured himself a sherry and lit a cigarette. He stood for a while, looking out of the sitting-room window down on to the Fulham Road below. More than three years had passed since the end of the war but it was still grim, grey austerity England. Chronic shortages, rationing – some of it even worse than during the war – utility goods, half-empty shelves and queues outside the shops. A little way along the road he could see a line of housewives with baskets hooked over their arms waiting patiently in front of a greengrocer's. Not such a very different picture from the queues in Berlin, except that this queue was much shorter and the women looked a lot more cheerful and somewhat better dressed. He could see them gossiping away to each other.

He was lucky and he knew it. He'd had a fairly tough war but so had thousands of men. And a lot of them had had no homes to return to and not much prospect of a decent job in Civvy Street. In addition to his service pay, he had a small private income set up out of family capital by his father when he was twenty-one. He had a car, kept in a garage round the corner – bought off a less fortunate fellow officer who could no longer afford to run it – and pretty good prospects in the RAF. He was expected to do well. All he had to do was keep running on the required rails. *You're sticking your neck out for some little fräulein? You've gone crackers, Michael.*

He finished the cigarette and phoned Celia at the flat she shared with another girl in Hans Place. When she answered, he could tell that she was very pleased to hear from him, though she kept it casual.

'Dinner? That sounds a nice idea, Michael.'

'I'll pick you up at seven, if that's all right.'

'I'll be ready.'

He went round to the garage where the Riley was housed. After a few tries and a bit of judicious nursing, the engine fired and he drove it over to Knightsbridge. Celia opened the door. She was wearing a rather elegant woollen frock and a double string of pearls round her neck that he knew had been a coming-of-age present from her parents. Her father was something very successful in the City, her mother a doer of good works, like his own. If the war hadn't intervened, he assumed that she would have done the London Season and dabbled in some kind of pleasant and undemanding job before getting married. Instead, she had gone into the WRNS as soon as she had been old enough and served throughout the duration until she was demobbed. Her job at the War Office was anything but undemanding, so far as he could gather. He also gathered that she was rather good at it.

He took her to a French restaurant that usually managed to serve a fairly decent dinner in spite of the five-shilling limit. They ordered onion soup and veal with a mushroom sauce, and while they waited they drank gin and tonics and smoked cigarettes. She was curious about Berlin. What was it like?

'It's in ruins,' he told her. 'Almost completely destroyed. The people live in cellars and wherever there's still a roof of some kind over their heads.'

'And now they have to endure this blockade. One feels very sorry for them.'

'They're not particularly sorry for themselves, as a matter of fact. They're rather like Londoners in that respect. They get on with things. If they didn't, this airlift wouldn't stand a chance. It depends on them, as much as on us. They could easily give up and settle for life under the Russians.'

She grimaced. 'Not much of an option. Not from what I've heard.'

'I certainly wouldn't choose it.'

'I can't imagine what it must be like to have your city carved up into pieces and run by different countries. Imagine if it had happened to London.'

'Unimaginable. And unthinkable.'

The waiter came with the onion soup, which was very good.

'What do the poor Berliners get to eat?' she asked.

'They seem to survive mainly on soup. But not soup like this. Cabbage soup or soup made with anything they can get hold of. The stuff we bring in by plane is nearly all dried, of course, because of the weight. Powdered eggs, milk, coffee, potatoes, cereals. We fly in flour so they can bake their own bread. We tried carrying biscuits once but they arrived as crumbs.'

'Do they get any meat?'

'In tins.'

'Cheese?'

He shook his head. 'None. But then they haven't had any since the war so they don't miss it.'

She said, 'You must find it all a bit of an irony, Michael?'

'You mean, considering I spent several years doing my level best to annihilate the very same people? Yes, I do. It's extraordinary to be in the exact opposite situation – trying to help them to survive. The Berliners call it *die luftbrüche* – the air bridge – you know. A bridge to the rest of the world. I suppose that's the way they see it.'

'Their only link.'

He nodded. 'And their only hope. The chaps who are doing the real work – the air crews actually ferrying in the stuff – seem to get a big kick out of it all. I rather envy them. Quite a challenge and some very tricky flying and they're doing a damn good job.'

'Do you miss flying?'

'Frequently.'

The veal was pretty good too – a welcome change after months of tinned meat – and the wine he'd ordered passable.

'You'll be going back?' she asked.

'As far as I know.'

'Do you mind?'

'No. I'd like to see the job finished. The Russians giving up.' In fact, the thought of not being sent back – perfectly possible given the vagaries of RAF orders – dismayed him.

She toyed with her wine glass. 'How long do you think it's going to go on?'

'No idea,' he said truthfully. 'Nobody knows. It depends on all sorts of things. Not least, on the Russians and no-one ever knows how they're going to behave or what they're going to think up next.'

'I hope it doesn't go on too long, Michael.' He knew that what she really meant was that she hoped he wouldn't be away for long, though she would never say so. Again, he asked himself how he felt about her. He liked her. He liked her very much. She was what people called a thoroughly good sort, the right kind of girl. He could understand why his mother was so keen. Even Tubby would probably approve, as far as he approved of any woman. If he asked her to marry him, he was fairly certain she'd say yes without the slightest hesitation. They'd probably be perfectly happy together. She understood service life and she'd make an ideal service wife. He'd certainly do everything within his power to be an ideal husband. He could ask her this evening and break the news to his parents at the weekend to make it an even bigger celebration. It would give them immense pleasure.

And yet, he knew that he wouldn't.

Although there had never been any definite, spoken understanding between them, he felt that in all decency he owed Celia some kind of explanation. But he could scarcely say, actually, I'm besotted with a German girl I met in Berlin. I hardly know her and she's far from keen on me, but I simply can't get her out of my mind. The whole thing's ridiculous, of course. But there it is. He said instead, 'By the way, Mother's invited you to lunch on Sunday – if you'd like to come over. She's asking your parents, too.'

'Is she killing the fatted calf?'

He smiled. 'She's browbeating the butcher. Would you like to come?'

'I'd love to.'

'Drinks before. She's getting some people in after church. You know the form.'

'I'll look forward to it.'

He drove her back to her flat and arranged to pick her up on Friday evening outside the War Office and give her a lift down to Surrey. He didn't kiss her at the door and she waved him a carefully casual good night as she went inside.

He spent the next day sorting through things in the flat, getting his uniform cleaned, his hair cut, his shoes mended, taking his old watch to be repaired, paying bills and answering the letters that had piled up on the mat. He also paid a visit to a model shop in Holborn that had miraculously kept going all through the war. After that, he looked up several old friends, went to drinks and to dinner and to the theatre. He was asked endless questions about Berlin and found that few people had any real idea or understanding of what it was like. For all the post-war austerity of life in London, there was no longer a dark shadow of oppression hanging over the city and its people; the battle for freedom had been won. In Berlin, the battle was still being fought; the outcome still undecided.

He was waiting outside the War Office in the Riley on the Friday evening when Celia came out. It was getting dark but she caught sight of the car at once and waved. He got out and watched her walking towards him – tall and smartly dressed in a costume and hat and carrying a small suitcase.

'Hallo, Michael.'

'Hallo.' He returned her smile easily. 'Let me take that for you.'

He put the case in the boot and held the door for her as she got into the passenger seat. They drove along the Embankment, down the King's Road, over Putney Bridge and out on the A3. Another of

Celia's virtues was that she never chattered aimlessly and, apart from the occasional remark, she sat beside him in silence. There was a quiet dignity about her that made him feel all the more guilty at the way he was treating her.

He turned off the A3 towards Epsom and Reigate. There was very little traffic and he picked up some speed, glancing at his watch. 'We should be there soon after six.'

She said, 'That's a very impressive-looking watch.'

'It's German. My service one packed up when I was out there and I got this one on the black market.'

'You don't mind wearing a German watch?'

'Actually, it rather amuses me. It's a *Flieger-chronograph*. A pilot's watch. The kid who flogged it to me swore it had belonged to a Luftwaffe pilot. Probably not true, but it's an intriguing thought. And it keeps very good time.'

'Is there a big black market in Berlin?'

'Huge. Unstoppable, really. Everybody seems to dabble, one way or another. The kid I got the watch from comes from a decent family but he's turned into a sort of Artful Dodger, living off the streets, trading in anything he can get hold of.'

'How did you come across him?'

'I happened to run into some chap I was at school with who knew the family. Dragged me along to meet them, much against my will. Both parents dead and only a senile grandfather. The children live in what little survived of their apartment. It's pretty grim, I can tell you.'

'Poor things.'

'Yes. Hard not to feel pity for them. Even when you know damn well the Germans deserved everything they got.'

'Some of them must have been against the Nazis. Tried to stand up to them.'

He was not my beloved Führer. I hated him. 'Yes,' he said. 'Some of them were. But look how many must have gone along with it all – with considerable enthusiasm. Hitler was a god. The Saviour of the Fatherland. The bringer of new glory and *liebensraum* in other people's countries, the chap who conveniently got rid of the scapegoat Jews. When they went around greeting each other with *Heil Hitler!* and *Sieg Heil!* they jolly well meant it.'

'But the children were innocent. How old is your Artful Dodger?'

'Hard to tell. Sixteen or seventeen. There's a younger brother of about eight or nine who's a semi-invalid and an older sister.'

'Is she much older?'

'I'm not sure. About nineteen or twenty, I think.' He realized that he didn't actually know how old any of them were. 'I'm not exactly sure.'

'Does she dabble in the black market too?'

'No. She works as a *trummerfrau*. She clears away the rubble from streets and bomb sites and cleans up bricks. There are gangs of women everywhere doing that. Very few able-bodied men around, you see.'

'What a dreadful job.'

'She doesn't seem to mind too much. The idea is that Berlin will be built again from the bricks they reclaim. It must make it seem something pretty worthwhile, at least.' Useful was the word she had used. He could see her, in his mind's eye, sitting at the wobbly dining table. 'It won't last for ever. So long as the western Allies can hang on in Berlin, the city has a reasonable chance of economic recovery. There'll be decent jobs eventually. She's well educated so she should be all right. The kid brother's the real worry. He's pretty ill. I doubt he's going to make it through the winter. I'm trying to arrange for him and the grandfather to be flown out, along with the other children and old people we're evacuating from our sector.'

'That's good of you, Michael.'

He shook his head. 'I'm not sure it's even going to be possible. They live in the wrong sector: the Russian one.'

Celia's parents' large Georgian house was on the other side of the village. He delivered her to the door and politely refused her mother's enthusiastic invitation to go in for a drink. She was as keen on an engagement, he suspected, as his own mother.

As he turned in through the gateway to his own home and saw the lights shining in welcome from the windows, he was conscious, again, of how fortunate he was. He had been born in the house, born with a silver spoon in his mouth some might say, and lived a privileged life of comfort and stability with devoted parents. He hoped that he had never taken it all for granted.

His mother had opened the front door before he got out of the car, his father close behind her. The dogs came to greet him – Muffy the ancient Labrador arthritically, Brandy the new liver and white springer spaniel puppy bouncing around as though she had springs on her feet.

A log fire had been lit in the drawing-room fireplace, the silk-shaded lamps switched on, the long chintz curtains drawn against the dark. His father opened a bottle of champagne. The return of the son: the only son and now the only child. He glanced at the silver-framed studio portrait of Elizabeth, Harry and Benjy in their prominent place on the sofa table. His sister sat with Harry beside her and Benjy on her lap and they were all smiling straight at him. He turned away. Even now, nearly eight years on, he found it painful to look at them.

The fishmonger had come up trumps with some sole fillets for dinner and there were fresh potatoes and vegetables from the garden and an apple charlotte afterwards. His father had opened a bottle of Pouilly-Fuissé. He ate and drank appreciatively, knowing the trouble that had been taken for him. It wasn't long before his mother brought up the subject of Celia.

'How was she, darling?'

'She seems very well.'

'Did you have dinner?'

'Yes. At a French restaurant. It was pretty good.'

'That must have been very nice. She's been promoted recently – did she tell you?'

'No, she didn't mention it.'

'I'm sure she's frightfully clever at her job – whatever it is. Just the sort of girl they like to have. She's coming on Sunday, isn't she?'

'Yes, she said she'd love to.'

'Her parents are coming too, so it will be rather a lovely get-together.'

She was watching him covertly for any hopeful sign; any hint he might drop that an engagement was in the offing. He wished very much that he had been able to give her that pleasure. Instead, he changed the subject.

After dinner, when his mother had gone to bed, he sat by the fire with his father, smoking and drinking a brandy saved for special occasions. They talked of Berlin – military talk that his father craved since his retirement: tactics, strategy, means. His father expounded his theory.

'The big mistake we and the Americans made was letting the Russians take the city. We were lagging behind them, of course. The German counter-offensive in the Ardennes in December had held us up and they gave us a real mauling there, but then the Americans found that bridge intact at Remagen and were over the Rhine by mid-March. The Germans had started surrendering in their thousands and by the end of the month we were only two hundred miles from Berlin. We should have pushed straight on. Top speed.'

'Was it as simple as that?'

'Yes, it damn well was. Montgomery wanted to go on and take the city but Eisenhower vetoed it. For some reason he didn't consider it strategically vital and he listened to Stalin. Excellent chap, Eisenhower, in many ways, but Stalin had him tied up in knots. So the Russians went in full steam ahead and the damage was done.'

His father saw the airlift as a military operation that would stand or fall by its efficiency. 'And there's no room for any compromise or shilly-shallying with the Russians, Michael. Pointless trying to placate them; they're slippery as hell. If they ever get control of western Berlin, the city's completely finished.'

He said, 'So far as I can see, the Russians want a separate Communist East German state with Berlin as the capital.'

'Damn right they do. Do you think the western Allies can hold out over the winter?'

'I believe so. If the weather gives us half a chance. The will to is certainly there.'

'How about the Berliners? The ordinary civilians? Are they going to cave in if the going gets really rough?'

'I don't think so. A few of them don't believe we've a hope of getting through the winter and are ready to give up. You know the sort of defeatist attitude: better a live dog than a dead lion . . . that kind of thing. But I think most of them will hold fast. They've had plenty of blandishments served up by the Russians to try and persuade them to give up the fight but, so far, they've resisted.'

His father grunted. 'Well, you have to hand it to them for guts, that's true. I'd never deny that. Fine soldiers. Bloody brave. Never cared much for them as a race, though – arrogant bastards. Can't trust them any more than the Russians, in my view. Of course, I can see the sense in propping them up against the Commies, but I must say it sticks in my craw a bit the way the Allies are falling over themselves to nursemaid them. The Yanks are handing out shoals and shoals of dollars to the very chaps who got us into the bloody mess in the first place. All this country got left with for its considerable pains was the Lease-Lend bill and a mountain of debts. It'll be years before we're back on *our* feet.'

He went on at some length, delivering judgements and putting the world to rights. Harrison wondered if he would eventually, in his turn, become like his father – entrenched in his views. Set, like concrete, in his ways. Whether he wasn't, in fact, pretty much like him already? Another brandy and the subject of Celia came up again. His father didn't waste time beating about the bush.

'Your mother's keen for you to settle down, of course. Perfectly natural. She seems to think you and Celia might make a go of it.'

'I'm afraid I may have to disappoint her.'

'Rather a pity. She's a first-class girl. You'd be a fool to pass her up, in my opinion, but, of course, it's entirely your call. You can't marry someone just to please us.' His father sighed. 'The trouble is your mother's never really got over losing Elizabeth and the boys, you know.'

'I realize that. None of us has.'

'Quite. Only, unfortunately, she's pinned all her hopes on you and she's very fond of Celia. Well, we both are. Very fond. The only thing I would say, Michael, is for God's sake be careful to pick the right one. If you want to get on in your career, don't go and marry some woman who's going to be a disadvantage to you. Know what I mean?'

He knew exactly what his father meant. Changing the subject, he said, 'I ran into a chap in Berlin who was at school with me. Someone called Nico Kocharian.'

'Odd name.'

'His father was Armenian. He speaks about eight languages and says he worked for British Army Intelligence Corps during the war. Would you be able to check up on that for me? Find out if he really did.'

'Something fishy about him?'

'I'm not sure. He's started up some kind of publishing business in the Soviet sector, doing school textbooks. It seems genuine enough, on the face of it, but he's an odd bird and I'm rather curious. I mentioned him to our Intelligence lot, of course, but they didn't seem too worried.'

'They're a law unto themselves, in my experience. You won't get anything out of them, either way. Play their cards close to the chest. But I can at least find out if he *was* with the Intelligence Corps. I'll get on to one of my contacts. Still keep in touch as much as I can. A finger on the old pulse. I'll let you know what I turn up.'

Before he went to bed Harrison stopped by the bedroom that had belonged to Elizabeth. It was much the same as when she had occupied it: the same furnishings and furniture, her books in the bookcase, the same pictures on the walls. He stood for a moment, remembering. She had been eight years his senior and he'd worshipped her devotedly when he was a child, trotting around after her like a small dog. As he had grown up, the devotion had stayed because she was one of the best people he knew. And when she had married and Harry and Benjy had been born, he had become a devoted uncle, revelling in the role. On leave from the RAF one day in January 1941 he had gone to visit them at their house by Wimbledon Common. He'd taken a present – a box of tin trains and track that he'd managed to find in a toyshop. He could see the boys running full tilt to greet him – and how excited they'd been about the trains. He'd got down on his hands and knees with them on the sitting-room floor. They'd built a long tunnel from books and a platform from wooden bricks and co-opted lead soldiers as passengers. The game had gone on until their bedtime. He remembered how reluctant they'd been to stop; how they'd called good night to him through the banisters as they had trailed upstairs; how they'd smiled and waved as they had reached the landing, before they turned away. He'd left later that evening to get back on duty. By midnight the London air raid had taken place. The house had received a direct hit from a high explosive and all three of them were dead: Elizabeth, Harry and Benjy. Tom, Elizabeth's husband, had been away serving in the Navy. A few months later he'd been lost at sea when his ship had been torpedoed by a U-boat and gone down in the Atlantic.

He shut the door on the room and the painful

memories and went on to his own room. In bed he lay awake, thinking about Lili. His father would certainly place her in the category of women who would be a disadvantage to his RAF career. Not just a foreigner, which would be bad enough, but a *German*. A former enemy. A girl who worked as a labourer on the streets, who had a brother who was a black-marketeer and who lived in a rat hole in Berlin. His mother would be dismayed and appalled; his father trenchant in his disapproval. But whatever they might think made no difference to him. It was, as his father had so correctly pointed out, his call.

Saturday passed agreeably. He slept late and strolled down to the pub for a pint before lunch. No matter how long he had been away or however grim his experiences, the White Hart remained the same. Same greeting from the same landlord, same regulars, same sort of talk, same sense of well-being and a mutual understanding that never needed putting into words. At lunch his father noticed the German watch and disapproved. 'Wouldn't be seen dead wearing that, if I were you, Michael. Not very good form.' He went on wearing it, nonetheless.

On Sunday they went to church and sang familiar and well-loved hymns, 'Praise my soul the King of Heaven', 'Thy hand, O God, has guided', 'Now thank we all our God', and listened to the vicar who had so annoyed his father by saying special prayers for the people of Berlin. This time he was preaching on the safer subject of faith, assuring his congregation that faith could move all obstacles in its path, even mountains. Harrison only half listened, his mind not in a fourteenth-century church in the English countryside but miles away in the ruins of Germany.

His mother had invited a dozen or so locals in for drinks after church, including, of course, Celia and her parents. He circulated dutifully, refilled glasses, lit cigarettes, made pleasant and innocuous conversation. Celia's mother buttonholed him for some time. He liked her well enough but he sensed that she was demonstrating a special claim on him and, after a while, he excused himself and moved on. Across the room, he could see Celia talking to his father and laughing at something he had said; it was very obvious that they got on extremely well and it was equally obvious what was expected of him, what they all hoped. Mrs Millis, the doctor's wife, fully recovered from her gallstone operation, laid an inquisitive hand on his arm.

'Is this little gathering for something special, Michael? I heard a rumour . . .'

'Not as far as I know,' he said. 'Can I get you another sherry?'

When the others had left, the two families sat round the table and his father poured his best claret. The butcher had excelled himself with a joint of beef. Roast potatoes, Yorkshire pudding, Brussels sprouts, queen of puddings to follow. A celebration. They raised their glasses to him, smiled at him: *welcome back, Michael*.

After lunch, his mother asked him to take the dogs for a walk. 'They could do with a run, poor things. Celia will keep you company while we old fogies sit down together.'

He concealed his irritation at the blatant manoeuvre with some difficulty. She meant well, but he was selfishly glad that the weekend would soon be over and he could escape back to London. They set out across the field behind the house with the two dogs. Celia had borrowed a pair of his mother's wellingtons and had tied a scarf round her hair – an expensive silk scarf that she wore loosely knotted at the point of her chin. She matched his pace, striding freely along beside him with her hands dug deep in her coat pockets. The field was surrounded by gentle hills and wooded valleys and the dying sun, with the fireglow light of autumn, had turned the trees to copper and gold. There was nothing in the world, he thought, more peaceful and lovely than the English countryside. During the war, the mere idea of it being desecrated by German tanks and jackboots had often spurred him on; he imagined that others had felt the same. Old Muffy stayed at their heels but the puppy raced off to explore the hedgerows. They reached the far end of the first field and stopped at the closed five-barred gate. Celia leaned against it, admiring the view. This is where I'm supposed to propose, he thought wryly. Not on bended knee in the mud, perhaps, but it would be the perfect moment and a perfect place to bring up the subject. He wished he could think of something decently truthful to say that would not hurt her feelings.

Before he could say anything, Celia spoke – not

looking at him but away down across the field, shielding her eyes against the low sun. 'I think it's much better if we're honest, Michael, don't you? Our parents both seem intent on marrying us off to each other – it's awfully obvious, isn't it? Bless them, they're not very subtle. But they've rather overlooked the fact that it might not be at all what you, or I, are planning. That they might have got the whole thing completely wrong.' She turned her head towards him, smiling. 'Will you be the one to disillusion them, or shall I? Or would it be kinder and wiser to say nothing?'

He said slowly, 'I think it would be better to say nothing.'

'I agree. There's really nothing to say, is there? They'll give up eventually. I'm sorry if it's an embarrassment for you.'

'It isn't. I hope it isn't for you.'

'Of course not. Let's just ignore it.' She looked away again. 'I can't see Brandy. Do you think she's gone off somewhere?'

He whistled for the spaniel who reappeared from a hedge and scampered towards them, tongue lolling. They set off back towards the house. The sun had sunk lower, casting long dark shadows, and rooks were wheeling and cawing over the woods, preparing to roost for the night. The perfect moment had passed and gone. He was grateful to Celia for her frankness and relieved that he had misjudged her feelings. She had seemed almost as anxious as himself to put an end to the situation.

'When are you going back to Berlin, Michael?'

'My leave's up on Tuesday.'

'Good luck, then. It sounds as though you'll be needing it over there.'

He nodded grimly. 'All the luck we can get.'

'I'll still write, if you like. Give you the home news.'

He glanced at her as she walked beside him; her face was calm and composed. 'Please do, if you get the time.'

Coming in to land at RAF Gatow, the Dakota passed low over the surrounding pine forests and the grey waters of the Havel See. It looked bleak and depressing – as though winter had already taken a firm grip in his absence – and it was raining. The Dakota touched, bounced and settled. It flashed past the two GCA cabins, ran on smoothly and turned towards the unloading apron. Besides passengers, Harrison's plane was carrying bags of mail, cigarettes, medical supplies, and an assortment of necessities – razor blades, candles, boots and shoes, socks and, ominously, a large consignment of hot-water bottles for the sick and elderly. Another plane had landed just ahead and there would be another close behind, and another behind that, and yet another . . . a continuous succession of them, as precisely spaced as beads on a string.

Harrison was out as soon as the door was open, down the steps and onto the wet and windswept tarmac. A reloaded York lumbered by, heading for the row of blue lamps that marked the taxi track. The Australian Air Force Dakota that had landed ahead of them was already being unloaded – a gang of German labourers heaving sacks of flour fast onto a backed-up lorry. Ten minutes was the calculated unloading time for a Dakota, seventeen for the Skymaster parked next door. Thirty minutes allowed on the apron for unloading and reloading. Fifty minutes, in all, from touchdown to take-off. That was the aim and, more often than not, it was achieved. Beyond the RAAF Dakota stood a brand new Handley Page Hastings and alongside it a row of civil aircraft painted with their company names: Eagle Aviation, Bond Air Services, Skyways, Westminster Airways, the Lancashire Aircraft Corporation. The motley collection contracted from seventeen private civil airlines to the airlift cause was another big headache: many of them were decrepit old machines with no spares or compatible equipment.

He threaded his way through the constant criss-cross traffic of heavy lorries and trucks, passing an RAF pilot and navigator who, from their black-streaked faces, had just brought in a consignment of coal. A group of Berlin children were waiting to board a Dakota, standing patiently among the rain puddles. He paused for a moment. They reminded him of an assembly of British evacuees that he had once seen during the war on a railway station platform in London. Pasty-white and tearful faces, pathetic bundles and baskets, luggage labels tied to buttonholes on shabby, make-do clothes.

He watched the German children begin scrambling up the aircraft steps, a harassed-looking RAF flight lieutenant at the top shepherding them in through the open door. They were the lucky ones, though, Harrison thought. They'd be out of it before winter really set in. A Tudor tanker had landed and was heading for the liquid fuel depot at the back of the unloading apron; beyond that lay the coal depot that was never still. The York's engines were bellowing at the end of the runway and it began its take-off run. He turned his head to see it climb into the sky.

Two hours later he was back on duty in the Operations Room.

The skeleton was of a small child. Lili had uncovered it, digging down with her spade into a heap of rubble. She had gone deep and turned over the broken bricks, almost as though she were digging for potatoes. But instead of potatoes, she had fetched up the bones of a small hand and arm. The bones were still attached to the rest of the remains which were buried deeper under a heavy block of masonry. The other *trummerfrauen* gathered around. After some discussion, they combined their strength to roll the block to one side and then began, very carefully, to scrape away the debris beneath, following the direction of the arm. It took some time before the rest of the skeleton was exposed.

The child would have been about three years old and was lying on its back with one arm outstretched, the other arm across its small ribcage, the head back a little. The bones were fleshless, long since picked clean by the rats, but scraps of blue striped material adhered to them in places and there was still hair on the skull – blond curls. Beautiful hair. The mouth, slightly open, as though in a laugh, showed perfect little white teeth. The women stared down in silence at first and then one or two of them started weeping.

It was dark by the time Lili had walked home. She let herself into the apartment and took off her head-scarf and her coat. Grandfather was dozing in his chair and Dirk sitting at the table, reading a news-paper and smoking a cigarette.

'Where is Rudi?'

He looked up. 'Lying down on his bed, reading a book. He's OK. What's the matter, Lili?'

'Nothing.'

'Yes, there is. I can tell by your face.'

She came and sat at the table with him and rested her head in her hands. 'We found the body of a small child in the ruins today. It upset me, that's all.'

'It's not the first you've found, is it?'

'It's the first child. So small . . . a little boy, I think. Perhaps three years old.'

'Forget about it, Lili. He died years ago. It's finished.'

'I wonder what happened to his mother and father . . . If they died, too.'

'Well, the father was most probably away fighting and is dead and the mother was very likely killed by the same bomb as her child.'

'Or she might have survived and never found him. Or the father came back from the war and could not find either of them. You know, like those notices people put up all over the city, begging for any news of someone. I stop to read them sometimes and it breaks my heart. I stand there crying . . .' Tears came into her eyes.

'You shouldn't read them. You're torturing yourself, Lili. Forget all about it. Have a cigarette. I found four packets at work today.' He meant, of course, that he had stolen them, but she had given up remonstrating with him. He lit one for her with his American lighter. 'You're tired, that's the trouble. You shouldn't do that crazy job any more. I'm always telling you. We'll find you something else. Perhaps with the Americans. They have German women working at Tempelhof.'

'What sort of work?'

'Waitresses, cleaners, in the kitchens, sweeping out the planes . . . It's not wonderful but it's better than what you're doing.'

'I don't mind what I'm doing. And I'm not sure I'd want to be a servant to the Americans. Or the British, either. Seeing that little child has reminded me of what they did to us.'

'The war is over, Lili, and the sooner you realize that, the better. The Allies are our friends, now – they have to be – and we have to be friends with them if we want to survive. It's stupid to think otherwise.'

She handed him the cigarette. 'You have this. I don't want it. I must go and see how Rudi is.'

He was curled up on his bed, reading one of Father's English books: *Oliver Twist* by Charles Dickens. Again, he had not been well enough to go

to school. 'This is a good book, Lili. I do not understand everything but enough to follow the story. I
am very sorry for Oliver. The English did not treat
poor orphans well.'

He was a poor orphan himself and in just as bad
circumstances. Worse, perhaps, because the story in
the book, she remembered, had a happy ending. She
said, 'Be careful you don't strain your eyes. The light
is bad in here.'

'Oh, I can see enough.'

Since reading was one of the very few things he
had to enjoy, it was unthinkable to stop him. 'I am
going to cook some supper. I'll call you when it's
ready.'

He didn't ask what it was; he had no real interest
in eating any more and in any case it was always the
same sort of thing. As she reached the door, he said,
'Do you think the squadron leader will come again
soon?'

'I told you, he went to England on leave, I don't
know when he'll be back.'

'I've been thinking more about what he said –
about my going away.'

'Yes?'

'I really wouldn't mind too much – if it wasn't for
long. Would there be books?'

'I'm sure there would be.'

'And the squadron leader thought it would be a
good idea, didn't he? You said that.'

'Yes, he did. He didn't think you should spend the
winter in Berlin. Nor do I, Rudi. Not the way things
are. But we must wait to see if it is possible for the

RAF to take you out. Since we are not in the British sector, it may be difficult. Nothing is promised.'

She went back to prepare the supper: cabbage, yet again, and some turnips, with slices of liver sausage and dumplings. She simmered it all in the big pot. One day, she vowed, I am never, ever going to eat cabbage again.

They had just finished eating and Rudi had gone off to bed when the doorbell rang and Dirk went to open the door. It was Nico.

He came into the room, smiling his toad's smile. Even from several feet away, she could smell the smell of him. 'Good evening, Lili. I hope I am not disturbing you?'

He always disturbs me, she thought. I am never at ease when he is in the room. They sat down round the table and she took the chair furthest from him and occupied herself with some mending. Nico kept his coat on against the cold. He had brought more things for them: a tin of American corned beef, some soap, some Nestles condensed milk. She wished he would stop and wanted to tell him so. Dirk, naturally, would not agree. He could never understand her dislike and distrust of Nico. *He's a good fellow, Lili. He helps us. You should be grateful.*

Nico produced one more item from his coat pocket – something in a flat paper bag. 'For you, dear Lili. Something rather special.' She put it down on the table. 'Please open it.' She did so, reluctantly, and found it was a pair of stockings. 'American nylons,' Nico said, his dark eyes fixed on her. 'I was sure you would be pleased by them. They are hard to come by, even for me.'

'Thank you.'

They were gossamer-fine but she knew she would never wear them because they were from him. That he had given such an intimate present repelled her.

Grandfather had got up to switch on the wireless and was turning the dial. There were the usual squeals and howls and the torrent of Russian propaganda from Radio Berlin, and then an American male voice soulfully singing some popular song. *I wish I didn't love you so* . . . Surprisingly, Grandfather, who had never listened to anything but Viennese waltzes and operetta, had taken happily to the American sector station, RIAS. He settled down again in his chair, nodding his head. Nico laughed. 'The old man likes it.'

She didn't care for the lack of respect. 'Grandfather has always loved music.'

'Forgive me . . . of course. He is a Berliner. Berliners always love music. And to dance, isn't that so? They love to dance.'

She shrugged. 'It's a long time since I saw people dancing.'

'Lili is tired and out of sorts today,' Dirk said. 'I have been telling her that she ought not to go on with that labouring work she does. We should find something else better.'

'I agree with you, Dirk.'

'There are lots of German girls employed at Tempelhof, but she won't listen to me.'

Nico was fitting one of his Turkish cigarettes into

his holder. He flicked his lighter and the smell of the tobacco burning joined the smell of cologne and hair oil. 'It so happens that I know a man who is in charge of the workforce at one of the Siemens factories. If you like, Lili, I will ask him if he could take you on. They have many women applying, of course, but he owes me a favour.'

'Thank you, but no, Nico.'

Dirk made a gesture of helplessness. 'She's crazy.'

'Well, at least she has had the good sense to remain here. It's much better for all of you – I told you that. You have food and you have electric light. Did you know that households in the western sectors are allowed only four hours of electricity in a day and their gas supply goes off every evening? A little bag of coal is all they are being given to last the winter and unless they can afford candles or kerosene they must sit in the cold and dark with just their hunger for company.'

'We know all about that,' she said. 'But they don't mind, so long as the Allies stay.'

He smiled. 'So long as they stay.'

Whose side are you on, Nico? She wanted to ask him that outright, but he would never have given a straight answer. Perhaps the truth was that he was on nobody's side but his own. 'I believe they will, don't you?'

He waved a hand. 'Who knows? In the meantime, you are in the right place. In the Russian sector there are lights and people do not have to stay at home in the dark. You should go out, Lili. Have some fun.'

She said coldly, 'With Russian soldiers?'

'Perhaps not. But there is the theatre. Only the other day I went to see the Red Army dancers at the *Deutsche Staatsoper*. They were quite remarkable. I could get some more tickets, if you would like to go.'

'No, thank you.'

'Ah, well. It was only a suggestion.' He drew on his cigarette. 'Have you seen our mutual friend Michael Harrison lately, I wonder?'

'Not lately.'

'He went to England on leave,' Dirk said. 'We don't know if he's come back. We've heard nothing. Have you any news of him?'

'No, none. Perhaps the RAF have sent him somewhere else. It's quite possible. Did you hope to sell him another watch, Dirk? Is that why you are so anxious to see him?'

She could see that Dirk was about to disclose the plan for Rudi and Grandfather and reached out with her foot under the table to kick him on the ankle. Her brother frowned at her. 'No. I have nothing as good as the Hanhart for him.'

'Perhaps he will come again to see *you*, dear Lili. I'm sure he must admire you.'

Dirk smirked. 'He admires her very much.'

'Who would not?'

'I keep telling her she ought to marry him and go and live in England.'

'Would you like to do that, Lili?'

'Dirk is talking nonsense to tease me. He finds it amusing.'

To her annoyance, Nico stayed an hour or more, smoking his cigarettes and encouraging Dirk to recount his stories about Tempelhof. The American dance music went on playing on the wireless with Grandfather nodding in time to it. Dirk, she well knew, had been dazzled by the Americans: by the abundance of everything and by the glamour. Whereas once he had been contemptuous, he was now full of admiration and envy. These days his speech was peppered with American words: with 'OK' and 'sure' and 'yeah'. She listened to him talking to Nico and speaking of one of the ground crew who dealt regularly on the Berlin black market with goods flown in by the airlift. In her eyes, this was contemptible but Dirk seemed impressed. The man's name was Hank and Hank not only traded his wares through his Berlin contacts but made forays himself in a jeep out into the countryside in search of other profitable deals: German cameras, porcelain, silver, clocks, barometers, paintings. 'I hope he is caught,' she said. 'He deserves to be punished.'

Dirk rolled his eyes. 'Lili doesn't approve. She's behind the times.'

Nico looked at her. 'Your sister remembers what life was once like – before it became commonplace to cheat and profiteer. Isn't that so, Lili?'

She bent her head over her sewing without answering him. It was another half-hour before he finally left and she could go to bed on the couch. She lay there, fretting. Supposing that the squadron leader never came back? Supposing that he had not really meant what he said about trying to get Rudi and Grandfather out and had done nothing about it? Every day it was getting colder and colder.

Grandfather already had a chill and Rudi's cough was worse. Some lucky homes in the Russian sector might have heating systems that worked and fuel to run them, but in the apartment the radiators and the broken pipes leading to nowhere were useless. The only warmth came from the old cooking stove in the corner which consumed more wood than they could ever find. Neither Grandfather nor Rudi would survive another winter in Berlin – she was certain of that. The squadron leader had thought the same which was why he had offered to help.

She tried to think calmly and rationally. The English set great store by honour – Father had told them so. An Englishman's word was his bond. The squadron leader had promised that he would try to get Rudi and Grandfather taken out of the city and he would therefore do his best to keep his promise. But supposing he had been sent away somewhere else and would never come back to Berlin? Nico had said it was quite possible. And the more she thought about it, the more convinced she was that that was what had happened. In which case, there would be no hope for Grandfather or Rudi.

Then she thought of something else. The other RAF squadron leader whom she had met at the Shakespeare play performance had had something to do with the arrangements for flying German civilians out from Gatow. He had been much older and rather fat and she could recall his face quite well – but what was his name? If she could remember it, she could go out to Gatow and ask to see him. If only she could remember.

*　　*　　*

'You're quite a stranger, Michael, dear boy. Haven't seen you in here for ages.'

'I've been pretty busy since I got back.'

'Time for a drink now, I trust? It's on me.'

'Thanks. I could do with one.' Harrison sat down in the armchair opposite Tubby.

'It's beer, beer or beer. Unless, of course, God forbid, you prefer lemonade. They've run out of spirits until the next lot gets flown in and heaven knows when that'll be. So much bloody Pom they haven't got room for the real necessities of life, I suppose. I told you it would happen.' Tubby signalled to a waitress. 'Have a good leave?'

'It was OK.'

'Blighty in one piece?'

'More or less. Things are pretty grim, though.'

'Will be for years. I'm sorry for all those demob chaps trying to pick up the pieces in Civvy Street. They must almost wish there was still a war on. I almost wish it myself sometimes. We all knew where we were then. Not sure I do any more.'

He understood what Tubby meant. Fighting the war had been straightforward. Now the enemy was no longer the enemy but had somehow become their ally against a former ally who had somehow become the new enemy. Weird. The beers arrived and the German waitress smiled brightly at him. They smiled a great deal these days. Well, for once they had something to smile about. The airlift was actually working. The improvised shambles at the start had developed into a highly precise and ordered round-the-clock operation. A non-stop procession of laden aircraft was flying into Gatow and Tempelhof and now into a third airport, Tegel in the French sector, which had been built in a matter of four months. The problems were still there, of course, and in plenty. The lack of spares and tools and of the most basic equipment, the nightmare of maintaining so many different aircraft, some of them obsolete and all with different characteristics and needs. Dakotas, Yorks, Skymasters, Tudors, Hastings, Haltons, Lancasters, Vikings, Liberators, Lincolns . . . Strictly practical difficulties, too, such as finding the sacks to carry the coal and converting enough aircraft to fly in the essential liquid fuel supplies to run the whole show.

And always the harassment from the Russian fighters invading the air corridors, buzzing Allied aircraft, performing wild aerobatics in their space, and from Russian searchlights beamed straight into pilots' eyes and from exploding thunderflashes. Everything short of actually shooting down an Allied aircraft which would constitute an act of war.

In spite of all the problems, there was a feeling now that they could go on with the airlift indefinitely. Keep going, come what may. No wonder the German waitress was smiling.

He raised his mug to Tubby in thanks for the beer. 'Any news on the evacuee front yet?'

'You mean about your fräulein's family? I was rather hoping you'd forgotten about them.'

'Far from it.'

'Bad idea to get mixed up with the natives, Michael. I wish you wouldn't.'

'My lookout, Tubby. Is there any chance of getting them away soon?'

'There's still a wait.'

'How soon?'

'December at the earliest.'

'They're not going to survive long if it's a bad winter.'

'I'm doing my best. Strictly against regs, though. Officially they're nothing to do with us. Not our responsibility at all. We've got enough of our own lot to worry about. Have you seen them since you got back?'

'I haven't had a chance to get into the city yet. Too damn much going on here.'

Tubby brightened. 'Maybe they've decamped? Happens all the time with these people, I gather. Fold their tents and disappear.'

'No.' He shook his head. 'It's their home. And they've nowhere else to go.'

The wolves' heads snarled at him but this time he felt more confident of a welcome. When Lili opened the door, though, his hopes were dashed; instead of smiling she looked stunned.

'Squadron Leader . . . I did not expect to see you ever again. We were very sure that you were never coming back to Berlin.'

He tried to explain. 'I'm sorry I haven't been able to get over sooner. There's been absolutely no chance. We've been awfully busy.'

'Of course.' She had stopped looking stunned now but she still hadn't smiled. 'I understand.'

'Are you going out?'

'No.'

'I just wondered – because of the coat.'

'Oh.' She smiled then – at last. 'I am wearing this because it is so cold inside. I'm afraid it's even colder than outside.'

'I don't mind.'

'Then come in, please, but you had better keep your overcoat on too. And your gloves. Rudi will be very glad to see you. Dirk is not here. He is working at Tempelhof on the evening shift.'

'How is Rudi?'

'Not so good.' She searched his face anxiously. 'Is there any hope of the RAF taking them out, do you think?'

'Probably not until December at the earliest. I'll do everything I can to make it happen soon.'

'You're very kind.'

Harrison followed her into the living room. Seeing it again, after his home leave and an interval of time, he was appalled afresh at how terrible it was. Miserable, cheerless, scarcely fit for human habitation. There were some new holes in the ceiling and he saw that they had tried to stuff them all with newspaper. And Lili had been quite right about the cold. It was bone-chilling.

The old man, asleep in his chair, was huddled up in a ragged shawl, a woollen scarf tied round his head and a rug tucked round his knees. Rudi, who had been sitting at the table with a blanket round his shoulders, leaped to his feet.

'Squadron Leader! I am very pleased that it is you. Lili thought perhaps you are not coming back.'

He said breezily, 'She thought quite wrong. I'm back and I've brought you something from England.' He handed over the cardboard box containing the aeroplane kit that he had bought from the shop in Holborn. Rudi took it in his hands, staring at the picture on the lid. He coughed. 'This is to make? To put together from pieces?'

'That's right. The instructions are in English, of course, but they don't look too difficult.'

'Will you help me – if I cannot understand?'

'If you like.' He smiled at the boy, thinking that he definitely looked worse. 'You know what the plane is?'

'No, I do not know this one.' He coughed again.

'It's a Tiger Moth. Made by an English company called de Havilland in 1931.' Harrison had searched along the dusty shelves in the London model shop to find a peacetime plane. 'It was mainly for training. Actually, I learned to fly on a Moth myself. It's a terrific plane. Great fun to fly.'

'Not very like a bomber.'

'No. Not at all like a bomber.'

'How long to learn to fly in this?'

'About ten hours. It's not too difficult.'

'And to fly a big bomber?'

'Much longer. You do it in stages. First a two-engined plane, then four-engines. The heavies.'

'One day I should like very much to learn to fly in an air force. If it is possible.'

'Perhaps it will be.' But he couldn't imagine how or when. There was no Luftwaffe any more and it was going to be a long, long time before the Germans were allowed to fly anything more than a kite.

The boy looked at the box again. 'Can we begin this now? At once?'

Lili intervened. 'Rudi, the squadron leader does not have time. He is very busy.'

'No, that's fine by me,' he said quickly. 'I'm off duty.' He put his cap and gloves on the table, sat down beside the boy and opened the box. 'I'll show you how to make a start.' He felt in his greatcoat pocket and took out a brown paper bag. 'I've brought some glue and sandpaper and a penknife and paints and brushes too. I thought red might be a good colour for the fuselage and white for the wings.'

He took the sheet of instructions from the box and laid it out, hoping he hadn't lost the knack of model-making. It was fiddly work, sanding down and shaping the rough wood and gluing small parts together, and the dim electric light wouldn't help. Lili brought some darning to the table and sat with them. All the time he was conscious of her there, sewing away quietly. It looked like a stocking that she was mending – one that already had several other darns. He wondered if the German women had had their own equivalent of Mrs Sew-and-Sew during the war. If they had had their sewing and knitting circles and their make-do-and-mend groups, like the women in England. He went on sanding down the lump of wood for the fuselage with Rudi watching him closely, and after a while he handed it over. 'You do some now.'

The boy managed pretty well, working away slowly and carefully with the sandpaper. He stopped and held the wood up. 'It is all right?'

'It's fine. Very good.'

He looked pleased and some colour came into his cheeks. 'I like to do this. It is good fun.'

He couldn't have had much fun in his short life, Harrison thought. In fact, probably none at all.

Lili looked up from her darning. 'I am sorry that I cannot offer you coffee but we have finished all our wood so I cannot make it.'

The old stove, he realized, must be the sole source of any heat of any kind. No wonder the room was like an icebox. 'Can you get more?'

'Dirk will go tomorrow to find some.'

He remembered the Tiergarten tree stumps, hacked down to the ground. 'Where?'

'He will go on the bike out into the country. He has made a cart that he can pull behind and he will fill that. We manage.'

We manage. But for how much longer? The boy kept on coughing, the old man, too, in his sleep. How much longer could they last, living in this sort of cold? And it was only November. The weather was bound to get worse. Much worse.

He stayed for more than an hour, helping to build the Tiger Moth. Eventually, Lili stopped her darning. 'I think it is time for Rudi to go to bed now.'

Her brother protested but in vain. At the door he turned. 'You will come back, sir?'

'It's a promise.'

The boy smiled and waved. For a second, Harrison saw two other small boys turning to smile and wave good night.

Lili said, 'It is warmer for him to be in bed. Also, he should not keep you here any longer. It is very cold for you too.'

'It doesn't matter to me,' he said truthfully. 'I've hardly noticed it.'

The grandfather stirred and coughed and muttered peevishly in his armchair. Lili rose to her feet. 'I must get him to bed, as well.'

He picked up his cap and gloves. 'I'll come back as soon as I can.'

She went to the door with him. 'Thank you for bringing the model, Squadron Leader. Rudi is very happy with it.'

He wished he'd brought something for her too – something English from England – but he hadn't been sure whether she would have been pleased, or even accepted anything from him. 'It was nothing,' he said. 'I'm really sorry I couldn't get here sooner. Things have been so hectic.'

'Dirk says it is also very hectic at Tempelhof. The Americans are bringing in a lot of coal in their planes.'

'We're bringing quite a bit in, too, actually,' he told her. 'Not as much as the Americans, of course. We haven't as many planes, but we're doing our best.'

'Do you fly yourself?'

He shook his head ruefully. 'I'm stuck on the ground these days, flying a desk.'

She looked puzzled. 'What does that mean?'

'Paperwork. Planning. Generally keeping the show on the road.'

'Do you believe that the Russians will give up in the end?'

'If we can keep going. And I can't see why we shouldn't. Of course, it rather depends on the weather this winter. And on the Berliners. Whether they can stick it out, you know.'

She understood him. 'They will. You can be sure of that. They see and hear the planes all day and all night and so they know that the *luftbrücke* is working.'

He fingered his cap. 'Well, I'll do everything I can for Rudi and your grandfather.'

'Thank you.' She smiled. 'I see you are still wearing your Hanhart watch. Do you like it so much?'

'It keeps jolly good time. I tried to get my other one repaired in England but I had to leave it with the watchmakers. It needs a new part.'

'It will take long?'

'Everything takes long nowadays in England.'

'I thought it would all be so much better there because you won the war.'

'Far from it. Things are still rationed and there are lots of shortages.'

'But it is not as bad as Berlin?'

'No,' he said slowly. 'It's not as bad as that.'

229

*　　*　　*

She heard Dirk coming in – much later than he should have been if he had come back straight from his shift. He always moved like a cat, scarcely making a sound, but she had been lying awake on the couch and heard the soft click of the front door. She got up, wrapping a blanket round her, and switched on the electric light. He stopped halfway across the room, blinking at her, like a hunted animal caught at night.

'I thought you would be asleep, Lili.'

'And I thought you would be home long before this. You must have finished work hours ago.'

'Don't nag. I stopped to have a beer, that's all. There's a new bar opened up near the airfield. All the Americans go there.'

'To trade on the black market?'

'No, for girls. Swarms of German girls, hoping to catch a Yank. Some guy plays the piano and they've got a singer. It's a real hot spot. The beer's not bad either.'

He looked at her with his most innocent expression – the one he wore when he was most guilty. And he could turn it on so easily. As usual, he was wearing his filthy old raincoat that made him look like a gangster. She wondered what its deep pockets contained this time. There was a tin box that he kept hidden under a floorboard in his room containing a small hoard of jewellery: the ruby ring, a diamond brooch, gold earrings and bracelets, a string of pearls, more rings. She had found it by accident when she had noticed that the board was loose.

He had spotted the model of the English plane on the table. 'So . . . I see that the squadron leader came back after all. That's good. I always thought he would. Did he say anything about Grandfather and Rudi?'

'He doesn't think the RAF will be able to take them until December.'

'That's not so long. Only two weeks away.'

His unconcern angered her. 'Rudi has been coughing all day, and now Grandfather, too. And this evening I couldn't even heat the soup for their supper because the wood was finished. We *have* to find some more tomorrow, Dirk.'

'Calm down, Lili. Don't worry, we will. I'll take the cart out first thing and fill it up. I know a very good place to look.' He put his hand in his raincoat pocket. 'By the way, I found some more coffee.'

The weather worsened steadily. The conditions at Gatow, coupled with the decreasing number of daylight hours, were already bad enough to threaten the airlift. Fog was the worst hazard: impenetrable, cold and clammy fogs that blanketed the airfield for days on end. The rain poured down in torrents, flooding the tarmac and causing all kinds of electrical faults to aircraft standing outside. And the snow was yet to come. A treat in store, as Tubby put it. The Sunderlands continued to fly in and out of Lake Havel with their precious cargoes of salt but it seemed only a matter of time before ice formed on the lake and put a stop to them. Out on the windswept wastes of the airfield, the RAF and the

German civilian labourers worked on doggedly in sodden clothing and miserable circumstances, guiding the aircraft in and out, unloading and reloading them, repairing them, refuelling them. And their crews went on flying, backwards and forwards. The Ground Control Approach directors sat for hours crouched over their radar screens in their cramped caravans without heating. Nobody complained. Nobody faltered. Nobody came even close to giving up.

Nico Kocharian phoned Harrison. 'Hallo there, Michael, old chap. How are you?'

'Fine, thanks.'

'I've managed to wangle some tickets for the opera this Friday. The Berlin Opera Company are doing *Tannhauser*. I wondered if you'd like to come along – as my guest, of course.'

'I'm afraid I won't be able to.'

'The tickets are like gold dust and it'll be a marvellous performance. Bit chilly in the house, of course, but people take rugs and blankets. Hot-water bottles, too, if they've got them.'

'Sorry, I can't get away. I'm sure you'll be able to find somebody else.'

'Quite sure you won't be able to?'

'Quite sure.'

'That's a pity.' There was a pause. 'Things going all right at Gatow?'

'Pretty well.'

'I hear you're all doing a terrific job.'

'The best we can.'

'Perhaps we could meet up for a drink sometime?'

A flight lieutenant was hovering with some papers, waiting to see him. 'I'm sorry but you'll have to excuse me. I'm right in the middle of things.' He said goodbye and put the phone down. He had spoken more curtly than he'd intended but there were more important things to worry about than Kocharian's feelings. He dismissed him immediately from his mind as he attended to the flight lieutenant.

His mother's chatty letters came from home and another world. There'd been a rather boring lecture on the Himalayas with coloured lantern slides at the village hall, a severe overnight frost had almost certainly killed off the Mrs Popple fuchsia, Mrs Lewis's daughter was expecting at last, and they'd played bridge with Celia's parents.

We haven't seen Celia since you were home, but her mother says she'll be down one weekend soon. Apparently she's been working very hard since her promotion. I'm sure the War Office appreciate what a wonderful asset she is. He smiled when he read this. His mother was losing hope but she had by no means abandoned it. Celia herself had written once: a friendly letter containing only the most general news and no hints or digs of any kind. His father, who communicated infrequently, had also written.

I made some enquiries about that fellow, Nico Kocharian, through an old Intelligence contact of mine. He tells me that he did serve with them during the war until he was demobbed in '45. He's an excellent linguist, apparently. In fact, I rather gathered that they thought pretty highly of him all round. I told them you'd run across him in Berlin, but they don't know anything about what he's up to there. Not that they'd say if they did. These chaps always clam up on you. Still, it doesn't sound as though he's anything to worry about.

He put the letter away, unconvinced.

When she had any soup to spare, Lili would take some to Dr Meier. The old man seemed to exist on practically nothing. But though she could see that he was growing physically even frailer, his mind remained clear. She had taken to sitting with him for a while in that dreadful cellar and talking. They talked about all kinds of things. He spoke of his long-dead wife, Frieda, and of his only son, Peter, who had died in the trenches of the First World War. All his photographs of them had been lost in the bombing. This had made him very sad, he told her. 'I have to rely on my memory alone to give me a picture of what they looked like, and my memory is not as good as it used to be. Music was always my consolation but now I can only hear it in my head.'

She found herself confiding in him about the Russian soldiers – telling him far more than she had ever been able to tell Dirk or any other living soul. He had listened to her in silence as she had struggled to find the words to describe how they had seized hold of her and dragged her into the ruins; how they'd slapped her and punched her and torn her clothes from her and held her down in the dirt so each could take a turn while the rest had watched and laughed. Seven, eight, nine of them – perhaps more. How afterwards they'd jeered at her and spat on her and urinated on her face and kicked her with their heavy boots before at last they went away.

When she had finished, he said quietly, 'You will never forget, Fräulein, so there's no point in trying. It's better to tell yourself that it belongs to the past, together with all the other terrible things that have happened to you. Think of it sometimes, if you must, but don't dwell on it. Look only forwards. Not backwards.'

'But I can never feel clean. It's a stain on me for ever. One that can never be taken away.' She touched the scar on her forehead. 'And this reminds me each time I look in a mirror. This mark is from them.'

'What happens to your body is not so important. It's your mind and spirit that count. The person you are, the way you live, the things you hold dear and true and keep faith with. *That's* what matters.'

Later she told him about the Americans. She was to be pitied for the Russians but the Americans had been of her own making, her own choice. She expected Dr Meier's shocked censure. Instead, he merely remarked, 'You did it for your young brother, Fräulein, and it can't have been easy for you. There are many women in Berlin who have had to do the same.'

They talked about Squadron Leader Harrison and his promise of help.

'He is doing this for you?'

'Not for me. For Rudi and Grandfather.'

'But it's really for *you*, I think. He is in love with you. Don't you realize that?'

'He hardly knows me.'

'He wouldn't need to. Only to see you. And once would do. The first moment I saw my wife I fell in love with her.'

She shook her head. 'You're wrong. He's never said anything. Not a word.'

'The English are reticent about these things, I believe. He wouldn't speak unless he thought you felt something for him, in return. Do you?'

'I hated him at first for what he was and what he had done. But it's hard to go on hating him when he is so kind to us.'

'It would be easy, perhaps, to love him instead?'

She answered the doorbell and found him standing there in the rain, soaking wet. He stepped into the hallway, taking off his cap.

'I came to tell you to get things ready for Rudi and your grandfather to leave the day after tomorrow.'

'They will really take them?'

'In one of the Sunderlands. The flying boats. They go from the Havel See. They have some room on the return journey.' He smiled at her. 'Rudi will like that.'

'Yes, he will. Very much.'

'Do you have suitcases? Or something to put their things in?'

'There is one suitcase for Grandfather. And we have an old canvas bag I could use for Rudi. There is not much for them to take.'

'I'm arranging for an RAF corporal – a Corporal Haines – to come and meet you with transport at the Brandenburg Gate. He will wait inside the British sector, just beyond the barrier. It's safer that way, in case the Russian guards cause any trouble. Can you get there all right, do you think?'

'Oh yes, we'll manage.'

He said apologetically, 'I'm on duty or I'd come myself.'

'We would never expect that. What time will the corporal be at the Gate?'

'Early. By seven o'clock.'

'We'll be there.'

'Do you think you'll get through the barrier OK?'

'Usually it is all right, so long as one has the correct papers. People go back and forth all the time. Working, visiting, shopping. The Russians make difficulties if they can – search everything for black-market goods, take their time, insult us. Sometimes they arrest people. You never know . . .'

'I'm sorry, but the corporal won't be able to wait.'

'I understand. Can I go with Rudi and Grandfather – to the flying boat? To say goodbye?'

'Yes, that's fine, but I'm afraid you'll have to get back here on your own somehow. I'm awfully sorry about that.'

'I will manage,' she repeated. 'Where will the flying boat take them?'

'To their base at Finkenwerder at Hamburg in the British zone. Then it depends what the medicos there think – hospital or a nursing home, or some kind of foster home. They'll be well looked after, you don't need to worry.'

'I'm not worried,' she said. 'Only grateful. Will you come and tell Rudi yourself?'

Eleven

Grandfather refused to be hurried. Lili had packed up their luggage the night before – his old leather suitcase, stuck about with tattered labels from journeys he and Grandmother had made long, long ago before the First World War, containing the few garments he possessed, all as clean and presentable as she could make them. The canvas bag had been filled with Rudi's motley assortment of clothing, some of his favourite books, his scrapbook, and the little metal Dakota that the squadron leader had given him. The Tiger Moth plane, being too fragile, had to stay behind. She had sworn to take care of it.

Dirk was on the night shift at Tempelhof and without him it was going to be twice as hard. She had risen in the pitch dark by five and bundled her grandfather out of bed, washed him in cold water and dressed him in his warmest clothes while Rudi got himself ready. Then she gave them both a piece of dry bread and a slice of sausage and some extra to carry in their pockets. She would have liked to heat some of the leftover soup for them to drink but the stove was out and there was no time.

It all took so long, with Grandfather so confused and querulous, and it was nearly six o'clock by the time they set off – Rudi carrying his bag and herself the suitcase. Grandfather tottered along unsteadily and they went at a snail's pace down Albrecht Strasse, under the U-Bahn archway, over the bridge across the See. It was still dark and the gas street lamps gave a poor light. Grandfather kept stumbling over things and she had to hold on to both him and the suitcase while Rudi clutched his other arm.

'We must go faster,' she kept urging. 'Please try to walk a little quicker, Grandfather. We mustn't be late. It's very important.'

Of course, he didn't understand why it was so important. He grumbled away and went on stumbling and they went no faster at all. She and Rudi half-dragged the old man down Friedrich Strasse. The ruins stood black and silent as tombs on each side and the only sound was the dragging shuffle of Grandfather's feet and the wooden click-clack of her and Rudi's urgent steps as they coaxed him along. At last they reached the point where the street crossed the Unter den Linden and they turned towards the west. Ahead, she could make out the great mass of the Brandenburg Gate – still so far away. Too far. It was already twenty minutes to seven. Grandfather had started to cough and stopped suddenly, sagging between them, and they struggled to support his dead weight. Once he was down, she knew they would never get him to his feet again. In desperation, she shouted at him harshly – something she had never done before – and went on berating him until he began to totter forward again, making small sobbing sounds. She was horrified to realize that he was weeping.

Their progress was agonizingly slow but, at last, they came to the Gate and passed under one of its mighty arches to approach the barrier. The British sector beyond the barbed wire, where every lump of coal for lighting had to be flown in, lay in complete darkness. Again, Grandfather stumbled, lurched, almost fell. A Soviet guard stepped forward and flashed a torch into their faces.

'What's going on? Who is this old fool? Is he drunk?'

Lili said, 'No my grandfather is not drunk but he is not well. We are taking him to stay with my aunt who lives in the British sector.'

'At this hour?'

'I have to go out to work later on. He must not be left on his own. His mind is not clear.'

'Where are your papers?'

She fumbled in her bag and handed them over. The guard beamed his torch onto them. On the other side of the boundary she could hear the noise of a vehicle – a car or small truck. She could see its lights approaching from the direction of the Tiergarten. The vehicle stopped and the headlights dimmed, leaving only the pinpricks of sidelights. The guard was taking his time with the papers, the way they always did. She dared not look at her watch in case it annoyed him into taking even longer, but she knew that it must be seven o'clock by now. *I'm sorry, but the corporal won't be able to wait.* At long last the papers were handed back and she urged Grandfather forward.

'Halt. Not yet, Fräulein. Not so fast. What is in that suitcase? Open it, please.'

She knelt down on the road and undid the case, fumbling feverishly with the rusty old clasps to lift the lid for him. The guard shone his torch and rifled through the contents, turning everything upside down, making a jumble of the neatly packed clothes and spilling some of them out onto the road. He kicked at the case, disappointed. 'The boy has a bag. He is going too?'

'Yes. He is my brother. He is also going to stay with his aunt.' She was gathering up the spilled clothes, piling them back in anyhow, fumbling again desperately to close the lid.

'What has he in the bag?'

'Show it to him, Rudi. *Quickly.*'

She heard the vehicle's engine starting up again, saw the headlights flick on and could have wept with despair. The corporal was going to leave without them. The guard had found the little Dakota and seemed amused by it. He held it up, spotlit in the torch beam, the metal shining. 'American plane. I have seen these. I shall keep it.'

'Yes, please keep it. You're most welcome. Can we go now? We are very late.'

'Take your old fool away. He's no use to anyone.' The guard shoved Grandfather hard in the back so that he staggered helplessly. She and Rudi grabbed his arms to steady him. The barrier pole went up and they hauled him across the white line and into the British sector.

The vehicle – a small truck – was backing and turning to leave. Lili let go of Grandfather, dropped the suitcase and ran towards it. She flung herself in front of the headlights, arms outstretched. There was a screech of brakes as it stopped only a foot or two away from her and the driver yelled furiously out of his window. 'Blimey, you want to get yourself killed?'

She went up to him. 'Corporal Haines? I am Lili Leicht. We were to meet you here.'

His tone changed. 'Thought you couldn't make it, miss. I was just about to push off. Couldn't hang about, see.'

She could barely understand what he was saying. 'I am sorry to be late. My grandfather and brother are here too. I will bring them at once.'

He got out and helped her heave Grandfather up into the back of the truck. Rudi scrambled up after him. 'You hop in, sweetheart. I'll see to the bags.'

The truck gathered speed down the East-West Axis between the desolate wastes of the Tiergarten. Grandfather slumped exhausted in a corner; Rudi's thrill at the ride was spoiled by the loss of his precious Dakota.

'Do you think the squadron leader could get me another one?'

'I don't know. Perhaps.'

'Will you ask him? You could send it to me.'

'I may not see him again.'

They headed west across the city, through the

borough of Charlottenburg and then to the south out into the suburbs and the dark pine forests towards the Havel See. From time to time the corporal shouted something over his shoulder from the front but she could neither hear nor understand him properly.

When they reached the shores of the lake, it was beginning to get light. Gatow airfield was close enough to be able to hear the constant roar of aircraft coming in to land and taking off.

'They don't never stop over there,' the corporal shouted. 'Night and day. One every three minutes. It's a bloomin' miracle they don't buy it more often.' He pointed across the lake to a pale shape floating on the water like a great white whale. 'Look, love, there's the Sunderland.'

There was a building beside the lake and more trucks and men in Royal Air Force uniform moving about. A group of children stood huddled together on the bank beside a pontoon, wearing lifejackets. The corporal helped her down out of the truck. 'Easy does it, miss.' Grandfather was shaky and babbling nonsense to himself. She had made a cardboard label for him and tied it to a buttonhole of his coat with string. *Wolfgang Leicht. Aged 79 years, 8, Albrecht Strasse, Berlin*. Another for Rudi, while he protested indignantly. An RAF sergeant came up with two lifejackets.

Rudi clung to her as she kissed him but she knew he was more excited than sad. She wrapped his scarf more closely round his neck and smiled at him though she wanted to weep.

'Write to me, as soon as you can. Tell me how you are.'

'I'll come back soon, won't I?'

'Of course. When the winter's over.'

Grandfather was plucking uncertainly at the label and at the lifejacket. 'What is happening, Irma? Where are we going, Irma?' He was muddling her, as usual, with Grandmother. She took his hands in hers. 'You're going on a holiday, Grandfather – just for a little while. These good people will look after you.'

She watched anxiously as he was led away by the sergeant and helped out onto the pontoon and into a barge. Rudi, at least, understood but poor Grandfather was completely bewildered. As the barge travelled slowly out towards the flying boat Rudi stood up, waving to her. She waved back cheerily with her handkerchief. It had started to rain: a cold, misty drizzle drifting across the water. In the early dawn, sky, water, and the low hills that sheltered the lake were a uniform dull grey, the flying boat out at its mooring a ghostly white.

A crowd of spectators had assembled further along the bank – Berliners come to watch. As the barge drew alongside the flying boat, one of the crew appeared at an open door and began guiding the passengers on board, lifting up the smaller children in his arms. The pilot was leaning out of his cockpit window high above, watching. She could see his RAF cap and the fur collar of his leather jacket. They seem kind, she thought, relieved. They are taking great care.

Grandfather was being helped through the entrance and Rudi turned round to give one last, excited wave. The door was closed and the four engines started up. The Sunderland surged forward with a roar, sending up a huge bow wave. It gathered speed, racing away across the lake until its nose lifted slowly from the water and rose, dripping, into the air. A mighty cheer broke out from the crowd along the bank, echoing round the hills. She stood, watching the flying boat steadily gaining height until it disappeared into the clouds.

The corporal said at her shoulder, 'They'll be all right, sweetheart. Don't you worry, they'll look after 'em.'

She wiped her cheeks. 'Yes. I know that they will.' With an effort she smiled at him. 'Goodbye and thank you for everything.'

A road led back through the forest, curving to follow a fence round the edge of the airfield. She could hear the constant noise of the planes and presently she was able to see one of them descending in the sky ahead. A Dakota exactly like Rudi's model. Behind it, higher in the sky, there was another, and behind that one, higher still, yet another. Further on, she came to a gateway onto the airfield, guarded by a Royal Air Force sentry. He stepped forward. 'Can I help you, miss?' She shook her head and walked on.

By then it was raining hard. After several miles the driver of a British army lorry stopped to give her a lift. She sat up in the front cab beside him, dripping wet and shivering, with her wood-soled shoes in a puddle of water. The driver kept looking at her, clicking his tongue. 'Catch your death, miss. You want to get back home fast as you can.' He spoke as though there was a warm, comfortable place waiting for her, perhaps with a nice hot bath and a cosy fire.

He dropped her at an S-Bahn station where she waited for more than two hours before a train came, packed tightly with workers. At Friedrich Strasse bahnhof where they had crossed into the Soviet sector, Russian guards held up the train while they demanded to see identification papers and searched for black-market goods. She was ordered to open her handbag, its contents rummaged through. A young man was found to have pockets full of packets of American cigarettes and was dragged off, protesting in vain. That could have been Dirk, Lili thought, watching his white and terrified face and listening to his cries.

She walked down the bahnhof steps and under the railway arch into Albrecht Strasse. The apartment was as cold as ice and the rain had leaked through the ceiling holes in several places. She stood miserably in her wet clothes. No Grandfather in his armchair. No Rudi at the table. No Dirk who should have been home by now but, naturally, wasn't. Emptiness. Silence. Loneliness. And, suddenly, fear – shaking not only from cold, but from near-panic.

She went over to the wireless and switched it on, desperate for company and comfort. Grandfather had left it tuned to the American broadcasting station. Somebody was speaking, in German, about the *luftbrücke* – about how well it was going, about how many tons of coal and food and supplies had been flown in, about how confident the western Allies and the western Berliners all were that they would get through the winter. On Radio Berlin, of course, the Russians would be telling quite the opposite story.

The speaker finished and she went to change out of her wet clothing. She had missed her work shift and so she would miss the hot soup and bread and the pay in East marks. When Dirk came back perhaps they would light the stove, except that the pile of wood was frighteningly low again. He would bring something with him; he always did. Something he had stolen or bartered with stolen goods. She could no longer find the strength to argue.

On the wireless, music was playing. American music, the kind that Grandfather had come to like so much. A crooner started to sing, *I'd like to get you on a slow boat to China . . .* She sat down in Grandfather's chair with his rug wrapped around her, closed her eyes and listened.

'They got away all right presumably, Michael.'

'Yes, I checked.'

Tubby put down his beer mug. 'That's it, then. You've done your bit. No need to worry any more. They'll sort them out at Finkenwerder. Both in hospital for a while, I should imagine.'

'Thanks for the help.'

'Glad to be of use, dear boy.' Tubby accepted a cigarette. 'You're not planning on seeing your little fräulein any more, I trust.'

'That rather depends on whether she wants to see me.'

'Of course she will, dear boy – if she's got any sense and I'm sure she has. You're her knight in shining armour – the one who can rescue her from the dark, dank dungeon. She won't be the only fräulein looking for a way out of Berlin, by any means. If they can latch on to a Yank or a British serviceman, they will, and if he's an officer with exceptionally good prospects, then that's a real piece of luck.'

Harrison said coolly, 'She's not remotely like that. Exactly the opposite, as it happens.'

'But you don't really know much about her, do you? She's *eine Berlinerin*. That means she's likely to be damaged goods. Almost a racing certainty, in fact. No blame attached. The women in this god-forsaken city have had a simply frightful time and they've had to survive somehow – keep body and soul together. The only thing they've had to sell is themselves.'

'I'm well aware of the situation.'

'Sorry. I can see I've spoken out of turn, but I considered it my bounden duty as an old friend.' Tubby leaned towards him earnestly. 'Think very carefully about it, for heaven's sake, Michael. Knowing what an upright, honourable chap you are, I doubt that you'd offer her anything less than marriage. You'd be a bloody fool to saddle yourself with a German wife with, or without, a past. That other girl in England would be a much safer bet.'

'Thanks for the advice, Tubby, but, frankly, it's none of your damn business.'

'Quite so. I stand corrected. No offence taken, I trust?'

'None whatsoever. Because I know you mean well. The other half?'

'*Now* you're talking sense. Whisky would be delightful – if they've got it.'

Twelve

Lili stared at the big pile of wood beside the stove. Not the scavenged assortment of broken branches and hacked-about lumps that Dirk usually brought back in his home-made cart, but a neat stack of sawn timber. Logs, cut small and ready for the stove. 'Where did you get this, Dirk?'

'Out in the country.'

She swung round to confront him. 'Where in the country? Where did you find wood like this?'

He said easily, 'A piece of luck.'

'What sort of luck?'

'Does it matter? You should be grateful, Lili. It will keep us warm for ages.'

'It matters to me – where and how you got it. And how did you bring it all back? Not in the cart – it's not possible. So, tell me. *Tell me.*'

He looked injured. 'There's no need to get so fussed. I got a lift in a jeep with one of the Americans from Tempelhof. He was driving out and he took me with him. We came across the logs by chance.'

'Where?'

'In a barn.'

'You stole them?'

'No, I didn't. As a matter of fact, I traded some coffee for them. And a few other things.'

'What other things?'

'Vitamin pills, medicines . . . the people were very pleased to have them. They had a sick child.'

'Where did you get them? Did you steal them, like the coffee?'

'No.'

'I don't believe you.'

He shrugged. 'If you must know, the Yank gave them to me. He was grateful. I've been showing him around. Interpreting for him. I've helped him quite a lot. Americans are generous guys, as you know. We loaded the logs into the jeep and he dropped me back here.'

'This American . . . is he the man you were telling Nico about? Hank – wasn't that his name? The one who steals airlift goods and does all those black-market deals?'

'He does a few. So what?'

'But he does much more than a few. He's like a real criminal and sooner or later he will be caught. And you will be caught too. If not by the Americans, then the Russians.'

'Oh, Lili, you're making such a fuss. I can look after myself. Haven't I always?'

'This is different from a little trading on a street corner. Different from pilfering the odd tin of coffee and some cigarettes, don't you see that?'

'There's nothing wrong in it. People get what

they want in exchange for things they don't need any more. Everybody's happy.'

She stared at him. He was chewing gum – the horrible American habit that he'd picked up lately – and he was wearing some kind of American peaked cloth cap on his head; she thought it looked ridiculous. What was the point of aping them? He was a German. A Berliner. He should be proud of that, in spite of everything. They had not all been Nazis, whatever people believed. 'Things? You mean the few precious possessions they have left swindled out of them by a man like Hank to make his fortune from their misfortune? A man who is using the *luftbrücke* for his own greedy ends. That's despicable. How can you have anything to do with him, Dirk? What would Father have said? And Mother? They'd be horrified. Heartbroken. How can you say there's nothing wrong in it? Have you changed so much?'

He stared back at her, his eyes hard. In the beginning, when he had begun his black-market peddling, there had been an airy defiance, some awareness of wrong-doing. Now there was no such awareness. No conscience. No regret of any kind.

'Mother and Father are dead,' he said. 'But you and I are still trying to stay alive. We've all had to change, Lili. You too. They wouldn't have liked what you've done either. You're no better than me.'

Nico called. Lili was home from work and she had just lit the stove when the doorbell sounded.

He was wearing a belted tweed overcoat, a hat of grey astrakhan and yellow pigskin gloves, none of which she had seen before. Where did he find such clothes? How could he afford them?

'May I come in, Lili?'

'I'm very tired.'

'I shan't stay long, I promise.'

He padded after her into the living room on leather-soled shoes and yet no-one had been able to buy them in Germany for years. 'It's starting to snow, did you realize?'

'Yes, I know.' She saw his eyes go to the stack of logs. Nothing escaped his notice.

'I see you have plenty of wood, at least. That's good. However did you find all that lot?'

'Dirk brought it from the country.'

'Amazing what he comes up with these days.'

She didn't answer. He was taking things out of the pockets of the fine overcoat. 'I have brought you a few oddments. Nothing very special.' He laid two tins of corned beef on the table, a bar of American Crystal White soap and a small dark blue packet. 'Raisins. I thought they might make a change. The RAF have been flying them in by the ton.' He smiled his wet-lipped smile at her. 'Perhaps they think the Berliners will be able to make Christmas puddings out of them.'

'Perhaps they do.' She started to slice a turnip for the soup, glad of something to occupy her. 'It's kind of you, Nico, but I keep asking you not to bring us anything any more.'

'Don't deny me that small pleasure, Lili.' He took off the fur hat and the pigskin gloves and laid them on the table. 'Is Dirk not home?'

'Not yet.'

He looked round the room. 'And no Grandfather? Or Rudi? I hope they're not both ill in bed?'

'They've gone away.'

'Gone away?'

'To stay with relatives for the winter. With cousins in the country. We thought it was better for them.'

'I didn't know you had any relatives, Lili. You've never mentioned them before.'

'They're on my mother's side.'

'I always thought you were alone in the world. And now, after all, you have country cousins. Where do they live?'

'A small village to the east of Berlin. We have never seen much of them.'

'But nonetheless, they agreed to take Grandfather and Rudi?'

'Yes, they did.'

'That was very good of them.' He was looking at her with his head on one side; he seemed amused. He knows very well that I'm lying, she thought. Why should I lie? Because I don't trust him, that's why. He talks with everybody, knows everybody. It's safer not to tell him anything.

'How is Dirk?'

'Quite well, thank you.'

'Still working for the Americans?'

'Yes.'

'Staying out of trouble?'

'Yes.' She was not going to discuss Dirk either.

'I have warned him to be careful, Lili. I know how you worry.'

'There are always things to worry about.'

'Poor Lili . . . it hasn't been easy for you, has it?' His voice was soft but she didn't want his sympathy.

'It hasn't been easy for anybody in Berlin.'

She scooped the turnip pieces into the pot of water and set it on the top of the stove. Nico wandered round the room. 'And how is Michael these days?'

'Michael?'

'Michael Harrison. Who else?'

'I haven't seen him for some time.'

'He's been up to his eyes, no doubt. I invited him to the opera recently but he was too busy to come. A great pity. It was a magnificent performance. I would have asked you, Lili, but your grandfather and Rudi were not at all well just then and I knew you would not leave them. Still, the next time you must come. They're doing *The Bartered Bride* soon, I believe. I'm sure you'd enjoy it.'

'I don't much care for opera.'

'I'm surprised to hear that. Dirk told me that your father and mother were always playing records of all the great operas. Do you still listen to them?'

'They were smashed by the Russians. So was the gramophone.'

'Of course . . . like everything else. So now you're reduced to listening to popular American music on your wireless.'

'I like it, as a matter of fact.'

'Not quite in the same class as Mozart or Beethoven or Wagner, though.'

'My father refused to listen to anything by Wagner. He was as bad as the Nazis.'

'But he still composed great music.' He smiled at her. 'Fortunately, since Smetana composed *The Bartered Bride* it would be quite all right for you to enjoy it.'

She added some sliced potatoes to the turnips and stirred them, hoping that he would leave soon, but instead he sat down at the table and lit one of his cigarettes.

'I don't suppose Michael has told you much about himself, has he?'

'There's no reason why he should.'

'I thought you might be curious to know more. The English don't usually talk about themselves. It's not the done thing. His father's a general in the British army. Rows of medals and a title. General Sir Arnold Harrison. He and Lady Harrison used to come to Speech Days at school – did I tell you that I was at school with Michael?'

'No, you didn't, but he said something about it.'

'Oh yes. We were both at one of those ancient boarding schools that the British upper classes pack their sons off to as soon as possible. Hideously uncomfortable, freezing cold and sound thrashings for any boy who steps out of line – and I had plenty of those, believe me. All in the best character-building tradition, of course. Michael's father's an exact older version of him – tall and handsome. Michael's a real chip off the old block, as they say.

The mother's beautiful in a very upper-crust English way. He's the only son and heir. Actually, there was a daughter as well but she was killed by the Luftwaffe when they bombed London. Her two little boys died with her as well.'

She stopped stirring. 'I didn't know that.'

'Well, Michael would probably be the last person to tell you – doubly so in the circumstances. His sister was beautiful, too. An absolute knock-out. I used to admire her from afar when she visited the school. She was quite a few years older than Michael. I think he rather worshipped her. Of course, I was never exactly a friend of Michael's. He was a year above me and very exalted. A prefect, head of the house, head of the school . . . he was like a god. A golden god. Very popular, too. Whereas, I have to confess, I was extremely *un*popular. I didn't conform and that's never a good thing at an English public school. I was no good at games and far too good at languages. Didn't fit into the mould at all.' He smiled wryly. 'The English don't mind foreigners, you see, but they have to know their place and I don't think I knew mine. They felt they had to take me down a peg or two from time to time.'

She said uncertainly, 'How do you mean?'

'Bullying. That age-old custom that the strong majority perpetrate on a weak minority. It's by no means exclusive to English public schools, to be fair. The Nazis, one could say, were the bullies to end all bullies. The supreme masters of the art. In England it's carried out in a variety of much lesser ways.

Quite amateur by comparison. I won't go into it – all rather boring – but Michael Harrison stepped in and put a stop to it in my case. The irony is that he can't even remember doing so, but I've never forgotten. And I never will.' Another wry smile. 'He doesn't like me, of course, and never has, but that didn't prevent him from saving my bacon. Fair play, you see, is another fine old English principle. Standing up for the underdog. Doing the decent, honourable thing at all costs. No wonder Hitler misjudged them so badly.'

'He admired them.'

'Indeed. But he never understood them. Most people don't. But they understand themselves very well.'

To her relief, when he had finished the cigarette, he put on his hat and the pigskin gloves and got up to leave. At the door, he paused. 'To the English you and I are both foreigners, Lili, and nothing can ever change that no matter how hard we may try. Do remember.'

She went on stirring the turnips and potatoes. He'd been warning her in his devious way – not that she needed it. With Nico, one never knew the reason for his actions.

Dirk came back soon after. He looked cold and fed up. 'Nico was here, wasn't he? I can smell his cigarette. Did he bring us anything?'

'Some corned beef. Some soap. Raisins. I hate him visiting.'

'Why? He's never tried anything on with you, has he?'

'No.'

'Well, then you've got nothing to worry about. Just take the things and be polite to him. It's worth it.' He flopped down at the table. 'God, I'm tired. I've been heaving bags of cement around all day.'

'Is it still snowing?'

'Yes, and if it goes on it'll ground the planes, that's for sure.'

She served the soup and slabs of black bread. Dirk hunched over the bowl, wrapping his hands round it for warmth. 'I'm thinking of giving up at Tempelhof. It's slave labour and for what? A pittance and a few scraps. A mug's game.'

'It's steady work. You'd be crazy.'

'Steady? For how much longer? Remember what it was like the winter before last? If that happens again, the Allies are finished here. Unless they can keep on bringing the stuff in at the rate they're doing now, they might as well give up and go home.'

'And leave their Berliners to starve?'

'It could be their only chance of survival. Once the Allies are out, the Russians will take over and feed them. Let's face it, it's probably a losing battle.' He tore at the bread fiercely. 'We've got to look out for ourselves, Lili. Find other ways.'

'Hank's ways, you mean?'

'Don't look at me like that. You needn't worry. I won't be seeing him any more. He's gone back to America. Look, he gave me this as a farewell present.' He groped in his raincoat pocket and flourished a cigar aloft. 'Havana. The real thing.'

* * *

The snow had stopped, thank God. It had settled across the airfield, covering the hardstands and the runways a couple of inches or so deep, and every available man and woman on the station, wielding every available broom and shovel, had cleared it within a few hours. There had been barely a pause in the flow of air traffic. Next time, Harrison thought, they were unlikely to be so lucky. Snow, though, wasn't as much to be feared as fog. Snow could be cleared away somehow, but nothing could be done about fog which had kept forming over the swampland round Gatow since the beginning of November, reducing visibility to almost zero. Planes could be guided down to earth by radar, but they still had to taxi about without crashing into each other or anything else. Twice the airfield had had to be shut down completely when pea-soupers had forced everything to a halt.

Christmas was five days away. Plucked and drawn turkeys had been flown in to provide a proper Christmas Day lunch in the station Messes, together with sacks of fresh potatoes for roasting and puddings and mince pies. A mouth-watering feast after months of dehydrated, tinned, salted, pickled food. And there wasn't a single person at Gatow, Harrison reckoned, who didn't thoroughly deserve it.

That night he attended the Christmas Dance in the Officers' Mess. A German band played their brass-pumping version of American swing and he danced with several WAAFs and diplomatic wives. Tubby, forced to do his seasonal duty, trundled gallantly round the floor. He could remember him at other Christmas dances on wartime England airfields, doing his stuff. Paper chains, tarnished tinsel and soft-eyed WAAFs who had imagined, with some justification, that it was every pilot's last evening alive.

One of the wives reminded him a little of Celia. She hadn't written for a while and a recent letter from his mother had provided the probable explanation. *Celia was home last weekend. We saw her at church on Sunday with her parents and she had some man with her. He's something at the War Office, apparently. Quite a bit older than Celia, by the look of him. He seemed pleasant enough but I don't think her parents are all that keen.* Which meant that his mother had decided it might be nothing to worry about. He hoped, for Celia's sake, that the man, whoever he was, was rather more than 'pleasant enough'.

There had been a time when he had thoroughly enjoyed Christmas. As a child he had looked forward to it for weeks. Later, he had enjoyed it all over again with Harry and Benjy, reliving it through their eyes. For the rest of the war, after they were gone, it had been a day much like any other, in spite of all the valiant efforts with paper chains and carol-singing. He had spent one Christmas bombing Essen, another Cologne. Men had died as on any other day.

On Christmas Eve he took one of the Volkswagen taxis into the city. The driver, an elderly man, was eager to be friendly with his few words of English.

'The RAF is wonderful! Berliners thank you very much. Thank you. Thank you. The RAF is our good friend.' The man's outpourings embarrassed him. Unreasonably, he had almost preferred the pre-airlift sullenness. In the same way, he disliked the offerings that arrived at the station in a constant stream of gratitude. The flowers, the hand-made, home-made gifts, the cards and letters all expressing German thanks. Heartfelt as they undoubtedly were, he was not ready to be a friend of the enemy.

The British sector was in the middle of one of its power rations and there were lights burning in windows. Berliners would be cooking, ironing, listening to the wireless for as long as the electricity supply lasted. No Christmas turkey or roast potatoes for the vanquished, though. Instead, boiled cabbage, reconstituted Pom, margarine scraped thinly onto bread. The taxi took him down empty streets. Snow still covered the city. It could be a bloody nuisance but it could also be merciful. Berlin, like an ugly woman wearing a thick veil, looked almost beautiful.

The Russian sector was as dimly lit as ever. The district might once have been the heart and soul of Berlin but it always struck him as infinitely grimmer and more depressing than the western sectors. It was not only the fact that the Russians had made so little effort to restore anything, it was also the inhabitants themselves. They seemed bowed down, resigned, defeated, as though they had abandoned all hope.

At Albrecht Strasse, he used his torch to show the way across the inner courtyard, holding the box he was carrying under his other arm. The wolves' heads' snarls were softened by their mantle of snow but when he tugged at the bell pull there was no response. He waited for a while before trying again. There was no glimmer of light from inside, no sign of life. He tested the iron handle. It turned stiffly and when he pushed, the door swung open.

The hallway was in pitch darkness, everything still and cold as a morgue. She's gone, he thought. Now that Rudi and the old man are looked after, she and Dirk have got out. How in hell am I going to find her? And then he heard the music: faint music. Guided by the torch, he found the door to the big living room and opened it. The room was in darkness, too. The music, he realized, was coming from the wireless up on the high shelf: Goebbels's propaganda-spewing *volksempfanger* broadcasting American swing instead. He even knew the tune. He traversed the torch beam slowly until it fell on Lili fast asleep in her grandfather's chair, wrapped up in a rug, her head resting on one hand. She looked like a child, with a child's vulnerability, and his heart ached with love and pity for her.

He put the box down on the table, went closer and spoke her name softly. Her eyes opened, blinked in the torchlight and she leaped to her feet with a scream of terror. When he tried to reassure her she only screamed louder, shrieking in German, clawing at him wildly. He dropped the torch in order to grab at her hands and protect himself. 'It's only me. Michael Harrison.' She stopped screaming at last. The torch had gone out but he could hear her

263

breathing hard in the darkness and feel her trembling in his grip. 'It's Michael Harrison,' he said again, very clearly. 'The squadron leader. It's all right. It's only me.'

After a moment, the breathing slowed and the trembling stopped. He let go of her.

Out of the darkness, she said, 'You gave me a very bad fright.'

'I'm most awfully sorry. I couldn't get any answer at the door so I let myself in. I found you asleep. I didn't mean to startle you like that.'

'It's all right. I couldn't see you properly behind the torch and I thought . . . I thought it was someone going to attack me.'

'It was damned stupid of me. I'm so sorry.' He groped around on the floor. 'I think the torch is probably broken.'

'I'll turn on the light.'

She moved away from him and presently there was the click of a switch and the two overhead bulbs came on. They stood looking at each other across the squalid room. The music was still playing softly on the wireless. 'Are you OK now?' he asked.

She nodded. 'Yes, thank you. I was listening to the wireless, you see, and then I must have fallen asleep. I was a bit tired.'

'You were working today?'

'A lot of work.' She brushed a strand of hair away from her forehead. 'I'm glad you came. I wanted to thank you for what you did for Grandfather and Rudi.'

'Corporal Haines told me everything went OK.'

'Yes. Everything went OK. Except that the Soviet guard at the barrier took Rudi's model Dakota – the one that you gave him. They do things like that. Take what they want.'

'I'll try and get him another one – for when he comes home.'

'Please, you mustn't bother. You have already done so much. Is the torch broken?'

'Afraid so. The bulb at least.'

'I'm sorry for that. It was all my fault.' She hugged herself, shivering. 'And I'm sorry that it is so very cold in here. The stove must have gone out while I was asleep. I'll light it again and make hot coffee, if you would like some.'

'There's no need.'

'But it's so cold. And I should like some coffee anyway.'

'Let me give you a hand, then.'

There was a stack of good logs in a corner, which surprised him. 'Dirk got them from the country,' she told him. She didn't say how.

The stove was very similar to the ones he had known in RAF Nissen huts and he soon got the fire going. 'We found it on a bomb site,' Lili said. 'It works quite well. We did have a real kitchen once, with a proper stove.' She fetched water from the bathroom and put it to heat in a saucepan. 'We have American instant coffee. Dirk brought it back, of course. He has gone out this evening – to a dance hall near here. He wanted to have some fun.'

'Not you?'

She shook her head. 'Russian soldiers go there.'

'Not much of a way to spend Christmas Eve – alone here, in the cold and dark.'

'Perhaps not. But it's better than dancing with Russians.'

'You don't like them?'

'I hate them.' She said it quietly, almost under her breath. 'As much as they hate us.'

She started to get out the saucerless cups, one with a handle, one without. He said, 'I brought you a Christmas present. It's on the table.'

'A Christmas present?' She sounded completely astonished. As though it was the very last thing she expected. 'What is it?'

He fetched the cardboard box from the table. 'Open it and you'll find out. I'm sorry it's not wrapped properly. It should have paper and ribbon but there wasn't any.' She took the box from him and opened the lid warily. 'It won't bite you,' he told her, smiling. 'You're quite safe.' He watched her feel among the wood shavings, playing lucky dip. She brought out one of the cups and stared at it. 'There are six of them,' he said. 'And saucers. And plates to match. It's a tea set really, of course, but I thought they'd do for coffee as well. You might as well use them now.'

She was still staring in awe at the bone china cup with its delicately painted pale yellow flowers and green leaves. 'It's so beautiful. Is it English?'

'Yes.'

'It came with you from England? You bought it there?'

He shook his head. 'You can't buy anything like

that in England now. It's all for export only. Actually, I got it in the Malcolm Club at Gatow. There's a kind of shop there, selling all sorts of things. Don't ask me how *they* got hold of them.' He looked at her with misgivings. 'Perhaps I ought to have brought food instead. Chocolates, or something.'

'No. Not at all. It is very wonderful to have something beautiful like this.' She turned the cup over. 'It's called Spring.'

'The flowers are primroses. The English countryside's full of them then. They grow wild everywhere.'

'So pretty. Thank you for such a wonderful present. I will use them at once.' She took out another cup and two saucers, set them ready on the table and smiled at him. 'Cups *and* saucers. We are very grand.'

They sat down on opposite sides of the battle-scarred table. The flowery cups, designed for dainty English teas on lace cloths in English parlours, looked absurdly out of place among the shrapnel hits. He offered a cigarette and lit it for her. The small intimacy pleased him, as it had done once before. He lit his own cigarette and put the lighter away in the breast pocket of his uniform. The music played on softly from the wireless – another wartime song that he knew well. There was another sound – a scuffling noise from the shadows. 'A rat,' she said calmly. 'There are many of them.' She lifted the teacup and gazed at it again. 'My mother had cups a little like these. They were German, of course, but they had flowers on them, too. The Russian soldiers broke them all.'

'Were you here in this apartment when they came?'

'Oh, no.' She looked away from him. 'We were hiding in one of the U-Bahn tunnels. We hid for many days – Grandfather, Dirk, Rudi and me – until we thought it might be safe. When we came back we found that they had been here. Almost everything was destroyed, or stolen.'

'I'm sorry,' he said. 'It must have been awful.'

'It was awful for all Berliners. I told you, the Russians hate us.'

With some reason, he thought, wondering what version Goebbels's propaganda machine had churned out of the Wehrmacht's brutal advance across Russia and the siege of Stalingrad. 'This room must have looked very different once.'

'Oh yes. It's hard to imagine, I know, but it was a very nice room, before the bombing. And, of course, there were other nice rooms in the apartment that were completely destroyed. This was our *salon*, you know, and on Christmas Eve all the family would be in here together – my parents, my grandparents, Dirk and I. Rudi was too small then to stay awake. My grandmother would sit over there on the sofa, my grandfather beside her. There was good furniture and velvet curtains at the windows, and pictures on the walls and a Bechstein piano. My father had many shelves of books. The Russians spoiled most of them but others escaped, as you see. So did my mother's hats.'

'Hats?'

'A whole trunkful of them – there in that corner, against the wall. She was a milliner and she made wonderful hats. Very French sort of hats. Very chic. Very expensive. She had a lovely little shop in the Dessauer Strasse. Rich Berlin ladies went there – until the war went badly for Germany and nobody bought hats any more.'

At what point exactly had the doubts started and the penny eventually dropped that the sainted Führer had got things horribly wrong? After the German defeat at Stalingrad in 1942? Or when the heavy bombing Allied raids had begun in earnest in 1943? Or had the hat-buying gone on even longer than that? Lili herself would have been around nine or ten at the outbreak of war – too young to have understood everything that was going on and yet old enough to have some clear memories. 'Do you remember what Berlin was like – in those days?'

She frowned. 'It's very difficult for me to think how it was. Berlin has been like this for so long – or so it seems. When I walk down a street I cannot remember what it looked like before the bombing. I pass the ruin of a shop and only if I try very hard can I sometimes think what it was. I remember perhaps that the window was full of beautiful boxes of chocolates with coloured paper, tied up in shiny yellow and pink ribbons. Or that another window had red meat and big, fat sausages hanging from hooks. Or in another there were elegant clothes on plaster models. I walk past the empty hole where I remember that there was once a restaurant which had a long glass case showing all the wonderful things to eat inside – big hams, lobsters and crabs, pies and pastry, cakes with coloured icing . . . So much of everything. And so much colour. And so many lights. That is what I remember most. Colour and lights. When the war started it went dark for years and years.'

As a Pathfinder, he had looked down often enough on a blacked-out Berlin – on a blanket of total darkness that had concealed a whole city and its three million or so people until the sudden brilliant flare from the coloured target indicators he'd dropped for the bombers following him. *Bomb on the green, bomb on the green*. He said, 'Where did you go during the raids? Was there a shelter here?'

'There is a cellar underneath. We used to go down into it. It seemed safe until one night the bombs hit the building directly.'

'But you got out?'

'Dirk and I did, with Rudi. My mother gave me Rudi and I carried him. The whole street was in flames and we ran down to the river bank to be by the water.'

'Your mother?'

She looked down at her teacup, tracing the outline of a primrose. 'She could have got out too, but my grandmother was completely hysterical and she could not make her move. So she stayed with her and they were both suffocated by the fire. Grandfather was found wandering about in the streets, out of his mind. We don't know exactly what happened with him. He could never remember.'

'I'm sorry,' he said. 'Very sorry.'

She lifted her head. 'Your sister and her two sons were killed. By German bombs. Nico told me. I am also very sorry about that.'

Harrison was silent for a moment, smoking his cigarette. 'What about your father? Was he with you in the cellar?'

'Oh no. He had died the year before. He had been arrested by the Gestapo. He was put in prison in their headquarters here, interrogated and tortured.'

The quiet way she said it was more affecting to him than any number of tears or lamentations. 'Why did they arrest him?'

She shrugged. 'They didn't need an excuse. He did not believe in Naziism and he was not afraid to say so. That was enough. He was a professor at the university, you know, and a social democrat. He would speak out openly against the Führer and the regime and he refused to make the Nazi salute. Of course, he was reported to the Gestapo. At that time people would betray their own brothers. Everybody was afraid for their own skins. That's how the Nazis ruled, you see – by terror. Everyone was terrified. And everything was in secret. Secret police, secret arrests, secret lists . . . It was horrible.' She looked away again. 'There were many people in Berlin like my father, though perhaps you do not believe it. Many people were against Hitler from the very beginning but, in the end, they could not stop him. And most of those who tried were murdered.'

'Did your father die in prison?'

'No. After two months he was taken to Sachsenhausen – a concentration camp close to Berlin. It was a terrible place.'

He pictured the newsreels he'd seen of camp liberations by the Allies. 'I can imagine.'

'The Nazis sent anyone there who opposed them – not just Jews. Nobody was safe. Nobody. And, you know, the Russians are doing just the same in this sector. The newspapers and the radio are run by the Communist Party, all the officials and the lawyers and the administrators are appointed by the Party, so are the police. Instead of being bullied by Fascists, it is now the Communists. There is not very much difference.'

It was a truly wretched city, he thought. So little hope. So little chance for the future. 'What happened to your father?'

'They hanged him.'

The brutality shocked but it did not surprise him. What could he say to her? Sorry, was useless. He was sorry. She was sorry. To keep repeating it was pointless. He was silent for a moment. He began to understand something of what it must have been like to make a lone stand against the Nazis. 'Your father must have had great integrity.'

She nodded. 'Oh, yes. Not everybody was like that. Only the very strong. Only the very brave.'

And yet, he still held the German people collectively responsible for allowing them to come to power in the first place. He doubted that he would ever be able to change that view.

'After this building was bombed, you and Dirk

came back to live here, with Rudi and your grandfather?'

'Yes. Some days later, when the fires had stopped
at last. We found that it was still possible to live in
these three rooms. We cleaned them and saved
everything we could. And we looked for things on
bomb sites to use – like the stove. We managed.
Until the Russians came.'

The victorious Red Army storming in to take their
grim and grisly revenge. Massacre, torture, rape.

He nudged the ash carefully off his cigarette into
the tin lid on the table. 'What did you do then?'

'We hid. In one of the railway tunnels. We waited
there for days until it was safe to come out. Then we
came back here again. The soldiers had taken everything they wanted and destroyed almost all the rest
so we had to start over again.'

He knew that she was only telling him a part of
the whole story, but he had no right to probe
further. On the wireless Bing Crosby had started
crooning, *I'm dreaming of a white Christmas* . . . He
listened to it uncomfortably. The sickly sentimen-
tality of the ballad with its visions of rosy-cheeked
children, sleigh bells jingling and happy home-
comings had a dreadful irony. The reality of a white
Christmas in 1948 Berlin was rather different. And
the Christmases that Lili used to know would never
come again. 'I'm surprised the Russians didn't take
your wireless.'

'They would have, but Grandfather carried it
with him to the tunnel, under his arm. He refused
to be parted from it. He was like a child with a

favourite toy. In the war it was a great comfort, you see. He trusted the BBC. He could only understand a few words of the English broadcasts, of course, but he would ask us what they were saying.'

The old man had trusted the BBC. That was quite a piece of confidence-placing, considering everything. He said quietly, 'You can trust me, too, Lili. I swear it.'

Her hand lay beside the English cup and saucer – the cut and callused hand of a *trummerfrau*. He reached out and lifted it to his lips and then turned it over to kiss the palm as well. He dared not look at her.

There was a loud noise from the hallway, the crash of the front door slamming, and she snatched her hand away. Dirk stumbled into the room and stood, swaying. He gave a sweeping bow. '*Guten Abend, gnadige Frau, mein Herr.*' He staggered forward and grinned foolishly at them. '*Frohe Weihnachten.* Happy Christmas.' Harrison moved fast to catch him as his knees buckled and he passed out.

'Vodka,' Lili said sadly. 'Cheap vodka. The Russians drink it like water. Can you help me get him to bed?'

He carried the youth into the small back room that he had shared with his grandfather and brother and laid him down on the bed. He'd weighed next to nothing – not more than about six or seven stone – and lying unconscious, bereft of his usual cocky bravado, he looked no more than a kid. A very skinny kid, dressed in shabby, too-large clothes, with big holes in the soles of his shoes.

Lili covered him with a blanket. 'I'll look after him now. Thank you.'

'Sure you can manage?'

'Oh, yes. He has done this before. He will sleep now until morning and most of tomorrow.'

'He'll have a frightful hangover.'

'I know. He won't care, though. He'll say it's worth it for some fun.'

Harrison had had some bad hangovers in his time and they had seldom seemed worth it, but he could see how a few hours of carefree oblivion on Christmas Eve in post-war Berlin might outweigh a splitting headache. 'I'd better go, then.'

She kept her head turned away. 'Yes, it is very late.' He collected his cap from the table. 'Be careful on the streets,' she told him. 'The Russians stop people at night. They can be very unpleasant.' She handed him his torch. 'I'm sorry this won't be any use now. Perhaps you can get a new bulb.'

'Perhaps.'

She said anxiously, 'Will that be very difficult?'

'I don't actually know, but it's not important.'

'But will you see your way?'

'Yes, I'll be fine.' He hesitated at the front door, wanting to say so much more but afraid to lose the small step he had gained. 'Do you mind if I come here again?'

'No. If you want to, it's all right.'

He smiled down at her. 'Good night, then.'

'Good night.'

He put on his cap and gloves, walked a few steps across the courtyard, stopped and turned. 'I almost forgot. Happy Christmas, Lili.' It was a ridiculous thing to say, of course. Almost an insult. But she answered him softly from the open doorway.

'Happy Christmas, Michael.'

Without the torch it was hard going. There were few enough street lamps and not all of those were working. There was no moonlight to help him and he had to navigate a path round piles of rubble. Nobody was about. No cars, no people, no sound of anything except for the steady crunch of his feet on the snow and the eerie moan of a bitterly cold wind that had probably come straight from Siberia. He reached the end of the street, passed under the railway arch and turned onto the bridge that crossed the river. On the other side, he made his way down an empty Friedrich Strasse. On other Christmases, in the past, the long street must have been a vista of brightly lit shops and restaurants with jolly models of St Nikolaus and healthy, happy Berliners crowding the pavements.

He turned onto the Unter den Linden and, as he did so, a figure stepped out of the darkness. '*Halt!*' A torch clicked on, the bright beam dazzling him. Another torch was switched on and showed him two men in the uniform of the east sector police, both armed with sub-machine guns. More German words were barked out – incomprehensibly. He said in English, 'I am an officer of the British Royal Air Force. Please let me pass.' They barred his way. '*Hände hoch!*' He raised his hands slowly. More German and waving of guns. The meaning was clear and he had no choice. He walked ahead and they followed, prodding him in the back with both the gun muzzles.

He was taken into the lower floor of a building off the street and put in some kind of small guard-room, the door slammed shut behind him and locked. There was no furniture of any kind and he lit a cigarette and waited, pacing up and down. He went on waiting – over half an hour according to his watch – and, losing patience, started to bang on the door. It was a further twenty minutes or more before, finally, he heard the key being turned in the lock and the door opened. The man who entered the room wore a badly cut civilian suit. He reminded Harrison of the Russian who had been so intransi-gent at Marienborn – the same stocky build, stubble hair and hard eyes. Harrison decided to deal with him in the same way.

'I strongly protest at this outrageous treatment of a British officer and I demand to be released im-mediately.'

'That is not possible.' The accent was Russian, not German.

'What authority do you have for keeping me here?'

His question was ignored. 'Your identification papers, please.'

He took his ID card out of his tunic pocket and the man scrutinized it minutely.

'Why were you in the Russian sector?'

'I fail to see what business that is of yours. There is no restriction on members of the Occupation Forces crossing into any sector of Berlin.'

'Everything that happens in this sector is our business, Squadron Leader. I repeat, why were you here and at this time of night?'

He spoke far better English than the chap at Marienborn and Harrison realized that he was not going to be quite so easy to handle. Even so, the whole thing was nonsense. The Soviets, he knew, had frequently abducted German civilians from western sectors, but never military personnel. There were no grounds for the Soviet sector police detaining him unless he had been breaking the law. 'I was visiting German friends.'

'What are their names? Where do they live?'

'That's irrelevant.'

'Their names, please. And the address.'

'I see no reason to tell you.'

'I'm afraid that you must remain here until you give us the information.' The Russian took a cigarette from a case and lit it. An English cigarette. Harrison had just smoked his last one.

He said coldly, 'That's absurd. You have absolutely no right to keep me here. None whatever.'

'What were you doing in this sector?'

'I've already told you. I was visiting friends, that's all. A social call on Christmas Eve, delivering a gift.'

'What sort of gift?'

'That's hardly your concern.'

'Black-market goods? It is illegal to bring such merchandise into the Russian sector. There are grave penalties.'

'It was nothing of the kind.'

'What, then?'

'If you must know,' he said, exasperated, 'it was china.'

'China? Porcelain? From Dresden perhaps?'

'*Dresden!*' He thought of that city in ashes. 'Hardly. From England. An ordinary tea set.'

'A tea set? A curious gift.'

'I fail to see why.'

'It was for a woman?'

'Yes, as a matter of fact.'

'A prostitute?'

'No.'

'Prostitution is not permitted in this sector. It is an offence against the regime.'

'I told you, it was not a prostitute. The gift was for the lady of the house.'

The Russian stared at him. 'Unless you can tell me the names of these friends who can corroborate your story, I am unable to release you.'

'That's completely absurd. Why should I lie about it?'

'Why should you withhold the names?'

He was not sure why, except to protect Lili and Dirk from any possible harm. Whatever happened, he refused to involve them. The Russians were capable of twisting anything to make trouble if it suited them, he knew that only too well. He was angry now. Angry and tired, and cold; the cell-like room was freezing. He also needed to pee. He looked at his watch. 'I'm due back on duty at RAF Gatow within a few hours. I suggest we finish this charade now. I have nothing more to say. And I should like my ID back, please.'

'May I see your watch.'

'My watch? What for?'

'It is most unusual. I should like to see it. Give it to me, please.'

He shrugged and undid the strap to hand it over. The Russian examined it closely. 'This is German. A pilot's watch. Very expensive. Where did you get it?'

'I bought it from somebody.'

'Who?'

He had intended to stick to the truth, if possible, but now he had to lie. 'A man in the street. A stranger. My own watch was broken and I needed to get another quickly. There are not many watch-makers left in Berlin.'

'It has the Nazi symbol on the back. The *Hakenkreuz*.'

'I'm aware of that. It probably belonged to a Luftwaffe pilot.'

'You have Nazi sympathies?'

'Of course I don't. Is that likely?'

'Then why do you wear their symbol?'

'It just happens to be on the watch, that's all. It rather amused me.'

'Amused you? You find the Nazis amusing?'

'For God's sake!' he exploded. 'I don't find them in the least amusing. But I'm a pilot, so it interested me. That's what I meant. It also happens to be an extremely good timekeeper.'

'Who sold it to you?'

'I told you. A stranger. A man on the street.'

'What street? Where?'

'I don't know the name.'

'In which sector?'

'The British sector.'

'What did you pay for it?'

'Some English cigarettes.'

'How many?'

'Three hundred and fifty, to be precise.'

'You carried all those on you when you met this man in the street? So many?'

'As it happens, yes. In tins. I needed to get a watch. Mine was broken. Cigarettes are common currency in Berlin.'

'So you made a black-market deal.'

'I prefer to call it an exchange. It's not exactly unusual. There are official Barter Exchange places everywhere.'

'It is illegal in this sector. We punish black-marketeers.'

'I found this watch in the British sector.'

'I do not believe you. I think that you got it from these friends that you have been visiting – the ones to whom you gave the English tea set. What are their names?'

'I am not prepared to tell you.'

'Then you must remain here until you do.'

He bit back his fury and forced himself to speak calmly. 'This is completely unreasonable and you know it. I'm an officer of the British Occupation Forces, due back on urgent duty. I have committed no crime and you have no authority to detain me. I demand to see whoever is in charge of this place.'

Instead of answering the Russian went to the

door and knocked on it. The door had been locked behind him and, again, Harrison heard the key turning as it was unlocked. The same two armed police entered the room and the Russian spoke to them in German. He turned to Harrison.

'These men will search you. Remove your overcoat and jacket, please.'

It was pointless to refuse. 'There's nothing to find.'

While one of them searched him, the other went through the pockets of his coat and tunic, tossing the contents onto the floor: his cigarette case and lighter, a handkerchief, his fountain pen, coins. A letter from his mother was handed to the Russian, who opened it and read it through. Harrison wondered grimly what he made of the daily round in an English village: the whist drive for the church roof, the Gardeners' Club outing, the verger's wife's sciatica and the Women's Institute talk on making artificial flowers out of scraps of material. The slim back leather wallet he carried in an inside pocket was gone through – notes and receipts scattered, a small white card handed over to the Russian.

'You know this man?'

'What man?'

'The man whose name is on this card. Herr Kocharian.'

He'd completely forgotten about it – had meant to throw it away ages ago. 'Yes.'

'You know him well?'

'We were at school together in England and I

happened to run into him here in Berlin. I hadn't seen him for years. He gave me his card.'

'You say you were at the same school?'

'That's right.'

'Then he is a friend?'

Harrison said cautiously, 'Not exactly.' He thought he could sense a subtle shift in the Russian's attitude but had no idea in which direction – whether to know Kocharian was an advantage or a disadvantage. Almost certainly the latter.

'But you have known him for a long time?'

'In a way.'

Nothing more was said. He was left alone once again in the room, the door locked. The card had been taken, so had his ID and so had his watch. He gathered up his scattered belongings and replaced his tunic and greatcoat. Since there was no chair, he sat on the floor, leaning his back against the wall. Although he could see no kind of peephole anywhere, he had a feeling that he was being watched, in which case he would not give them the satisfaction of looking rattled. In fact, he was not so much rattled as plain furious. The east sector police had no right and no reason to detain him; it was simply yet another ploy to make life difficult for anybody from the western sectors. Unfortunately, though, it was a game they played without any rules.

He was well aware that they could keep him locked up for hours, perhaps days, even weeks, if they chose. Maybe months or years. Frequently people they arrested simply disappeared. Any trumped-up charge would do and black-marketeering would be a convenient one for them to use. Having Nico Kocharian's card in his pocket was probably the nail in the coffin. Ludicrous though it had all seemed at first, he could be in real trouble. Not only his career but his freedom could be at stake. But there was no question of him divulging Lili's and Dirk's names. None whatever. A police raid on the apartment in Albrecht Strasse would certainly turn up evidence of Dirk's black-market activities. Both of them could be arrested and anything could happen to them – deportation to Russia as slave labour, imprisonment in a camp like Sachsenhausen.

More time passed, but without his watch he was not sure how much. The need to pee was now urgent and he got up and banged on the door. No response. And he could hear nothing from outside the room. He needed a cigarette, he needed to pee, he needed to get out and get back to Gatow in time to go on duty. He banged hard on the door again. This time, after a moment, he heard the key turn in the lock and the door opened. Nico Kocharian entered the room.

'I gather you're in a spot of bother, old chap.'

He stared at him suspiciously. 'What the hell are you doing here?'

'Getting you out. Vishnyakov rang me and I've been persuading him that he's made a big mistake.'

'Vishnyakov?'

'The fellow who's been asking you all the questions. Not much of a bedside manner, I'm afraid, but his bark's worse than his bite. He'd got it into his head that you were up to some black-marketeering. I told him the idea was completely absurd. That you were of unimpeachable character and reputation. A wartime hero of the RAF, with medals to prove it. Actually, he'd already noticed the medals.'

'How is it that you have so much influence?'

'I happen to know him rather well. I'm sure I mentioned that I know a lot of people in Berlin. And I keep in with them. And up with them. It pays to. By the way, here's your ID back.'

'The bastard took my watch as well.'

The Hanhart watch appeared from a coat pocket. 'Returned with his apologies. I think he took quite a shine to it. You're jolly lucky to get it back.' He held open the door. 'Shall we go?'

'You mean they're releasing me?'

'Oh, absolutely. You're perfectly free.'

They passed the two policemen in the corridor and Nico said something aside to them in rapid German. There was no sign of the Russian.

Outside it was snowing again, small, icy flakes swirling about, stinging his eyes. Harrison said curtly, 'Well, thanks for bailing me out.'

'Don't mention it. I owe you – remember? I like to pay my debts. I take it you were visiting Lili, though, of course, wild horses wouldn't have dragged it out of you. Very gallant and very wise. But not so wise to be wandering around the Russian sector at night. Do be more careful in future, Michael. I can usually help, but not always.' He held out his gloved hand. 'The sector border's just at the end of this street – you'll be all right now.'

Harrison shook the proffered hand reluctantly. He should have felt gratitude; instead he felt only the same dislike and suspicion. Spy? Double agent? Or just a smart-alec wheeler-dealer on the make? He looked back once on his way down the dark street, but the Armenian had already vanished.

Thirteen

Dr Meier had taken to his bed. He looked so white and still that, at first, Lili thought he was dead. Then he opened his eyes.

'I've brought you some soup, Herr Doktor.'

He smiled weakly. 'Thank you, Fräulein. You are very kind.'

'It's still hot. Will you have some now?' She helped him to sit up in the iron bed and held the bowl so that he could drink from the side. She could see that it was a great effort for him. 'Are you ill?'

He nodded. 'For several days now. First a cold, then it got worse.'

The grey blanket that covered him was thin and worn. 'Do you have any other blankets?' He shook his head. 'I'll bring more.' She went on holding the bowl until he had finished the soup, drinking very slowly in small mouthfuls. 'And I'll bring more soup.'

He lay back, seeming exhausted. 'No . . . it is not necessary. I shall soon be up and about again.'

He would soon be dead, she thought, if she didn't do something. She fetched his long overcoat from a hook beside the door and spread it over the blanket. The stove in the corner was stone cold, the enamel bucket standing beside it empty. 'I'll bring some wood too.'

He started to protest but she carried the bucket away with her, and the empty bowl. The apartment was only slightly warmer than Dr Meier's cellar but they still had enough wood to keep their stove burning for several more days. She filled the bucket and went into the bedroom where Dirk was still asleep. He had come in late the night before, the worse for drink again. Since he'd stopped working at Tempelhof it was happening more and more frequently. Every evening he would go out, and in the day he would disappear with his case and refuse to tell her where he was going or what he was doing. He brought back a steady stream of black-market goods and more pieces of jewellery that he hid in the tin box under the floorboard and, his prized possession, a portable wind-up gramophone with a lid full of records that he played over and over again.

She pulled the top blanket off him and he woke up and rolled over with a groan.

'What is it, Lili? What are you doing?'

'Taking one of your blankets.'

He made a grab at it. 'What the hell for?'

'For Dr Meier. He's ill and he needs it. I'm giving him one of mine too.'

He sat up, peering at her with bloodshot eyes. 'You're crazy! We need them.'

'We can spare them now that Grandfather and Rudi aren't here.'

'No we can't.' He made another grab and caught hold of the blanket edge. 'I'm keeping mine, thanks.'

She tugged it away sharply. 'No, you're not. I'm taking it to him and some of our wood. He's got none at all. He'll freeze to death if we don't help.'

'Who cares?'

'*I* care, and so should you, Dirk. You would have helped him once. What's happened to you?'

'I've learned that if we don't look after ourselves, nobody else will,' he said. 'That's what's happened to me. If we give away our blankets to that old fool, it's *us* that will freeze to death. I've learned sense.'

'And you have forgotten how to be a human being.'

She took two blankets, the bucket of wood, some more soup and a hunk of bread back to Dr Meier. The street was still covered with snow and slippery with patches of ice, and she had to go carefully with her burden. The old man was still lying in bed and she covered him with the extra blankets and got a fire going in the stove. He had turned his head towards her.

'You are very kind, Fräulein. You have a good heart. It's sad that life has been so cruel to you. I ask myself what the future can hold for you, here in Berlin.'

She knelt, watching the flames taking hold. 'It's the same for us all.'

'No. It's not at all the same for me. I'm near the end of my life so for me it doesn't matter, but you are young. It's different for you. You shouldn't stay here. You should try to go somewhere else where things will be better.'

'My home is here. This is all I know.'

'The English squadron leader . . . does he still come to see you?'

'Yes.'

'Have you learned to love him, instead of hating him?'

'Yes,' she said. 'It was easy. Just like you said.'

'Does he know?'

'No. I don't think so.'

'If he did, he would take you away. Make you his wife. Give you a good life in England.'

'He's never spoken of it.'

'But he will – if you give him some sign.'

She stared into the fire. 'I don't believe it could work. We could never be happy.'

'Why not?'

'Many reasons.'

'Tell me one of them.'

'I know that his family are very respectable. Nico Kocharian told me all about them. His father is a British army general and titled. General Sir Arnold Harrison. What would they think of me? An unknown German girl from the ruins of Berlin?'

'I'm sure they would love you.'

She shook her head. 'I'm quite sure they wouldn't. I'm not at all what they must wish for their son. They would be shocked. And they would want to know more – to find out everything about me. They would suspect the truth and they would despise me.'

'You've never met them, so you can't know they would be like this.'

'It would be natural. And they wouldn't be the

only ones. The English people would talk about me. That German girl, they'd say, she must have tricked him into marrying her. Used him to escape from Berlin.'

'Let them say it.'

'And then there is my brother, Dirk.'

'Yes?'

'What would I do about him? He's only seventeen. I couldn't leave him.'

'Then take him with you.'

'You don't understand. He's become like a common criminal – doing deals on the black market, stealing, always in bad company and getting drunk. He lives like one of the Berlin rats and the very worst thing is that he sees nothing wrong in it.'

'All this would change in England.'

She shook her head. 'I'm afraid it might not. That he would bring disgrace on Michael and his family. And there's still Rudi and Grandfather. After the winter they'll come back and must both be looked after. How could I take them all with me? You see it's quite impossible.' She shut the stove door and got to her feet.

Dr Meier looked up at her from his pillow. 'Everything is possible, Fräulein. Show the squadron leader that you love him. Give him some sign and the rest will follow.'

She heated the soup and gave him a bowl of it with the bread, promising to return the next day. Dirk's bed was empty, the bedclothes thrown back in a heap, and he was nowhere in the apartment. As she remade it, her foot caught against the case he'd left underneath. She pulled it out, set it on the bed and tried the clasps. For once, he had forgotten to lock them and she opened the lid.

The case was full of small glass ampoules with a needle at one end. She picked one up and read the word on the glass: *morphine*.

She confronted him on his return; waited for him with the case laid on the table in the big room. It was evening and dark before he came back and stopped dead when he saw it there. She stayed sitting in Grandfather's chair and watched the dismay and the guilt and then the anger on his face.

'You've no right to touch my case, Lili.'

'You left it unlocked,' she said. 'And I opened it because I was curious. I wanted to find out what sort of dealing you were up to. Now I know. Morphine.'

He faced her defiantly. 'So, now you know. So what?'

'Where did you get it?'

'From one of the Yanks,' he said. 'I met him at that bar near Tempelhof that I told you about. They're morphine syrettes – that's what they call them. The American Air Force issued them to bomber crews in the war to use if any of them got wounded on a mission. This guy got hold of a load of them somehow and I did a deal with him.'

'What sort of deal?'

'A few watches. It was a bargain.' He patted the case. 'I can get some good stuff with this lot.'

'Have you used any of it – on yourself?'

'I've tried it once or twice. It's a good feeling.'

'Like when you're drunk?'

'It's a lot better than that and there's no hangover. Don't look so grim, Lili. It's harmless enough. You should try it yourself.'

'It's addictive,' she said quietly. 'You know that. Drugs ruin people's lives. And now you're dealing in them. I can't believe it of you, Dirk. I can't believe that you could stoop so low.'

'Can't you? Well, I have. And I'll go on doing it, if I get the chance. There's nothing you can do about it.'

'Yes, there is. And I've already done it.'

'What do you mean?'

'Open the case.'

He snapped open the clasps and lifted the lid.

'I threw them in the river,' she told him. 'The whole bloody lot.' She stood up then, walked across to her brother and slapped him as hard as she could across the face.

The snow went away and was replaced by heavy rain and more fogs. In the very worst weather, the three-minute landing interval, with one take-off in between, had to be increased to every six minutes. But the airlift routine had now become so fine-tuned that pilots landed within ten seconds of their expected time of arrival throughout the whole twenty-four hours. Two American Skymasters had crashed during January but, miraculously, there had been no accidents at RAF Gatow.

Tubby, normally a sceptical agnostic, decided that God had come down firmly against the

Russians. 'Definitely on our side, dear boy,' he told Harrison. 'There's no other explanation.'

'Maybe it's just a question of damned good flying and a whole lot of hard work, discipline and determination from a great many people.'

'That, too, of course. But, mark my words, the Hand of God's in there somewhere. No doubt about it. We're going to make it.'

At some point, over the long, weary months since the airlift had begun, with the constant battle against the weather and the struggle with endless trials and tribulations, the feeling that they could make it had hardened into a certainty. The western Berliners realized it and the Russians must surely do the same, eventually.

Harrison had a letter from Celia. *Dear Michael, I wanted to give you the news of my engagement to Richard Anstruther. He works at the War Office in the same department and I have known him for quite a while. We're planning to get married next summer and I do hope you'll be able to come to the wedding . . .*

A letter from his mother arrived the following day. *Celia told me that she is writing to tell you of her engagement. I won't pretend that I am thrilled because, as I'm sure you realize, I have always rather hoped that you and she would get married one day. She would have been the perfect wife for you.* He wrote back – congratulations to Celia and commiserations to his mother.

He'd been twice recently to the apartment in Albrecht Strasse. On the first occasion there had been nobody at home and on the second, Dirk had opened the door and told him that Lili was in bed with a bad cold. He had looked unwell himself, Harrison had thought, and thinner than ever, his ragbag clothes hanging on him like a scarecrow's, and he had seemed ill at ease. 'She will be very sorry not to be able to see you, sir.'

He had wondered, walking away, whether the truth was that she had not wanted to see him at all.

'I'm not sure if he believed me,' Dirk said. 'Next time you can tell him yourself.'

'I'm sorry.'

He looked at her stonily. 'You're crazy to put him off. He's your passport out of here. You've got him hooked like a fish. All you have to do is reel him in and your troubles are over.'

'Don't talk like that, Dirk.'

'Like what?'

'You know what I mean.'

'OK, so you're not just using him. You're in love with him and he's in love with you. That's wonderful. So, why won't you see him?'

'I'm afraid,' she said.

'What of? That he'll find out about you? Why should he? Nobody else knows but you and me. Just keep your mouth shut.'

'He's already asked me about what happened when the Russians came.'

'What did you say?'

'That we hid in the tunnel until it was safe to come out. But supposing he wants to know more?'

'He won't. It would be rude to keep asking personal questions and the English are always polite. Stick to your story. We hid until it was safe. We survived. Then the Allies arrived. That's all you need say.'

'I'm not sure I could live with that.'

He said impatiently, 'For God's sake, Lili, do you want to throw away the chance of getting out? Spill the beans and ruin the whole thing? How stupid can you be? He's a nice guy. I like him. In fact, I like him rather a lot. I've quite forgiven him for dropping all those bombs on us. When he calls again, I'm saying you're in.'

He went off to his room and slammed the door. He was still very angry with her for what she had done with the ampoules, and most especially, she knew, for slapping him. She had hurt his feelings and his pride as well as his face.

Nearly three weeks passed before the squadron leader came back. Lili had begun to believe that he never would and while half of her was relieved, the other half was wretched. Then, one evening, the bell rang and when she opened the door he was standing there. He said in his quiet way, 'I hope you're better, Lili.'

'Much better, thank you. Please come in.' He followed her into the living room. Dirk was out and she was thankful, because of how he might behave in his present mood and what he might say. 'I'm sorry, it's just as cold as ever in here.'

'I don't notice it.'

'Will you have some hot coffee – in the English teacups?'

'Only if you have some to spare.'

She set the pan of water on the stove and waited for it to heat up. 'I've had a letter from the hospital in Hamburg where Rudi is. I was afraid they would say he had tuberculosis but he hasn't. They are giving him treatment for malnutrition, then he will go to stay with a family nearby.'

'And your grandfather?'

'He's in a nursing home. They are taking care of him.'

'Everything will get better. Winter will soon be over and the blockade won't last for ever.'

'How much longer, do you think?'

He frowned. 'It's hard to say. As long as it takes the Russians to realize that we can go on with the airlift indefinitely, I suppose. That could be just a few months away.'

'Then you'll have won.'

He smiled faintly. 'I'm not sure I'd use those words exactly. It might be truer to say that at least we won't have lost – lost Berlin, that is.' He groped in his coat pocket. 'I've brought you something. I hope you like it.' He put it on the table. The orange wrapper had the words CRUNCHIE in large white letters. 'It's chocolate outside with a sort of honey-comb inside. Rather good, actually.'

'Thank you. You're very kind.'

'How are you managing with food and things?'

'All right, thank you.'

'Is Dirk well?'

'Oh, yes.' It was better not to talk about Dirk. Better not to mention that he was no longer working at Tempelhof. Better to say nothing.

She measured out the coffee and poured on the hot water. He carried the primrose cups and saucers to the table for her and, as before, they sat on each side. He offered her a cigarette and lit it and, as he did so, his hand brushed accidentally against hers. On Christmas Eve he had taken hold of her hand and kissed it. Perhaps she had read too much into that? Perhaps he was not in love with her at all? Perhaps it had only been pity or kindness or sympathy?

He put the lighter away in a top pocket under his overcoat, buttoning the flap. 'I had a spot of bother with the Russians on my way back the last time I saw you. The east sector police stopped me and marched me off at gunpoint. I was locked up in a cell and it took a hell of a time to get out of there.'

She was horrified. 'I'm so sorry that this should happen. You must always be very careful with them. They are dangerous people.'

'They thought I was up to some kind of black-marketeering – or at least that's what they pretended to think. It was probably just an excuse to cause trouble.'

'How did you persuade them to let you go?'

'I didn't. Nico Kocharian did. They searched me and found his business card in my wallet. He seemed to have quite a bit of influence with them. He's a pretty odd sort of chap, isn't he? What do you know about him?'

'Very little. He met Dirk one day in Alexander Platz and bought a watch from him, and later Dirk brought him home here. He is a publisher of school books, so he told us, and I think he has been in Berlin for about two years. He comes here from time to time and brings us things.' She shivered. 'To tell the truth, he frightens me. He is . . . *unheimlich. Ein unheimlicher Man*. I don't know how to say this in English.'

'Creepy? Sinister?'

She nodded. 'Yet he has never done us any harm. Only tried to help.'

'I think you should be careful of him.'

'You don't like him either, do you? He knows that. He told me so himself. But he also said that you were good to him at the school in England. You stopped the other boys mistreating him.'

'I can't honestly remember, but he certainly wasn't awfully popular and probably came in for a fair bit of bullying. He was an awful show-off, you know, and that never goes down terribly well. I'm afraid English boarding schools can be pretty tough places, if you don't really fit in.'

'It is very important to do that in England? Fit in?'

He said slowly, 'I was talking about schools and schoolboys.'

'He told me a little about your family too,' she said. 'About your parents. Your father is a general in the British army.'

'He's retired now, actually.'

'Was he a good general?'

'Yes, he was rather.'

'And he must be very proud of you, of course. Your mother as well.'

He smiled. Whenever he did so his face lost its stern look and softened. 'Well, I don't know about that.'

'I am sure they are.' How differently her mother and father would feel if they could see what had become of Dirk and of herself. Not proud at all. Ashamed. 'Where do they live in England?'

'In a village in Surrey – that's in the south of England. It's nice countryside around. Hills and woods . . . rather beautiful, in fact.'

'My father used to say what a beautiful country England was.'

'Well, it is, in parts. Not all of it, of course. Some bits are quite ugly.'

'It's the same in Germany, too. Some of it is beautiful and some is very ugly – like Berlin now.'

'One day it will be rebuilt.'

'Yes, one day. And London? Is there much destroyed there?'

'Quite a bit. Nothing like here, but I expect it'll take years to get it all done.'

'My father thought London was a wonderful city. Very historic.'

'It's not very wonderful at the moment,' he said. 'But I love it. I have a flat there – an apartment.'

'I hope it's better than this one.'

He smiled again at her feeble little joke. 'It's not very big – just two bedrooms – but it suits me. It makes a good base when I'm home.'

'You have a kitchen?'

'Yes. Quite small, but it's got everything one needs.'

'And a bathroom?'

'Yes.'

'With hot water?'

He nodded.

She sighed. 'And central heating?'

'Yes, that too. Mind you, fuel's still scarce in England so it's not always at full chat, but the place keeps quite warm. There's a pretty good-sized sitting room and a dining room. I haven't bothered too much with the decoration and furnishing, being just me, but it could be made jolly nice.'

She thought wistfully of the apartment in London: a proper kitchen, proper bedrooms, proper bathroom, sitting room and dining room, no holes in the ceilings, no rats, no leaks, no horrible flies. Warmth. Comfort. Safety. And him.

'I think you'd like it there, Lili,' he said quietly, as though he knew just what she was imagining. 'And I'd take care of you. For always.'

His left arm rested on the table, close enough to see that there was a crown and eagle on each of the three shiny Royal Air Force buttons on the thick cuff of his overcoat.

'Lili?'

Give him some sign and the rest will follow.

She put out her hand and touched his sleeve. She thought, I know this is wrong. I know it, but I can't help it. The next moment he was at her side, pulling her to her feet and into his arms.

Fourteen

Dirk had brought back something wrapped in newspaper. He dumped it on the table. 'Don't go and throw *that* in the river.'

There was blood oozing through the paper – dark red, almost black. The sight and the smell turned her stomach. 'What is it?'

'What does it look like? Meat. Part of a cow. The backside. It was slaughtered a couple of days ago.'

'Where did you get it?'

'You always ask that, Lili. From the country. There aren't any cows wandering round Berlin, in case you haven't noticed. Do you want it, or not?'

'Yes, of course. I'll cut it up and cook it.' She carried the disgusting parcel over to the table by the stove and started to unwrap it. The hunk of raw flesh looked horrible and a lot more than two days dead. She started to saw at it with the carving knife. Dirk lit one of his American cigarettes.

'So, have you made up your mind yet?'

'Don't keep asking that.'

'Well, the squadron leader wants you to marry him, doesn't he? From what I saw the other night it looks like you've well and truly landed him.'

Neither of them had heard Dirk come into the room – not until he had coughed loudly. Far from being embarrassed, Michael had said easily, 'I've asked your sister to marry me, Dirk. I hope you don't mind.'

Her brother had grinned. He was slightly tipsy, she could tell, but not so much that it really showed. 'Not at all, sir. I hope she's said yes.'

'Lili has asked for some time to think about it. She wants to be sure.' Michael had smiled down at her. 'See what you can do to persuade her to take me on.'

The stink of the meat was almost making her retch. She went on cutting into it doggedly.

'Supposing that I *did* go to England, Dirk, would you come with me?'

'Me? Go and live in stuffy old England? No, thanks. I don't think it would suit me at all, do you? Can you see me settling down quietly, behaving like an English gentleman? Playing by their rules? Fitting in with the squadron leader's respectable English family? Sipping tea out of little china cups like he gave you? Making polite conversation? After all we've been through?' He cocked his head on one side, looking at her. 'No, I didn't think you would see it.'

'You might go to university there. Study law – like you were always meant to do.'

'You've overlooked something, Lili. A small point. I haven't studied a thing for nearly five years. I've forgotten everything I learned at school. It's too late now.'

'It's not too late. Not if you don't want it to be. You could catch up, Dirk. You're very clever. You always got such good marks.'

He stood with one hand thrust in the pocket of his raincoat, the other holding his cigarette, shoulders hunched. Like a Chicago gangster. 'I was nine, ten, eleven, then. I'm not that kid any more. I'm past sitting in class and doing what teacher tells me. Or anybody else. If I went anywhere it'd be to America. The new world, not the old one.'

'Anyway, I couldn't leave Grandfather and Rudi. That's impossible.'

'You wouldn't have to. They could go to England too. The squadron leader would arrange it. He arranged things for them once, so he'll do it again. He'd do anything for you. Rudi could go to school in England – it's not too late for him. He'd grow up an English gentleman. And Grandfather probably wouldn't know or care where he was.' Dirk picked up his case. 'I've got to go out again now. Don't ask me where, Lili, because I'm not going to tell you.'

He went, banging the front door loudly behind him. She went on cutting, her hands crimson and sticky with blood.

If any one single thing could be said, in future years, to have saved the city, Harrison reflected soberly, it would not be the airlift itself, nor the morale of the citizens, but the weather. The records showed that average winters in Berlin consisted of months of extreme cold, with bitter winds from Russia and Poland. Prolonged severe frost could have iced up engines, torn up runways, and burned up fuel stocks faster than they could possibly have been replenished. But General Winter had been on their side, after all. In the month of January there had been mainly clear skies and no bad frost, and more tons of supplies had been flown in than in any previous month. February was proving equally obliging. With spring and summer lying not so very far ahead, the Russians had lost their chance to take the city at its weakest time – in the darkest, coldest months with food and fuel so scarce.

At the very beginning, the airlift had been seen as a desperate and temporary measure until some craven agreement could be made with the Russians. Now all that had changed. It had been shown that the city could be supplied from the air for as long as it was necessary. Now the question was not how long the western sectors could hold out, but how long it would take the Soviet Union to give way, and on Allied terms. The talk was now not just of keeping western Berliners alive but of improving their lives with better food, more medical supplies, more coal, more fuel and more raw materials and machinery so that more things could be made for export, and there was even talk of flying in some consumer goods to brighten everyone's dreary existence.

Tubby, who was still quite convinced of God's Hand intervening, kept referring pointedly to the calm seas at Dunkirk.

'Same thing then. The Channel's usually appallingly rough and what happened when they were taking off the troops? Calm as a millpond for a week. A miracle.'

'I'd no idea you were so religious, Tubby.'

'Nor had I, dear boy. Perhaps it's a symptom of old age. The nearer one gets to meeting one's Maker, the more one starts to think about things one never thought about before – if you follow me.'

'I'm not sure I do.'

'No need to worry your handsome head about it. You've a long way to go before you get to that stage. They'll be retiring me soon, you know. Putting me out to grass.'

'What'll you do then?'

'God knows. I've been in the RAF since I was eighteen, so it's going to be a bit of a wrench.'

'Gardening? Golf?'

'Can't stand either. Don't know what I'll do. Life's going to be jolly dull, one way and another. Lonely, too.'

'How about finding a wife?'

'I'm too old a leopard to change my spots. No woman would have me. Are you still seeing that fräulein of yours, by the way?'

'Yes.'

'Is it serious?'

'Yes. Extremely. I've asked her to marry me.'

'What did she say?'

'She wants some time to think.'

'She'll say yes, in the end. She'd be a fool to turn you down. You're mad, Michael. If you *must* get yourself spliced wait until this business is all over and you're back in Blighty, then get yourself a nice, sensible, uncomplicated English girl. Somebody who knows the drill; no skeletons in the cupboard; everything above board and tickety-boo. Doesn't even have to be a good-looker, so long as she's not hideous. All cats are grey in the dark.'

In spite of himself, Harrison smiled. 'How would you know, Tubby?'

'So I'm told, dear boy. So I'm told.'

He *was* mad. He knew that in his heart. It was mad to have got involved with the Leichts in the first place, crazier still to have fallen so deeply in love with Lili, but he had every intention of ignoring Tubby's sound advice.

She had asked for time. Fair enough, he'd give her all the time it took, but he was going to make damned sure that she married him in the end. So far as he was concerned, none of the practical difficulties that worried her about her family mattered. He could take care of it all: Dirk, Rudi, the grandfather. God knows, he'd had plenty of practice in finding solutions to thorny problems. He thought about it when he had the time, lying awake at night, dog-tired from long hours on duty but unable to sleep for thinking about her. A decent boarding school in England for Rudi, a nursing home probably for the old man – one nearby – so Lili could visit him easily. Sorting Dirk out wouldn't be quite so easy – he was a law unto himself – but he'd manage something. The flat would be too small, of course, so he'd have to sell it and buy somewhere larger.

'And then there is me,' she'd said, turning her

head away from him. 'What would your family say about me?'

'They'll be delighted to see me married at last.'

'But to a German girl? To someone they know nothing about? And with such problems?'

'They'll still be delighted.' He knew that, in fact, they would be anything but delighted, though they would conceal it from her, if not from him.

She had shaken her head vehemently. 'I think they would wish you to marry an English girl. Somebody quite different. Someone who has not lived through the war in Berlin.'

Damaged goods was how Tubby had described it, and it was probably what she meant. He'd heard the horror stories for himself. The atrocities and mutilations, the raping of every female that the Russian soldiers could get their hands on when they took the city. *Frau komm!* If there was something to tell, let her tell him when she was ready to tell him, or maybe never, if that was her wish. It would make no difference at all to him.

Dr Meier was sitting up in his chair and looking a little better. Lili stoked up the stove and put the soup she had brought to heat. When it was warm enough, she gave it to him and stayed while he drank it, sitting on the other chair beside him. After a few mouthfuls he paused.

'This is very good.'

'It's swedes, that's all, with a little carrot. Dirk brought home some meat and I made a stew but the meat was so bad I had to throw it all away.'

'What a pity.'

'Dirk thought I had done it on purpose and he was very angry, so we had another quarrel. We're always quarrelling these days.'

'How sad for you.'

She nodded and was silent while he drank some more soup. 'The squadron leader has asked me to marry him. I said that I couldn't answer him yet. I have to think.'

'What about?'

'About everything. Dirk, Grandfather, Rudi. And me. Most of all me. He knows so little about me and I can't tell him the whole truth.'

'Why not?'

'Because I know that if I did he would never feel the same about me again. I would lose him.'

'How can you be so sure of that?'

'Dirk thinks so, and so do I. He might say that he understood and perhaps he would really believe that he did, but, deep down, it would change everything. He is so very correct, you see. So very English.'

Nico called and she let him in reluctantly. In the living room she did not invite him to sit down and remained standing herself, at a distance. He took his hat off and laid it on the table and then his gloves beside it. Michael always did the same, but his hat was not made of expensive fur and his gloves were dark and plain, not yellow pigskin. 'Is Dirk in?'

'No.'

'Is he all right?'

No, he's not all right, she wanted to say. He's all wrong. 'Why do you ask?'

'I'm rather worried about him, you see. He's been drinking too much vodka, Lili. I see him sometimes in the bars. And when he's drunk, he talks too much. It's always dangerous. People listen.'

She said, alarmed, 'What does he say?'

'Oh, he rambles on, like drunks do. Not too keen on the Russians, is he? I can understand that, but it's wiser to keep one's mouth tightly shut.'

She wondered if Dirk had rambled on about her and how much Nico himself had listened.

He went on, 'He's still doing his little deals, of course. Some not so little.'

'He doesn't tell me what he does.'

'Well, he should be careful these days. Pass that on from me. The east sector police are very vigilant. And quite unpleasant. Did you hear what happened to Michael on Christmas Eve? Poor chap, they locked him up in a cell. They thought he was a black-marketeer. *Michael*, of all people! The most upright and honest chap I know. Ridiculous! Fortunately, they discovered that he had my business card in his wallet and I was able to vouch for him.'

'I'm sure he was grateful.'

'I happened to know the Russian in charge there rather well, otherwise things might have been a bit tricky. I've warned Michael not to go wandering about this sector at night any more.' He smiled his toad's smile at her. 'Of course, I can see the attraction right in front of me, and I don't blame him, but it can be very dangerous.'

'I expect he realizes it now.'

'No, I don't think he does. He doesn't quite understand that Berlin is not like London, or like any other city in the world. That *nobody* is safe – not even an officer in the Royal Air Force.'

She said, 'If that's all, Nico . . .'

'Don't worry, I'm going now. But you'll warn Dirk to be more careful, won't you?' He picked up his hat and gloves. 'And Michael, too.'

He could tell from the way her face lit up that she was awfully glad to see him, and that gave him hope. She looked so pale, he thought. So small and thin and fragile and dressed in such pathetically worn and shabby clothes. In the living room there was yet another hole in the ceiling with a tin bucket placed strategically beneath it. 'The hole is too big to fill with newspaper,' she told him, 'but the bowl will catch the leaks.'

The whole room looked worse than ever – even more squalid and depressing. Harrison faced her grimly. 'You can't go on living here, Lili. It's simply not on.'

'Not on? What does that mean?'

'It means I won't let you.' He went over to her and put his hands on her shoulders. 'You asked for time to think and I've given it to you. Weeks of time. Now, I want an answer.' She turned her head away and he turned it back firmly. 'Look, Lili. It's very simple. I love you and I want you to be my wife. I swear that I'll do everything in my power to make you happy.'

311

'But would I make *you* happy?'

'You can't imagine how much.'

'In spite of everything?'

'*Because* of everything. Every single thing about you. There's nothing that I'd want to change. *Nothing*. Do you understand?' She nodded and he waited a moment and then went on. 'So, will you, or won't you?' He shook her gently, 'Answer me, Lili. And the answer had better be yes.'

People who said that the English were cold and unfeeling had got it all wrong. When he had finally let her go, he had made her sit down at the table and held her hands in his and told her that he would make all the arrangements for them to be married as soon as possible. While he had talked she had watched his face and seen how happy he was, how the stern look had vanished completely, how tender the expression was in his eyes. 'I've never thought to ask before,' he'd said, 'but what religion are you?'

'We were brought up as Roman Catholics,' she'd told him. 'But it's years since I have attended Mass. There's been nowhere to go.'

'I'm Church of England, I'm afraid. But I don't see that mattering, do you? We're both Christian, we just belong to different clubs. We could have a civil wedding – unless you don't like the idea?'

'I don't mind.'

'Nor do I. Simpler to arrange and no fuss.'

'I have nothing to wear.'

He'd laughed at that. 'It doesn't matter a damn

what you wear, Lili. Not to me. You could wear an old sack for all I'd care. But, if you like, we'll try and find you something special. There must be some pretty frocks somewhere in Berlin. And pretty hats.'

'The hats are here. My mother's – in the trunk over there.' She'd opened it and shown him the beautiful treasure store and tried several on for him to approve, until he had chosen the one he'd liked best. And then he'd begun to kiss her again.

'Where will we live?' she'd asked when she could speak.

'Well, I'll try to wangle a bit of leave for a honeymoon and take you to England. We'll go somewhere you're bound to like – Cornwall, probably. I know a terrific place where we used to go on holidays when I was a child – a fishing village on the south coast. And there's a nice old inn there where we could stay. There'd be plenty of good fish to eat and Cornish butter and cream – we'd fatten you up in no time.'

'Like a pig?'

He'd smiled and stroked her hair. 'No, nothing like a pig. Just making you fit and strong again. You'll love it in Cornwall. The scenery's beautiful and the sea air's wonderful. We can go for long walks . . . you do like walking, don't you?'

'I've never really done that – except for walking in the Tiergarten.'

'I bet you'll enjoy it. It'll be spring by the time we get there and so the weather should be warming up and all the flowers coming out.'

'Primroses? Like on the teacups?'

'Yes, primroses. Lots and lots of them.'

'I should like to see them. They look so beautiful.'

'They are. They grow all along the country lanes and paths. We have a rather nice saying in English – the primrose path. It means the easy, pleasant way. Doing only things that make you happy, that you enjoy.'

'It sounds so wonderful. But I can't imagine that any more.'

He'd kissed her hands. 'I'll find a primrose path for you, Lili, I promise.'

She'd said to him, half-serious, half-teasing: 'For you it should be easy. You were a pathfinder in the war – isn't that so? That's what you were called.'

'How did you know?'

'Nico told me. He said you were amazingly brave and devoted to duty – those were his words. I remember very well.' She'd sighed. 'And so, when we have been to England and seen the beautiful primroses, you must come back to Berlin? It will be your duty?'

'I'm afraid so. Until I get another posting.'

'What would I do?'

'Well, I'll try to find a place for us near Gatow, off-station, if it's possible – somewhere with enough room for Dirk as well. And for Rudi and your grandfather when they come back. When the time comes for us to go to England, I'll arrange for Rudi to go to a good school there and for your grandfather to go into a nursing home close by so you can visit him every day.'

'And Dirk?'

'Don't worry, I'll talk to Dirk and sort out what's best for him. What he wants to do. I'll make sure that he's all right.'

All at once, it had seemed quite simple; she had been agonizing over nothing. Everything was going to be fine. Then he'd asked suddenly about the scar on her forehead – touched it and asked how she'd got it. When the bomb had hit the house, she'd blurted out in panic. It had happened then. He had asked no more questions and so she had had no need to tell any more lies.

He'd frowned and clicked his tongue. 'I've forgotten something. A ring. You must have an engagement ring, but God knows where we'll find one.'

Here, under Dirk's bed, she'd thought to herself wryly. 'It doesn't matter. I don't need a ring.'

'Yes, you do.' He'd tugged at the gold signet ring on his little finger. 'This will have to do until I can buy you a proper one in London.' It was too big for her fourth finger and so he'd slid it on to the middle one of her left hand and then kissed each finger in turn. And then her mouth for even longer. They might have ended up on the couch if he hadn't finally stopped and smiled and said he'd better leave before anything like that happened. With him, it would have been so different. But perhaps, then, he would have guessed the truth about her? What would she say if he ever asked, straight out? Would she be able to lie to him as easily as she had lied about the scar?

She looked at the ring now, holding her hand up

in front of her to see it gleam in the dim electric light. It felt heavy on her finger. There was an engraving of a swan with wings half outstretched. His family crest, he'd told her when she'd asked about it. His parents had given it to him when he'd come of age. It had belonged to his grandfather once. What would this so-respectable and respected family think of her?

Dirk came home much later, after she had gone to bed. She heard him blunder into the room and knew that he was drunk again.

Fifteen

'You're looking like the cat that's got the cream,' Tubby told him. 'Let me guess what that means. Wedding bells? Your little fräulein has said yes.'

'Right first time.'

'Well, I've never seen you so joyful, Michael. You're positively glowing, so it must be a good thing after all. Congratulations. When is the happy day to be?'

'As soon as I can cut through all the usual red tape and get things set up.'

'Am I invited to the ceremony?'

'More than that, I want you to be my best man – if you don't mind.'

'Mind? I'd be delighted. Forget all my gloomy prognostications, I shall be right beside you. May I kiss the bride at the appropriate moment?'

'Certainly. Tell me, Tubby, have you any idea where the hell I could find a women's dress shop in Berlin? Does such a thing still exist?'

'It's not my habit to shop for women's clothes, dear boy. I suggest you go in search of a WAAF and ask her if she's got any ideas.'

After a good deal of WAAF-hunting he found a radar operator who was almost as petite as Lili and put the problem to her. She blushed scarlet, as if he had made an improper suggestion, but told him that though she didn't know of any dress shops, one of the German civilian cleaners was very good at sewing and made frocks to measure from black-market material for the price of a tin of coffee or a packet of cigarettes. After more persuasion and more blushing, she agreed to arrange a meeting with the German seamstress and to act as a model. It pleased him very much to think of surprising Lili with a brand new and beautiful frock to wear at their wedding – something that would go well with the bewitching hat she had fetched out of the trunk.

In the middle of these plans and preparations, the station commander sent for him.

'Sorry to be the bearer of bad tidings, Michael, but we've just received a signal. I'm afraid your father has suffered a stroke and been taken to hospital.'

It took a moment to sink in. 'Is it serious, sir?'

'Serious enough for you to go home at once. I'm giving you compassionate leave, of course. Get back to England on the first flight out that can take you.'

He flung some things into a case and sat down and wrote a note to Lili before he went in search of Tubby. He ran him down at his desk and told him the news.

'Frightfully sorry, dear boy. How ghastly for you. Anything I can do?'

'As a matter of fact, there is.' He held out the

envelope. 'Could you take this to Lili? I've put the address on it. I can't get in touch with her any other way. There's no time to get over there and they've no phone and God knows how long it would take by post, or if it would ever reach her. Would you do that, Tubby?'

'Of course, old chap. Glad to. I'm just wondering if I'll ever be able to find it. Not too sure of my Berlin bearings except for the landmarks and the Officers' Club.'

'Get one of the VW cabs to take you. They'll find it.'

'Consider it done. I'll pop over the first chance I have.'

He got a seat on an Avro York flying to Bückeburg. It was carrying five other passengers besides himself and crates of light bulbs bearing the proud stamp *Made in Blockaded Berlin*. They took off to the west with another York aircraft airborne immediately ahead and the one following already starting its take-off run: the never-ending cavalcade down the central air corridor out of Berlin.

'Fräulein Leicht?'

He looked familiar to her: a short, plump man in Royal Air Force uniform with the same sort of cap as Michael's, the same markings on the shoulders of his greatcoat and the same rows of polished gilt buttons. He had a moustache, though – big and bushy – and he was much older. She opened the front door a little further. 'Yes?'

'I'm Squadron Leader Hill. We met at the performance of *Measure for Measure* last summer.'

'Of course, I remember now.' What could he be doing here? 'Would you like to come in?'

'Only for a moment. I have a taxi waiting for me out in the street.'

He removed his cap and followed her into the big room. She saw how shocked he was at the sight of it, though he quickly recovered. He groped in his coat pocket and held out an envelope. 'Michael asked me to come and give this to you. He's been called away suddenly and there was no time to do so himself.'

She took it from him fearfully. 'What has happened?'

'His father has had a stroke, I'm afraid.'

'A stroke? Please, what is this?'

He frowned. 'Awfully sorry, but I don't know the German word for it. It happens suddenly . . . blood clot in the brain, I think. Loss of speech, movement, all that sort of thing . . . People can recover perfectly well, of course, if it's not too serious.'

She understood what he meant. 'And is this stroke serious?'

'I rather think so, or Michael wouldn't have been sent for. He'll have told you all about it in the letter, I'm sure.'

'Do you have any idea when he will be coming back?'

'Not the foggiest, I'm afraid.' He moved towards the door. 'Well, I ought to be getting back.'

'Thank you for bringing the letter.'

'Glad to be of help.'

At the front door she said, 'Do you mind if I ask you something, Squadron Leader Hill?'

'Fire away.'

'Did Michael tell you that he has asked me to marry him . . . and that I have accepted?'

'Rather. Congratulations. I ought to have said so in the beginning.'

'But you didn't,' she pointed out. 'You didn't say anything about it at all. You don't think it is a good idea, do you? You think it is a very bad idea – for Michael.'

He looked her straight in the eye. 'To be perfectly honest, my dear, no, I don't think it's at all a good idea. It's not your fault, but I don't think marrying you will help Michael's career or bring him happiness. But it's none of my business, and perhaps I'm quite mistaken. He doesn't often get things wrong. One thing I can tell you for sure is he's a jolly decent chap. The best. And he'll make a damn good husband.' He held out his hand. 'Goodbye Fräulein Leicht. I wish you well.'

She watched him stride away across the cobbled courtyard – a portly, straight-backed and dignified figure.

From Bückeburg, Harrison boarded a Dakota that took him on to Northolt aerodrome. He picked up a taxi into London, collected his car from its garage and drove straight down to the hospital at Reigate. His father was in Intensive Care and still unconscious, his mother sitting at his side. When he came into the room she got to her feet and collapsed into his arms, weeping. It was a while before she managed to get herself under control. She wiped her eyes with his handkerchief.

'I'm, sorry, darling. It's all been so awful . . . It happened so suddenly. We were having dinner and one moment he was perfectly all right – talking about you as a matter of fact – and the next minute he just keeled over. It was such a terrible shock. I thought he was dead, at first – a heart attack, or something – and then I could hear him breathing – that awful noise, like now.'

. He sat her down again gently and went to the other side of the bed. His father lay very still with his eyes closed. Every breath he drew had a harsh rasping sound, as though each one was a great effort. The man who had always been so vigorously in command of himself and others, all at once reduced to helplessness. 'Has he regained consciousness at all?'

His mother shook her head. 'No. They don't seem to be sure if he ever will.'

'Have you spoken to the doctor in charge?'

'Only for a moment. He just said that they're doing everything they can. The nurses have been wonderful and very kind. Would you like a cup of tea, or something? They'll get you one.'

'No, thanks. I'll just go and see if I can have a word with someone. Find out a bit more.'

The ward sister was brisk and efficient. 'You'll need to talk with Mr Clark, the consultant neurologist. If you'd like to wait a few minutes, I'll see if he can be found.'

He was shown into some kind of office down the corridor and after a good deal longer than a few minutes, the neurologist appeared. 'Squadron Leader Harrison? Sorry to have kept you. Do sit down.' The prognosis, he learned, was uncertain. 'That's the trouble with strokes, you see. It's always hard to predict the outcome. So much depends on the patient and there are factors that are difficult to assess accurately. The General's stroke was certainly quite severe, but I've known patients make a very good recovery from worse ones. The brain has some remarkable recuperative powers and other parts can take over damaged areas, given time.'

'And if that doesn't happen?'

'Again, it depends on the extent of any permanent damage. Partial paralysis, speech impairment . . . down to the very worst picture which is no recovery at all. The next six to eight weeks will show us. I'm afraid we must wait patiently and see what happens. You're on leave, I take it? Where are you stationed?'

'Berlin.'

The neurologist raised his eyebrows. 'Berlin? Good heavens. All part of the airlift, I suppose. How's it going over there?'

'Pretty well.'

'From what we're told in the newspapers, you chaps are all doing a first-class job. Performing a miracle. Think you're going to be able to stick it out?'

'I don't see why not.'

'Glad to hear it. Personally, I don't care too much about the Germans, but we can't let the Russians get the upper hand, can we?'

They drove home. Mrs Lewis had left the drawing-room fire laid ready and he lit it, sat his mother down and poured her a large gin and tonic. She was still tearful, but more composed. 'Sweet of you to come so quickly, darling. It's a big comfort to have you here. Will you be able to stay for a bit?'

'As long as I can,' he promised. 'The RAF are very decent about these things.'

'Can I have one of your cigarettes?'

'Of course.' He lit it for her.

'What's happened to your signet ring, darling?'

'I left it in Berlin.' It wasn't the time to tell her about Lili. He would do that later on.

'So long as you haven't lost it.' She managed a smile. 'There's one good bit of news, anyway. Celia's broken off her engagement.'

'That sounds rather bad news.'

'Well, you know what I mean, darling . . .'

He knew only too well. 'What happened?'

'I'm not too sure. I expect she decided he was Mr Wrong, after all. I never liked him much, I must say. Rather a dull sort of type.'

'Better to find it out now than later.'

'She might be home this weekend. We could ring and see.'

He said firmly, 'I rather think we've got enough to cope with at the moment, don't you?'

Dr Meier was improving slowly. Lili went every day to take him whatever food and fuel she could and to chat with him. The chatting did the most good of all, she thought. He seemed to enjoy her company and she always stayed as long as possible. Once she had suggested that he moved into the apartment, though she knew that Dirk would be furious, but he had refused.

'I am very grateful to you for such great kindness, Fräulein, but no. It is better that I remain here.' She was always Fräulein and he treated her with an old-world courtesy. When she had told him of her engagement he had smiled and said how pleased he was for her. 'I should very much like to meet your squadron leader when he returns from England. I speak some English and so we could converse a little.'

In his letter Michael had written that he had no idea when he could be back, only that it would be as soon as he could. *Take care of yourself while I'm away, Lili, until I can take care of you.* She was glad of the hard work in the ruins. It occupied her days and, at night, exhaustion helped her to sleep. But she always lay awake for a while first, thinking of him and wondering how his father, the General, was and if he had told his family about her and what they would have to say.

Dirk came and went with scarcely a word. The suitcase was always with him and never left unlocked. Every so often he would dump something else on the table: sausage, bacon, a bar of soap, a tin of American ham, a jar of peanut butter, another hunk of meat – pork this time and fresh enough to eat. She had stopped asking questions because he never gave answers.

And then, one night, he didn't come home.

She had gone to bed early, even more tired than usual, and slept soundly. In the morning she went into his room and saw that the bed was empty. He didn't come home that day, or that evening, or the next night, or the night after that.

After five days, Harrison's father recovered consciousness. The hospital had telephoned first thing in the morning and, hurrying downstairs to answer the ringing in the hall, he had expected to hear the worst. Instead, the news was good. His father was not only conscious but able to speak a little. He drove his mother to the hospital and they found him, eyes wide open, talking to the nurse. The speech was slurred and he kept mixing up words but it was intelligible. His mother burst into tears again – tears of relief this time. The neurologist was cautiously optimistic. 'Early days but, with luck, he may make a good recovery. He'll need treatment and lots of rest and he'll have to take it easy for a long time. Nothing strenuous. No excitements. Peace and quiet. One has to remember the danger of a second stroke.'

By the fire with his mother, after dinner that evening, he broached the subject of his return to Berlin. 'They need me back as soon as possible. Do you think you can cope with things?'

'Of course, darling. It's quite different now. I'll be fine. Celia telephoned from London, by the way. She wanted to know how your father was. So sweet of her. Will you try to see her before you go back?'

He said steadily, 'There's absolutely no point

going on about Celia, I'm afraid. I'm not going to marry her. I'm going to marry somebody else. I would have told you before, but it was hardly the right time with Father so ill.'

She stared at him, open-mouthed. 'But who, darling? I'd no idea there was another girl you were seeing! You've kept it awfully dark. Do I know her?'

'No, you don't know her. You've never met her. You couldn't have done because she lives in Berlin.'

'*Berlin?* Good gracious. Is she one of the WAAFs or something? I remember you saying in one of your letters that there were several of them on the station.'

'No, she's not a WAAF. She's not English, she's German.'

He saw it register and the dismay that followed. '*German!* Michael, you're not serious? You can't possibly marry a German girl, darling. It would be madness. Complete madness. You can't really mean it.'

'I'm afraid I do really mean it.'

The dismay was now horror. 'But who is she? How did you meet her?'

'Her name is Lili. Lili Leicht. And I met her at her home in Berlin. I happened to come across a chap who was at school with me, quite by chance, and he knew her and introduced me.'

'What chap?'

'It doesn't matter. You wouldn't remember him. The point is, Mother, I love her and I want to marry her. And I hope you'll be glad for me. She's a wonderful girl. You'll like her very much.'

'I know I shan't. And I can't be glad for you. She could ruin your career, your whole life. Haven't you thought about that? How much it would harm you to have a German wife, in your position in the services? She wouldn't care, of course. All she'll care about is catching an English husband, getting out of Berlin.'

'If you knew her, you'd also know that's not so. I've had the greatest difficulty in persuading her to marry me.'

'Playing hard to get is one of the oldest tricks in the book. You've given her your signet ring, haven't you? That's what you've done with it. How could you, Michael? How *could* you? That ring belonged to your grandfather. He left it to *you*.'

'I gave it to her until I can buy her a proper engagement ring, that's all.'

'You'll never get it back. She'll go and sell it, or something.'

'That's uncalled for.'

'Well, what do you know about her? Next to nothing, I should think. Does she live with her parents?'

'They're both dead. Her mother and grandmother died when we bombed Berlin and her father was hanged by the Nazis for refusing to kowtow to them. She's only nineteen and she's had a pretty rough time.'

'A rough time? Plenty of people here in England had that during the war – thanks to the Germans.'

He said quietly, 'It's impossible for you to imagine how bad it was in Berlin – unless you've seen it with your own eyes. And still is. They survive from day to day, living in the most appalling conditions in the ruins.'

'To think of you marrying a girl from such circumstances! Does she have any other family at all? Any background?'

'She has two brothers and a grandfather who live with her.'

'And how old are *they*?'

'Nine and seventeen. The grandfather is elderly. I'm not sure of his age.'

'And what will happen to them? I suppose she wants you to look after them all too and you've agreed? No wonder she set her cap at you. You were the answer to her prayers.' His mother began to sob hysterically. 'This is too much, Michael. I can't bear it . . . first your father and now this horrible news. For God's sake, don't tell him. It'll kill him. Promise me you won't say anything to him.' She clutched at his arm. '*Promise* me.'

It took her hours to find the right place; hours of walking up and down streets and searching for some sign. He'd given her a business card once, but, of course, she had thrown it away. She was on the point of giving up when, at last, she came to a half-ruined building standing alone in a street and saw another card, just the same, pinned up outside the entrance. *Phönix Verlag, Phoenix Publishers, Édition Phénix*. Even then, her courage almost failed her. 'You have no choice, Fräulein,' Dr Meier had said. 'You must ask him for help. He is the only one who might be able to give it.' The door was unlocked. Lili opened it and stepped into a bare, dark hallway. Another door stood a little open and she could hear Nico's voice beyond. She pushed open the door a bit further. He was speaking on the telephone, sitting at a desk; behind him there were shelves containing books. As soon as he saw her, he slammed down the receiver and jumped to his feet. 'Lili! Is there something the matter? You don't look well at all. Sit down, sit down.' He fussed around her.

She sank onto the chair. 'I'm all right.'

'A cigarette?'

He was hovering too close, one hand on her shoulder. In spite of the need to be polite to him, not to offend, she couldn't help shrinking from his touch. 'No, thank you.'

'I hope you don't mind if I do.' He took his hand away and went to sit behind his desk again. He fitted one of his Turkish cigarettes into the holder and lit it. 'Something must be very badly wrong for you to come here. Tell me what has happened.'

'Dirk is missing,' she said. 'He hasn't been home for nearly a week. I've heard nothing from him. Not a word.'

'Is that so unusual? He's very independent.'

'He never tells me where he's going or what he's doing but he always comes home. This is the first time he hasn't done so. And for so long. I know something must have happened to him.'

'And you have come to *me* for help? I'm astonished. Why not to Michael?'

'Michael is in England. His father has been taken seriously ill.'

'I'm very sorry to hear that. So, poor Lili, you're on your own with nobody but me to turn to. That's a terrible situation for you.' He leaned forward with his arms on the desk, the smoke spiralling upwards from the cigarette and nauseating her. 'Now, tell me, what's Dirk been up to lately that makes you so especially worried?'

She told him about the morphine ampoules, the dealings with the Americans, the locked suitcase. 'I've tried to stop him but it's hopeless. He won't listen to me.'

Nico smiled faintly. 'What self-respecting young man of seventeen would listen to his elder sister? Naturally, he knows better.' He turned and lifted the telephone receiver. 'The most likely thing is that he has been caught and arrested by the police. In which case I may be able to do something about it.'

He spoke first in German and then, at some length, in Russian. Lili tried to guess from the tone of his voice and the look on his face if there was any news, but it was impossible. Nico never gave anything away. At last he put down the receiver. 'It's as I thought. The east sector police arrested him several nights ago. He was carrying a suitcase crammed with black-market goods.'

'Where is he? Can I go and see him?'

'Unfortunately not. He was kept in the cells for a while for questioning and then moved.'

'Moved? Where to?'

'To Sachsenhausen.'

'*Sachsenhausen*. Oh, God!'

'The Russians have started to use it again. A convenient, ready-made prison camp. Try not to distress yourself, Lili. I promise you that I will do everything I can to get him released. You must trust me. It's by no means hopeless.' He put his head on one side. 'I see you're wearing Michael's signet ring. Too late to try and hide it. I take it that this means happy news?'

'There's nothing to be happy about,' she said desolately. 'Not any more.'

Harrison went alone to say goodbye to his father. He had been moved to another room – comfortable and pleasant with a Constable print on the wall and a window overlooking some quiet gardens. He was propped up in bed against a backrest and a mound of starched pillows, complaining about being kept there. 'Damned stupid . . . bored to death lying here.' His speech was still very slow and indistinct, each word obviously a difficulty.

'They think you should take it easy for a bit, that's all.'

'Lot of . . . nonsense.'

He sat down beside the bed. 'I've brought you a couple of books from home – when you're up to reading.'

'Can't seem to . . . read . . . yet.'

'It'll come in time. They're pretty pleased with the progress you're making.' He put the two volumes of war memoirs away in the bedside locker. 'I'm off to London today, then back to Berlin.'

'Good of you to stay . . . so long . . . meant . . . a lot . . . your mother. And . . . me.' His father turned his head away towards the window. 'Damned proud of you . . . Michael . . . war record . . . everything . . . want you . . . know that.' His voice faltered and Harrison saw his hand reach up clumsily to brush away the tears that were trickling down his cheeks. It was the first time he had ever seen him cry.

He drove up to London later that evening. The flat was silent and cheerless, the only offerings in the store cupboard tinned baked beans or sardines. On impulse, he phoned Celia. Her flatmate answered and he waited for her to come to the phone, wondering if he'd been an idiot to call her. Presently he heard the receiver being picked up and her clear voice speaking.

'Michael? How nice to hear from you. How are you?'

'Fine, thanks.'

'I heard you were over. I'm so sorry about your father. Is he any better?'

'Much improved, I'd say. The outlook seems quite hopeful.'

'I'm awfully glad. That's wonderful news. So, you're off back to Berlin now, I expect?'

'Very early tomorrow morning. I'm at the flat in London tonight. Actually, I wondered if you'd be free for dinner this evening?'

There was a slight pause, then she said, 'Yes, of course. That would be lovely.'

'I'll pick you up about eight – if that's OK.'

'Look forward to seeing you.'

He took her to the same French restaurant as before. She looked much as always, he thought – well groomed and attractive – though she'd done her hair a bit differently, he noticed. It was longer and softer and it suited her rather well. Made her seem more vulnerable, more feminine. He raised his glass to her.

'Thank you for turning out this evening. Sorry it was such short notice.'

She said easily, 'It's always nice to see you, Michael. We're old friends, aren't we?'

He nodded. 'I was sorry to hear your engagement didn't work out.'

'Just one of those things.'

'Any particular thing? None of my business, of course.'

'Not really. I simply realized – in time, thank goodness – that it wasn't right. I'm afraid I hurt Richard a lot but I couldn't go through with it. No excuses. My big mistake.'

'Easy enough to make.'

'Not really. I'm not proud of it. I ought to have known from the beginning – actually part of me *did* know but I didn't listen to myself.' She set down her glass. 'That's enough of that. Have *you* any plans yourself in that direction, Michael? I sort of get the feeling that there is someone.'

He said slowly, 'Yes, actually there is but I have to ask you not to say anything about it to anyone else at the moment.'

'I promise I won't. Who is she? The girl in Berlin? The one you told me about when you were last home on leave? The one who works in the ruins?'

He was amazed she'd remembered. 'I've forgotten what I said . . .'

'Not much. But from the way you said it, I rather guessed she already meant quite a lot to you.'

'Yes, she did. And she does, even more now.' He smiled. 'You seem to know me pretty well, don't you, Celia?'

'Well, we've known each other for a long time, haven't we? More than twenty years. On and off. I ought to have some idea of what makes you tick. I'm very happy for you, Michael. I know that she must be a wonderful girl.'

'She is. And with the most tremendous courage.'

'From what you told me, she's had a pretty rotten time for years.'

'You can't imagine how rotten. I was trying to explain to my mother, but of course, it's impossible for her to understand. She was absolutely horrified when I told her about Lili. Appalled about the whole idea. A *German* girl! Disaster for my career, no background, on the make, and so on . . . you can picture it.'

'Yes, I'm afraid I can.'

'I had to promise not to tell my father – for the time being anyway. She's terrified he'd have another stroke on the spot.'

'I don't believe he would, Michael. I think he's made of sterner stuff than that. He might not like the idea – at first – but he'd come around to it. And he'd trust your judgement.'

He smiled again and touched her hand lightly.

'Thanks, Celia. Even so, I'll keep my promise for the moment – until he's stronger. I daren't risk it.'

She looked down at his wrist. 'You still have your Luftwaffe watch.'

'I've got rather used to it, and I haven't had a chance to pick up my old RAF one yet. Actually, it nearly caused me a spot of real bother recently.' He told her about being arrested by the police and locked up in a cell.

She looked alarmed. 'Isn't it better to stay out of the Russian sector?'

'It's where Lili lives. Besides, we're perfectly entitled to go there, so long as we carry our ID, though it's not exactly encouraged. The Berliners go to and fro across the sector borders the whole time, of course. They're the ones usually at risk. The Russians have a nasty habit of making off with various civilians they claim are breaking the law, but the blockade's put a bit of a curb on their activities.'

'What happens to the people they take?'

'Nobody knows. They just disappear.'

She shivered. 'How much longer will you have to stay there?'

'No idea. Until the blockade is lifted, I imagine. And, before you ask, I've no idea when that will be either. When the Russians finally see sense and give in.'

'Will you get married in Berlin?'

'That's the general idea. I was in the middle of going through all the rigmarole to arrange it when I was called home. The plan is that we come home to live here as soon as possible.'

'You'll be saving Lili, Michael. Getting her away from that hateful place.'

He said drily, 'Actually, I've had the dickens of a job persuading her to agree to leave it at all. It took some convincing to get her to marry me.'

'Does she know about what you did in the war?'

'Oh, yes.' He nodded. 'We had quite a set-to about that in the beginning. I've often thought that maybe it was my Lanc that dropped the bomb that hit her home – when her mother and grandmother died. Pretty far-fetched considering the numbers, but still. We bombed the city to smithereens, as you know – us and the Americans between us. Literally smashed it to pieces. You can't really imagine how terrible it is until you actually go there and see it. But I believe we were right. Absolutely right. It was the only way to exterminate the Nazis.' He paused and ran a hand through his hair. 'Anyway, I don't think Lili holds it against me any more.'

'Do you hold anything against her – as a German, I mean? I was thinking of Elizabeth and the boys, for instance.'

'How could I possibly blame her for that? Of course not.'

'That's all right, then.'

He drove her back to her flat and stopped the car outside. 'Thanks for this evening, Celia. And for everything.'

'Everything?'

'Yes, everything. Being so decent always. And so sane.' He hesitated, not knowing how to put it. 'I hope I've never hurt you in any way. I should hate to have done that.'

'Of course not. And I wish you all the happiness in the world, Michael.'

He leaned across and kissed her gently – first her cheek and then, because it was so close, her mouth. 'Thanks again.'

She got out of the car and walked quickly to the flat entrance. He waited to see if she would turn to wave, as she usually did, but she went straight inside without looking back.

Sixteen

Being completely alone in the apartment at night had begun to terrify Lili. She lay awake listening to every sound – the rats running, the water dripping, every creak and rustle and movement in the ruined building. The Gestapo had come to arrest her father late at night – in the same way that they had come for the Jewish family above – hammering on the door and shouldering their way into the apartment. Brutal men with brutal faces. Her father had offered no resistance but he had been roughly handled just the same. Punched and kicked. She became convinced that the Russian sector police would come to get her and drag her off to the camp at Sachsenhausen. And she tortured herself imagining what might be happening to Dirk there, the dreadful state he might be in, the fear and misery that he might be suffering.

When the doorbell rang late one evening she was too frightened to answer it. It rang again, and then again – a loud, insistent jangle echoing through the apartment. She crept into the hall, heart thudding, and heard Nico's voice outside. 'Lili, it's me, Nico.

Open the door, please. I have some news for you.'
She had never before been glad to see him – a fact
which did not escape him. He put an arm around
her shoulders. 'Poor thing, you have been in great
distress, I can tell.'

In the living room he took off his fur hat and the
pigskin gloves and laid them side by side on the
table. 'Sit down, Lili, and I will explain the situation
to you.'

She sat down slowly, her eyes fixed on his face,
which told her nothing. 'Have you seen Dirk?'

'No. They won't allow it. All I can tell you is that
he is there in the camp and that he is alive.'

'Are you sure? He is alive?'

'Yes, I'm sure. I always know when they're lying.
He's still there and he's still alive. Look, they gave me
his lighter to return to you.' He handed her the
American Zippo lighter with the dent in one side.
She would have recognized it anywhere. 'At first, they
wouldn't play ball – not at any price. The prisoner is
guilty of black-marketeering and he must pay the
penalty. An example must be set, and so on . . . It's
possible, they said, that he may be sent to a labour
camp in Russia. In which case, of course, we are
unlikely to hear of him again. I found myself, for once,
with no cards to play. Something that doesn't often
happen.' He smiled at her. 'And then I remembered
the signet ring on your finger, and I realized that
perhaps, after all, I had just one. Not an ace, or a king
or queen, but quite a useful card nevertheless.'

He was talking in riddles. 'What do you mean?
What card?'

He fitted a cigarette into his holder and lit it. 'I mentioned your engagement to a British squadron leader at Gatow. They were rather interested.'

'I never said that we were engaged.'

'But you are, aren't you? Michael has asked you to marry him and you have said yes.' He wagged a finger at her. 'It's no use denying it. I always know when you're lying, too. You must understand, Lili, that the Russians are extremely anxious to learn anything and everything they can about the western Allies in Berlin, particularly in the present circumstances of the blockade. Even the smallest details can be useful to them. The little pieces from different sources all add up to make the whole picture. I suggested to them that in exchange for your brother's release you would be willing to provide them with some of those details about the Allies. To tell them any little thing you learn through Michael.'

She stared at him. 'You mean, *spy* for them? I'd sooner be dead.'

'It's not your life that's at stake, it's Dirk's, remember. You want him back, don't you?'

'Of course I do.'

'Then listen to me, please. It's a game, that's all, and I will show you how to play it. You give them little morsels – trivia. They won't expect you to know state secrets. Just bits of this and that. Nothing of any great importance. Berlin is full of such exchanges between the sectors. Everybody likes to know what's going on in the other ones.'

She said angrily, 'I never talk about such things with Michael.'

'He's in love with you, Lili. Very deeply in love. A man in love will discuss anything with his beloved – if she knows how to encourage him.'

'I could never do such a thing. I refuse to.'

He shrugged and picked up his hat and gloves. 'Then you leave Dirk to his fate. Think about it, Lili. Let me know if you change your mind.' He walked away towards the door.

'*Wait*. Please, Nico.'

He stopped and turned. 'Yes?'

'I can't,' she pleaded. 'I can't do it. I couldn't deceive Michael.'

He looked at her, his head on one side. 'Couldn't you, Lili?'

Dirk has been blabbing when he was drunk on vodka, she thought in panic. Nico knows it all. She drew a long, deep breath and said quietly, 'Anyway, Michael wouldn't tell me anything. You don't realize the sort of man he is.'

'I assure you that I do. Probably much better than you. Naturally, he would never knowingly betray his country. Not a chap like Michael. Not in a thousand million years. But I'm sure you've talked about the airlift with him – in a general way. You've asked him how it's getting on, when the British think it'll be over, how they feel about it, their morale, all that sort of thing . . . and he's told you. Not in great detail, just nice little snippets to pass on to our Russians. As I said, all quite trivial and no harm done, but interesting enough to persuade them that you could, perhaps, find out more eventually. Do you see? Of course, you put yourself at some risk

– you do understand? But you have never been afraid to do that, have you, Lili? And if you want to save Dirk . . .'

She said coldly, 'Whose side are you on, Nico? I've always wondered.'

'Whose side? Dear Lili, I'm on nobody's side. You came to me and I'm simply trying to help you, that's all. Isn't that what I've always tried to do?'

'Good evening. You are Fräulein Lili Leicht?'

'Yes.'

'My name is Anatole Silogov. May I come in, please?' He spoke good German but with a strong Russian accent and he looked like a Russian – high-cheekboned and with ice-grey eyes. He wore civilian clothing: a heavy, belted overcoat over a suit and a broad-brimmed felt hat: ugly, ill-fitting Russian clothes. Without a word she led the way into the living room and he glanced around briefly. She had the impression that in that short moment he took note of everything. He did not remove his hat.

'Please sit down, Herr Silogov.'

'I prefer to stand.'

He produced a packet of cigarettes and a box of matches from his coat pocket. 'Do you smoke?'

'Not Russian cigarettes, thank you.'

'You like American ones perhaps? The kind that your brother traded?' She said nothing and waited while he tapped one end of the cigarette against the packet a few times before putting it in his mouth and striking a match. He blew out the flame and replaced the dead match carefully in the box with

343

fingers stained yellow from nicotine. 'Your brother has been arrested for black-marketeering and is in Sachsenhausen prison camp. You know that?'

She nodded.

'Black-marketeering is viewed by the authorities as a very serious crime. One that must be stamped out. It is very probable that your brother will be sent to a labour camp in Russia for many years.' The cigarette smoke drifted towards her, rank as rotting weeds. She still said nothing. 'We have been given some information about you, Fräulein Leicht, that is of interest to us. Is it true that you are on intimate terms with a Royal Air Force officer by the name of Squadron Leader Harrison who is based at Gatow airfield in the British sector of Berlin?'

'I'm acquainted with him, yes.'

'It's our understanding that your relationship is rather more than that, Fräulein Leicht. That you are engaged to be married.'

The signet ring was well hidden in a bag of flour. 'You're misinformed. There's nothing official. Nothing at all.'

'But you are sleeping with him?'

'That's not your business.'

'Come, Fräulein Leicht. He visits you here frequently. Your grandfather is senile, your younger brother a chronic invalid. Squadron Leader Harrison went to the considerable trouble of arranging for them to be flown out of Berlin by the British. He is your lover.'

She shrugged. 'He's very useful. He brings extra

food, presents, chocolate, cigarettes . . . I don't discourage him.'

'Of course you don't. No Berlin woman would be fool enough to do that. You string him along. And you talk with him . . . pillow talk. The squadron leader naturally speaks almost no German but you speak excellent English. French, too, I hear. What do you talk about?'

'All kinds of things.'

'Have you discussed the blockade?'

It's a game, that's all. You give them little morsels – trivia. They won't expect you to know state secrets. 'Occasionally.'

'And what does Squadron Leader Harrison say? What does he tell you about the British transport of supplies to Gatow by air?'

She hesitated.

'What does he say, Fräulein?'

'He says that they can keep going indefinitely.'

'So can the blockade. What else does he say?'

'He thinks that now the winter's nearly over, the blockade will probably be lifted within a few months.'

'Why does he think that?'

'I suppose because he believes the Russians will realize by then that it can't work.'

'And what else does he believe?'

'I don't know. That's all he has said on the subject.'

'I don't believe you.'

'It's the truth. It's a dull subject to me. We talk about other things.'

'Such as?'

She shrugged again. 'I really don't remember.'

'The weather perhaps?' He seemed almost amused. 'Don't the English always like to talk about the weather?'

'He talks about England sometimes.'

'What does he say?'

'That the countryside is very beautiful.'

He drew on his cigarette. He had never once taken his eyes from her face. 'And when did you last see Squadron Leader Harrison?'

'More than a week ago. He's on leave in England. His father was taken ill.'

'The father who is General Sir Arnold Harrison. Recently retired from the British army.'

Nico, she thought bitterly. Nico has told them all these things. The Russian said, as though he knew exactly what she was thinking, 'It's not very difficult for us to find out, Fräulein. One can look it up in a moment. When is Squadron Leader Harrison returning?'

'I've no idea. When his father is better, I expect.'

'And he will come hurrying here to see you as soon as he can.'

'Perhaps.'

'In which case, we should like you to continue your pillow talks and to relay these to us.'

'And if I do?'

'Your brother, Dirk, will be released from Sachsenhausen and allowed to return here.'

'And if I don't?'

'You will never see him again.'

She steadied herself enough to reply quite calmly. 'What would you want me to talk about?'

'You will be told.'

'He might suspect.'

'Love is blind, Fräulein Leicht.'

'If I am to do this, then my brother must be released now. Immediately.'

'You're in no position to bargain, Fräulein.'

She met his eyes without flinching. Eyes that seemed to probe into her mind, detect every lie, divine every thought. 'I don't trust you, Herr Silogov. I want to see him back home, alive and well. Before I do anything.'

In the silence that followed, she held her breath. He smoked the cigarette, staring at her. She could not tell whether he was angry or amused, or what he was thinking. Or deciding.

Dirk came home that night. Lili had gone to bed and was lying in the darkness, unable to sleep. At first she thought the scraping, scratching noise from the direction of the hallway was a rat, but it went on and on. She got up to investigate and found that it came from outside the front door.

When she summoned the courage to open the door, her brother fell inwards at her feet.

He slept for more than twenty-four hours. She had managed to drag him to his bed and wash the blood from his face, but there was nothing she could do about the bruises and the two missing teeth and the split lip and the black eye. When, at last, he woke up she fed him with warm soup and a little bread. She spooned the soup in carefully, trying not to hurt his swollen mouth. When he began to speak, it was a mumble.

'Bastards kept beating me . . . asking questions.'

'What sort of questions?'

'Where I'd got the stuff, names, places . . . didn't tell them, though, Lili.' His one open eye gleamed triumphantly at her. 'Not a thing.'

She knew he expected her to be proud of him but she said harshly, 'They were going to send you to a labour camp in Russia, do you realize that? For years. Perhaps for ever. I warned you what might happen.'

'Anyway . . . they let me go.'

'Because of Nico. I went to him for help. I had to.'

'Good old Nico . . . knows everyone . . . can always fix things.'

'Oh, yes, he can always fix everything. They came here. One of the Russians. To see me.'

The gleam faded. 'You? What for?'

'To get me to spy for them. In exchange for letting you go.'

'Spy . . . *you*? How?'

'They want me to find out things from the squadron leader. About the British at Gatow. Everything I can. And tell them. I said that I would. That's why they let you go.'

'Oh, Lili . . .'

'You have to get out,' she said. 'As soon as you can. Out of Berlin. Nico says you must and he's right. Ask your American friends at Tempelhof to help you get away in one of their planes. Give them everything you have. All the jewellery in that box you've hidden . . . *everything*. I'm not going to betray the squadron leader, Dirk. Not even for you. And when the Russians realize I'm not going to help them, they'll come and get you. You must go at once so that you'll be safe. Far away. Go to America, if you can. You've always said how much you'd like to.'

He looked very scared and uncertain suddenly – the small kid brother again from years long ago when something had gone badly wrong. She wanted to break down and weep but she had to be strong.

'I can't, Lili . . . won't leave you.'

'Do you want to end up in a labour camp in Russia? You must go, Dirk.' She felt in her pocket. 'Look, here's your lighter. Nico brought it back.'

'Took it away . . . the swine.'

She fetched a packet of Camels and put one between his bruised and split lips. She spun the Zippo wheel with her thumb and held the flame to the cigarette's end for him. 'Have one yourself, Lili,' he urged her, the way he often did. 'They're good.' She took another from the packet and lit it, keeping her hand firm and steady because Dirk was watching her.

'You'll be all right, Lili, won't you? The squadron leader . . . he'll marry you. Take you to England. Rudi and Grandfather too. I'll come and find you. It's not such a problem.' He seemed almost jaunty, his eye bright again. He even tried to smile at her, though she could tell that he, too, was close to weak

349

tears. He blinked them away. 'We'll survive, won't we, Lili? Somehow we always survive.'

Harrison spent some time at RAF Honington in Suffolk, a nerve centre for the needs of the airlift squadrons, before he flew back to Berlin in the middle of March. From the air, Lake Havel looked as cold and grey as before, the landscape just as lifeless, but the worst of the winter was over. In his absence, the airlift had continued without cease and, in spite of some bitter weather towards the end of February and hurricane-force winds in early March, tonnage records had been broken and the fifty-thousandth German civilian had been flown out of Gatow. Station morale was high, the mood quietly confident. Tubby, when he encountered him in the Mess, was positively jubilant.

'Got 'em licked, dear boy. No question about it. We're in Berlin to stay. Here's to us.'

Harrison raised his glass, too, but less jubilantly. The headaches were still there – aircraft maintenance one of the worst. Engines and airframes were badly overstrained by non-stop flying with maximum loads and there was still a chronic shortage of mechanics, tools, spare parts and basic equipment needed to keep the planes flying. The whole show, he reckoned, had been a damn fine-run thing from the start and would go on being so until the finish. No letting up. No resting on laurels. No premature celebrations. They couldn't afford to relax for a moment.

'Went to see your little fräulein and deliver your *billet-doux*,' Tubby told him. 'Shocking place she lives in. Shook me to the core, I can tell you.

'I know. I should have warned you. Was she all right?'

'Seemed to be. More or less. She asked after you, of course. Wanted to know if I'd any idea when you'd be back. I'd no clue, naturally.'

'I wrote to her several times from England. God knows if she'll have got the letters.'

'One certainly feels the post in that sector might be somewhat unreliable. Well, I dare say you'll be popping over to see her, as soon as you get the chance. Set the wedding day yet?'

He shook his head. 'There's so much bloody red tape, not to mention everything else going on. You still think I'm mad, don't you, Tubby? It's written all over your face.'

'I'm just worried for you, dear boy. Wouldn't like you to make a mistake.'

'I'm not making one.'

'Well, you know best. Who am I to utter a word – an old bachelor like me? By the way, I almost forgot to mention it – that charming little WAAF radar operator gave me a message for you. About the frock.'

She opened the door to him and threw herself straight into his arms. He held her close for a long time, stroking her hair, soothing her. After a while, he led her inside, closing the door behind them.

He was shocked to see how ill she looked. How pale and drawn, eyes red-rimmed either from exhaustion or crying, or perhaps both. He made her sit down at the table and held her hands in his while she told him about Dirk being arrested and taken to Sachsenhausen.

'I had to ask Nico for help. I didn't know what else to do. He went to see the Russians at the camp and in the end they let Dirk go.'

He said grimly, 'I wonder how he managed that.'

She bent her head. 'I don't know.'

'Never mind. The main thing is that Dirk's free. Where is he now?'

'He's gone.'

'Gone? Where?'

She told him, then, about the Americans at Tempelhof who had arranged to smuggle Dirk on board a plane flying to Frankfurt in the American zone. How he was going to try to get to America from there and ask for asylum.

Harrison said, 'Well, he'll be much safer out of Berlin. So will you, Lili. I'm taking you away from here as soon as I can.' He held out the brown paper package that he had brought with him. 'Something for you.'

'What is it?'

'Your wedding dress.' He watched while she undid the string and opened up the paper. 'I hope you like it.'

She stared down at the soft folds of cream-coloured silk. 'Oh, Michael . . . Is it *new*?'

'Brand new. Made specially for you.' She seemed almost stunned. 'When did you last have a new dress?'

'I can't remember . . . years and years ago. I really

can't remember . . . Where did you find such a thing?'

'I have ways and means – like Nico – only rather more straightforward ones. I'm sorry it couldn't be a proper wedding one with a long train and everything, like brides are supposed to have. It was the best I could do. Hold it up against you.' She did so, and he could see how well it would suit her. How lovely she would look. 'Will you try it on for me?'

'That would be very unlucky.'

He smiled. 'In that case, you'd better not. You're not wearing my ring any more.'

'It was too loose,' she said. 'I was afraid of losing it.' She went over to the cupboard by the stove. 'I hid it in the flour. Here it is, quite safe.'

'Well, I've something to replace it soon.' He took the small box out of his greatcoat pocket and opened it. He'd chosen the plain gold wedding ring from a jeweller's in Bond Street. 'She has very small hands,' he'd told the man at the counter, who'd fetched one of the female assistants to try it on. Her hands had been very small, too, and soft and white, without a single mark or blemish. Hands that had never toiled among ruins. 'Let's see if this fits all right or we'll have to get it altered.' He slid the ring onto the fourth finger of her left hand. 'Is it OK?'

'Oh yes.'

'Sure?'

She nodded. 'Here is your ring to take back.'

'No, you hang onto it until the day we're married.' He put the wedding ring back in its box and replaced the signet ring on her middle finger.

'When we're in England we'll go to a jeweller's together – the same place where I bought the wedding ring – and I'll buy a proper engagement ring for you. You must choose whatever you want.'

She started to cry and he had to get out his handkerchief to wipe away her tears. Then he held her close again and kissed her. And went on kissing her. The love he felt for her overwhelmed him and he wanted so much to take her to bed. He sensed that she wanted it as much as he did – that it would have been easy. But not now, he told himself firmly. Not yet. Not in this godforsaken, miserable rat hole. That wasn't how he wanted it.

The Russian, Silogov, came to the apartment again. Lili had begun to hope that, after all, he might have decided that she was no use to them. She had dared to think of the future that could lie ahead – marriage to Michael, a home in England. Happiness, far away.

'Good evening, Fräulein Leicht.' This time he didn't ask permission to enter, but pushed his way past her. There was another man with him in police uniform, following at his heels. A German. She stood frozen in terror while the policeman made a rapid search of the whole apartment. The Russian moved to stand in front of her.

'Where is your brother, Fräulein?'

'He left,' she said. 'Disappeared, with all his belongings. I don't know where he went.'

'You're lying.'

'I'm speaking the truth. He was very afraid. One

day I went to work and when I came back he had gone. I have heard nothing from him since.'

He stared at her for a moment before he turned away and spoke sharply to the German, who left the room. She heard the front door open and slam shut. Then he said, in different, friendlier tones, as though the man had been an impertinent and unwarranted intrusion, 'Sit down, please, Fräulein. We can talk now.' She sat at the table and he took the chair opposite: Michael's chair. 'Cigarette?'

'No, thank you.'

'Which brand does Squadron Leader Harrison smoke, I wonder. Player's? State Express? Senior Service? Du Maurier, perhaps?'

'I've never really noticed. Player's, I think.'

He struck a match to light his cigarette and then blew it out slowly, replacing the dead match carefully in the box, as he had done before. 'He has returned recently from England and we know that he has visited you. What did you talk about this time?'

'Nothing in particular. His father's health. The weather in England.'

That amused him. He actually smiled. 'I told you that the English love to talk about the weather. Did he bring you anything? A present?'

We know that he has visited you. They must have been watching. Waiting. Don't lie. There's no point. 'Yes, he brought a frock.'

'A frock? What a charming gift. And very surprising. Quite un-English. Was it a nice frock?'

'Yes, very nice.'

'I should like to see it.'

She fetched the frock which she had hung in the cupboard in Dirk's bedroom and held it up in silence. He looked at it consideringly, his head on one side. 'Charming. You interest me even more, Fräulein.' He reached out to finger the hem. 'This is a gown that a man would buy for a woman he loved and respected. How he sees her, or wishes to see her. On a pedestal. You may put it away now, thank you.'

When she had sat down again, he said, 'What else has he given you?'

Don't lie. Tell the truth or he'll catch you out. 'A tea set.'

'A tea set? That's even more surprising but, of course, the English drink a lot of tea. What kind of tea set? Did he bring it all the way from England for you?'

'No, I believe he bought it at Gatow. At something called the Malcolm Club.'

He nodded. 'Yes, I know of this. May I see this tea set? Or a piece of it.' She brought him one of the cups and he inspected it gravely. 'Delightful.' He turned the cup over. 'Spring. I believe the spring in England is quite spectacular. What flower is this, do you know?'

'It's a primrose.'

'Is that so? I've never seen one. Very pretty.' He gave the cup back. 'It's clear to me that Squadron Leader Harrison holds you in the highest regard, Fräulein Leicht. And yet you say that you are not engaged to be married? Isn't that his signet ring that you're wearing?'

Her mind had been so numbed by fear that she had forgotten all about the ring. 'It belongs to him, yes.'

'He gave it to you to wear?'

'For a while.'

'As a token of his love. There can be no other reason. Did he also ask you to marry him?' She was silent. 'Fräulein Leicht, I asked you a simple question. Has Squadron Leader Harrison asked you to marry him?'

'He spoke of marriage.'

'Of course he did. It would be useless to deny it. The man who gave such a charming gown and so domestic a tea set to any woman undoubtedly has marriage in his mind. Especially a man like your squadron leader. We know something of him, you see. A distinguished war record. DSO, DFC. A member of the legendary Pathfinder Force of No. 8 Group in the Royal Air Force. A man of courage. A man of honour. Also, a man who will have played a considerable part in reducing this city to rubble. Were you aware of that?'

'Yes. I was aware of it.'

'But you still welcomed him into your home, and your bed. You've come to terms with it, shall we say?'

'Yes.'

'No grudges borne?'

'No.'

'You must be in love with him yourself.'

Her instinct was to deny it and yet she dared not do so completely. 'I find him attractive.'

357

He stubbed out the cigarette in the tin lid ashtray and took another from the packet, lighting it with a match. She watched him blow out the flame and put the match neatly back in the box. He always replaced it the opposite way from the unused matches. 'You find him attractive. So, when he asked you to marry him, what did you reply?'

'I asked for time to think.'

'How wise. What is the old saying? Marry in haste, repent at leisure. So true. But, of course, you would be very foolish not to accept such an advantageous offer. What an agreeable life you would lead. So comfortable. So secure. Well fed. A loving English husband.' He looked round the room. 'The contrast could hardly be greater. There is nothing to keep you here. And now that your brother has gone, there is even less. Nobody else left for you to worry about, except yourself. Both your parents, of course, are dead. Your mother in the bombing, your father at the hands of the Nazis. Your father was a staunch opponent of the German National Socialist Party, isn't that so?'

'He was against Hitler, yes.'

'Your mother, too?'

'My mother was a milliner, Herr Silogov. She made beautiful hats. She was not much concerned with politics.'

'And you?'

'I was too young.'

'But old enough to understand a great deal. Surely your father must have preached the evils of fascism to his family. Taught you of the dangers? He had many Communist Party friends in Berlin. You must have known that?'

'He had many friends of all kinds.'

He drew on the cigarette, watching her. 'Millions of Russians did not shed their blood in the war in order to have western capitalists step straight into the shoes of the Nazis, Fräulein. I'm certain that your father would not have wanted that to happen either. He would have been on our side, don't you think? He would have been as opposed to capitalist greed as he was to the Nazi creed.'

'I don't know.'

'But naturally, he would have been. He was a man of very strong principles. Indeed, he died for them. And so, in helping us, you will be honouring his memory. We had a bargain, you and I, remember? I have kept my side of it and your brother was released. Now, it's your turn to keep yours.'

She swallowed. 'What do you want me to do?'

'You will accept Squadron Leader Harrison's offer of marriage, of course – if you have not already done so, which I think you have. And you will tell us everything you learn about the British Royal Air Force in your new life with him. Not from a military point of view – you are unlikely to learn very much about that – but from the human angle. The gossip. Find out who has some weakness, some indiscretion, some guilty secret they would be very anxious to keep dark. Adultery, homosexuality, dishonesty, debt . . . we should like to hear of it.'

She told herself that she had only to pretend to agree with him, that was all. Pretend. Once she had married Michael and got away, there was nothing they could do. Dirk was safe, Rudi and Grandfather were safe. Later, she could tell Michael what they had tried to make her do and he would understand why she had had to agree.

'I'll try.'

He smiled. 'You will have to do a little better than that, Fräulein. We're not quite so gullible, you know. You will have to try very hard. Otherwise we shall have to tell Squadron Leader Harrison some unpleasant truths about you. Things that he does not yet know.'

'What . . . things?'

'That you were raped by a gang of Russian soldiers after the fall of Berlin. He might forgive you for that – it was hardly your fault – but how will he receive the news that later on you sold yourself willingly to a number of American servicemen, like a common whore? How many was it? Five, six, seven? More? That's quite a tally of men who have had the pleasure of knowing you. What will General Sir Arnold and Lady Harrison think of their new daughter-in-law, I wonder, when that comes to their ears? Most interesting of all, what might it do to the squadron leader's very promising career when all the juicy details leak out about his German wife's past? Of course, if we feel like it, we can also add the edifying snippet that your brother is a drug dealer. He was carrying drugs when he was arrested, you know.'

She had leaped to her feet while he was speaking and he looked up at her coldly. 'You had better sit down again, Fräulein. There is nowhere for you to go and we have not finished talking yet.'

'Get your best blue pressed and ready, Tubby. It's all fixed for the day after tomorrow. A civil ceremony. Over and done in a few minutes.'

'Count on me to be present and correct, dear boy. Have you got a ring?'

'I bought one in England. And it fits.'

'Splendid. Any leave?'

'They're giving me a forty-eight. We'll have a proper honeymoon in England later on. I've found a small apartment not too far away from here. A bit grim but it's clean and weatherproof. After what Lili's been living in I expect it'll seem like a palace to her.'

'You've got it all worked out. Nothing more to worry about. All's well that ends well.'

Harrison guessed that Tubby still had his own reservations but he was carefully hiding them. He wished he could count on his parents in the same way. Now that his father was out of hospital and on the road to recovery, he had written a letter, telling them that he was marrying Lili Leicht. He would have much preferred to talk to his father about it in person, face to face, but that was impossible. All he could hope was that they would both accept a *fait accompli* and welcome Lili, if not exactly with joy, at least with kindness and understanding.

'I'm collecting her at Albrecht Strasse tomorrow, with all her gear, such as it is. Thank God, she'll soon be out of that place.'

'I'll drink to that, dear boy. And make it a double, will you?'

The left-hand door was standing slightly ajar. He pushed the wolf's head gently so that it swung inwards, and stepped into the hallway.

Silence. 'Lili?' No answer. He took off his cap and went on into the living room. Someone was sitting in the grandfather's chair – not Lili but an emaciated old man dressed in a long overcoat and a black beret covering silver-white hair, gnarled hands resting on the arms. A complete stranger. As Harrison hesitated, the old man spoke in slow but clear English with a heavy German accent.

'Squadron Leader Harrison? Please allow me to introduce myself. My name is Dr Meier. I am a friend of Fräulein Leicht. I also live in Albrecht Strasse. Forgive me for not standing, but I have not been well.'

He said abruptly, 'Where is she?'

'Not here. She asked me to wait here for you. Please sit down, if you will.'

'No, thank you.' He stared at the old man with foreboding. 'Why isn't she here? She's expecting me. Is something wrong?'

His questions were ignored. 'She has asked me to speak to you, on her behalf.'

He said again, more roughly, 'Where is she?'

'Not here, I assure you.'

He went to look in the rooms beyond – the one where Dirk had slept and the bathroom. Both were empty. He pulled open a cupboard and found that empty too. Then he went back into the big room. The stranger was still sitting where he had left him.

'Where's Lili?'

'I regret that I am not able to tell you.'

He went over to the old man, seized hold of the lapels of his overcoat, and yanked him up out of the chair. It was like lifting a bag of bones. 'I think you'd better tell me. Damn quickly.'

'If you will be good enough to release me, I will explain.'

He held on for a moment longer, glaring at him. The old man met his eyes, showing no sign of fear, no emotion other than a calm politeness. What could he do to him, anyway? He let him fall back into the chair. 'All right. Explain. What's this all about?'

'Fräulein Leicht has asked me to tell you that she has changed her mind. She does not wish, after all, to marry you.'

He said quietly, 'I don't believe you. What's happened to her?'

'Nothing has happened to her. But she has decided that it would be better if you and she were not to marry. She does not think that it would bring happiness, most especially to yourself. If you will remember, she expressed some grave doubts on the subject to you before. For you to marry a German girl, is perhaps not such a good thing.'

'We've sorted all that out,' he said slowly. 'Talked it over. There's nothing for her to worry about.'

'She is not so sure.'

'What is she not so sure about?'

'She is afraid the past would come between you.'

'What do you mean – the past? I don't give a damn about the past.'

'But Fräulein Leicht does.'

He stared at the old man. 'Where is she?'

'I am unable to tell you.'

'I must speak to her. Talk about all this.'

'It will not be possible. You must respect and accept her decision.'

'*Like hell!*' he said furiously. 'I won't accept it. I want to see her. Talk to her myself.'

'She will not see you. Never again.' The old man indicated the table. 'She left the gown you gave her and the English tea set, and also your ring. Please take them, Squadron Leader, and go, like an officer and a gentleman. There is nothing more to be said.'

The brown paper package, neatly retied with its string, lay beside the cardboard box that had held the tea set, also tied with string. His signet ring was on top of the box.

'Christ almighty . . . Why didn't she tell me herself? Why ask you to do it?'

'She knew that you would be unwilling to accept the decision. That you would try to change her mind. It's easier for her like this. For both of you.'

'Did she leave a letter – a note of some kind?'

'No. Nothing like that.'

He picked up the ring and pushed it back onto his little finger. He said bitterly, 'Tell her she can keep the rest.'

*　　*　　*

He passed the place quite by chance as he walked through the streets. His mind was in miserable turmoil and he scarcely noticed where he was going. He'd stopped at a bar and downed several vodkas, overpaid and walked on, turning at random in the vague direction of the Brandenburg Gate. It was almost dark and he knew it was risky to be in the Russian sector but he didn't care.

He noticed the flight of steps going downwards from the pavement. No different from hundreds of others in Berlin leading to foul basements and cellars, except that something about these ones rang a bell and when he shone his torch down it showed an odd-looking door at the bottom, repaired with planks of wood, nailed in a criss-cross fashion so that it resembled a portcullis. *Der Keller*. Nico's seedy dive.

He recognized the unsavoury type who opened the door and immediately tried to shut it again. Harrison stuck his foot in the closing gap. He said pleasantly in English, 'I'm looking for Nico Kocharian? Is he here?'

'Perhaps. Perhaps not.'

'I'll see for myself, then, shall I?' He shoved the man aside and made his way into the cellar, through the thick fug of cigarette smoke and beer, past the crowded tables, the flickering candles, the heads turning to stare. The Armenian was sitting alone at a table at the far side, under one of the archways. He glanced up from his drink.

'Michael, my dear chap! Good gracious, I didn't think you liked this place.'

'I don't. I thought I might find you here.'

'And here I am. *Me voici*! as the French say. What will you have to drink? It's on me.'

He dragged a chair away from the next-door table without asking and sat down. The three-piece band was pumping out some jolly German tune by the rickety stage. 'Schnapps, and I'm paying, thank you.' He signalled a waiter and gave him the order. People were staring. He ignored them all.

'Cigarette?' Nico said. 'No, of course, you prefer Player's. Well, at least I can light it for you. I'm still rather curious, Michael, I must admit. What did you want to find me for?'

He drew hard on the cigarette before he answered. 'Lili and I were to be married tomorrow. I went to the apartment in Albrecht Strasse to collect her and found some old man waiting for me instead, a Dr Meier.'

'Oh yes, I know him. A pathetic old soul who lives just down the street. Lili takes him soup from time to time, so Dirk told me. She's very kind-hearted.'

'He gave me a message from Lili.'

'Did he?'

'She's called off the wedding. Changed her mind, apparently.'

'Oh dear. I thought you were looking rather upset, old chap.'

The waiter brought the schnapps and set it in front of him. He paid for it on the spot and drank half in one go. 'What I want to know is, did you have anything to do with it?'

'With Lili changing her mind? *Me*? Absolutely

not. She would never ask my opinion or confide in me. She doesn't like me, you see.'

'She went to you for help when Dirk was arrested.'

'She was obliged to. There was nobody else. You were far away in England, Michael – not that you could have done anything, actually. Even *I* had a sticky time getting him out of that camp.'

'I'm interested. How *did* you manage that, exactly?'

'You have to know how to deal with the Russians, you see. Speak their language in more ways than one. Fortunately I do – as you'll remember from that time when you got into a spot of bother with them yourself.'

He waited a moment, smoking his cigarette. 'Why is Lili so afraid of marrying me?'

'Afraid?'

'Is it because of something in her past? Something she doesn't want me to find out?'

'Every Berliner has things in their past that they would prefer to forget. Every single one of them.'

'I don't give a bugger about her past. I was going to give her a future.'

Nico spread his hands. 'Of course you were. You were going to rescue her from the ruins. Ruins you had unfortunately helped to create. Very romantic. Very chivalrous. Only it wasn't quite that simple, as it turned out, was it? Things very seldom are in this city. I blame myself for taking you to the Leichts' apartment in the first place, only you needed a watch. But I should have warned you.'

'Warned me?' he said sharply. 'What about?'

'About Berlin.'

The orchestra had finished its folksy German tune and began a long roll of drums. A spotlight flicked on, trained on to the makeshift stage. People began clapping. 'You're in luck, old chap,' Nico said, smiling at him and clapping too. 'Helene's about to start her act.'

The transvestite, dressed in Dietrich garb, materialized from the shadows into the spotlight's glare and stood before the microphone. The husky voice began.

Ich bin von Kopf bis Fuss auf Liebe eingestellt . . .

He had forgotten how good she was. Almost as good as the real thing. After a while she left the stage to move among the tables, smiling, touching, teasing . . . He knew long before she came to their table that she had already spotted his uniform from the stage and singled him out. He went on smoking and waiting while she came closer and closer, table by table, reached them and stopped in front.

Falling in love again . . .

She draped herself across his lap, lying back to look up into his face, the long legs in black fishnet stockings provocatively displayed. *What am I to do, I can't help it . . .* He could smell strong perfume, mixed with sweat and greasepaint; see the grotesque

368

mask of make-up, the malicious eyes, the glistening, parted lips; hear the salacious laughter from the other tables. Her hand caressed his cheek, and the long, red nails dug into his skin; he felt her draw blood. She leaned closer until her mouth nibbled at his ear. She whispered something disgustingly obscene in English.

He thrust her off his lap, so hard that she fell backwards onto the floor. As he elbowed a way out through the tables there were angry cries, fists shaken; a hand grabbed hold of his arm and he shook it off savagely.

Outside, the street was dark and silent. He stood for a moment, breathing in clean, cold, sobering air, before he walked on towards the Gate.

'I'm afraid I have to disturb you again, Fräulein Leicht.' She stood aside to let the Russian, Silogov, go past her into the living room, and he sat down in Grandfather's armchair and struck a match to light a cigarette. He gestured to her politely. 'Sit down, Fräulein. We may as well be comfortable.' She did so, at a distance, at the table. 'I understand that you and Squadron Leader Harrison are not to be married, after all. No wedding bells. No comfortable home in England. You changed your mind.'

'How do you know?'

'We have informants everywhere. They tell us the things we wish to know.' He replaced the spent match in its box and poked the lid shut. 'Why did you change your mind?'

'I decided that I would not be happy in England.'

'I see. And the squadron leader accepted your decision?'

'Yes. You can tell him anything you like about me. It won't matter any more.'

'And the gown? What about the beautiful gown?'

'He wanted me to keep it.'

'And the English tea set?'

'That, too.'

'The spoils of war.' He smoked his cigarette, considering her. 'Did you keep the ring as well?'

'No, he took it back.'

'He was upset, no doubt?'

She said dully, 'I imagine so.'

'I'm sure he was. Extremely. You hurt his heart as well as his pride.' She said nothing. 'So, what will you do now, Fräulein?'

'Go on, the way I was before.'

'Living here, all alone.'

'There's nowhere else.'

'Toiling away as a *trummerfrau*?'

'There's no other work.'

'Not much of a future.'

She was silent while he continued to stare at her for a moment.

He said, 'We know that you speak excellent English. Also very good French. That you are intelligent and well educated and very presentable. We know everything about you. Your talents are quite wasted at the moment and I have been considering the problem. I feel responsible, you see.'

She remained silent. They knew everything about her. Nico had told them things, certainly. Perhaps even Dr Meier? *We have informants everywhere.* She could never trust anybody again.

He went on smoothly, 'A number of the old Berlin industrial companies in the British and American sectors are beginning to start up again – to find their feet and expand. They will be needing more staff – clerks, secretaries, translators. It would be quite a simple matter to find you a post with one of them. Can you type? Do shorthand?'

She shook her head.

'But you can learn. It can be arranged. An intensive course. It could also be arranged for you to move from here into something much pleasanter. An apartment in one of the fine new buildings that are going up in this sector. Central heating, a kitchen, a bathroom with running water – hot and cold. All the modern amenities. New furniture. And extra rations.'

'My grandfather and brother will be coming back when the winter is over.'

'The apartment will have room for them too.'

She hesitated. 'And extra rations for them?'

'Of course.'

'And in return?'

'A little information from time to time. To keep us up to date with things on that side of Berlin. That's all. We like to know what's happening in any industry over there.'

'And if I choose not to do this?'

He shrugged. 'It's not a disaster. We can always find alternative employment for you, Fräulein. You could be directed by the state into some kind of rather less agreeable work – compulsory employment, you understand. Mining, for instance. In Russia women are regularly used for heavy labour.' He paused and flicked the ash from his cigarette onto the floor. 'And then, of course, there are the camps.'

She felt so tired. Too tired to go on with the struggle. She had run out of strength and out of courage. She no longer cared what happened to herself – whether she lived or died – but there was still Grandfather and Rudi. *Take Rudi. Look after him, whatever happens*. The sacred trust.

Seventeen

The Russians lifted the blockade at one o'clock in the morning of the twelfth of May. Railways and highways to Berlin across the Soviet zone of Germany reopened and the first trucks and trains, draped with banners and garlands, began the hundred-mile journey to and from the city. At a meeting of the City Assembly in the Rathaus, people stood in tribute as the names of the fifty-four men – American, British and German – who had died in the airlift were read out, and huge crowds began to gather in the square and the neighbouring streets outside to celebrate.

A deputation of Berliners arrived at RAF Gatow to make speeches of thanks, give presents and flowers, sing songs and embrace every blushing airlift pilot or crew member they could find, and many others as well. Tubby, who had been hugged and kissed by several *Berlinerinnen*, appeared in the Mess dishevelled and greatly touched. 'Considering we reduced them to dust not so very long ago, it's jolly moving to see how grateful they are now, don't you think?'

Harrison said, 'They can thank themselves – for not giving up.'

'*Their* finest hour,' Tubby agreed. 'And the dawn of a brave new era. No more being beastly to the Germans. We stand shoulder to shoulder from this day forward. And have you heard the best news of all, dear boy? No more bloody Pom. *Fresh* potatoes from now on. Hallelujah!'

He said slowly, 'The only trouble is, Berlin's still an island set in a Soviet sea. That hasn't changed and we can't change it. Their troubles aren't over yet, Tubby – not by a long chalk. I have a feeling the Russians aren't going to stop playing silly buggers.'

He was proved right. The petty interference in road and rail and barge travel continued and so, in consequence, did the airlift – though without quite the same grim intensity. There had been an amazing victory. A triumph against all the odds. And the winter was over, the weather warm. Some street markets appeared, selling fresh vegetables and fruit unseen for months or years – lemons and oranges, cucumbers – and fresh fish.

People sat in the sunshine outside cafés and some of the coffee they drank was real, not ersatz.

He had been out to the apartment in Albrecht Strasse in the hope of finding Lili there and talking to her. He had rung the bell again and again and hammered with both fists on the doors until, at last, he heard the sound of somebody the other side. For a moment, he had expected that it would be Lili who opened it to him. Instead, it had been an old woman. A hag out of Grimm, dressed in black with a knitted scarf tied round her head. She had spoken no English and he had floundered with his few words of German.

'Is Fräulein Leicht at home? May I speak with her? *Ich möchte si gerne sprechen, bitte.*'

'*Nein, nein.*' She had shaken her head emphatically at him. '*Sie ist ausgezogen. Ich wohne jetzt hier.*'

Ausgezogen meant gone away. And he had understood, I live here now. When he had started to ask where Lili had gone, she had slammed the door shut in his face. He had rung the bell several more times and hammered on the door some more, but the old woman had refused to open it again.

He had gone from there to Nico Kocharian's office, where the door was open and he had walked straight in. He had found the inner room empty. No desk, no chair, no telephone and bare bookshelves. No clue of any kind as to what had happened or where the Armenian had gone. The only evidence of his occupation the lingering smell of Turkish cigarettes, hair oil and exotic cologne. He thought of his father's comment: *I rather gathered they thought pretty highly of him all round.* The Intelligence chaps generally knew their stuff. The whole truth about Kocharian, he realized, would probably never be known.

In early June he learned that he was to be posted back to England. Tubby, occupying his usual chair in the Officers' Mess bar, sighed when he heard the news. 'I'll miss you, dear boy. When are you off?'

'First thing in the morning.'

'Put in a good word for me when you get back, will you? Ask around and see if there's a place for an ageing pen-pusher. Something nice and cushy, if you can manage it.'

He smiled. 'I'll do what I can.'

'I've reached the conclusion that there's no place like home.'

'There's certainly no place like Berlin.'

'Praise be to God for that mercy. The trouble it's all been.'

'Yes,' he said. 'But worth it.'

'I've been thinking about that little fräulein, Michael . . .'

'What about her?'

'Well, if you want my opinion – and I can see by your face that you don't – she did you a good turn. Best thing all round. Of course, you don't look at it that way now, but give it time. Give it time.'

As the Dakota took off soon after dawn and climbed into the sky, he turned to take one last look in the direction of the ruined city before it vanished.

In London the trees were in leaf, flowers in bloom, the grass in the parks a fresh new green. It looked better than he had seen it for years. A little less war-worn, a little less weary, a little more prosperous. At the mansion flat he sorted through the accumulated post: a couple of letters, some circulars, two party invitations, another to a wedding. There was a postcard from the watchmakers: at long last his Omega was ready for collection.

He poured himself a drink and lit a cigarette and stood at the sitting-room window, looking out down onto the Fulham Road. They were still queuing at the greengrocer's – a patient little line of housewives with their shopping baskets over their arms, waiting for their turn – but the queue was shorter than he remembered.

He wondered how London would have looked through Lili's eyes. What would she have thought of it? Would she have liked it? Would she have been happy – as he had so wanted her to be and believed he could make her? He had gone through all the stages of rejection: disbelief, misery, rage, and, finally, resignation – though he would never understand. He would have risked anything and everything for her. Yet, after all, she had not been ready to do the same for him.

He finished the cigarette and the drink, lifted the telephone receiver and dialled a number. He listened to the ringing tone and to the clear, English voice answering at the other end.

'Celia? It's Michael. I'm back.'

Epilogue

1961

The newspaper boy was late with the morning paper. He heard it flop onto the mat and went into the hall. As he picked it up, the banner headline caught his eye and the photograph beneath it, splashed across the front page. The children were shouting from the garden but he read on, lost in the past.

Celia came into the house. 'Tom's fallen off his bike and cut his knee. Blood everywhere but it doesn't look too serious. Apparently he collided with Billy going round a corner – they ran slap bang into each other, silly idiots. I'm just going for the first-aid kit.'

She came down a moment later, carrying the tin, and stopped at the foot of the stairs. 'Is anything the matter, Michael? You look as though you've seen a ghost.'

He dragged himself back to the present. 'They're building a wall.'

'A wall? Who? Where?'

'The Russians,' he held up the newspaper. 'Right across Berlin. A huge concrete wall along

378

their sector border. No-one can get in or out.'

'It sounds perfectly dreadful. Poor Berlin.'

'Yes,' he agreed. 'Poor Berlin.'

There was another yell from the garden and sounds of a furious argument. Celia sighed. 'I'd better go and see what on earth's happened now.'

He smiled at her. 'Let me know if they need their heads knocking together.'

She smiled back. 'Don't worry, I will.'

He watched her hurry off. He had always liked her and the liking had steadily deepened into love. She was a marvellous wife and mother and he was grateful to her for so many things, not the least for being such a good friend and companion.

He looked down at the newspaper again, at the photograph of the huge wall with its guard towers and fencing and barbed wire and floodlights.

He thought of Lili and he wondered, as he had wondered constantly over the years and would always wonder, what had become of her.

Lili could see the wall from the window of the apartment on the fifth floor. She had watched it being built almost overnight. Troops of the National People's Army had sealed the sector borders with barbed wire and workers had begun tearing up roads and constructing a great barricade of concrete blocks, topped by a high metal fence. The wall was cutting the city into two halves, making two separate cities – East and West Berlin. They were bricking up the doors and windows of houses along its perimeter, digging vehicle traps and putting up floodlights and sensor fences and chain-link fences. And they were building guard towers and bunkers and runs for guard dogs. She had seen it all happening.

The door opened and Manfred came into the room.

'Lili? What are you doing?'

'Looking at the wall.'

He stood beside her, putting his arm round her shoulders, and grunted. 'That'll keep them out all right.'

But she knew that the wall had been built to keep the East in, not the West out: to staunch the haemorrhage of people fleeing Communist Germany. Naturally, she didn't say this aloud. It was very likely that the apartment building was wired with hidden microphones and, in any case, Manfred would not agree with her. And he would be upset. He was a good Party member – sincere and principled. She had learned to respect that and to toe the line herself. She did what they asked. It was simply another form of survival – a lesson well taught long ago. *Das überleben*. In the end, that was all that mattered.

'You should sit down and rest a little,' he told her gently. 'Shall I make you a cup of tea?'

He was always thoughtful. Always considerate. She thanked him but instead of sitting down while he went into the kitchen, she stayed at the window. In the opposite direction, eastwards, across Berlin towards Russia, she could look at all the other ugly concrete apartment towers, identical to the one they lived in, sprouting like weeds in a flat wasteland of bomb sites and rubble. Once, soon after they had been married, she had suggested to Manfred that they might move to live in the west of Berlin. He had been shocked by the idea, dismayed that she should even consider it. 'Our future is here, Lili,' he had told her. 'Not in the fascist west.' Now it was too late. No-one could leave. They were all prisoners.

She could hear the clink of cups from the kitchen, the spluttering hiss from the kettle on the stove, Manfred moving about. He was a good husband, a decent man, and she was grateful to him for many things – not the least, for his company and his friendship. When she had met him she had been utterly alone and lonely. Dirk was far away in America, Grandfather in his grave and Rudi at university in Hamburg. It was a kind of love. Another kind.

The baby would be born within a month. She had stopped work to be ready, just before they had started on the wall. Later on, when the baby was older, she would be given other work to do; told what they wanted from her. Whatever happened, she would take care of the child as she had taken care of Rudi. Do the best she could for it in a grim world. So, too, would Manfred.

He came in from the kitchen, carrying a tray. To please him she went to sit down. 'Your English cups,' he said, smiling at her. 'I know how you like them.' She gazed at the pretty china cup in her hand. Primroses flowered in England in the spring,

Michael had told her. There were lots and lots of them growing wild everywhere in the countryside. He had promised to find her a primrose path.

She still thought of him almost every day and wondered, as she would wonder for the rest of her life, how things might have been.

THE END

A SELECTED LIST OF FINE NOVELS
AVAILABLE FROM CORGI BOOKS

13855 X	ELLAN VANNIN	*Lyn Andrews*	£5.99
14036 1	MAGGIE MAY	*Lyn Andrews*	£5.99
14058 9	MIST OVER THE MERSEY	*Lyn Andrews*	£5.99
14060 0	MERSEY BLUES	*Lyn Andrews*	£5.99
14448 7	DREAM CATCHER	*Iris Gower*	£5.99
14449 5	SWEET ROSIE	*Iris Gower*	£5.99
14450 9	DAUGHTERS OF REBECCA	*Iris Gower*	£5.99
14537 8	APPLE BLOSSOM TIME	*Kathryn Haig*	£5.99
14538 6	A TIME TO DANCE	*Kathryn Haig*	£5.99
14567 X	THE CORNER HOUSE	*Ruth Hamilton*	£5.99
14410 X	MRS HONORIA WEST	*Ruth Hamilton*	£5.99
14770 2	MULLGAN'S YARD	*Ruth Hamilton*	£6.99
14220 4	CAPEL BELLS	*Joan Hessayon*	£5.99
14535 3	THE HELMINGHAM ROSE	*Joan Hessayon*	£5.99
14691 7	THE PARADISE GARDEN	*Joan Hessayon*	£5.99
14868 7	SEASON OF MISTS	*Joan Hessayon*	£5.99
13910 6	BLUEBIRDS	*Margaret Mayhew*	£5.99
14492 4	THE CREW	*Margaret Mayhew*	£5.99
14693 5	THE LITTLE SHIP	*Margaret Mayhew*	£5.99
14822 9	OUR YANKS	*Margaret Mayhew*	£5.99
14655 2	SPRNG MUSIC	*Elvi Rhodes*	£5.99
14715 X	MIDSUMMER MEETING	*Elvi Rhodes*	£5.99
14792 3	THE BIRTHDAY PARTY	*Elvi Rhodes*	£5.99
14671 4	THE KEYS TO THE GARDEN	*Susan Sallis*	£5.99
14747 8	THE APPLE BARREL	*Susan Sallis*	£5.99
14867 9	SEA OF DREAMS	*Susan Sallis*	£5.99